ASHES, ASHES

JESSICA GOEKEN

A MORTALS & SHADOWS NOVEL

ONE

I SHOULD HAVE KNOWN it wasn't a typical werewolf when its front claws shredded my jeans and left trails of fire racing over my entire body. But in the middle of a fight, details like that get pushed aside in favor of trying to stay alive. The beast is the biggest I've ever hunted down, and I've yet to even draw blood.

"Ventus," I hiss as it springs toward me again. The rush of wind stops the creature in midair. Ideally, the spell would throw it backward, but it's still a work in progress. The half-second respite is enough. I dive toward the beast, and we collide once again as it lands back on the ground. Its balance is off just enough from the drop, while mine is perfect. My silver knife is silent as it slides under the beast's chin.

Instead of slumping into a pool of blood, the beast explodes in a cloud of black ash.

Shit. Hellhound.

For a moment I just stand there, dumbfounded. A hellhound? Seriously? How did one of those even cross over? They don't possess that much power. It was supposed to be a werewolf. Cut-and-dried, kill-the-beast kind of mission. After tracking the creature through four full moons and a trail of dead co-eds, there was no reason to suspect it was anything else.

Raucous laughter has me shelving the problem-solving for later. It's a good thing I don't have a body to dispose of, because I'm officially out of time. Students are pouring out of the stadium doors across the parking lot, and a girl lurking around with a big knife and bloody jeans is likely to draw attention from even the most inebriated among them. I smile at them grimly before backing farther into the shadows. Lucky bastards. They'll never know how close they came tonight.

Two streets later, I'm far enough away from the crowds to check out my injury. The four deep slashes have left my thigh looking more like a package of hamburger than human flesh. They're still bleeding more than I'm comfortable with, and they're way too hot to the touch. I can just imagine what could happen to an untreated hellhound scratch. Under my breath, I mutter the words that will cleanse the wound, the first in a long list of first-aid spells any novice magi can cast. Nothing happens.

I repeat the spell, blaming myself for its failure. I don't do well with the more delicate magics. Nothing happens. I do it again. Same result. *All righty then. We do it the hard way.*

The hard way involves me tearing the sleeves off my shirt to bind the gashes. The pressure makes the bleeding stop but does nothing for the fire burning on my skin.

The phone call comes next. The manor is number one on everybody's speed dial.

"Adrienne. What's up?"

"Dixon? I thought Heather was on phones tonight?"

"She and Andrew got a call. They didn't say much, but it sounded important. They left in a hurry."

"Uh-huh. Well, I just called to check in. Let them know I'll be home soon, okay?"

"No way. Tell me what happened first. Did you find the wolf?"

I hesitate. I should really tell the McGinnises first, make it official and everything. But something this strange isn't something I want to keep to myself too long, and who knows when they'll make it home? "Fine, yes, I found it. But it wasn't a wolf."

Silence on the other end as he waits for me to drop the other shoe.

"It was a hellhound."

"A hellhound?" His voice gets nervous and excited at the same time. "Are you sure?"

I try not to be offended. "I'm sure."

"But that would mean...this is big, Adrienne."

"I know. Someone brought that hellhound over, and we're going to have to find out who. But not tonight. I'm not expecting any more excitement, so get some sleep, okay? It's late. Make sure Liza gets to bed, too."

"I think she's already in bed. I haven't seen her since dinner. She couldn't stop yawning."

"All right. I'll be home soon. I'm taking the long way, so it might be a little while."

He sighs. "Again? What about school tomorrow?"

"You can drive."

"You know, someone's eventually going to notice I'm only fifteen."

"No, they won't. You're too good. I'll see you tomorrow."

I hang up before he can answer. It won't be the first time Dixon's driven to school when I haven't made it home on time, but it won't be a problem. Perception magic is his strong suit. My grades will take the bigger hit. Fall semester just started, and I'm already racking up unexcused absences. Still, after a hunt like this one, I like the extra travel time to decompress. Even my injury, painful as it is, isn't enough to make me rush home.

The city bus drops me off at the airport, which is fairly deserted at this time of night. I can't help glancing up at the moon beaming down from overhead. Most people enjoy full moons. They're beautiful, I can admit that. But too many people have died under them for me to ever enjoy them.

My glamours aren't nearly as good as Dixon's, but they're good enough to convince the lady at the ticket counter that I'm clean and my clothes are intact. The platinum card in my wallet helps sell it. I can't get a flight out until the morning, but I buy the ticket anyway. Heather won't be pleased, but Andrew will understand. He's combat magic, like me. He gets it. It's more than the physical exertion of the fight. Taking another life, even one that needs to be taken, it does something to you. Drains something out of you.

It's nearly noon by the time I finally make it home, exhausted and feverish. Heather's waiting for me at the kitchen table, her chestnut hair pulled back in a tight bun and her freckles stark against her pale face. Waiting to lecture me, no doubt. The McGinnises are pretty cool, for house parents, but they like things done a certain way. Protocol says I should have come through the Shadow Plane and made my report in person, as soon as possible. The trip that took me half a day could have been done in minutes, and I could have slept in my own bed last night instead of a plastic chair at the airport. We've had this conversation so many times I can recite both parts verbatim.

"Sit down." Heather wastes no time getting the show started.

"I know what you're going to say, but—"

"This isn't about last night. I mean, it is, but it's not what you think."

Heather's going off script? It's enough to make me keep my mouth shut and take the indicated seat at the table. I sink into the hard wooden chair, ready to get this over with so I can crash.

"Andrew and I were called out last night, which you already know, because Dixon told you."

She pauses, but I'm pretty sure it's not so I can answer. I've never seen her so agitated.

"There was...an incident. At a girls' school in Vermont. Several students were murdered."

Murdered?

Heather reads the question in my eyes before I can figure out how to say it without sounding callous.

"It's our problem because they were killed with magic."

Shit. "But that means..."

"We don't know who did it yet." That's a big deal. At any given time, there are only a couple dozen magi in the entire country, so we're a pretty tight-knit group. And murder? Not exactly encouraged.

"Andrew and I are going to...Adrienne? Are you okay?"

"Hmm? Oh, just tired. It was a hell of a fight. Why?"

"You look pale."

I do? My glamour must be slipping.

I let the glamour fall, and Heather gasps. "What happened, Adrienne?"

"I got hurt. It's no big deal. I was going to ask you to look at it when we were done here. My first-aid spells were on the fritz last night, so I couldn't heal it."

"Show me." Heather's voice has gone still and serious.

"Really, it's not that big of a deal," I say again as I unwind the binding on my leg. "It looks pretty bad, but once you work your mojo, I'll be good as new."

When I finally expose the gashes in my thigh a stream of fresh blood comes oozing out. The skin around the scratches is shiny and puffed up.

"Oh my goodness," whispers Heather as she reaches a hand out tentatively in my direction. Her cool fingers brush against my thigh, making me see stars. I know I'm going to faint a half second before it happens. My eyes roll back in my head and Heather's arms wrap around me as I slide out of my chair.

I'm in my own bed when I come to, swathed in blankets with a giant poof ball covering my face. The poof ball notices I'm awake and begins to vibrate. With gentle fingers I lift the poof ball, also known as Pong, Liza's familiar, and move him to the warm indention my head left on the pillow. The black tabby accepts the relocation with grace and allows me to scratch him under the chin.

"Where is everyone, boy?" Pong opens one eye, as if to see if I really expect him to answer, then promptly falls back asleep.

I scramble out of bed and stretch, reveling in the way my body feels. It's achy and sore, a testament to what I accomplished last night, and my injured thigh is tender but whole once more. My fever is gone, my head is clear, and I'm starving.

There's no one in the kitchen, but someone left me a sandwich wrapped up in the fridge. My money's on Andrew. Not that Heather wouldn't make me a sandwich; Andrew's just more empathetic. I wasn't asleep long, and Liza and Dixon aren't home from school yet. Andrew is also absent, but I find Heather dozing on a couch in the downstairs living room, absentmindedly stroking the wing of a glorious macaw.

"Heather?"

"Hmm?"

"Thank you. For my leg."

"Do you know why you couldn't heal it?" Ever the teacher, Heather rarely explains something outright. She'd rather I try to work it out for myself first.

"I was already worn out from the fight, and I'd been struggling to cast even before that. I hit the hellhound with a wind spell and it barely held it at bay. Manipulation magic is hard for me on a good day, let alone in those circumstances."

"That's a good guess." Heather still doesn't open her eyes, but Cerise, the macaw, hasn't stopped staring me down. I swear, bird familiars give me the willies. "But that's not it."

"What else could it be?"

"Sit down."

Heather finally sits up, dislodging Cerise from her perch on the cushion, and meets my eyes with a serious expression. "It wasn't any deficiency on your part, not the injury and not your struggles with manipulation magic. There are few magi who would have been up to the task. As it was, even I couldn't do it alone. I required help from Cerise. What do you know of hellhounds, Adrienne?"

My answer is a monotone, rote memorization out of a textbook. "They're killing machines. They have little power of their own, relying on brute strength and ferocity, and do the bidding of whoever summons them. It's been at least two centuries since the last confirmed hellhound sighting."

"Do you know where they come from?"

"Deeper than the Shadow Plane. They have no magic of their own and lack the ability to cross planes unaided." I'm only a level-two magi, so my education is still lacking, but Heather's question makes me doubt my assumption.

Her next words prove me correct. "They come from the Ashen Plane."

A chill runs down my spine. There are many planes of existence between here, the Mortal Plane, and the Ashen Plane, which is pretty much what most people would refer to as hell. The creatures there are what nightmares are made of.

"Creatures from the Ashen Plane have a certain immunity to the magic we can access here on our plane. Your scratches from the hellhound were protected by powerful enchantments that had to be broken before I could even begin to heal the wounds. Your tardiness coming home compounded the issue, allowing the wounds to fester and infection to spread. You could have died, Adrienne."

Heather's always been good about saying just the right thing to make me feel bad about myself. She waves off my reply, though. "I'm not going to scold you. There are bigger things we need to talk about."

"Someone summoned it."

"Yes. That hellhound didn't get here on its own. The lives it has taken..."

She trails off, and we both sit in silence for a moment. It took longer than usual for us to track down what we thought was a werewolf, which was both endlessly frustrating and incredibly heartbreaking. As each full moon approached, the atmosphere in the manor got tense and agitated. Whoever summoned it is responsible for the lives it took, but that doesn't make any of us feel any better for failing to save them.

"They're going to pay, Heather. I'm going to make sure of it."

My words bring her out of her memories. "Yes, yes you are. That's what I wanted to talk to you about earlier. Andrew and I will be leading the investigation into the girls' school murders. I'd like you to track down our summoner."

"Me? Like, just me?"

"Just you. I'm putting you in charge of this investigation. You're nearly eighteen. It's time you began to take on more of a leadership role, and you're already intimately acquainted with the details of the case. It'll be good for you."

"I won't let you down." *I might let her down.*

"See that you don't. You killed their little pet, but don't expect that to be the end of it. If they summoned one hellhound, they're capable of summoning another. Find them before that happens."

Heart racing, I leave Heather and speed down the hall. I wait until the door of my room closes before I allow my thoughts to run wild. *My own mission! I'm finally running my own mission!* The ecstasy soon wears off, though, leaving doubt in its place. *How can she do this to me? I'm not ready for this!* And worse: *What if more people die because I'm not ready for this?*

I can't wait in my room until the others get home. I'll go insane if I don't work off this nervous energy. I change clothes quickly and fly back up the hall, down the stairs, and into the utility room in the basement. The manor is magically protected against influence from the Shadow Plane, and this is the only access inside the house. It doesn't lead to the whole plane, more like our own private pocket universe. The run down here has my pulse up, and it takes a minute to calm myself and prepare for the transition. It's a lot more dangerous over there. Taking two deep, slow breaths, I rein in my emotions, order my thoughts, and slip into the Shadow Plane.

Two

I MAGINE TWO DIFFERENT WOMEN, late at night, tired from a long day, families safe and asleep in their beds. They each hear a noise, a mysterious bump in the night. One of the women considers the noise, dismisses it, and goes on in to bed. Her family remains safe.

The second woman gets nervous about the noise. She turns on lights and checks every corner of the house. She never finds a reason for it, so she goes to bed jumpy and afraid. Her family is no longer safe. She let the shadow in.

Shadows are ever seeking to gain a foothold in the Mortal Plane. They can't do much; they whisper in people's ears, they influence people's emotions, always seeking to sow distrust and fear. Enough fear, enough influence, and a shadow can become strong enough to cross over. Most are benign; they want to get into people's heads but don't cause physical harm. Some, though, are malevolent.

The Shadow Plane and the Mortal Plane are the most closely connected of all the planes that make up totality; the deeper you go, the more obscure the planes become. For an experienced traveler, moving through the Shadow Plane is a lot like watching your favorite movie in black and white instead of color: familiar, understandable, but not quite right. There are no buildings or other marks of civilization, as the primary inhabitants, the shadows, don't need them. The vibrant colors of the Mortal Plane are muted to a somber hue, and the pieces of the landscape blend into one another.

Magi have been utilizing the Shadow Plane for centuries. Magic works better here. No one knows exactly why, but the prevailing theory is that life is less anchored here. Regardless, most of our training is done on this side. Normally I would encase myself in wards before traveling between planes, but not to go to the training room. Our pocket universe, tucked away as it is, is safe. There's a fleeting moment as we're between planes that we're vulnerable, but I utter the phrases that will allow me to pass through unmolested.

I find Andrew in the training room, pummeling the snot out of a practice dummy. Magic has its uses, but so does good old-fashioned hand-to-hand. Andrew resembles Heather so much they could be related: chestnut hair, only a few shades darker than hers, and a smattering of freckles. His eyes are blue, though, where hers are hazel bordering on green. "Want some real competition?" I call out, breaking Andrew's concentration.

"Sure! You know anybody?"

"Funny. Just give me a few minutes to warm up."

My few minutes turns into half an hour as my muscles protest against my stretches. By the time I return to the training room Andrew has abandoned the dummy and pulled out a pair of bow staffs.

"How are you feeling?" he asks as he tosses me a staff.

"I feel good." The staff is smooth and heavy in my hands. "Sorry," I add as an afterthought. "I screwed up. I didn't know how bad the injury really was."

Andrew brushes me off, then attacks without warning. I block his blow as a reflex, right foot sliding back to stabilize my balance. Then we're off, dancing across the floor, the sound of the staffs colliding soon joined by our panting breaths. It's been a while since I trained with a bow staff, and it shows. Moments later Andrew sweeps my legs out from underneath me, planting me on my back on the mat.

"Again?"

I kick out at him in response, and he gives me room to get back to my feet. The next round we move more slowly. I attack first this time, making an obvious play that Andrew doesn't fall for. I knew he wouldn't, though, which is why it works. Andrew moves to block the blow he thinks is coming, while I follow through on my "feint". The blow catches him across the middle, knocking the wind out of him.

"Nice shot," he wheezes.

"Again?"

We spar for the next half hour, neither of us really gaining the upper hand. Andrew trained me well, and we're pretty evenly matched, except for brute strength. Andrew holds back just enough to not crush me while still presenting me with a challenge.

"Enough." Andrew calls the halt when we're both gasping for breath and have sweat pouring down our backs. The bout was just what I needed to work out the kinks from last night.

A glance at the practice dummy Andrew was wailing on earlier tells me he needed it just as much as I did.

"Andrew?"

"Hmm?"

"Do you want to talk about it?"

"Talk about what?" He can't fool me. I look pointedly at the practice dummy, whose head is nearly completely detached and will need to be restuffed before it can be used again.

"Heather told me about last night."

"I'm sure she left out the gory details." He sighs and runs a hand through his damp hair. "They were just kids, Adrienne. Eleven and twelve years old. And they were butchered like animals."

"How do...how...Heather said they were killed by magic?"

"How could we tell?"

"Yeah."

"Magic isn't natural to our plane. It leaves a mark, every time it's used. It may have been a blade that struck the killing blows, but magic was somehow involved. Heather will figure out how, and hopefully from there we'll be able to figure out who."

A troubled look comes into Andrew's eyes, something more than just the tragic deaths of those girls. It takes me a minute, but I finally figure it out. "It's going to be someone you know, isn't it?"

"Most likely. There are some magic users other than the magi, but they typically possess very little power. Whoever committed this crime isn't an amateur."

I don't know how to answer that, so I don't say anything at all. The silence stretches until it becomes too long to break without sounding awkward. Thankfully, we're saved by a disembodied voice booming out, "Adrienne Young! You've got some explaining to do!"

"Can't he deliver a message normally?" Andrew mutters and shakes his head, and the air between us becomes normal again.

"Then he wouldn't be Dixon," I answer, heading toward the door while Andrew begins to collect the scattered pieces of the practice dummy.

Dixon is waiting for me in the utility room of the manor. "Look, I'm sorry about school today, but you know I wouldn't have left you guys alone if I didn't think you could handle it—"

"That's not it." Dixon's clearly agitated, bouncing up and down so hard his glasses keep sliding to the end of his nose. "Mr. Sanders caught me in the hallway. He gave me this."

I don't have to read the paper Dixon thrusts into my hands. "Dix—"

"You're failing chemistry! How can you be failing already? It's barely October!"

"Keep your voice down, would you? I'm handling it, and I don't need Heather on my tail." I steer Dixon toward the stairs, talking as I walk. He's only two years younger than me, but I still stand head and shoulders taller than him. I'm tall for my age, and he's short for his, causing a striking difference.

"How are you handling it? Are you doing extra credit or something? Because Mr. Sanders didn't say anything about—"

"Okay, fine, I haven't exactly figured it out yet, but I will, and Andrew and Heather never need to know. I just need some time."

Dixon gets serious. "What happened, Adrienne? You're not dumb enough to flunk."

"Things have just gotten away from me, that's all. I've missed some classes, and I really dropped the ball on some lab reports."

"Adrienne!"

"Give me a break! Chasing a werewolf, remember?"

"Werewolf?" Our journey has brought us into the kitchen, where a stranger stands in the middle of the floor watching Liza rummaging through the refrigerator. The bulb inside highlights Liza's coffee-colored skin and dark brown, disheveled hair, reminding me that I had promised to redo her braids before school this morning.

"Oh, um, just talking about a movie. Who are you?" I ask, sending Liza a weighted glance. There's nothing in the house that will give away our secrets, but we usually tell each other when we're having guests over to prevent situations exactly like this.

"I'm Violet. Liza and I are study-buddies." Her smile is so wide I can count all of her shiny, perfectly spaced teeth. Her clothes are covered in designer labels and her platinum-blonde hair looks like it was done by a professional.

I giggle. I can't help it; it just slips out. Study-buddies? Who says that? Out of Violet's view, Liza rolls her eyes. "Science project. Something about a comet. We won't be long. I want to hear more about your movie." Liza's glance carries a message of its own: *Don't you dare talk about last night without waiting for me.*

Liza leads Violet out of the kitchen, and I giggle again as I hear Violet questioning her on their way down the hall. "Why are you interested in a werewolf movie? I've always thought they were kind of lame. I really didn't think you'd be the type of person who…"

"Poor Liza," I mutter and shake my head, snagging a yogurt out of the fridge.

"You should probably wait to eat that," Dixon advises.

"Why?"

"You stink."

Dixon ducks the swipe I take at his head, but he's not wrong. I take my yogurt with me, scarfing it on my way back to my room. As I pass Liza's, I can hear the duo through the door, Violet prattling on about her family's summer home at Martha's Vineyard and Liza trying vainly to redirect her.

I crank the hot water and let the shower run while I undress, examining myself in the mirror. I'm what Heather likes to call a "late-bloomer": on the cusp of turning eighteen, and still resembling a willow tree more than a woman. The muscles under my skin are lean and defined, the natural consequence of workouts like the one I just had. I do like my green eyes. In a face as pale as mine, they almost glow. The one thing I definitely have going for me is my hair. Thick and curly, it falls in a black, tangled mess all the way to my hips. I get it from my mom.

The steam eventually fogs up the mirror until I can no longer see myself. The thoughts of my mom have soured my endorphin high, leaving me mired in the past. Heather and Andrew took me from my family when I began to exhibit signs of power at the tender age of eight. My parents consented, of course. How could they not? They couldn't even touch me without getting electrocuted or tossed across the room. Once I was in control of myself, I tried to re-establish contact, but the damage was already done. I still talk to my mom, sometimes, but each conversation is a struggle. I think they're afraid of me.

Violet doesn't leave until Heather kicks her out so that we can eat dinner as a family. "I can't believe you told Dixon about the hellhound last night and not me," Lisa accuses as we fill our plates.

"You weren't around. Dixon said you went to bed."

"I was around!" A confused look crosses Liza's face, and I can see the wheels turning behind her delicate features. "Actually, no. That's not right. Yeah, I must have fallen asleep." I don't have time to respond before we sit down, and the conversation drops.

Case talk is forbidden at the table, even for Andrew and Heather. House rules. Instead, we hear the incredibly boring details of Liza's science project while eating faster than normal, intent on getting the meal over with so we can get to work. Heather and Andrew are a team. Liza and Dixon are unofficially my team. They're both too young to be in the field yet, but they act as my support staff whenever I'm hunting a beastie. They'll probably never do what I do, either. As a combat magi, I do the physical stuff. Dixon's strength is in perception magic, and Liza's a prodigy. She's truly incredible. She's mastered everything the magi have set before her, but her preference is for manipulation magic. I kind of suck at both of those. They're too delicate and subtle. I'd much rather smash things.

If Heather and Andrew notice our haste, they don't comment on it. If Andrew's face is any indication, he's still dwelling on the girls' school murders. They're probably in as much of a hurry to work on their own case as we are on ours.

Once dinner is over, the three of us convene in the living room. I retrieve the case file from my room and spread the contents across the coffee table. There's nothing in it that points to magic, but if anyone got their hands on it they would be very concerned about my extra-curricular interests.

"So, when the attacks started, we thought it was a werewolf. The killings were savage, done on the full moon, with canine teeth. It was a safe assumption."

"We know all of this," Dixon interrupts, shoving a handful of popcorn into his mouth.

"Let her finish," Liza interjects. Pong purrs contentedly from her lap. "She's making a point."

"Yes, I am. We evaluated the killings on the assumption that the killer was a werewolf. Now that we know it wasn't, we need to start from the beginning." I wipe my sweaty hands on my pajama pants. The only difference between this meeting and the dozens of others just like it is that this time Andrew isn't sitting behind me making sure I don't miss anything. It changes everything. Namely, it's giving me performance anxiety.

"Werewolves are people. They change at the full moon, but they're not inherently monsters. Most of them control their bloodlust and live relatively normal lives. Once they start killing people, though, we take them out." None of us need the lesson, but again, it's about starting from the beginning.

"The hellhound has only ever been a beast. We were looking for a pattern, some logical reason why a werewolf would target these specific schools. Boston College. NYU. Penn State.

George Mason. Attacks happened at a lacrosse game, a Take Back the Night rally, and two different concerts. The only similarity was large groups of students. I got lucky last night when someone placed a 911 call reporting a stray dog on campus." It was the closest thing we'd had to a lead. I pause, considering how differently last night could have gone for those kids spilling out of that stadium.

"We need to look at the data again. Our killer wasn't a werewolf. It wasn't even the hellhound. It was the summoner. The hellhound only went where the summoner told it to go. That's a completely different motive than a werewolf attack. There's a pattern. We just have to find it."

Dixon's eyes light up as if Christmas just came early. Popcorn forgotten, he scoots over to the coffee table, anxious to get started.

Liza is less certain. "We've been poring over all of this for three months. Why do you expect to find something now?"

I can't tell her that the same thoughts have been plaguing me. "Our perspective is different this time. We may be looking at the same data, but we're doing it with a different starting point. I expect to find something because, well, because we have to."

Not exactly a rousing motivational speech. I can see it on their faces. Their excitement from this afternoon was purely about hearing the details of my fight with the hellhound. Now, faced with the same daunting task we couldn't even figure out the first time, their enthusiasm is dwindling.

Inspire them.

"Come on, guys. We've got this. If there's one thing I can do right, it's kick a beastie's ass. I'm a silver-knife-wielding, lightning-bolt-throwing, hellhound-slaying, badass super chick." I pull out my best pep rally voice. "So, we're going to find the pattern. We're going to find the summoner. And then I'm going to kick their ass!"

Andrew's voice comes echoing down the stairwell. "Remember, Adrienne, you're on dishes tonight! And use the soft scrubber on that skillet so it doesn't scratch!"

So much for being a badass.

THREE

M{R. SANDERS IS WAITING} for me the next morning, hovering by my locker like some kind of flying insect. It's early, and I'm still shaking off the remnants of a dream I can't quite remember, so flying insect is the best I can do. He's scowling.

"Good to see you back in class today, Ms. Young. I trust you are feeling better?"

I don't know what excuse Dixon gave for my absence yesterday, so I just smile and nod. *Although, Dixon could probably whip up a ghost version of me to make it seem like I'm in school. That way I won't be "absent" as much, and this doesn't happen again. No, that wouldn't work. He'd have to make it talk and answer questions and stuff, and-*

"Ms. Young?"

"Hmm?" I cringe as Mr. Sanders's scowl deepens.

"Care to share what's going on in your head that's so terribly interesting?"

"Not really."

"Well then. Did you manage to get the letter I sent home yesterday signed by your guardians?"

The emphasis he puts on "guardians" tells me exactly what he thinks of my situation. It's common knowledge that Heather and Andrew aren't our parents. The cover story is that the manor is a group home, which is close enough to the truth. Some people, like Mr. Sanders, apparently, take that to mean we're degenerates unfit for civilized society. I don't correct him. My track record in his class supports his theory, and it's not like I can tell him the truth anyway.

"I have it right here." It took me half an hour to get Andrew's signature just right on the paper. It was a little piece of manipulation magic that Liza could've done in a flash, but I didn't want to get her involved. Despite our extenuating circumstances, Heather and Andrew expect us to put in our best effort and get good grades. No way I'm telling them I'm failing chemistry.

Mr. Sanders looks disappointed. "Very well. I look forward to seeing you in class."

He turns on his heel and marches down the now-empty hall, paper clutched tightly in his fist. Sighing, I slam my locker shut as the bell rings overhead. *Great. Now I'm late for English.*

Later, Dixon beats me to lunch and saves me a seat at our table. "How'd it go?"

"Mr. Sanders hates me. But he did give me a project to do for extra credit." I flop my backpack onto the chair beside me and it lands with an audible thud.

"All of this is for chemistry?" Dixon hoists my bag up, testing its weight, while various classmates filter into the seats around us. It's not common for seniors to mix with sophomores, but thankfully, neither of us is popular enough for it to matter.

"Not just chemistry. Also English, geometry, and Spanish."

"You turning into a brain or something?" Dixon's friend Vinnie cracks up at his own joke and doesn't seem to notice that no one else is laughing.

I shrug it off, trying to deflect the attention. "Just need to get my grades up. College, you know?"

The mention of college sets off a flurry of conversation at my end of the table, and I pretend to pay attention as I poke at a flavorless beige lump on my lunch tray. College. I have no idea what I want to be when I grow up.

Being a magi doesn't have to influence my future. In fact, it's not supposed to. Saving the world is not everyday stuff. Most magi spend the bulk of their lives in non-life-threatening situations; but, they're expected to respond when the need arises. Even Heather and Andrew have "real" jobs. They work from home, online, which leaves them free to see to our training and respond quickly when something goes magically awry.

The use of magic in our careers is strictly regulated. For instance, there's a magi on Wall Street named Mick Eggers. He's absolutely not allowed to use magic to influence the stock market in any way whatsoever. However, if he spills coffee on his tie, he's more than welcome to use manipulation to fix it, or perception to make the people around him not even see it. Then there's Willow. She's Native American, and in her late seventies. She's a veterinarian on her reservation in Montana, and she uses magic every day. Manipulation magic, mostly. Healing bones, closing wounds. Her clients are astounded at the miracles she can work on their pets.

That being said, our first and foremost duty is to protect people. Secondary to that is to protect our secrets. And my life will be more involved than most. There are exactly five combat magi in the country that I know of. Myself, Andrew, a guy named Mason Chandler, and two others, both of whom are very old. Any magi can fight a monster, but us combat magi are specifically trained for it.

"What about you, Adrienne?" The question comes from Kelsey, a girl who's been trying to be my friend since she moved here two years ago. She's nice, but you can only be so close with someone when you can't let them completely into your world.

"College? I don't really know. I don't even know what I want to study." The conversation moves on without me, but my thoughts linger on the recent college "visits" I've had. NYU. George Mason. Boston College. Penn State. The blood spilled there makes me shudder. *If I never see another college campus again it'll be too soon.* Still, everyone at the table seems to have a plan. They make me feel directionless. Unfocused.

A hand on my shoulder startles me out of my pity party before I can sink too deep. "Adrienne? I overheard you talking to Ms. Rochester and thought you might like to borrow my geometry notes?" The hand belongs to Alex, our school's star running back and the guy I've had a crush on for the past three years.

"Sure. Thanks." Unable to hold his eyes, my own drop to the notebook in his hand. *Why do you always do this? Why can't you just look at the guy?* By the time I look up again he's already moving away, making me kick myself. *Not that it matters. You can't date him anyway. Can't date, can't go to college, can't have any friends…*

The bell rings before I can wander any farther down my "poor me" path. Dixon turns down the south hallway toward his locker, and I continue on toward fifth-period economics. The one class I'm not on the brink of flunking, but only because the teacher never assigns any homework.

I meet up with Dixon again after school, where Liza waits for us by the car. The junior high lets out twenty minutes before the high school, and it's easier for her to walk across the street than for us to drive over and pick her up. Dixon starts to ask her about her day, but before he can get the words out, Liza squeals and grabs my elbow.

"Adrienne! Look!"

I whirl, eyes scanning the parking lot for imminent danger, but see nothing out of the ordinary. "What?"

Liza's voice is dangerously close to swooning. "By the silver pickup. He has a motorcycle."

A motorcycle? My pulse quickens. It takes a moment to locate Alex among the throng of cheerleaders clustered around the bike, but I don't stop looking until I do. My breath catches as he throws his head back in a laugh, long blond hair artfully tousled around his face. Apparently one of the bimbos is funny. I scowl. I could make him laugh. I did, once. We could be good together. Even our names sound good together. Adrienne and Alex.

Dixon makes a gagging sound and plops into the passenger seat. Liza and I linger, watching the bimbos slowly filter away. As the crowd thins, I get a good look at Alex's flashy new bike. I have enough danger in my life as it is, but something about a motorcycle still makes me go all tingly. When they're all gone,

Alex looks up, straight at me, and catches me staring at him. Neither of us looks away.

Maybe it's my lingering bad mood from lunch. Maybe it's the motorcycle inspiring me to be reckless. "I'm going to do it."

"What?" Liza squeaks.

I don't answer. I'm too busy moving forward before I chicken out again. Alex watches me walk toward him, a half-smile turning his mouth up at the corner. I know exactly what I'm going to say. *Nice bike. Do you have plans for this weekend? Maybe you'd like to do something after the game?* Simple, direct, and easy.

Instead, what comes out is, "Weekend game plan something bike?"

Blood rushes into my cheeks as I die right there on the pavement. Alex just stares at me, looking puzzled.

"Sorry." I spin on my heel and have to keep myself from running away as fast as I can, which is pretty darn fast.

I'm halfway back to the car when his voice comes from right behind me. "Adrienne!"

I stop and turn, eyes trained on the ground.

"You want to go out with me sometime?"

Slowly, I let my eyes rise until they meet his. My voice takes a moment to find its way out of my mouth. "Are you sure?"

He smiles again, that heart-stopping, head-spinning, makes-the-whole-world-stand-still smile. "I'm sure."

"Okay." I don't know how the word comes out. My head is still trying to wrap itself around what's happening here.

"Cool. I'll call you."

"Okay."

Liza's grinning from ear to ear when I finally make it back to the car. "That was so cool!"

"Uh-huh." Numb, I stare at the steering wheel a moment, trying to remember what to do next.

"Adrienne?" Dixon's annoyance breaks my trance. "Are we leaving or not?"

"Oh, um, yeah. Buckle up." Somehow I get us home without killing us all.

My senses come crashing back down the moment we get home. Something's off; all of us can feel it. No matter what happens during the school day, magi duties take priority. My fluttery feelings vanish as sobriety settles in.

There's a conference going on in the living room. Heather and Andrew are sitting among a small collection of other magi. The three of us hover in the door, unsure about whether we should intrude.

Andrew spots us first. He excuses himself and hurries over. "Hey, guys, how was school?"

"What's going on?" I ask, ignoring the question. My eyes sweep the room. I know most of the magi present, by name at least. My gaze snags a moment on Mason Chandler. He's only a few years older than me and was living at the manor when I got here. This must be his first council meeting. They have him tucked in a corner, taking notes. The badge on his chest gleams, like he came straight from work.

"We're discussing the girls' school murders. We shouldn't be too much longer." The voices in the living room die down to a barely discernible hush as the occupants become aware of our presence.

Andrew ushers us upstairs without giving us any more information. By unspoken agreement we convene in Liza's room, but only because it's the first one we come to. I'm unprepared for what I see when I walk in. The room is completely covered in sunflowers. Actual, growing sunflowers. They're sprouting from the carpet and climbing the walls, obscuring every inch of the lilac paint underneath.

Dixon whistles softly. So, he didn't know either.

Liza notices us noticing. "They relax me. Help me sleep."

I'll lecture her about the obvious display of magic later. "Something's wrong."

"Yeah. Heather's never had the council here at the manor before." Dixon plops onto Liza's bed. "It must be bad."

Liza settles into a seated position on the floor, legs crossed in some kind of yoga position. "Let's find out."

"How do you plan to do that?"

She doesn't answer me, just closes her eyes and begins to take long, even breaths. Dixon and I shut up. She's using techniques we've all been taught when attempting a difficult piece of magic. She intones a chant under her breath, one I can't hear. It doesn't matter. The words she's using don't matter. Magic is all about intent. The words only help us to focus our mind and channel that intent into our desired outcome.

It only takes a moment. Liza stops speaking abruptly, and a stack of paper materializes out of the air and drops to the floor in front of her.

Dixon and I scramble to join her. "What did you do?" I ask, grabbing for the papers. My mouth drops open as I realize what I'm holding. "You stole their case file?"

"No. I just copied it."

"You...copied it." Liza's nonchalance isn't fooling anyone. Whatever she did, it's an impressive piece of manipulation magic. I look once more at the sunflowers. She's getting stronger.

Silence reigns in the next few minutes as we pass around the pages. Heather and Andrew are thorough, and there are a lot of notes to go through. The notes I can handle, but when I get to the pictures, my stomach heaves. I've never killed anything human. This is...this is...exactly what Andrew said. Butchery.

I force myself to study the pictures anyway. Those girls deserve my whole attention, despite my squeamishness. When I can't look anymore, I pass them to Dixon and start reading through Andrew's notes. His penmanship is small, neat, and precise, much different from Heather's smooth and flowing script. Most people assume Heather wears the pants in their marriage. Generally, they're right. She's a stronger magi and typically takes the lead in the field, which can't help but carry over into their personal lives. But they'd be wrong to assume that makes Andrew weak. His strengths are different from hers, but no less for it. It's why they're such a good team.

"Here." Liza begins to read out loud. "Though magic was present at the scene, we have been unable to determine its source. The traces of it are faint, indicating that it is either old or the user is very weak. Upon closer examination, its signature does not belong to any magi that we know of, nor even to any human being."

"What exactly does that mean?" Dixon asks, without raising his eyes from the photo he's studying. He squints, turning the page to look at it from every angle.

I chime in. "I think it's pretty clear. Not only do they not know who did it, it seems the killer isn't even human. At least, the magic doesn't belong to a human user."

"That doesn't make sense," Liza objects. "The girls were killed with a blade. Obviously a human did that."

"Got it!" Dixon exclaims, punching the air. He finally looks up, eyes wild. "They weren't killed by magic."

"Um, what?"

"Look here." He shoves the other papers aside and lays the picture down so Liza and I can see it. It's one of the accessory photos, with the only hint of a crime being a few splashes of blood on the grass. The picture is concentrated on a section of crisscrossing sidewalk, with a little bit of the garden in view around the edges. Broken pieces of statuary are scattered about, and a basket is upturned on the ground.

"What are we looking at?" I ask. Liza leans back against the bed, happy to let me do the talking.

"You know how I spend a lot of time in the library?" We both nod. I'm the muscle. Liza's the prodigy. Dixon's the brain. "I just finished reading a compendium of obscure branches of magic, most of which aren't practiced or even recognized anymore. Not that they're not valid, just obsolete."

"Your point?"

"Two things are out of place." He indicates the broken statue and the basket.

"How is a broken statue out of place in a garden?" I'm trying to see what Dixon sees, I really am.

"What if it's not a statue? What if it's a shrine?"

"A shrine?"

"Yeah." He becomes visibly excited. "And the ground around the basket has tiny little specks. I can't make them out, but I'm guessing it's some kind of bread."

"And together these mean?"

Dixon's eyes shine. "Worship. It's holistic, and gentle, and not entirely human. Heather and Andrew can't pin the magic down because it wasn't done by a magi. It was done by the girls."

FOUR

"**W**HAT ARE THE CHANCES those girls were working magic on the same night a hellhound was summoned? And on a full moon, no less?" It didn't take long for my thoughts to make this jump. Dixon's still downstairs explaining his theory to the council. Liza's sprawled across her bed as I pace restlessly across her floor.

"You think the girls summoned the hellhound?"

Do I? If they didn't, it's one heck of a coincidence. But how would a bunch of children have enough power to pull a hellhound all the way out of the Ashen Plane? Even on a full moon...

"The full moon," I mutter, mostly to myself.

"What?"

"The full moon," I repeat, louder, stronger. "We're complete idiots."

Liza huffs. "Maybe *you* are."

I pace faster, my words speeding up to match. "We're still thinking werewolf. Of course werewolves kill on the full moon. But it wasn't a werewolf."

Liza bolts upright. "So why did it kill on the full moon?"

"Exactly."

"Because whoever summoned the hellhound is weak. They needed the extra *oomph* the full moon would give their magic to be able to pull it over."

I sober quickly. "So, it really could have been those girls. That could be good. At least, that would mean it's over."

A shrill whistle cuts through the sudden silence in the room, startling both of us. Liza and I stare at each other a moment, then recognition comes.

"Your phone!"

"Alex!"

I lunge at my backpack, still sitting by the door where I dropped it. I dig the phone out of the front pocket on the fourth ring and manage to answer just before it goes to voicemail.

"Hello?" I ask breathlessly.

Alex notices. "Adrienne? Are you okay? You sound strange."

Stupid! Don't screw this up!

"Yeah, I'm fine. What's up?" It's a good thing I'm skilled at calming my body on demand. I put that training to work now, forcing my heart to slow and my voice to stay even. It's an abrupt shift from magic and hellhounds to boys and dates, and it takes me a moment to hear Alex's next words.

"Okay. I wanted to see if you have plans for this weekend. I think you may have told me you were coming to Friday's game?"

My words in the parking lot come rushing back to me as my face heats again. "Um, yeah, I was thinking about it."

"Cool. How would you like to go out for a burger after?"

"With you?"

He laughs. It's not a mocking laugh, though. "Yeah, with me. Kind of like a date."

Stay cool. You knew he was going to ask you out, remember? Be cool. I swallow hard. "I'd like that."

"Cool. So, I guess I'll see you at school tomorrow."

"Yeah, see you tomorrow."

Liza squeals when I hang up the phone. "I can't believe you have a date with Alex!"

"I know!" I allow her girlish fervor to wash over me and sweep me away. We laugh and squeal together, jumping up and down like children.

A few more minutes of giggling passes, then I allow my mind to shift gears again. *This back-and-forth is going to give me a headache. I need to solve this case so I can go back to my life.* "We should get downstairs."

Liza follows me back down to the living room, where Dixon is still trapped. Having heard him out, they're now discussing his theory while ignoring his physical presence. Liza and I slip in and join him in camaraderie. Heather notices us and beckons us to hold on a minute while an older magi finishes speaking.

"There is still the issue of the murdered students. Even if they were the ones working magic, which I have not yet heard enough evidence to convince me of, they did not kill themselves. There is still a killer who needs to be caught."

"No one has forgotten the killer, Walter, least of all me. But Dixon's idea has merit, and I believe it warrants further scrutiny." Hearing Andrew come to Dixon's defense makes me smile.

"Adrienne?"

My turn already? My throat goes dry as all eyes turn to me. "The full moon." Flustered, I blurt out the thought the same way it came to me upstairs.

Mason pounces on my moment of weakness. "Is that all you have to say? We're all aware the girls were killed under a full moon, so just go on back to your room. I'm sure you have homework to do."

I scowl at him, my hackles rising. It's too easy for him to get under my skin. *I can't believe I actually let him...nope. Not going there.* Just thinking about him touching me makes my skin crawl. Instead, I say the words that will put him in his place. "I killed a hellhound last night."

A collective intake of breath circles the room. Apparently Heather hasn't gotten around to sharing that tidbit yet. "It's been raised every full moon for the past four months."

"It took you four months to kill it?" Mason says, unwilling to be impressed like everyone else.

"I didn't know it was a hellhound. I thought it was a werewolf. You know, with the full moon and everything," I sneer back.

"The point?" Walter speaks again, his annoyance loud and clear. I think his last name starts with an H, but I can't place it at the moment.

"The point. Right. Why would someone need the full moon to raise a hellhound unless they weren't strong enough to do it otherwise? What if..." I can barely bring myself to say it. "What if it was the murdered girls?"

Dixon is looking at me like he's offended he didn't get to hear my idea before everyone else. Liza is half hiding behind me, still shy in the presence of so many magi. Andrew has a thoughtful expression, while Heather is showing hardly any emotion at all. *She was already thinking it.*

"You think a bunch of adolescent schoolchildren pulled a hellhound from the Ashen Plane using benign worship magic and used it to go on a killing spree?" asks another magi I met once but didn't bother to remember. Tara? Tamara? Whatever her name, her sour face and snarky tone are going to stick in my memory this time.

Well, when you say it like that...

I look around the room once, registering the hesitation on most of the faces. It's almost enough to make me back up, say I was mistaken, and flee upstairs. But no. This hellhound is *my* case, and I *will* fight for it. "I think it's possible, but it's too soon to know for sure." I take a deep breath, readying myself to switch from ideas to action in my first attempt at being assertive. "I need to see the scene."

"Just breathe, Adrienne." Andrew's words have no effect on me whatsoever. I'm so far out of my depth that I'm having trouble just standing still. *Examining a crime scene? Especially a murder scene? I don't belong here. What am I even looking for?*

I hug my leather jacket tighter against the nighttime chill. Under the cover of darkness, Andrew and I survey the open garden path. Yellow crime-scene tape still flutters from the bushes around us, although the physical evidence of what happened here has all been taken away. The glamours we're using will hide us from prying eyes, but it's much more difficult to trick people out of seeing movement in the grass and shadows against the ground. Hence the darkness.

"You have every right to be here, Adrienne. The council holds no power over you." Andrew continues to mutter assurances under his breath, knowing how the words of the council will have taken root inside. The other magi were not pleased when I insisted on seeing the crime scene. Most of them aren't yet sold on any of the "wild theories" us "children" have dreamed up.

"Your friend Walter would disagree with you. I believe his exact words were 'perverse interest bordering on voyeurism.'"

"Walter Henderson and I have clashed many times before, and doubtless we will clash again. His opinions don't change the fact that the council exists for discussion and guidance only. They can't tell you what to do unless you break the law."

Having the right doesn't mean I want to be here. The bodies may be gone, but I can see them anyway, burned into my memory. The details Dixon fixated on are gone, too. The statue, the basket, the theoretical bread. If I didn't know any better, I would find the location peaceful. A few night-blooming flowers are still holding out, unwilling to submit to the onset of autumn. Dew covers the sweet-swelling grass. A cobbled walkway meanders from the south, the direction of the dormitory, splitting in two as it chases each horizon.

"I'm ready," I say quietly, catching Andrew's attention. He's staring intently down at the grass, seeing things not studied in a picture.

"Do you remember the spell?"

"I remember. Whether I can cast it or not is another story." I spent the bulk of the evening with Andrew in the training room attempting to master this spell before we set out. It's the same one he and Heather use to detect magic. It's a fairly simple reversal of perception magic for the average magi. I'm not the average magi.

It takes me almost twenty minutes to successfully cast. I feel it take hold, then the air around me begins to gently hum, as if a storm were moving in. Unbidden, the tiny hairs on my arm stand up with a static charge.

"It feels familiar," I tell Andrew in confusion.

His teacher face is back in place. "What does it feel like?" he asks.

I close my eyes, allowing the sensation to wash over me. "Like...home. Like the manor, and dinner, and training, and...it's you. You and Heather."

"Yes. We worked a lot of magic here the other night. Look deeper."

I close my eyes this time. Heather and Andrew's magic is floating on the surface. The older magic will be fainter, fading away until in a few days nothing will be left at all.

"What does it feel like?"

The older magic is harder to pin down, like trying to fish the right pair of socks out of the dresser without turning on the light. I think I have it, though. "Like...Light. Earth. Darkness. Wait, how can it feel like light and darkness at the same time?"

Andrew chuckles despite our grim surroundings. "You're beginning to understand the difficulty Heather and I are facing."

It's a humbling reminder that while I may be chasing an idea, Andrew is chasing a very real killer. This crime scene is a lesson for me, but it's his responsibility.

"Do you think they're connected?" I've avoided asking him this question all evening, afraid of how he might answer. Even if they think I'm dead wrong, he and Heather will let me chase my tail and make every mistake in the book.

"I think your idea has merit, but at this point, who can say? I'll admit, I don't know anything about worship magic. Dixon's reading books that haven't been opened in decades. But this is for you to decide, Adrienne. If you feel like there's a connection, don't let anyone dissuade you."

"So, basically, trust myself?"

"Basically, yes."

"Great." Trusting myself doesn't come easily. Killing a beastie? Sure. Making a judgment call? Not so much.

"There's something else I want to do, while I'm here."

"What did I just say?"

"Trust myself?"

"Exactly. You don't need my permission."

"Okay then." I'm still holding on to the feeling of the older magic. I don't want to sit on the wet grass, so I move over to the walkway and settle down where all three paths meet. A small bundle in my jacket pocket holds a few strips of cedar wood, bound together with a sprig of vetiver grass. "Ignis," I mutter, and the bundle begins to smoke as I lay it on the ground before me. Fire is combat magic. For the next several minutes I simply breathe the smoke in, allowing it to soothe my nerves and sharpen my focus. I sink deep into my seat, hands resting limply on my knees, and allow myself to find that place of perfect serenity within. For a spell this complicated, I need all the serenity I can get.

The spell is a concoction of Liza's, thrown together in the hour after dinner before darkness fell. Her confidence in my ability to cast it is flattering, but I didn't have any time to practice. Hence the props.

With an effort, I ignore the minutes ticking by. Andrew won't mind the delay, but the longer we stay, the more likely we'll be discovered. I can't think about that, though. *Perfect serenity, remember?*

The smell of the cedar wood brings back memories of the first time I attempted to cast a spell. I was nine, and had been living at the manor for a couple of months, studying the mechanics of magic. Heather and I were sequestered in the training room, cedar wood burning in a censer. I was supposed to be lighting a candle and set the hem of her dress ablaze instead. The memory makes me smile, and with it, everything clicks into place.

I begin the incantation just as Liza had me memorize it, the flowing poetry foreign on my tongue. It's how she thinks. I prefer power words, spells I can cast in an instant during a fight. Despite my struggles I stay completely focused on my intentions, framing the words around what I want to happen. I reach the end and wait, but there's nothing. Sighing, I take a deep breath of cedar, center myself, and begin again.

The cedar wood is a smoldering pile of ash by the time I successfully cast Liza's spell. Falling backward, I lay panting on the walkway, stitches crawling up my back from holding my posture.

Andrew's face appears above mine.

"How long?"

He checks his watch. "Three hours."

I groan. Liza and I are going to have to have a talk about her faith in me.

"What does it do?"

I answer between panting breaths, arching my back to stretch out my spine. "It puts a tracer on the magic's signature. If that particular magic is used again, I'll know about it."

"Liza?"

"Liza."

"Neat."

I give my back one last long, good stretch, and my fingers scrape against a large stone on the walkway. I pull it closer, then scramble upright as I realize it's not a stone.

"Look at this!"

I hand it to Andrew and watch him closely examine it. It's obviously broken off of something; it's smooth on one side and jagged on the other.

"It looks like fired clay. Like pottery."

"Like something a student might make in art class? Like a shrine?"

Andrew hands the piece back. "Keep it safe. It could be nothing, or it could just be the proof you need."

I tuck the piece deep into my jacket pocket as I follow Andrew out of the garden. When the school is a safe distance behind us, we drop our glamours and melt into the darkness behind a copse of trees. I pull my wards tight as I enter the Shadow Plane. I can feel them like a second skin, encasing my entire body in magical protection. Magi aren't taught until level two to enter the Shadow Plane for just this reason. Over here, we're like juicy steaks to the shadows. If given the chance, they'll eat us up and leave us a quivering ball on the ground, too afraid to move. Or worse, use us to hitchhike back across to the other side.

The spells to master moving through the Shadow Plane are difficult to learn but easy to employ. Minutes after entering in Vermont, Andrew and I emerge in Massachusetts. The manor lies just outside Salem, and the irony isn't lost on us.

It's past midnight by the time we finally arrive home. *So much for getting started on that extra credit.* The manor is a bit creepy in the dark, large and brooding. Something's extra weird tonight, though. Liza's light is still on.

Five

PONG MEETS US AT the door.

"Hey, handsome. Why aren't you upstairs with Liza, huh?" I scoop him up into my arms. "Oof, you've put on weight."

Andrew frowns and takes Pong from me, hefting and poking at him. "Hmm. I think you're right. He does seem a little heavier. That's interesting."

"Why?" The word barely fits around the massive yawn that takes over my face. *Bed. Sleep.* "Liza's just been feeding him too much."

"Remember that familiars aren't actually animals, Adrienne. Pong isn't really a cat. His size is a manifestation of Liza's strength. If he's getting bigger, it means Liza's getting stronger."

"Oh. Good for her, then." It's hard not to sound whiny when I'm this tired. And when it comes to familiars, it's extra hard to not devolve into whiny mode. Not every magi has a familiar, but we all want one. Liza's the youngest magi in a century to have one.

Pong races me up the stairs, leading me to Liza's room. The door is shut tight, no light peeking out from underneath. Maybe I miscounted the windows.

I knock quietly and crack open the door. Light blazes into the hallway. *She put a perception spell on her own bedroom door?* "Liza?"

"Come in."

Liza's sitting cross-legged on the floor staring blankly at a magazine. Pong rushes to her and nuzzles her under the chin.

"Keeping secrets?" I ask, pointing behind me at the door.

"I didn't want to disturb anyone." Her voice is weak and heavy, and the eyes she raises to mine are bloodshot.

"What's going on?" I ask, all teasing vanishing in my concern.

"Can't sleep." She says it lightly but can't hide the troubled look in her eyes.

I lower myself to the floor beside her and wrap an arm around her shoulder. This close, it's easy to make out the tiny silver scar against the dark skin of her shoulder. A dog bite, from when she was little. "It's more than that. Talk to me."

She sighs and leans heavily into my side. "I used to get nightmares a lot when I was little. I hadn't had any for a while, though. I thought they were over."

"What are the dreams about?"

"I don't remember. But they scare me."

Magic comes so easily to Liza that sometimes it's hard to remember she's still a twelve-year-old girl. A frightened, lonely, twelve-year-old girl.

"Shh," I whisper, pulling her in tight. I scoop an arm under her knees and carry her to her bed, curling myself around her.

"Averte." The light goes out, and I feel her body relax against mine. "You're safe here with me. I'll protect you."

"Aaah!" The scream echoes through the manor, waking us all more effectively than Liza's alarm clock, which from the flashing time has been going off for more than fifteen minutes. I bolt from the bed, barely registering that Liza isn't there, tangling my legs up and tripping over blankets in my half-asleep haste.

I'm fully awake by the time I hit the staircase. Andrew and Heather come rushing in from the other direction and fall in behind me. "Downstairs," Heather gasps.

"Where's Dixon?" Liza asks, meeting us at the bottom. Her voice is high and frantic, the half-eaten muffin in her hand forgotten.

We don't have long to wonder. Dixon must have screamed incredibly loudly for us to hear him from all the way down in the utility room. His voice leads us to him, casting the same containment spell over and over.

Something got in.

We crash into the room to find him battling a shadow. Rather, desperately trying to keep it at bay as it charges for the door. I'm the first one in, crying out "Quae!" as I understand what's happening. It's a different containment spell than Dixon was attempting, but the outcome is the same. The shadow becomes locked, bound in both place and plane.

Liza goes to Dixon, who's panting and shaking. Andrew and Heather examine the shadow.

"What happened?" Heather asks Dixon, firmly but not harshly.

"I—I don't know. I was getting some practice in before school, and it's like it was waiting for me to come back."

"Your wards?"

"I did my wards just as I always do. It didn't ride me back. It was like it was already in between planes."

Heather purses her lips. "That's not possible. Someone had to bring it over."

Dixon is adamant. "It wasn't me."

"It's interesting," Andrew interjects, defusing the situation. "It didn't want you. It wanted out. Why would a malicious shadow work so hard to cross over and not go after the obvious target?"

Heather is not easily mollified, but she doesn't question Dixon again. With a wave of her hand, she banishes the shadow back to where it belongs. "This bears looking into. I'll examine the door and make sure our wards remain intact. For now, you all need to hurry or you'll be late for school."

School. Great. I yawn widely and follow Liza and Dixon back upstairs.

"Why wasn't your containment spell working?" Liza asks Dixon. "I thought you learned it months ago."

"I did. But the shadow was fighting so hard. I just couldn't catch it."

"No," I interject, trying not to sound too harsh. "That wasn't it. The problem was your control."

"But I know that spell by heart, I just—"

"Doesn't matter. You can practice all you want, but it's just practice. You didn't have control over your own mind and your own emotions, so when it came time to put that practice to work, you failed. Control is the foundation of combat magic. If you ever want to get out in the field, you have to master that."

We rush through our showers as fast as we can, but the minutes continue to slip by. It's nearly eight o'clock by the time we're all downstairs stuffing muffins into our backpacks.

"We're not going to make it." Liza panics, rushing for the door.

"We'll be fine." I stop her, making her sit down and actually tie her shoelaces. "We'll just have to go through the Shadow Plane."

Liza's eyes go wide. Dixon starts to object, but I raise a hand to stop him. "None of us can afford to be late, but especially not me. If you're not comfortable with it, you can take Liza in the car and be late. But I'm going."

"I'll be fine," Liza insists, before Dixon can say anything. "I've been in the Shadow Plane with Heather before."

"In training," he asserts. "You're not cleared to be there. If anything were to go wrong—"

"Nothing's going to go wrong. I'll stay with Adrienne, and she'll cover me with her wards. Right?"

Her question is directed at me. "We'll be fine. And we'll make it to school on time, and everyone wins. All right? Let's go."

Outside, I squeeze Liza's hand tightly as we shift into the Shadow Plane. After this morning's excitement, I'm on high alert, but no shadows are waiting to ambush us on the other side. There are a couple in the distance, but they're not interested in us at the moment. I take a few steadying breaths and lead us forward. Liza presses in close, squeezing back just as tightly. So long as we stay in physical contact, I'll be able to protect her. She's so proficient in magic she's not even on the chart, but because of her age and inexperience, Heather and Andrew decided to keep her on the Mortal Plane. She's only been a practicing magi for about a year.

Magic isn't genetic. No one knows where magi come from, or why only a handful are born to each generation. When magi children are identified, it's the guardians' job to track them down and train them. Liza's a special case. Her mother was a magi and used magic to hide Liza from the guardians. It wasn't until her mother died, suddenly and unexpectedly, that Heather and Andrew even learned of her existence.

Liza's usually bright and open face is drawn by the time we re-enter the Mortal Plane in the parking lot of the high school. I normally wouldn't make such an obvious entrance, but there's so much chaos in the parking lot that I didn't think we'd get noticed.

"Adrienne!"

My name being called by a deep male voice has my footsteps faltering. A moment later Alex catches up. "Hey. I didn't see you guys pull in."

What do you say to the guy you embarrassed yourself in front of yesterday but have a date with tomorrow night? I don't look directly in his eyes or else I truly won't say anything at all. Instead I keep my eyes on Liza, pretending to be watching her intently as she crosses the street to the junior high.

"Oh, yeah. My car's making this funny sound, so Andrew dropped us off." The lie comes easily. Hiding who I am is as natural to me as breathing.

Dixon takes off, leaving me alone with Alex. I finally look at him, and he's smiling like he's incredibly happy to see me. If I don't watch myself, I'm going to get utterly lost in those stormy blue eyes. The way he's looking at me makes me feel like I'm being tossed in a tumultuous sea, clinging to a piece of plywood and trying desperately not to drown. I don't know what he's planning to say, but I preempt him before I can screw up and say anything that'll make him decide he doesn't want to go out with me after all.

"I really have to get to homeroom, so I'll see you later, okay?"

I rush inside as the warning bell rings. Alex calls out behind me, "See you in geometry!"

Seriously, Adrienne? You've had conversations with the guy before. Whole conversations! Remember that presentation you did together last spring about Attila the Hun? It wasn't this hard then! My inner monologue turns into dialogue when I snap at myself, *Yeah, but this is personal! There's nothing romantic about Attila the Hun!* I don't have time to figure it out now. I slip into English class as the second bell rings, barely escaping yet another tardy.

Alex is waiting for me when I get to geometry. "Hey, Adrienne."

I expected this, so at least the weight of his presence doesn't take me by surprise. "Hey, Alex." *So far, so good.*

Then the rest of the football team comes in. At least, that's what it feels like when they descend on Alex and start launching questions at him about tomorrow's game. He falls into conversation with them easily, and why wouldn't he? They're his best friends. I back away until I'm outside of the circle and make my way to my usual desk.

To my surprise, a moment later Alex slides into the desk next to mine. "Sorry about that. Guys can be a little thick-headed this close to a game, and I'm including myself in that. I didn't mean to ignore you."

"No, it's fine. I didn't have anything to say anyway."

Kelsey enters the class and starts walking my way, stopping dead in her tracks when she notices Alex sitting in her seat. After a long once-over she flashes me a smile and a thumbs-up, then heads to the empty seat at the back of the room. She's not the only one who's noticed that something's off. Alex's friends are looking back and forth between him and his usual desk, now taken by Kelsey, and one of the cheerleaders that was hanging all over his motorcycle yesterday is glaring daggers at me. I can feel the tips of my ears start to burn under their scrutiny.

The bell rings, and Ms. Rochester is writing on the board when a tiny paper football bumps up against my hand. *A note? Seriously?* I snatch it up and unfold it under my desk, out of sight.

It's from Alex. *Can we talk later? I feel like things are getting off on the wrong foot.*

Writing is easier than actually talking. *It is a little awkward. It doesn't help that everyone keeps staring at us.*

Ms. Rochester calls three students to the board, and his reply takes several excruciating minutes to come. *We do seem to have caused a commotion.*

I don't have a chance to respond. Ms. Rochester spends the rest of the hour lecturing in my direction, as if she knows I'm not really paying attention. I keep my eyes trained on her, studiously ignoring Alex on my left, which is no easy feat. I can feel his gaze on me, but I'm too chicken to turn and meet it.

The bell rings, and Alex stays by my side as we surge toward the door. "I need a moment," he mutters into my ear, grasping my elbow and steering me into an alcove under the stairwell. I don't object. My desire to be near him is at war with my certainty that he's making a huge mistake, and if I don't get it sorted out, I'm going to be completely useless all day.

"You're having second thoughts, aren't you?" he wastes no time in asking, picking up where his note left off.

The words come more easily this time. "Maybe. I don't know. The way they were all looking at us, like we'd grown second heads or something. Why did you ask me out? Why now?"

"Did you forget that you tried to ask me out first?"

"Is that what this is? A pity date?"

Alex heaves a sigh and runs his hands through his hair. "Is it that hard to believe I'm attracted to you?"

I miss a breath. And another. When I try to speak, nothing comes out.

A small smile comes to his lips. "I thought you were gorgeous when I first laid eyes on you freshman year. Aren't you attracted to me?"

His smile gives me boldness. "Of course I am."

"Then what's the problem?"

"Why now?" I don't know how he hears the question with the cacophony in the hall, but he does. "You can have anybody you want. Why me? Why now?"

"Why now? Because you never seemed interested in me before. You rarely meet my eyes, you're polite but distant when we happen to be on the same project, you can't wait to escape if we get left alone. Then there was that debacle in the parking lot yesterday, and I realized I had it backwards."

My face heats again as he accurately describes our interactions over the past few years. "You noticed all that, huh?"

"I noticed you." Dimly I hear the bell, but I can't bring myself to care. "You have no reason to be insecure. I think you're beautiful, and smart, and interesting, and I'd like to get to know you better."

"I'd like that."

"Good to know."

For a moment we just stare at each other. His words tumble through my head; I had no idea he'd given me that much thought. I hear him call me beautiful again, and a smile tugs at the corner of my mouth.

Alex leans in close. "I'd love to know what that smile means." His words, softly spoken, echo strangely in the silence outside our alcove.

Silence?

"Crap! I'm late to chemistry!"

Six

I SLIP OUT OF the Shadow Plane just behind the bleachers and take a quick look around to make sure no one saw me. Not anticipating how packed the school's parking lot would be on a game night, I got here too late to get a spot. I had to park at the junior high, and the whole process put me at risk of missing the beginning of the game. So, a quick hop across planes saved me a ten-minute walk.

I tug nervously on the sleeves of my brown leather jacket and stare down at my jeans and boots. Not for the first time I wonder if I'm dressed okay. For a football game, yes. For a date? Probably not. For a date after a football game? I have no idea.

I spot Kelsey at the top of the bleachers, and she eagerly waves me over. As I climb the stairs, my mind wanders back to the first time I met Alex: first day of freshman year, and he was the new kid in class. Gorgeous, of course, and he ended up in the seat next to me.

Whatcha working on? I hadn't noticed the seat was even occupied, instead drawing out diagrams of fencing positions for Andrew. Caught off guard, I scrambled to cover the paper as I met his eyes, and he smiled. Not a mocking smile, but a compassionate one, like my current state was all his fault for startling me. That was the moment I fell in love with him. Not real love, of course, but the kind of infatuation that only not-quite-fifteen-year-old girls can feel. I don't remember what I said in response, but it made him laugh a little.

He wasn't in any more of my classes that morning, and by lunch the jocks had claimed him. Football tryouts that afternoon planted him firmly in their camp, and I lost any tenuous hold I might have held on his attention. My own training with Andrew took up most of my time and attention anyway, and I didn't have the social graces to win his friendship back. So, like many teenage crushes, we drifted into different circles, sometimes ending up in a class or two or working on a project together, and he was always so nice to me, but I didn't dare try asking him out.

The announcer calls out Alex's name, reminding me why I'm here. I watch him trot onto the field amid cheers and whistles and I can't help the smile that crosses my face. He scans the crowd, and although there's next to no way he can see me, I like to think he's looking for me anyway. Settling in, I keep my eyes trained on Alex as the rest of the team joins him on the field.

After the game, there are only a handful of people left on the bleachers when Alex comes looking for me. His hair's still damp from his shower and for a moment I melt into a little puddle inside my boots.

"Hey, you look great. Ready to go?"

"Sure."

We begin the long walk to the parking lot and I cast about for something to say. He beats me to it. "So, what did you think of the game?"

"You guys did great. The way you kept catching the ball and keeping it away from the other team. And you. You catch really well. And the—the—tackler guys, they did good, too."

He laughs, a high, clear note. "This is your first game, isn't it?"

"Is it that obvious?" His teasing doesn't make me blush this time. It actually feels kind of good.

"Only to someone who actually knows how to play football."

"So, basically everybody."

We reach his car and he opens the passenger door for me.

"What, no motorcycle?"

"I didn't think a motorcycle would be the best choice for a first date. If you'd like I can bring it next time, though."

He thinks there's going to be a next time! "So, where are we going?"

"Well, the team usually goes to Eddie's, so I thought we'd drive out a ways and go to Bullseye instead."

Is he hiding me? I don't answer, letting the sting settle in nice and deep.

Alex sighs as the silence stretches. "I thought we decided no more insecurity, remember? If we go to Eddie's, this'll become a team dinner instead of a date. I'd rather spend tonight with just you."

"You're right. I'm sorry. It's easier to believe you don't want the other guys to see you with me than to believe you just want some privacy."

"I'll have to see what I can do to change that."

His words send chills up my spine. He shoots me a wild grin and cranks the radio up. I throw my head back and laugh as Bon Jovi comes blaring through the speakers, the eighties rock unexpected but not unwelcome.

My cell phone chirps in my jacket pocket. I pull it out and flip the ringer off, ignoring the notification from Dixon. *Sorry, guys, I'm off duty tonight.*

"Everything okay?" Alex asks, almost shouting to be heard over "Livin' on a Prayer."

"Just Dixon. Nothing that can't wait."

An hour later, we're scarfing down fries when the conversation eventually turns to just how many classes I'm close to failing.

"How is that even possible? You're too smart to be failing classes, especially senior year."

"The jury's still out on smart. But I'm not a very good student."

"Yeah, I've noticed you're out a lot. I just assumed you get sick easy or something." His words have an implied question and his eyes are heavy with expectation, but I can't give him an answer he'll be satisfied with.

I try to keep it light. "Nah. Just a lot of family stuff. The absences wouldn't be so bad if I kept up with the homework, but I've really been dropping the ball there, too, and I don't even have a good excuse for it. I'm drowning in extra credit assignments."

My phone buzzes in my pocket again, the third time since we sat down. Alex doesn't seem to notice. "If you'd like, I can help you get caught up. Kind of like a study date."

"Kind of?"

"Okay, an actual study date. I just didn't want to say it that way and make you think I meant something else."

"What would I think—oh. That."

"Aaand things just got awkward. I'm sorry. I'm going to run to the bathroom, and when I get back we'll pretend it never happened, okay?"

My phone buzzes again and doesn't stop. Annoyed and distracted, I snatch it open and snap at Dixon on the other end. "What?"

"Didn't you get my texts? It's coming right for you!"

"What is?"

"I don't know, but it's huge and pissed off. You need to get out of there."

"Slow down, Dixon. What is going on?"

A growl reverberates through the diner before Dixon has a chance to answer. Dropping my phone, I spin to face the kitchen, where the sound of claws scraping against the tile floor has joined the menacing growl.

Alex chooses this moment to return from the bathroom. "Adrienne, I'm really sorry about saying-"

"Stop right there." My words come out like a bite, drenched in authority and expecting to be obeyed. A complete one-eighty from how I was talking to him just a few minutes ago.

"Adrienne—"

"You need to leave. Right now." I raise my voice. "Everyone, out!" Without waiting for a response, I hurdle the counter and dart for the little red box mounted on the wall. The wailing siren gets their attention like my command didn't. I don't look back at Alex as I stalk toward the swinging doors to the kitchen.

I don't make it. The doors suddenly burst open and something scaled and slimy lunges at me. I hit the ground and roll, coming up a few feet away as the creature crashes into the counter instead. One look is all I need. "Took you long enough. Guess I didn't cut quite deep enough, did I?"

I never found a name for the lizard-man-crocodile thing that's standing before me, but I did learn that beheading it is the surest way to kill it. Last spring I ran the gamut through a whole nest of them in the Everglades where they were munching on tourists. My swing went wide on the last one, burying the silver machete I was using deep in its hide and allowing it to escape back into the swamp. I hunted it for four more days before giving up, trusting it would die of its wounds. I was wrong.

The creature roars and lunges for me again, three-inch claws slashing for my throat. I duck and dodge again, keeping it contained behind the counter and out of the open space of the diner. As I pass under its outstretched arms I catch a slight glint of silver peeking out from the bulging red scar across its chest. My machete.

"Frigus," I mutter, thrusting my arms toward the lizard creature. "Frigus. Frigus. Frigus." The creature roars at me again but doesn't lunge, the cold taking effect and slowing its movements.

"Adrienne!" Alex's shout breaks my concentration, and a chair comes sailing over the counter and smacks the creature across the snout.

In the blink of an eye the creature swarms over the counter and takes Alex to the floor. "Alex!" My shout is too high-pitched, too frantic. *Control!* I follow, bounding over the counter, expecting to see Alex lying in a pool of blood with his arms ripped off.

Instead, he's climbing to his feet, the creature twitching on its side and trying to get traction on the slippery floor. I don't hesitate. Hauling back, I scream "Collido!" and drive my hand forward, palm out, right into that piece of machete. With a sickening, slurping sound the sliver of metal comes flying out the creature's back, cleaving it in two. Alex throws up as brownish sludge oozes across the floor.

When he's done, he looks up at me with a confused and horrified expression. "What was that?"

I allow my composure to slip a little. "I—I don't know. You know that urban legend thing, about people flushing baby alligators? Maybe it's that." It's not the first time I've had to fake it. I'm not great at it, but in the moment, it's usually enough to pass. Most people want to dismiss the strange and latch on to any semi-reasonable explanation.

"Yeah. Maybe." He's still looking at me like he has no idea who I am.

We wait for the police and give our statements. I repeat the alligator story, planting the idea that maybe it was mutated by pollution or something, letting my magic flow into my words. It's not a true spell, but it'll encourage their minds to see a deformed alligator when they look at the body. Alex is quiet in the meantime, gaze flickering between me and the diner behind us. *He doesn't believe the alligator story.*

Eventually we're cleared to leave. The mood is completely destroyed, but I give it a shot anyway. "I had a good time tonight. Before, you know."

It takes him a minute to respond. "Yeah. I was having a good time, too." His tone is even, but he won't meet my eyes. That's it. My relationship is over before it even got off the ground.

Better to save him from the awkward drive home. "You know, my boots are a mess. I'd hate to get this stuff all over your car. I think I'm just going to walk home, okay?"

For half a second it seems like he's going to object. Claim it's not safe, or insist on being the gentleman. But he doesn't. "Okay."

"I'll see you Monday, then."

"Yeah, see you."

I walk away before either of us can feel any worse about whatever just happened between us. I can feel his gaze on me as I go, but I don't turn back around. I hold it together while I retrieve my car and make the short drive back to the manor. Dixon is waiting for me in the driveway.

"That was amazing!" He throws his arms around me in an uncharacteristic hug.

"Explain."

He doesn't need any qualifiers. "It was nosing around the manor this evening. That was the first time I texted you. It couldn't get past the wards, and that pissed it off. I thought it might cause some trouble, so I cast this really cool spell. It was kind of like mounting a camera on its head. I watched it follow the route we take to school, then visit the football field, then head into town. Then I saw you through the window of the diner, and I realized it was hunting you."

"Where are Heather and Andrew?"

"Out. Hunting their own killer, remember?"

"They have new leads?"

"They're not talking about it." Dixon gives me a once-over, taking in the gore coating my boots and the lower six inches of my jeans. "I saw your fight. You were good."

"Thanks." I'm glad it's dead, but I took no pleasure in the kill tonight. The walk helped me decompress and process the fight, but did nothing for the emotions swirling inside.

"What are you going to do about Alex?"

I sigh and sit down on the steps, tugging off my grimy boots. "Nothing yet. He's probably never going to talk to me again."

"But what about the magic exposure?"

Boots gone, I roll the hems of my jeans all the way up to my knees, sealing the gunk in until I can get them off and dispose of them properly. "If he decides to spread it around, I'll have to deal with it, but until then, I'm going to pretend it never happened and hope he does the same. He's not the first person to witness me killing a monster. Most people don't get a good enough look to really know what they saw. The ones that do know how crazy it will sound if they run around blabbing about it. Somehow, I don't think Alex is the blabbing type."

I can feel Dixon's eyes on me as I get up and walk my ruined boots over and dump them in the garbage can. Like his magic, he's too perceptive for someone his age. "If you want to talk about it..." He trails off, leaving the invitation open-ended.

"Not tonight. I just want to go to bed."

He holds the door for me, then follows me into the kitchen. We part ways at the stairs, me heading up to bed, and him heading back down to the utility room. Whatever project he's wrapped up in is sure taking up a lot of his time. I crack Liza's door and find darkness and silence, so I don't disturb her.

In my own room, I peel off my jeans and leave them in a wadded heap on the bathroom floor. As long as they don't start to stink I'll deal with them tomorrow. I take a quick shower to rinse off the sweat and grime of the fight, then swaddle myself in the comfiest flannel pajamas I own. When I'm finally in bed the tears I've been holding back since Alex stared at me in the diner begin rolling down my cheeks. I'm not a crier. I really hate doing it. I extra hate being put in the position where I want to do it. Crying over a guy is so cliche.

Remembering my phone is still on silent, I grab it off the nightstand and flip the ringer back on. Apparently a text came through while I was in the shower. From Alex. *Tonight was weird. I want to talk to you about it. I'll call you when I'm ready.*

Talking is good, right? Right?

SEVEN

"ADRIENNE, I FOUND SOMETHING."

"What time is it?"

"Early."

I groan. The dream I was having lingers, giving me the uneasy feeling of being followed. Dixon sinks onto the edge of my bed, tipping me forward and unearthing my head from the depths of my pillow. I can feel my phone still clutched in my hand where I fell asleep reading Alex's message, over and over again. I crack my eyelids. No sunlight is streaming in my window.

"Go away." I snuggle back in, preparing to go back to sleep.

"No. Come on, it's important. It's about the summoner."

My eyes fly open. I drag myself out of bed, muttering under my breath. "This had better be dang important, waking me up before dawn on a freaking Sunday, or I'll beat you into a bloody pulp."

I splash some water on my face to wake up, then stumble after Dixon into the hall.

"I'll grab Liza."

"No, let her sleep. We can fill her in later." He gives me a questioning glance that I ignore. If she wants to tell him about her sleep issues, she will. "Show me what you have."

Dixon takes the lead, meandering down the hall to his room. He's shirtless, wearing only a pair of pajama pants, and I can't help but notice how much he's starting to fill out in the shoulders. *Looks like puberty is finally hitting. Maybe he'll get lucky and shoot up another half dozen inches.* Poor Dixon. Being the shortest guy in his class hasn't been easy for him. He's been at the manor for about three years now. Just like his growth, his magic manifested later than normal, but he's certainly not weak. His magic lacks the blunt force of my combat magic and the creativity of Liza's manipulation magic, but his perception spells have a finesse and delicacy that's unmatched.

Dixon's room is the polar opposite of mine. Stark and uncluttered, it's nearly devoid of personal possessions, like he never fully moved in. Or doesn't think he'll be here very long. Growing up in the foster care system will do that to you.

"So, I've been trying to determine what made the summoner target the specific schools they did." Dixon's talking as soon as I close the door behind me.

"And?"

"Nothing. The schools don't matter."

"You got me out of bed for this?" I don't even care how he determined it. It could've waited until later. Much, much later.

"Check this out." Dixon wakes his laptop up and turns the screen around for me to see. On it is a very complicated-looking spreadsheet.

I yawn and squint at the page for a minute, then give up. "Summarize it for me."

He visibly perks up. "Okay, so I listed out all of the colleges and universities in the New England area, including Pennsylvania, because of Penn State. I couldn't find any obvious connections, so I backed up and looked at the dates of the attacks and matched them with the schools."

"Skip to the end," I say, rubbing my temples. Sometimes his intellect makes my head spin. "I don't need to know how you got there."

"Okay. The chosen schools were hosting large events on the night of the full moon, guaranteed to draw in at least hundreds, if not thousands, of people. The attacks weren't about a message or a target or a vendetta. They were about the body count."

Now I'm awake. *Hellhound. Body count. Young, fertile victims.* "Shit. Someone's collecting souls."

"Shit."

I give him the stink eye for his language, but don't comment on it. "We need to wake up Andrew."

"Oh, he's already awake. He's down in the training room. At least, he was about an hour ago when I took a break from this." He gestures at the laptop, but I just stare at him.

"You were up all night working on this?"

"Yup."

"And Andrew was up all night?"

"Since they got home, yeah. This one's really getting to him."

I sigh. "Am I the only one who sleeps in this house anymore?"

I head for the door, but stop when Dixon starts to follow. "I got this. You need sleep."

"But—"

"Sleep." I start to leave again, but come back and give Dixon a quick hug. "Thank you. This is big, and you are amazing."

Andrew has relocated to the kitchen by the time I make it downstairs, having stopped in my own room to shower and dress now that I know I'm not getting back to bed. He's sitting at the table, cup of coffee in front of him, papers strewn across the entire surface of the table.

"You need sleep," I admonish him, pouring my own cup of coffee. I rarely drink it, but today feels like it's going to be one of those days.

"That's what Heather says."

"She's a smart woman."

There's a silence while we both sip at the hot nectar. I'm itching to discuss my case with him, but he just looks so worn out, so...old.

"You're staring at me."

"Sorry. I wanted to talk to you, but it doesn't seem like a very good time."

"You can always talk to me, Adrienne." He straightens the page he was reading then looks up at me, expectant. "What's on your mind?"

I briefly explain what Dixon found, and he begins nodding as he understands. "So I think the summoner is a soul-collector, but that can't be right, can it? I mean, nobody does that anymore." It's a wonder I even know about it. It was mentioned only briefly in a reading assignment Heather gave me ages ago.

"It's an ancient practice, that's true. But magic is still magic, whether it was used yesterday or a thousand years ago."

"That's not good." He doesn't respond, and I give voice to my next thought. "It wasn't the murdered girls, was it? They didn't summon the hellhound."

"Doubtful. There would be no reason for them to be collecting souls. Other than the worship theory, Heather and I have found no hard evidence they were experienced magic users. Their lives appear to be those of normal, boarding-school children."

"This is bad. Very, very bad. Someone only collects souls so that they can do one piece of very big, very bad magic. They're weak now, attacking on the full moon, but at the rate they're going they won't be weak for long. If I don't find the summoner, more hellhounds will come, and they'll only grow stronger." My resolve breaks. "I can't do this, Andrew. This isn't a simple find-the-summoner case anymore. It's a big, important case, and I'm not the right person to solve it. I can't do this." My last words come out in a whimper.

Andrew slams his hand down on the table. "Enough, Adrienne. You're not a child anymore, so stop acting like it."

I reel back in my chair as if he'd slapped me. "I'm not acting like a child, I just—"

"Do you have any idea where Heather and I were last night? Breaking into the FBI. The freaking *FBI*, Adrienne! You see this? All these files?" He waves his hands over the table. "Murders. Just like Vermont. Eleven of them from the last year, all across the country. More, stretching back almost a decade, and they're getting more frequent. I don't know how we missed them all this time. I'm hunting a serial killer, Adrienne. A serial killer who can do magic. So don't sit there and whine about how you can't handle your little summoner. It's one poor, little summoner. Grow up, and do your job."

Andrew doesn't give me a chance to respond. He gets up from the table in a huff and storms out of the kitchen, papers flying off the table in his wake. He's never spoken to me like that before. My very short night and stressful morning catch up with me, and I burst into tears.

I don't know how long I sit moping miserably at the table, but the kitchen is full of sunlight by the time I finally dry my eyes and blow my nose. Andrew's papers are still where he left them. Staring at the papers, I feel something inside me tighten up. *I'm not going to sit here feeling sorry for myself all day. I need to get out of here. Do something productive.*

Andrew's rebuke stings, but he was right. This is what I've been trained for. Granted, I'm better at pummeling the bad guy after he's already been found than doing the finding, but investigative work is part of my level two training. So far, I've been relying on Dixon to put the pieces together for me. It's time to do some research on my own.

First, I make some calls, which are not well received. Apparently not even magi appreciate being woken up early on Sunday. The two council members I manage to contact have no specific knowledge about soul collecting, but promise to look into it and let me know. I leave messages for the rest.

One avenue exhausted, I head downstairs to the library adjacent to the training room. The stores of knowledge contained in this room are astronomical, but I assume what I'm looking for isn't going to be in the regular textbooks. In a matter of days we've discovered evidence of worship magic and soul collecting, both ancient practices that aren't even taught anymore. Only Dixon could have caught them. He prowls the forgotten shelves of the library for fun, pouring over tomes that haven't been opened in decades. The layers of dust broken only by thin lines where he's removed a book here and there are testament to that fact.

But as Andrew said, just because they've fallen out of style doesn't mean they're no longer effective... With that in mind, I select a book and start reading.

My level one education taught me the basics: what magic is, how to use my magic, the role of the magi, and the planes that make up totality. Level two goes deeper, expounding on the foundations and guiding principles of magic and training my magic to be stronger and more effective. Since I'm combat, my curriculum was expanded to include a whole encyclopedia of beasties. That's where my education stalled. I have the knowledge portion down, but my practical magic has always been weak. I have a few combat spells that I can wield with abandon, but the other disciplines are a struggle on my best of days. Even Dixon has passed me, achieving level three earlier this year.

Studying has never been my strong suit, but the books I read now are fascinating. The ancient magi were connected to the earth and each other in ways that today we can only dream about. It doesn't stop with worship magic and soul collecting. There's soul searching, and alchemy, and mimicry, and so many more. I read until my head swims, little bits and pieces of information sticking themselves in wherever they can find room, until I just can't take it anymore. I didn't find anything particularly useful in hunting down my summoner/soul collector, and I can only stay immobile for so long. My body needs to move.

More than that, my body needs to hit things. My fight last night with the lizard-creature got my hackles up. My fight this morning with Andrew messed with my head, and my prolonged but ultimately unfulfilling study session has me itching to do something I know I can do right.

Before I leave the library I murmur the spells that will show me where magical disruptions are. Not every disruption is a monster. But since monsters don't belong in this plane, their energy jars against the energy of mortals and can give away their location if one knows how to look. It takes a while to find one. I've been on the ball lately, taking out my frustrations of not being able to catch my 'werewolf' on any other creature I could find. By keeping well away from humans, the lizard-creature slipped through the cracks as it made its way north.

Loaded down with silver, I come out of the Shadow Plane in the Pine Barrens of southern New Jersey. After taking a few moments to orient myself in the dizzying sprawl of towering pine trees, I begin tracking my quarry.

An hour later I find my monster holed up in a hidden den tucked beside a lake. It's not a normal lake, though. A perfect circle, it looks like it was intentionally carved out of the ground with skill and precision. And it's the most brilliant shade of blue. Not a single pine needle floats on its unbroken surface, though the forest canopy is so thick as to nearly block out the sun. Blade in hand, I advance on the den, well aware of the dangers of attacking an unknown beastie in its own lair. It doesn't seem to know I'm here, though. On silent feet, I pass into the darkness and murmur the one perception spell I can usually do with ease: a slight alteration of my eyes to give me a modicum of vision in the darkness. It's not true night vision, but it allows me to see just enough to not step on anything I don't want to be stepping on.

I find my prey sleeping, huddled in a tight ball in an open space at the end of a narrow passage. It's not often I get such a close look before I'm fighting for my life, and I let my eyes rove over the creature's body. Long, leathery wings. Two legs, ending in wicked-looking hooves. And the head of a...goat? *Holy cow! The Jersey Devil is real!*

Scattered throughout the room are various bone fragments and discarded offal and scraps of clothing. A human skull at the far end solidifies my resolve. It's killed someone. It needs to die.

"Ignis!" My scream reverberates off the packed-earth walls. The devil comes awake fast as fire races through the chamber, setting the thick carpet of dried grass and pine needles ablaze. A high-pitched and unearthly yell meets mine, and the devil leaps at me.

The devil doesn't stand a chance. In such confined quarters its wings are useless, and between the smoke and lingering sleepiness its attacks are reckless and desperate. I don't let it suffer. I parry one blow, two, meeting deadly hooves with the flat of the knife in my hand. When it snaps at me with jagged fangs I slide my knife up under its jaw, severing the head with a quick twist.

I let the den finish burning behind me as I leave, obscuring the evidence of the creature. It was a clean kill, but not a strenuous battle, and left me feeling somewhat unsatisfied. Eying the creepy lake one more time, I slip into the Shadow Plane and head for home.

EIGHT

“**M**Y LIFE IS OVER! I’ll never be able to show my face at school again!” I thump my head down on the desk.

“It’s not that bad. Really. Here, I’ll help.”

“You can’t help me. Nobody can.”

“Buck up, Adrienne. Do you want to pass history or not?” Kelsey’s glaring at me when I raise my head, eyes stinging from staring at a computer screen for the last several hours. I arrived home from my monster hunt to find her in the kitchen, having forgotten she’d volunteered to help me muddle through my extra credit assignments and get my homework back on track. I managed to explain away the dirt and sweat by saying I’d gone for a run, but I’ve been distracted all afternoon, torn between my disastrous date with Alex and the investigation I’m making no headway on. Not that I can explain that to Kelsey.

“Hey, this section is actually pretty good.” She pauses to stuff a handful of chips in her mouth, then continues reading.

I lean back to rest my eyes and my bedroom door flies open.

“Whatcha doin’?” Liza saunters in, making herself at home on the end of my bed.

“Homework. I told you that already. Now get out.”

Liza pouts, and Kelsey comes to her defense. "Be nice, Adrienne. Liza, would you like to read Adrienne's history project?"

"No!"

"Yes!"

Kelsey hoists the pages out of my grasp and turns them over to Liza. "We're studying the civil rights movement. Adrienne's assignment is to pick two influential people from that era and imagine a conversation between them. She then has to act out the scene with a volunteer from class."

I swipe at the pages again, but Liza knows me too well and scoots out of my reach. Thwarted, I settle for glowering at Kelsey instead, who pretends not to notice. "That's it. I'm not turning it in. I'll just flunk."

"Oh no you won't." Dixon's words precede him through the door, which Liza left open behind her.

"Anyone ever heard of privacy? Get out!"

No one has a chance to respond. All three of our phones go off at the same time, an identical buzzing sound they've never had a reason to make before.

Liza and Dixon bolt from the room. My pulse thunders in my ears as I haul Kelsey to her feet. Somehow, I manage to sound halfway polite, if abrupt. "I'm sorry, Kelsey, I completely forgot this thing that we all have to do tonight. It's a family thing, so you need to go home, and I'll see you at school tomorrow, okay?"

I hurry her to the door, fending off her questions and nearly shoving her outside. Liza and Dixon are behind me as I turn around.

"How bad is it?"

"Bad." Dixon's got his phone up, examining the alert. "Andrew hit the panic button, and now neither of them are responding."

"Where are they?"

Dixon rattles off coordinates, keeping pace as I race down the hall back to my bedroom. Faster than I thought possible, I strip off my pajama pants and scramble into work clothes. A quick trip downstairs and I re-emerge loaded down with silver blades of varying sizes. I'm out the door six minutes after the alert went off.

"Adrienne!"

"What?"

"Cerise is gone."

"Shit." I race outside the reach of the manor's wards and cross into the Shadow Plane.

Even here, the trip takes too long. Andrew's alert came from outside of Albuquerque, New Mexico, smack dab in the middle of nowhere. I stumble as I land on the red sand and look around wildly. Dixon was right. It's bad.

The ground is scorched and gouged, evidence of Andrew's attacks. The air is charged and tingles against my skin. Heather and Andrew lie prone in the sand, unmoving. Kneeling next to them is a tall, blond-haired man, limbs lean and roped with bands of muscle. His hands are at Heather's throat.

"Hey!"

That's all the warning I give. I attack before he even looks up, adrenaline and rage fueling my magic. Lightning sprays from my fingers as I throw them in the man's direction. He's lifted off his feet, landing hard several yards away. I race to my guardians' sides and drop to my knees. Their faces are peaceful, as if in sleep, and there's not a mark on their bodies. I place a finger under each of their chins. No pulse.

Pain shoots through my entire body, and then I'm the one being thrown backward. My heart skips several beats.

"Not pleasant, is it?" The man advances on me, lightning crackling between his fingers.

Fine. I'll play. I call the lightning again, sharpening my focus and pushing more power behind it. See if he gets up from this one.

I channel the bolt through my palm instead of my fingers, launching it straight toward his torso.

It doesn't connect. Reaching out, the man somehow catches the bolt, absorbing it into the skin of his hand. "Is that all you've got, little mage?"

I don't have time to figure out how he did it. "Not even close." My hands fly of their own accord, launching spell after spell. Wind. Fire. Water. He deflects them all, a smile on his face. *Who are you, you bastard?*

Time to change tactics. If my magic can't touch him, maybe my silver can.

"Ventus." I cast the wind spell again, directing it at the ground at my feet. Sand flies into the air at the force of the gale, swirling around us in a hazy red tornado. I race forward, blade drawn.

He's faster than me. The sand doesn't seem to be affecting him in the slightest. He deflects my blade and sends me stumbling behind him. He doesn't come after me, though.

Instead, he waits for me to catch my balance and turn to face him again.

I let the sand die down. It's not working, anyway. "Who are you?"

"My name does not matter. Only my mission."

"Your mission is over, and I'll need something to write on your headstone."

He nods deeply. "Very well. Give me your name, and I shall give you mine, and then we shall see who is dying tonight."

Unbidden, shivers run down my spine. He isn't my typical opponent and this isn't my typical fight. If it weren't for the two bodies lying on the ground, I'd be tempted to turn tail and run. "Adrienne Young."

"My given name has been lost, but there are those who call me the Immortal."

That one throws me. Silence fills the space between us as I figure out how to respond to that.

"Fine. Don't tell me. I can kill you just as dead without it."

I attack again, darting under his arm and aiming a blow at his ribs. He counters, as I expected, and I spin away, only to come at him from the other side. He's expecting this, too, and this time his block sends me stumbling. Again, he doesn't follow through but waits for me to recover.

I attack again. And again. No matter what moves I pull out he has something to counter. One by one he sends my blades spinning through the air until only one remains in my hand. Chest heaving, sweat running down my back, I glance once more at Heather and Andrew, gaining strength and focus from their bodies. Centering myself, I attack again.

Before my blow lands a rush of wind descends on the man from above, on the wings of a multi-colored whirlwind. Cerise lets out a piercing cry as she connects with the man's face, talons gouging red rivers down his cheeks. I scream with her, ducking beneath the man's flailing arms and driving my blade up underneath his ribcage.

With a roar the man flings Cerise to the ground. She flops for a moment, then lies still. He stares down at the hilt of the dagger protruding from his chest, then raises his eyes to mine as I stand gasping before him. I watch for the light in them to go out, but it doesn't. He simply draws the dagger out, blood squelching around his fist, and casts the blade on the ground at his feet.

"Enough! I have humored you, little mage, but my patience is at an end." An unseen force drags me to the ground, pinning me against the sand. No matter how I struggle I can't get free. Terror washes over me. *This is how I die.*

The man returns to Heather and Andrew, moving more slowly than before but otherwise seemingly unaffected by his injuries. He looks them over, then begins to gather Heather into his arms.

"What are you doing? Where are you taking her?" Despite my impending doom I need to know.

His voice is soft when he answers. "Somewhere she'll be safe."

"Safe? What are you talking about? You already killed her, she'll never be safe again!" My voice rises high, tipping into hysteria. What's he waiting for? Why hasn't he killed me yet?

"No. She merely sleeps." Then he vanishes.

His words have barely registered before he returns, alone. He collects Andrew.

"She's not dead?" I can't keep the hope out of my voice and curse the weakness I'm showing him. But when he turns to me his eyes are sad.

"I do not kill magi. You are too important to the peace in this world. But they would not have stopped hunting me and need to be removed."

What kind of serial killer talks like that? Regardless of what he says, he's still standing there with Andrew hanging limply in his arms. I say the cruelest thing I can think of. "You'll kill children, but not magi?"

"It does not please me to kill children. But they needed to die for their service to her."

Wait, what? "Her? Who's "her"?"

"Goodbye, little mage. I hope, for your sake, that we do not meet again."

"No! Wait! Bring him back!"

My pleas fall on empty sand. The force holding me down lifts as tears pour from my eyes. *I failed. They needed me, and I failed them.*

The last thing Andrew and I did was fight. Now they're gone, and I have no idea how to begin finding them. The realization settles in my chest like a weight, and suddenly I can't breathe. *What do I do now?*

Sometime later it occurs to me that I need to go home. Liza and Dixon are waiting for me to come home. They're waiting for me to bring Heather and Andrew home. The wave threatens to engulf me again, but I hold it at bay. I need to go home.

A flash of color in the oncoming darkness catches my attention. I scoop up the body of the macaw, cradling it against my chest. It isn't really Cerise. The familiar who occupied the bird has fled. In my head I know that, but looking down at her broken form I see Heather vanishing from my sight all over again.

I manage to get myself under enough control that I feel I can handle the Shadow Plane without getting eaten alive. As soon as I cross over the shadows are on me, held back only by the strength of my wards. The sheer amount of magic we were throwing around on our side has attracted them, and the emotional turmoil radiating off me must smell like Thanksgiving dinner. They may not be able to touch me, but they can follow me, and they do.

I finally make it home, leaving the shadows behind where they belong. Tucking the macaw tightly against my chest, I take a deep breath and open the door.

NINE

—·—

"I'M GOING TO GET them back."

Recounting what happened to Liza and Dixon, choking on the words, forcing my lips into the correct shapes, nearly tore me in two. Watching them understand, and their faces as disbelief and grief took over, made me wish I'd died rather than having to bear this news. But then something unexpected happened. My grief began to dissolve. Shift. Harden, into a burning fury deep in my gut. I *will* get them back. And I'll kill anyone who gets in my way.

Dixon's the first one to speak. "We need to call someone. The council—"

"Screw the council." Dixon flinches at the force of my interruption.

Liza tries to make the peace, sniffling, trying to hold back her tears. Trying to be strong. "Adrienne, they need to know. Heather and Andrew are gone, and if they're really, you know..."

"What? If they're really what?"

"You said it yourself. Andrew didn't have a pulse, and, and, Heather was, and, then Cerise—" She breaks. She can't help it.

Her weakness, her insinuation, is like gas to my smoldering anger. "They're not dead!"

Dixon wraps an arm around Liza's shoulders and rests his other hand on mine. "Let's all calm down, okay? Let's sit down, and take a minute, and talk this all through, okay?"

I shrug him off. I can't sit. I can't rest. I have to do something. "Whatever. Call the council if you want to. When you're ready to actually do something, come find me. I'll be downstairs."

I finally know how Andrew was feeling when he dismembered half a dozen practice dummies. I don't even bother warming up. I drive my fist into the punching bag, putting every ounce of strength I have behind the punch. My fight with the Immortal wore me out, but as I know from experience, there's always a reserve of strength buried somewhere. I wail on the bag, dredging up every last bit of energy I can muster. The tears come back. Sad, angry tears that fill my eyes and blur my vision and run unchecked down my cheeks. I keep going, punishing the bag for my failure to save them. Punishing myself.

When my arms won't swing anymore I collapse on the floor, letting the burning of my muscles and the stinging of the sweat in my eyes wash my emotions clean. The exertion, the familiarity, brings clarity. I become aware of my audience sometime later. How long they've been watching, I don't know, but there are dried tear tracks beneath their red, swollen eyes.

"I have a plan." My voice is rough, my throat raw.

"What do you need us to do?"

"Liza. I need you to work a spell. Heather and Andrew are out there. Somewhere. He said he was putting them somewhere safe. I need you to find them."

"Adrienne, I don't know—"

I keep talking, over her objection. I already know what she's going to say, and I don't care. "It's perception magic. If you can't handle it, Dixon can help, but you're the strongest magi here. You have to be the one to work it.

"Dixon, I want you to go through all of Heather and Andrew's work on this case. They caught up to the Immortal. We need to know how they found him."

"What are you going to do?"

"I'm going to learn more about our opponent. He called himself 'the Immortal'. If that's the case then someone, somewhere, has come across him before."

It takes me two days to read through every single journal in the library. Not every magi keeps a journal, of course, but many do. I have my own upstairs, detailing the fights I've been in and the creatures I've killed. For posterity. Over the years journals tend to find their way into the manor's library and mostly just sit around, ignored and unopened.

My back cracks as I stretch it, and my neck doesn't turn all the way to the left. My body protests as I try to stand, and it takes a few minutes to be able to fully uncurl it out of the chair-shape it's adopted.

Physical aches aside, my mental health has stabilized. The mania that drove me down here has taken a backseat to practicality and focus. It's time to go back upstairs.

I find Liza and Dixon in Heather's study. Saturated as it is in Heather's presence, they deemed it the best place to launch their tracking spell. I dump the three journals I brought with me on the desk and move to the far corner, where a large, ornately carved wooden perch sits. On it rests a tiny, sleek-feathered canary. The miniature bird looks out of place compared to the sheer size of the macaw, but her presence is reassuring. If Heather were dead, she wouldn't be here.

"Hey there, Cerise," I croon to the bird. She cocks one eye at me, then buries her head back beneath her wing. I stroke her back, then turn my attention to the others, leaving her to mourn in peace. Dixon is reviewing a page of handwritten notes while Liza mutters to herself, her eyes closed. Pong lies purring in Liza's lap, joined with her in working her spell. To anyone else this scene would look like just an ordinary girl cuddling with her cat.

"You're alive." Dixon's attempt at humor falls flat. "Cerise came back this morning." The bird's presence is both a joy and a blow. Heather's alive, but even Cerise doesn't know where she is. They've been together fourteen years. No wonder our canary isn't singing.

"Well?" I can't keep the hope out of my question as I gesture at his notes.

He's quiet as he answers, not wanting to disrupt Liza's concentration. "I found most of their research here in the office, but I don't know how it's going to help. Andrew's been tracking killings he believes the Immortal committed over the last few decades, and there are a lot. There's no obvious pattern to them, but if I study them a bit more I might be able to come up with something. It looks like Heather was working the magic angle, but her notes are written in a coded shorthanded, and I can't read them. One thing I was able to glean, though. You remember the magic at the girls' school? Several of the other crime scenes also showed traces of magic. The evidence is scant, because they weren't all investigated by magi, but it's interesting."

"Nothing on how they tracked him down?"

"Sorry, Adrienne."

Liza's chanting dies down, and I turn to her as she shakes her head and opens her eyes. "How's it going?" I ask.

Her voice is steady but tired when she answers. "I found them."

"What?" The question comes out as a shout. "Why didn't you tell me? I have to get ready, I have to go—"

"No." Liza's word stills me, though my thoughts are still whirling. "It's not that simple. I found them, but I didn't find them."

"You're not making any sense."

She sighs heavily and peels herself off the floor, dislodging Pong, who rumbles his displeasure. "I found them in the sense that I found their energies. They're alive, and stable, and still on this plane. But I can't physically locate them. They've been warded against me. Adrienne, the strength of those wards...I've never seen anything like it."

Now that she's standing in front of me I can see the swollen bags under her eyes. I'm sure my face looks much the same way. I dozed off reading a few times, but I haven't intentionally slept. I don't know what all Liza and Dixon have been up to up here, but I'm guessing they did much the same thing.

"Can you break through?"

"I'm sorry, Adrienne. Even with Pong's help, I'm...I'm just not strong enough." The words hurt her to say. They hurt to hear. I want to scream at her. *You're supposed to be a prodigy! You're the one who's supposed to be able to do stuff like this!* I bite the words back. They'll only make her feel worse.

"What about you?" Dixon joins us, eying the journals. "You found something?"

"I found three somethings."

I lay the journals out side by side, touching each as I describe their authors' contact with the Immortal. "This guy, Arthur Theodore, came across him in the fifties. He was investigating some mysterious objects that showed up at a pawn shop in New York. They ended up being fakes, but the Immortal was there, asking about the same objects. When Theodore took an interest in him, the stranger left."

"How do you know it was the Immortal?"

"Theodore left a sketch. Trust me, it's him."

"Okay. Next?"

"Next is Martha Crowell. She worked as a librarian at the British Museum in the eighties. She recorded a rumor she heard from a colleague, a friend of a friend of a friend type deal. The account is sketchy, but it tells of a man who has walked the earth for more than four hundred years. He never stays in the same place for long, and tends to show up in places where big magic is going down. Says he's cursed. She recorded the story as an interesting legend, but didn't give any credence to it.

"Last is Jeremiah Winthrop. He was in India in 1990 when the Andhra Pradesh cyclone hit. He slipped into the Shadow Plane and managed to evade the storm, but stayed in the area afterward to aid in the relief efforts. He describes a tall, thin man that he witnessed swimming through the flood waters, lifting entire houses and pulling survivors to safety. Believing him to be a magi, he tried to approach him, but every time he got close the stranger vanished. Winthrop shifted into the Shadow Plane, but the stranger wasn't there. He was just gone."

Liza and Dixon are both quiet when I finish my recitation, digesting everything I've said.

Liza speaks first. "So, he's old."

"Really old."

"He called himself 'the Immortal'. Maybe he really is immortal?"

"No," I interject. "He said that other people call him that."

"Does it matter who calls him that?" Dixon, ever the voice of reason. "For the sake of argument, assume these accounts are all talking about the same man, and that man is this 'Immortal'. We know he's old. We know he's strong, unnaturally so, even for a magi. But there's nothing there about him being violent. He was helping those people in India, and when magi have approached him, he avoided them. So, why now? What's changed?"

None of us have an answer. We stare at each other in silence, but we seem to have hit a dead end. On everything. We can't find

Andrew and Heather. We know more about the Immortal, but we're no closer to finding him or understanding his actions.

"Dixon," I finally say, breaking the silence. "I think it's time to call the council."

A guilty look flashes across his face. "Um, I kind of already did."

"You did? When?"

"Sunday night. After...well, after."

I try to ignore the sting of betrayal that shoots through me. My words the other night came from anger and helplessness, but he should have at least told me. "And?"

"And nothing. Nothing important, anyway. That's why I didn't tell you. They're going to investigate, and in the meantime, we're supposed to stay here and behave. Go to school. Stay out of their way."

Yeah, like that's going to happen. "So, basically, they're treating us like children?"

"We are children, Adrienne. Liza and me, at least."

"That's not...Ergh!" My hands ball into fists at my side. "How dare they just push us aside like that? Like we have nothing to offer? Like we're not affected?"

"Don't worry about them, Adrienne." Liza's hand is cool and gentle on my arm.

"Yeah. Like I said, they're not important. They can't stop us from finding them on our own." Dixon's encouraging smile is contagious, and I feel my cheeks stretching to match his. I almost feel like we can actually do this.

Then I remember that we still have nothing to go on and my smile falls. "All right, guys. Let's get some rest, and get back at it later. Maybe we'll come up with something new in our dreams."

My bed is disheveled, the books Kelsey and I were using Sunday night still strewn across it. The mess throws the events of that night sharply into my mind, and tears spring into my eyes. *No. No more crying. This is a time for action.*

The pep talk doesn't help, but thankfully my body rescues me. I snuggle under the covers, books thumping to the floor as the blankets beneath them lift, and crash into sleep before I can cry anymore.

I only sleep for a few hours before my stomach wakes me up again, trying to eat itself. Another thing I've neglected. Through the grogginess I see the notification light on my phone blinking.

I have a text from Alex.

Hey. I've missed you at school. The other night was bad, but I hope you're not skipping on my account. I think we should give it another shot. Brent is having a Halloween party next week, and I was thinking we could go, if you'd like to. Please call me.

Halloween. Halloween! I shoot out of bed, adrenaline chasing the clouds from my brain. My thoughts tumble over themselves as the cascade of pieces fall into place, and I struggle to put them into a cohesive order before running through the house and calling for Liza and Dixon. Something is going to happen on Halloween. Not only is it a ceremonial event, it practically calls out for people to do magic.

I quickly decide not to wake Liza and Dixon. They still need their sleep, and this isn't urgent news. As much as I'm dying to share it, it can wait. My stomach, however, cannot.

I needn't have worried. Liza and Dixon are both in the kitchen when I make my way downstairs. They obviously haven't slept yet.

"Why are you guys still up?" I fight back a yawn to ask the question.

"Tried. Couldn't sleep." Liza's words trigger a touch of concern, but I'll have to ask her about it later.

"What about you?" I ask Dixon.

"I wanted to put some time in on my project downstairs. I haven't since, well, obviously, but I don't want to neglect it for too long."

"What are you working on anyway? You know what, never mind. You can tell me later. I've had an epiphany." I pause while Liza extricates herself from the fridge, making sure I have their full attention. "Next week is Halloween."

I'm a little bummed that they don't immediately get it, but then Dixon's face lights up. "Big magic on ceremonial days. You think the Immortal is going to make an appearance?"

"It's more than that. Bear with me, then tell me if what I'm saying makes sense. I think everything is connected. The Immortal mentioned a "her". I didn't make the connection at the time, but he said he killed those girls in Vermont because they were serving "her." You called it, Dixon. They were practicing worship magic. And at the full moon, because they needed the power boost, right?"

Dixon nods.

"Okay, assumption time. If those other killings showed traces of magic, it stands to reason they were also worshiping this "her", and that's what drew the attention of the Immortal.

Someone weak, who needs the power of the full moon. You know who else needs the full moon? The summoner."

Liza gasps, her sleep-deprived state making her fumble for words.

"It's all connected," Dixon agrees, gears turning in his head. "I think you're right on target, Adrienne. It's all about amassing power. Souls that are sacrificed convey great power. And the summoner used the hellhound to sacrifice a lot of souls. Worship also bestows power on the one being worshiped. More disciples means more power. Someone, this 'her', is pulling all the strings. If the Immortal has been hunting her for decades, then this whole thing is bigger than we thought."

"Much bigger. And Halloween is coming."

"Halloween would be the perfect time to launch something big." Liza's finally caught up. "So, what do we do?"

"We prepare. We alert the council. They deserve to know."

"What about Andrew and Heather?"

I hesitate before answering, knowing how bad my words are going to sound. "We're not giving up on them. I *will* get them back. But they're safe, for now."

"How can you—"

I cut Liza off. "The Immortal doesn't kill magi. He told me so, and after reading the journals, I think I believe him. Besides, he already had his chance to kill them and he didn't do it. We've run out of options, so I think we need to move their rescue to the back burner while we focus on Halloween. To that end, we also need to keep anyone else from finding out they're gone. The school, the neighbors, the police. If anyone finds out there are three minors living alone in this house and our guardians vanished without a trace this place will be crawling with social workers, and we'll get whisked out of here before we can blink."

"How do we do that?"

"Well for starters, we're going back to school tomorrow."

TEN

PULLING OFF A MASS delusion is a difficult task in the best of circumstances, and we're definitely not working under the best of circumstances. After talking it over, we agree that dealing with a two-day unexcused absence without involving Heather and Andrew is a worse plan than just convincing the entire school we weren't even absent.

Dixon crafts the spell, and the three of us spend four hours in the training room getting it as nearly perfect as possible. It's exhausting, and frustrating, and only leaves us about five hours to sleep before we have to roll out and get ready for school. In addition to the delusion, we pull into the parking lot wielding glamours to hide all evidence that we've been awake for nearly three days. To the people around us, we look perfectly rested and ready to learn.

We're early enough that the lot is only half full, and by parking at the back end I can lessen the chances of anyone noticing us vanish out of the car. Seconds later we pop out of the Shadow Plane and into the library's computer lab. Dixon locks the door just in case, even though the lab doesn't open until lunch. "Ready?"

The three of us join hands, Liza in the middle to act as our epicenter. Physical contact carries weight in magic, and while we can't actually combine our strength, our contact with Liza will boost her casting power while we cast simultaneously with her. We have to be in perfect sync to pull this off.

I feel the exact moment our spell goes into effect. It's an immediate deadening of the air around us, like stuffing cotton balls into your ears. A fraction of a second later the delusion rolls forth, spreading out from us in a wave, washing over every single person present on the property and spilling over into the junior high school across the street. Liza sags backward into my arms, and I barely catch her as my own fatigue flares up. A moment later she's back on her feet, catching her breath and examining our handiwork.

Erasing someone's memory is extremely difficult, and controlling a person's thoughts is nearly impossible, way beyond even Liza's skill set. Doing it to an entire building full of people is out of the question. Our delusion works differently. It encourages people to make an assumption. They may not specifically remember seeing us for the last two days, but they'll assume we were here, because there's no reason why we wouldn't have been here. It's a subtle and delicate nudge on the conscious mind, but it's the best we could do with the time and experience available to us. I just hope it's enough.

"Remember, guys, business as usual. We've been here the whole time, and everything's just fine at home. Don't do anything to draw attention to yourselves."

"We're not the ones you have to worry about." Dixon's quip is dry but, unfortunately, right on target. If anybody is going to screw this up it's probably going to be me.

My first test comes in the form of Alex, of all people. He's leaning against my locker, waiting for me with a nervous look on his face.

Alex catches sight of me, and I plaster a smile on my face to mask the churning emotions inside. I haven't seen him or spoken to him since our disastrous first date what feels like a lifetime ago.

"Hey." His voice is low and hesitant, making me feel guilty and giddy all at the same time.

"Hey." There's a brief pause while we stare at each other, trying to decide who's supposed to speak next. "I got your text."

He lets out a breath. "Good. I feel like I haven't even seen you this week, and I wanted to talk to you, but I didn't know if you wanted to talk to me. Especially since you didn't answer."

Seeing Alex this insecure is a new experience for me, and it strangely helps me to relax. "I want to talk to you, too. We don't really have time before homeroom, though. Sit with me at lunch?" The invitation surprises us both. Sitting together at lunch will make a statement to the entire school that I'm not sure we're ready to make.

"I'd like that." His smile is genuine this time as he reaches out and briefly touches my hand. Then he's gone, swept into the chaos of the hallway and leaving me to scramble to collect the books I need before the bell rings.

Somehow the morning goes by smoothly, even chemistry. Mr. Sanders spends the entire class giving me sidelong glances like he suspects I'm up to something but he hasn't figured out what it is yet. I listen attentively to his lecture and slip out at the bell before he can pin me down.

Before I know it it's lunchtime. I haven't forgotten my lunch date with Alex, and as I enter the cafeteria my heart starts to pound. *Am I supposed to sit down and let him find me? Or am I supposed to go find him? What if he's already sitting with someone? What do I do if someone wants to sit with me before he sits down?*

Alex appears at my elbow while I hover in the doorway, instantly silencing the questions swirling around in my head.

"Shall we?" He gives a mock bow and extends his arm, making me laugh. I can feel the eyes on us as we cross the cafeteria and take up residence at an empty table at the far end. It's as close to privacy as we're going to get. As I sit down I catch sight of Dixon heading our way. He does a double take when he sees Alex and shoots me a questioning glance. I shake my head, and he veers off toward another table.

"So, I—"

"Hold that thought." My phone is vibrating on the table, the caller ID telling me it's not something I want to answer in front of Alex. "I need to take this. I'll be right back."

The hallway behind the cafeteria is clear, but depressing in shades of gray and grayer cinder block. "Finnigan. Thanks for calling me back. What do you have for me?" One of the newest members of the council, Finnigan immigrated to the U.S. only a couple of years ago from Ireland. I don't know him well, but he's the closest thing the council has to an expert on evocation.

"Dia duit, Adrienne. Afraid I don't have much. There's no way to track your summoner unless they're actively performing magic."

"Shit." That was my biggest hope, and now it's gone.

"One thing that may be helpful, though. Not any novice can pull a being from the Ashen Plane. It takes a lot of skill."

"That can't be right. My evidence points to the summoner being weak and needing the power boost from the full moon." My words make me suddenly very aware of the acoustics back here, and I make a mental note to lower my voice.

"Even the strongest of magi would need a power boost to pull off such a summoning. But I was referring to skill, not strength. The evocation itself is complicated and nuanced, requiring a great understanding of magical theory to succeed. It also requires aids beyond those used for simpler evocations. Most notably, a piece of ash retrieved from the plane itself."

A piece of ash retrieved from the plane itself? What the hell? "Where would someone find something like that?"

"Counterfeits abound, but a genuine article? I've never located one."

Looks like almost everything I assumed about the summoner is wrong. Strength and skill. It almost has to be a magi...

A moment later I remember Finnigan is still on the phone, no doubt waiting for me to react. "That's...a lot to take in. Thank you for calling. If you think of anything else..."

"It is a pleasure to help. It is not often my studies get to be put to practical use. My own magic is not strong, so I have little field experience. It is good to be useful."

"You have no idea how useful you've been. I mean it, Finnigan. This is…it's important. You have my gratitude."

"Before you go, I heard about the McGinnises. I am not actively involved in the investigation, but I want you to know that you have my condolences. I am sure their loss has been very hard on you, and I pray that they are quickly recovered."

"Thank you. I have no doubts they will be." *Even if I have to do it myself.*

Alex is behind me when I hang up the phone. I didn't even hear him approach, testifying to how distracting Finnigan's news was. "That sounded important."

"Yeah, um, family friend. He's helping with a….genealogy project." The lie doesn't roll off my tongue easily, and Alex hears it for what it is. His instant scowl tells me I'm about to lose him. "Okay, not a genealogy project. But still a family friend. And it was important, just not something I can tell you about right now."

It's the best I can do, but Alex's next question comes from a completely different angle. "Is there something going on here? Between you and…Finnigan?"

I close the distance between us, and he doesn't pull back. I can't take the hurt in his eyes. "Did it sound like there was?"

He finally meets my eyes. "Not really. It's just, you're being cagey, and—"

"And it's making you paranoid? Especially after you haven't heard from me in a few days?"

"Something like that."

"Isn't a little mystery a good thing? I promise, there's nothing romantic between me and Finnigan. I barely know him, and he's way too old for me anyway. He's at least forty. At least."

Alex's smile is back. "Good."

"No more insecurity, remember?"

"That's only for you."

We're back. Now if only we could stay this way, innocent and teasing. "Alex, about the other night—"

"Don't."

"Don't?"

He takes a deep breath, as if preparing for a speech. "That's what I wanted to talk to you about. Saturday night was...weird. I don't really understand what happened, and I don't know if I want to. What I do know is that I still like you, and I still want to spend time with you."

He cuts off abruptly, as if he'd planned on saying more and suddenly decided not to. The silence feels like he's waiting for me to say something, but I don't know what. At least it seems like he's not going to be running his mouth about magic, so that's good for both of us. "I want to spend time with you, too."

Alex looks briefly disappointed, but moves on. "You're kind of a badass. Where did you learn moves like that?"

I don't even have to lie about this one. "I've been taking martial arts since I was a kid."

"That's really sexy."

"Really?" No one's ever described me as sexy before.

Alex's voice drops and his eyes zero in on mine. "I've been trying to focus on the good memories of that night, instead of the scary and confusing ones. Watching you move like that is a good memory." He pauses, and his gaze wanders down to my lips. "Would it be bad if our first kiss was in the hallway behind the cafeteria?"

We're at the kissing stage? When we did we get here?

He laughs. "I'm not going to kiss you right now. I want to, but I'm not going to."

"Why not?"

He laughs again. "Because I don't think we're there yet. And I want something more romantic than the hallway behind the cafeteria."

Tension drains out of me. I don't like being flustered, and Alex is too good at doing it to me. I search my brain for a safer topic. "You said something about a Halloween party?"

"Yes, Halloween. It's next Tuesday, and Brent is having a party at his house. His parents know about it but won't be there, so it's likely to get a little rowdy. Oh, and you have to dress up."

"And you're sure I'm invited?" Brent plays on the defensive line, making him one of Alex's circle.

"He won't kick you out if you're with me." I don't know what my face looks like, but Alex winces. "That didn't come out right."

"No, it's fine. I get it." Not being popular has never bothered me, at least, not until I started dating the most popular guy in the school.

"They just don't know you. Give them a chance. For me. Please?"

I already have plans for Halloween. Stopping a killer takes precedence over a cute boy. Even a really, really cute boy. I find myself agreeing anyway. We don't even know what's going to happen yet, and I can figure out how to make it work. "Okay, I'm in."

"Great."

Whatever he's about to say next is drowned out by the bell, which rings obnoxiously loudly in this echoey hallway.

"Crap! I didn't get to eat lunch!" Alex and I dart back into the cafeteria, where our table sits suspiciously empty.

"I didn't, either. I was too busy being jealous and paranoid."

"Well, at least you're honest." I make the joke as I scroll through manipulation spells in my head, trying to come up with something I can use to stave off my hunger. Liza could probably turn her notebook into a sandwich or something, but I'd be lucky to conjure myself up a breath mint.

"Here, come with me. I might have something." Alex leads me to his locker, and after rummaging around in the depths of his backpack, hands me a plastic water bottle full of some blue liquid.

"What is this?" I ask, unscrewing the cap and sniffing the contents. It smells kind of fruity, but nothing I recognize.

"It's an energy drink. I keep it handy for after practice."

"What's in it?" I sniff the bottle again.

"Nothing bad, I promise. Drink it. It'll help." I give him a suspicious look that makes him laugh. Man, I could listen to him laugh all day. "Trust me."

I take a sip, and it's surprisingly good. It's cool, even after living in Alex's locker, and tastes like several flavors of gatorade all mixed together. Who knows, maybe it is just a whole bunch of gatorade mixed together. "Thanks."

"No sweat. You'd better go. Don't want to be late."

"Yeah, that would be bad." I pause for a minute and just look at him, thinking about how sweet he is. How far we've come since this morning. I say it again, softer this time. "Thanks."

ELEVEN

WHATEVER IS IN ALEX'S energy drink is magic. I should know. It somehow keeps my stomach from rumbling for the rest of the afternoon. I'm not full, by any means, but I'm not dying of hunger, either. I'm going to have to get that recipe.

Magic gatorade notwithstanding, I'm completely dragging by the time the final bell rings and I can gain the security of the car. I let the glamour fall, impressed that I was able to keep it intact all day. Okay, most of the day. I lost it sometime during fifth period, but nobody seemed to notice and I got it back in place quickly. Dixon climbs into the passenger seat, looking even worse than I feel. Even with how little sleep I got, he and Liza got less. Liza joins us a minute later, and I finagle us out of the parking lot as fast as I can.

As I drive I can feel Dixon's eyes on me. "What?"

"You know what."

I sigh, not in the mood for games. "Nothing happened, okay? I was on my best behavior, and no one noticed a thing. Not even Mr. Sanders."

"Good." He leans his head against the passenger window, staring blankly out the glass. A quick check in the rear-view mirror shows Liza already asleep, neck bent at an unnatural angle as her head bobs up and down.

We make it home in record time, and I use the last bit of my strength to haul Liza out of the backseat. She doesn't wake up, not even when I dump her unceremoniously on the couch. No way I'm carting her up those stairs.

As I come back through the kitchen I notice the little red light blinking on the answering machine. We're probably the only house in town that still uses a landline. I hit the button and a voice I've come to dread fills the kitchen.

"Mr. And Mrs. McGinnis. This is Mr. Sanders, from North Point High School. I'm calling about Adrienne. I have some concerns about her recent performance in my class, and I would like to meet with you to discuss this in the near future. Please give me a call at the school so that we can set something up. Thank you."

He sounds so *polite*. I shudder, trying to get his voice out of my head. The manor is my safe place. His voice doesn't belong here.

"I thought you said you didn't do anything." Dixon's voice precedes him into the kitchen.

"I didn't!"

"Then why is he calling?"

"I don't know. Maybe because I'm still failing?"

Dixon's look says he doesn't believe me. "And it's a coincidence that he happened to call today?"

"Who knows." I suddenly find it hard to stay on my feet. "I'm going to go lie down."

"You have to deal with this," he calls after me.

"I'll figure it out later!" Surprisingly, we don't wake up Liza, and I'm able to stagger upstairs in peace. Not for the first time I wonder if this struggle to keep things normal at school is worth it. Now, with the summoner issue and the missing guardians issue, I can't help thinking I'd be better off without the hassle. My bed is inviting, and I only pause to kick off my shoes before climbing in.

The sun is down when I wake up. I stare out the window in confusion, trying to figure out what's going on and why I'm awake. The blaring sound of my phone ringing finally gets my attention, and I dig the cursed thing out of my pants pocket.

"Hello?" My voice sounds more like a chain smoker than like me.

"Adrienne?"

"Alex?" Crap. Crap crap crap.

"Are you okay? You sound funny."

"Hm? Yeah. Just...sleeping." My brain isn't functioning. I should be charming and witty, but all I can summon is coherent, and even that's a struggle.

"Already? It's only eight o'clock."

Only eight o'clock? "Not feeling well."

"Oh. Sorry. You know, I thought you looked a little tired at school."

Guess my glamour wasn't as strong as I thought it was. "What's up?" My eyes are trying to close again and I'm finding it hard to focus.

"I just wanted to see if you wanted to do something this weekend. Halloween's almost a week away, and I want to see you before then."

"Aww, that's sweet." *Did I just say that out loud? I really need to get off the phone before I say something even stupider.*

Alex chuckles. "So, is that a yes?"

"Mm-hm. See you then. Buh-bye."

I'm back asleep before making the conscious decision to hang up the phone. I let the tide pull me under, deeper and deeper into the sleep I so desperately need. My dreams are tangled, the night I killed the hellhound playing backward and forward, slowing down then speeding up, like someone studying a tape of it. I can almost feel the viewer, a subtle presence in my head that I can't quite define.

The next time I wake up I'm less confused. My bedside clock reads eleven thirty. I stretch luxuriously, my muscles stiff after lying in the same position for so long. As I reach my arms up over my head, my hand bumps something under my pillow and knocks it to the floor. My phone.

I snatch it up, taking a moment to wonder why my phone was under my pillow. *Oh no. Alex.* The problem is, I can't remember what either of us said. He did send me a text, though. *Please please please don't be anything bad.* My fingers shake as I swipe the message open.

You must really be out of it. Hope you feel better soon. We'll talk tomorrow, okay?

I must really be out of it? What did I say? *I'll find out soon enough, I'm sure.*

There's nobody in the hall when I open the bedroom door. I creep to Liza's room, cracking the door open. She finally made it into bed, and even in the dark, I can see the enhancements she's made throwing creeping shadows across the carpet. The sunflowers are still there, subsisting off air and magic, I guess, but now they've been joined by miniature palm trees in the corners of the room. The windowsill sports a small herb garden, blooming right out of the window frame and trailing down to the floor. Pong slinks among the plants, an imitation jungle cat. He purrs when I notice him, rumbling like a diesel engine.

Dixon's room is next. He's asleep, too, laptop open on his bed as if he drifted off in the middle of working. I slip silently into his room, intending to close the computer, when the still-lit screen catches my eye. No wonder the screen is still glowing; it's actively running a program. Computer stuff is essentially Russian to me, but I can tell that it's some kind of algorithm running against a map of Europe. *What's Dixon looking for? Is this his mysterious project?*

"Adrienne?" Dixon's voice is muffled and sleepy.

"Sorry. I didn't mean to wake you up. Go back to sleep."

"Do you need something?" Dixon is coming awake fast, a trait we've all developed over the last few years.

"No. I was just checking on everybody. Go back to sleep."

Ignoring me, Dixon squirms around and switches on the reading light clipped to his headboard. The dim light makes his skin look even darker than it already is. A handful of blackheads have sprouted across his cheeks since I saw him last. His light brown eyes go immediately to the laptop, skimming the information before clouding over in disappointment.

"What is it?" He looks so young and vulnerable I can't bring myself to leave him alone. Instead I climb into bed with him, making myself comfortable propped against his spare pillow. "Talk to me."

He almost doesn't tell me. I see his lips form the words that will send me away, but this late and this tired he can't hang on to his tough guy facade. "I'm looking for my parents."

The words steal my breath, and it takes a moment for me to get it back. "Your...parents. But Dixon, I thought...I mean, Heather said..."

"I know what Heather said. She told me my parents were dead. They died right after I was born. I have the death certificates to prove it."

I wait, knowing he's not done.

"Death certificates are all I have, Adrienne. No pictures. No documents. No anything."

"Oh, Dixon. I'm so sorry that you don't have those things. Maybe we can get in touch with your case worker, see if they can come up with any—"

"You don't get it." There's fire in Dixon's voice when he cuts me off. "I'm not upset because I don't have them. I'm pissed off because they don't exist."

Don't exist? "You lost me."

Sighing heavily, Dixon gives me a look that says he can't believe he has to explain it to me. "I started looking a while ago. Casually, you know, just curious about who they were. What they were like."

Tough guy facade is back. The big sister in me wants to hug Dixon tight and tell him it's okay that he wants to know about his parents. He wouldn't welcome it, though, and I'd lose the camaraderie we've found here in the dark.

"I looked up the names Heather and Andrew gave me. They're fake. There's no record of Charles and Leticia

Leavengood anywhere. I went through all the paperwork I have. I called the case worker. I called my foster homes. No one can tell me—"

Dixon's voice breaks, and I finally get my opportunity to hug him. He lets me, but doesn't return it. A second later, he pulls back and keeps talking like nothing happened. "They might be dead, just like I always thought. Or there might be something else going on. I don't know who they are, Adrienne. I don't even know their names." Then, softly, "I don't even know my own name."

The pain in his voice kills me, but he won't look me in the eye. "So, the computer..." I let my question trail off, giving him as much time as he needs to respond.

"I was able to authenticate my birth certificate. Even if the names aren't right, the date and location are. The computer is running a facial recognition program for everyone caught on security footage in every hospital in Cook County, Illinois on the day I was born."

He says it so simply, like that's something every fifteen-year-old is capable of doing, and I marvel once again at his enormous brain. I'm about to tell him so, when a crash from downstairs has us both scrambling to get free of the covers. Downstairs, we find a shattered living room window alongside a brick with "freak" emblazoned on it in hot pink lipstick. Outside, tires squeal as the vandal peels away from the curb.

"Are you going to call the police?" Dixon asks as he examines the window, then starts muttering under his breath. Liza could have done it more easily, but in the end the result is the same: the pane is once again whole and in place.

"No, I don't think so."

"Why not?" The question comes out on a yawn as Dixon's exhaustion returns with a vengeance.

Throwing my arm around his shoulders, I lead him back toward the stairs, brick still clutched in my hand. The dirty looks I've gotten from many of the girls at school swim in my head. "I don't think it's a serious threat. We need to keep a low profile, remember?"

At the door of Dixon's room, I kiss him gently on top of his fuzzy hair, something I haven't done in a while. "You should get back to bed. Get some more sleep. I need you on your game tomorrow."

"What's tomorrow?"

"Our visitor showed us tonight that we have a vulnerability in the wards. Without Andrew and Heather here we need to make sure we're protected. I need you to go over the wards for the manor and figure out how to keep human intruders out just like we do monsters."

"I don't think I can—"

"Liza can cast it. You just need to tell her what to do."

"Okay." He yawns again, a big, jaw-popping yawn. "Night, Adrienne."

"Goodnight."

TWELVE

HALLOWEEN. TUESDAY AFTERNOON, WE'RE having the same argument we've been having for the past week.

"It's just a party, guys. I'll be a phone call away, and I can respond instantly if anything happens."

"If?" Liza squeaks. "If? You were pretty certain something big was going to happen tonight before you had a date, and now it's only "if"?"

Dixon's against me, too. "She's right. Anything could happen tonight. We've been practicing spells all weekend, just trying to cover all our bases. Going out isn't worth the risk."

"And sitting at home is going to accomplish what? There's nothing for me to do here, and I'll go stir crazy waiting around. Our feelers are already out there. We'll be alerted the second anything happens." It's actually a pretty cool setup, designed by Dixon, of course. Like the alert on our phones, there are now spells laced through various communication networks that will alert us to anything matching our criteria. Tonight, our criteria are pretty broad. Big magic, homicides, creature sightings. We've covered it all. Dixon's laptop will be running algorithms continuously, sorting and rating the information and sending updates to our cell phones. How he integrated magic and technology I'll never know, but he'll be meeting with the council later this week to walk them through how he did it. It could revolutionize how magi practice magic.

"I don't like it. You need to be home." Liza's appeal is almost enough to sway me. Almost. Of all of us, she's taking Andrew and Heather's absence the hardest. She's back to not sleeping well, her grades are slipping, and she's overall just looking a bit haggard.

"It's going to be okay." I hug her tight, trying to comfort her while being firm in my decision at the same time. "Midnight is the big draw on Halloween, right?"

"Yeah."

"The party will be long over by then. I'll have my phone on me at all times, I promise. As soon as something happens, I'm out of there. The Shadow Plane will get me there just as fast as if I'm leaving from the manor. And you guys will be safe here. Dixon made sure of that. We've planned for everything, okay? We're ready. Is it really so bad if I want to have a little fun before everything goes sideways?"

And with that, I've won. They're still not happy about it, but they stop trying to convince me to stay. Liza helps me finish getting ready as I wait for Alex to get here. My makeup is dark, sticking with the Halloween theme and making my green eyes pop out even more than normal. My lips are a deep, blood red, and a French braid pulls my hair away from my face. The effect is startling. I don't often wear make-up, and the face in the mirror is somewhat foreign to me.

The past week with Alex has been perfect. We've hung out every day at school, been to the movies twice, and I even went to Saturday's game. We've talked, we've laughed, and we've had a lot of fun. The one thing we haven't done is kiss. He said he wanted to wait for the right time, and I'm getting a little antsy.

I know the standard trope for Halloween costumes: lingerie with animal ears. No way I'm wearing that. I tried to be as practical as possible while still making Alex think I'm sexy. And knowing I may need to fight at a moment's notice, my costume needs to be conducive to traveling heavily armed. So, I'm going as Zena: Warrior Princess. The sword across my back and the knives in my boots are perfectly acceptable.

The crunch of gravel outside tells me Alex is here. A wave of nerves washes over me, and I stare down at my bare legs, fighting the sudden urge to throw on a pair of jeans instead. *Easy, Adrienne. Ignore the fact that you haven't worn a skirt in four years. You can't sit up here all night. You have to see him eventually.* The skirt was the only problematic part of the costume. I fixed it though, by slitting the leather up to my hip and throwing bike shorts on underneath. Now I can still kick monsters in the face.

Dixon has to call me twice before I descend the stairs on wobbly legs. Alex is waiting in the kitchen, and the slow once-over he gives me makes all doubts about my costume vanish. "Wow. You look great."

"Thanks. You too." Guys don't have to be sexy on Halloween, though I don't think Alex could stop being sexy if he tried. He got a haircut today, faded up the sides while staying long on the top. I have to resist the urge to walk right up to him and run my fingers through it. Tonight he's going as a bank robber, complete with striped shirt and canvas bag with a big dollar sign on it.

Alex escorts me outside, where he stops and looks me over again, this time with decidedly different intentions. "Um, are you going to be able to ride the bike in that?"

In response, I cross to the motorcycle, throw one leg over it, and waggle a finger at him in a "come hither" motion. It's a move I never would have tried without practicing several dozen times on the bench in the training room for just this moment. It must have worked, because I execute it flawlessly.

"Oh my. Be still my heart." Alex takes his time walking over to the bike, gaze sliding up my leg, and it occurs to me that I may have gone too far. We're definitely not ready to be doing any of the things that just crossed his mind. A moment later the tension between us is gone, and Alex climbs onto the bike in front of me. "Ready?" he asks, then turns the throttle. The motorcycle roars to life beneath us, and we go speeding into the night.

Brent lives on the outskirts of town, like we do, but on the complete opposite side. Alex has to slow down as we cross through town, avoiding groups of kids already out trick-or-treating. At the sight of them, a small lump forms in my throat. Being a magi means bearing the burden of knowledge. I know everything that could happen to those kids tonight, and just hope that if the worst should happen, I'll be there in time to stop it.

The party is in full swing by the time we arrive. Music blares out of the open windows, teenagers are prowling across the yard with cups in their hands, and someone's car alarm is going off. Alex maneuvers the bike toward the long driveway, then abruptly changes his mind and parks one street over. "Is this okay?" he asks as he helps me off the motorcycle. "I don't want it to get knocked over or anything."

"This is fine." Even at this distance I can feel the bass line pounding in my chest.

He gives me a beaming smile. "Ready?"

"Not really." Now that we're here my nerves are back. I know the guys on the football team slightly better now than I did a week ago, but definitely not well enough to call them "friends". And this will be my first social gathering with them outside of school grounds. And on Halloween, no less. Anything could happen.

"It's going to be fine." Alex leans down and for a moment I think he's chosen this moment, inconsequential as it is, and I tilt my face toward his. But he only whispers, "You really do look amazing," then takes my hand and leads me up to the house.

"You want anything to drink?" he asks as soon as we get inside.

"I don't drink," I answer, realizing I'm in the minority. One keg is already empty and being replaced by another. Even if I wanted to, it wouldn't be tonight. No drinking on duty.

"Neither do I," he answers, and relief rushes through me. "I'll grab us some water."

The bottle he pushes into my hand is cool to the touch, and I open it gratefully. The temperature may be chilly outside, but with all the bodies pressed in here it feels more like the Caribbean.

"Hey, Alex. Adrienne." My name is slightly less cordial rolling off Daphne's lips. Hot pink lips, the same color I've seen recently on a brick thrown through my living room window. She's wearing the requisite lingerie and bunny ears. Alex doesn't seem to notice my cool reception. "Glad you made it." She takes a sip out of her red plastic cup, eying our water bottles. "Can I get you a drink?"

Alex is all class when he answers, "No, thank you, we're good." He ignores her pout and pulls me close, killing my impulse to take some kind of petty revenge on her. "Want to dance?"

He doesn't give me a chance to respond before dragging me into the middle of the living room where our classmates are clustered around rubbing against each other.

"I don't think I know how to dance," I confide to him as he releases my hand. I take a moment to watch the couple beside us. His arms are flying in all directions while her hips swing wildly from side to side. "Yeah, I can't do that."

"Don't worry about them. Just do what I do."

I shift my attention back to Alex to find him shuffling a bit and kind of bouncing up and down. He looks a little ridiculous, and I let out a giggle. "I think I can do that."

Two songs later, I'm feeling much more confident in my dancing skills. Alex has broken out some moves that tell me he was going easy on me earlier, and we've been joined by Brent and a handful of other people I'm becoming increasingly more comfortable around. To my surprise, I'm having a really good time. I'm even laughing. Not to mention sweating. Even in my skimpy leather, a light sheen of sweat covers my exposed skin.

Alex's hair is damp, pushed back from his eyes in a fashionably tousled kind of way. We lock eyes as the song ends and a slow one takes its place. Without a word he reaches out for me, and I step into his arms.

Alex's hands on my back send shivers up my spine. He holds me close, closer than is probably necessary. I let my arms rest against his neck, fingers absently running through the fine hairs there. He's not much taller than I am, and doesn't have to lean down very far to rest his forehead against mine.

"Are you having a good time?"

"I am." Our voices are soft, contained in the little bubble we've created.

"I'm glad. I love seeing you smile. It makes you even more beautiful."

"You're not exactly an ogre yourself."

That makes him chuckle. He takes a little breath, and his eyes drop to my lips. *This is it.* Time slows. I can feel him leaning in, and I close my eyes in anticipation.

Before our lips touch, a bell goes off in my head. Not a metaphorical "something isn't quite right here" bell, but a literal bell, echoing through my brain. Crying out, I cradle my head in my hands and stumble back. Alex reaches for me, confusion etched across his features, but I turn away from him. The other dancers move around me, too absorbed in each other to notice my passage. The air feels suddenly stifling, the heat that was so sensuous moments ago now threatening to suffocate me.

Outside, I can finally breathe again. *What in the hell was that?* My first thought is of attack. Someone, another magi maybe, is after me. But no, my wards are still intact. I rarely have my wards up in the Mortal Plane, but well, Halloween.

Halloween. Magic. That's it! The girls' school murders feel like a long time ago, but I did put a magical tracker on their worship magic. Now, someone is using it again. Once I identify the alarm the ringing bell fades away, replaced by what can only be described as magical GPS. I know, somehow, exactly where the magic is being used.

I'm steadying my nerves and about to enter the Shadow Plane when Alex's hand closes on my elbow. I'd completely forgotten about him.

"Adrienne? Are you okay?" His worried eyes search my face, looking for some explanation for my bizarre behavior.

"I'm fine. I'm sorry, but I have to go."

"Go? What? What's going on?"

"Look, I can't explain right now, but something's come up. I'll call you later, okay?" I turn away, not wanting to look at his face when he looks so hurt and vulnerable. I shake off his arm and stride away, moving away from the house and anyone who might notice me suddenly vanishing into thin air. I pick up my pace into a jog and gain the relative quiet of the park across the street. There are people here, too, but they're engaged in more intimate activities and paying no attention to me. Pushing deeper, I angle for a thicket that appears unoccupied. It's much darker beneath the trees, and I can't make out the source of the heavy breathing, but that means they can't see me, either.

The moment I left Alex, I put him out of my mind, focused solely on the mission. I should have known he would follow me. Should have done something more to make sure he didn't.

Maybe then I wouldn't have felt his hand closing on my arm again as I cross into the Shadow Plane. I turn to look at him, and regret knifes through me at the emotions I see there. Fear, confusion, worry. I use my free hand to latch onto his wrist. "Don't let go!"

Like I did with Liza, I wrap Alex tightly in my wards. As long as we maintain physical contact, he'll be safe.

"Adrienne?" His voice shakes, though I can see he's trying to keep it all together. His eyes roam wildly, taking in the barrenness of the Shadow Plane, the shifting of the light in the gloom even though no light source can be seen. The shadows themselves flock to us, drawn by his fear.

"Alex, look at me." The authority in my voice snaps his eyes back to mine. The last time he heard me use this tone was on our first date, when I slaughtered a lizard creature right in front of him. I can almost see the memory replaying in his mind. "I'm going to protect you, but you need to do exactly what I say, all right?" I wait for him to nod before I continue. "As long as we stay in physical contact, they can't hurt you. Stay with me, and whatever you do, don't let go. Okay?"

"Okay." He's silent as we move through the Shadow Plane, placing his feet delicately and watching the shadows moving with us. He slows me down, but there's no way I'm leaving him behind. More bells go off in my head, and I log their locations, but none of them feel as strong as the first one. The minutes drag on, until I finally feel like I'm in the right place.

"Hold on tight!" His vice-like grip on my arm tightens even more, and I wince as his nails dig into my skin. With another breath I cross back into the Mortal Plane, on yet another college campus.

I dislodge Alex, who shrinks back and stares at me. "What the hell was that? Where are we?"

"San Diego State." I ignore the first part of the question. If Alex forgives me for this, I'll explain it all to him later. "Stay here."

I take off at a run, eyes darting to and fro, looking for my target. The street we've landed on looks like Greek housing. The GPS in my brain leads me to the Delta Zeta house, halfway down the block. Thinking of the girls' school, I ignore the house completely and circle around to the back. It's enclosed in a privacy fence, which I'm up and over in a single bound.

There, in the middle of the backyard, a circle of sorority girls kneels in the dirt, heads bowed and hands uplifted. There are no sidewalks like in the girls' school garden, but there are manicured pathways lined with familiar-looking herbs. The circle encompasses a junction where three of the paths meet. The girls are chanting. I take a step forward, and a thud lands behind me. Whirling, I find Alex crouching in the dirt. He didn't land as gracefully as I did, but he's not a star athlete for nothing.

"You have a lot of explaining to do."

"Not now." I turn away from him, again, as my attention is drawn to movement across the yard. Not the girls. Something bigger.

"You." His voice rumbles out of the darkness as I stride forward to meet him.

"You," I answer back, gaze riveted on the form of the Immortal as he steps into the moonlight. With measured movements, I reach a hand behind my head and draw my sword.

Thirteen

THE SWORD IS NEW. Relatively speaking. I haven't used it since my initial training years ago. Knives and hand-to-hand come more naturally to me, so I rely on them most often. But as our last confrontation proved, I can't deal the Immortal any lasting damage with them. I could barely even get close. I had to think bigger. So, while Dixon and Liza worked on spells and detection, I spent the last week re-familiarizing myself with the weapon. Now, the blade gleams in the moonlight, fresh sigils inscribed along its length. It's an ancient language, one no longer used but associated with our familiars. When I couldn't touch the Immortal, Cerise could. The inscription speaks of rending and freeing, of cleansing and making whole, and will hopefully help to cut through any wards or enchantments the Immortal has woven around himself.

As I heft the sword, my shoulders tingle with a soreness that hasn't quite faded completely away. But my hand closes securely around the hilt, and the weight pulls comfortably on my arm. I move forward, placing myself between the Immortal and the girls. They don't seem to notice any of us.

"You're not going to hurt them."

"They have been corrupted, and must be cleansed." There's no anger in his voice, no animosity. I'm reminded again of the scant information we have about him, and the assumptions we've made. He doesn't want to kill these girls. He just believes he has to.

"We can find another way."

"There is no other way."

He moves first, charging toward me with a speed that amazes me. Last time, he barely moved. This time, it seems he's changing tactics. I sidestep, crouching low and slashing at his legs as he passes. I'm too slow. He races past me and heads straight for the girls.

"No!" I don't think, I just move, racing after him and slamming my whole weight into his back. Surprisingly, I connect, knocking him off balance and to the side.

The collision sends me veering off into the middle of the circle, tripping over ankles as I go. None of them move. Their chanting continues, rising in volume and tempo. I land hard in the grass and slide, bumping my head on a garden statue. A garden statue?

The thought doesn't have the chance to fully form before the Immortal is back on target, rearing up behind a redheaded student. The glint of the blade in his hand has me responding with my own. I catch his downward swing on the edge of my blade, wincing as the sword jumps in my hand. But it holds. Deflected, his arm skitters to the left, and I follow up with a roundhouse kick to his chest. He's strong, but so am I. The difference between this fight and the last one is this time, I'm not trying to kill him. If I can hold him at bay...

"Alex!" I call out, as the Immortal stumbles back half a step. It's enough time for the statue thought to finish materializing. "Smash the shrine!" I have to hope he hears me, because I don't have time to check. The Immortal is glaring at me with death in his eyes, promising pain if I don't get out of his way. I puff out my chest and brandish my sword at him in response.

I still can't best the Immortal. We both know that. But with my handy new sword, I'm able to at least fend off his attacks, and maybe save those girls' lives. He tries to dart around me, but I'm expecting it this time and move to intercept. I slash at his chest, which I know he'll block, and allow the weight of the sword to carry my body around in a complete circle, giving me a split-second view of the yard. Alex is standing in the middle of the circle, hands out, fending off his own attacks from enraged sorority girls. He must have succeeded. "Get them out of here!" I scream the command into the air, counting on the words to find their way to him. The Immortal's blade connects with mine, making my jaw snap shut and jarring my whole body.

He roars and swings at me, hard. I block it, but fall for the same trick I used on him just moments ago. As soon as our blades touch, his fist connects with my jaw, sending me sprawling. As I hit the ground I see him sprinting away from me, toward the girls who are now fleeing back inside the sorority house.

"No!" My mouth doesn't open the way it's supposed to, so the word doesn't come out. I scramble up from the ground, hands slick with dew, but it doesn't matter. I'm too far behind him; I'll never reach them in time. Not that that stops me from giving chase.

I make it half a dozen steps before the world explodes around me. The force of the blast hurtles me back, slamming me into the privacy fence. The Immortal goes flying, too, and his airborne form is the last thing I see before my head snaps back and the world goes dark. I'm back when I hit the ground and scramble to get my feet beneath me before I'm attacked again. The Immortal has regained his, faster than me again, and now stands facing off with...Alex?

Alex's arm shoots forward and something pink sails through the air. It hits the ground at the Immortal's feet and a wisp of pink smoke puffs upward. The Immortal lunges forward, ready to obliterate anything standing between him and his target. In this case, Alex. I try to scream, to warn him, but my jaw still isn't working right. I lurch forward, but can't keep my balance and tumble back to the ground. Alex is backing up now, not fast enough, and flinging his hand again. Two more puffs of pink smoke wrap around the Immortal's legs. I can only gape in horror at what I'm sure is about to happen.

Then the unexpected happens. The Immortal stalls, wobbling on his feet. A breath later he crumples to the ground and lies still. Alex barely looks at him before rushing over to me.

"Adrienne! Are you okay?" His hands hover over my head, reluctant to touch me. "Can you hear me?"

I try to sit up and show him I'm fine, but it probably looks more like a fish trying to swim on land than the graceful rising I had pictured. The worry in his face deepens. I try to reassure him, but my mouth is stuck shut and won't open.

"Hold on. I can help. Just, lie still, okay?" From the pocket of his pants he pulls a small glass vial, amber-colored liquid swirling inside. Sliding his hand cautiously behind my head, he tilts it forward and presses the vial to my lips. "Drink."

My jaw still doesn't respond, but I'm able to part my lips enough for the liquid to dribble in. It's warm and sweet on my tongue, and slides down my throat like honey. I feel its effects almost immediately. The pain in my jaw eases, and my mouth pops open. My swirling, pounding head stops swirling and pounding. And I'm able to sit up.

"What—"

Alex cuts me off with a tight hug. "He won't be out long. You should deal with him first, and we can talk after."

"Right." Business first. But later, definitely have to talk to Alex. I'm not the only one who has things to explain.

My phone is ringing, somewhere. It must have gone flying at some point during the fight. My costume is severely lacking in pocket space, so I'd tucked it in the old standby: my bra. I don't immediately see it and choose to ignore it rather than hunting through the grass for it.

The Immortal is still where Alex left him, sprawled haphazardly in the grass. His breaths are deep and even. *He looks so...normal.* If he were walking down the street, strangers wouldn't immediately think "threat!" when they saw him. He could pass for a graduate student on any college campus. And I hate to even think it, but he's handsome. Classical lines emphasize his strong jaw and high cheekbones, and piercing blue eyes peek out from under heavy lids.

"What are you going to do?" Alex interrupts my wonderings.

"I don't know. He's stronger than me, much stronger, and when he wakes up he's going to be pissed. Nothing I do to him will hold him."

"Are you going to kill him?" Alex's question is matter-of-fact, and it makes me pause. *We really don't know each other as well as we thought we did.* I knew I was holding back from him, but it never occurred to me that he was holding back, too.

"He's not the bad guy." The words seem strange, considering he's a serial killer, but I can't argue with the feeling of truth in them. There's more shades of gray to this story than are visible from the surface.

"Then I have something that might work." Alex jogs to his bank-robber bag, the one with the dollar sign, rifles through it, then returns. He hands me three vials, this time colored blue-black. "Here."

"What are they?"

"A strong paralytic. If they work, they'll immobilize his body from the neck down, so, he'll still be able to talk."

"Neat trick." I'm working hard to compartmentalize right now. It's hard, standing over an unconscious man with my new boyfriend discussing ways to magically restrain him. It's a lot to deal with.

"That's if they work. There's no guarantee they will."

"Will they hurt him?"

"No."

"Then let's do it."

Alex helps me haul the Immortal into a lounge chair and prop him up. Then like he did for me, he braces his head so I can pour the contents of the vials into his mouth. This is no time for caution; I use all three. When we're done I sit staring down at him, just for a moment.

"Who is he?"

"I don't really know."

"Then how do you know he's not the bad guy? I may be wrong, but wasn't he trying to kill them?" Alex gestures at the house, which I've completely forgotten about. The windows are dark, and the night is still and quiet.

"It's complicated. Hey, does something feel wrong to you? Where did the girls go? Shouldn't they have called the cops or something?"

"Hmm." Alex moves toward the patio's sliding glass doors, and after a moment, I follow him. Either the potion worked or it didn't; me hovering over the Immortal isn't going to change the outcome.

The house is eerily quiet. Something is making my skin crawl, and it doesn't take long to find out what. Alex finds a light switch first, and as the lamps come on I see them.

The girls lie on the floor where they fell, some in the hall, some on the stairs, one just to the side of the door. We walked right past her. I kneel down next to an overweight brunette and check for a pulse, already knowing I won't find one. The blood running from her nose and eyes is still wet, seeping into the plush violet rug beneath her head.

Alex has gone deathly pale. He hasn't moved from the wall, hand still on the switch, frozen in place, eyes unseeing. I can't blame him. I felt much the same when I saw my first dead body.

I stand back up and go to him. "Come on," I nudge him, guiding him back outside and sitting him down on the patio. "There's nothing we can do for them."

"She killed them, didn't she?" The Immortal is awake.

"Who is she?"

"She is Enodia, Melinoe, Trimorphe. Cthonia and Trioditis. The ancients called her "The Nameless One", they feared her so."

"Stop talking in riddles. What happened in there? Why are a dozen girls dead?" My voice has risen to a shout, and I don't care. The Immortal is here, and helpless, and has the answers I need, and I'll be damned if I'm not going to get them.

"She is jealous, and vengeful. They did not complete their ritual, and she punished them."

My blood turns to ice. "I did this?"

The Immortal doesn't answer, just studies me, much as I was studying him earlier. "You do not serve her. Why do you protect her acolytes?"

The question helps to center me. *Learn now. Deal later.* "I protect human life. No matter their sins, those girls didn't deserve to be butchered."

"That is an interesting way to see it." He genuinely means it. I can see it in his eyes.

Now that we're having an actual conversation, I'm having a hard time feeling animosity for the Immortal. I'll still oppose him with every fiber of my being if he tries to lay a hand on an innocent ever again, but he's actually a reasonable person. "Tell me. About her. About you. About your mission."

He studies me, as if gauging my worth. Deciding if I can be trusted.

I pass. "Your history books call it the Golden Age of Athens. More than two thousand years ago. A human sorceress thought herself a goddess, and demanded she be worshiped as such. Her cruelty was limitless, and her thirst for power unquenchable. In time, she was defeated, and banished from this plane. Banished, but not destroyed. She seeks, even now, to restore her power and return to her former glory."

It's a short speech, but enough to send shivers down my spine and raise gooseflesh on all of my exposed skin. A heaviness falls across my mind like a shadow, and I shake my head to clear it.

"Who is she?"

"She has many names, as I've already mentioned. Most people today know her as Hecate."

The almost church-like silence of the night is shattered by my ringing phone. Again. Upon reflection, it's been ringing almost nonstop for the last several minutes. I was just too absorbed with the Immortal to notice. "Hold that thought." I follow the music to where my phone lies vibrating in the damp grass, but it cuts off before I can answer. The screen shines when I pick it up, showing me exactly how many calls and notifications and alarms I've missed. "Shit! It's Halloween!"

Dixon's yelling before I can get a word in. "Where the hell have you been? Do you know what's been going on out there? How could you do this, you said you would answer your phone, you said you would be there..."

I let him run out of words, trying to absorb it all while he vents. The laptop has been going crazy, there have been attacks all over the country, he's been trying to call me for the last half an hour, and Liza's missing.

"Whoa, Dixon, slow down," I finally have the chance to say. "I'm sorry. I got tangled up with the Immortal, but I'm heading home now, and—"

"The Immortal? Are you okay? Geez, no wonder...you know what, never mind, just get back here."

Dixon hangs up, and I stare at the phone, dumbfounded. Then his words sink in. *Liza's missing?*

I turn to head back up to the house and find the Immortal standing directly behind me. To my credit, I don't scream, but barely.

He doesn't attack, just stands there, leaving me to wonder if the paralytic potion actually worked or if he just let me think it did.

I have an idea. "I believe we're on the same side. This Hecate. She's hurting people?"

He nods.

"I need to know more. In order to fight her. To win. I could use your help."

"I have hunted Hecate for more than two thousand years. What help could you be to me?"

"If you haven't beaten her yet then you're obviously not doing it right. And I'm not going to stop, so you might as well keep me from getting myself killed."

He bristles at the insult, but doesn't argue the point. "I will consider your proposal."

"Great, I guess. Let me give you—"

"I know where to find you, Adrienne Young."

He turns his back to me, proving once again how non-threatening he finds me, and strides away back across the grass. I ignore him. I can't stop him from going, and I have more pressing issues to deal with. I collect my sword from where it landed after being wrenched from my hand, returning it to its sheath on my back. I don't have time to examine the site as well as I'd like to, so I snap a couple of pictures with my phone to look at later.

Then I collect Alex. He's still shaky, but his color is better and he seems to be in control of himself again. He gave me space as I talked to the Immortal, but I could feel his eyes boring into my back, keeping watch.

The last thing I do before we leave is call 911, slipping inside to use the landline in the office. I'm in and out in less than two minutes, leaving the phone off the hook. The cops will show eventually.

"Come on, we're going home."

"We need to—"

"Not now." I've said that way too many times tonight, and it'll be a while before I can stop saying it. "Things are bad at home, and I have to get back. Remember, don't let go."

I wrap my arms tightly around Alex, keeping him secure as I cross into the Shadow Plane.

FOURTEEN

"WHERE IS HE?" DIXON accosts me at the door before I have the chance to come inside.

I thrust Alex through in front of me, using him to knock Dixon out of the way. He's pale and shaky from our second trip through the Shadow Plane. The shadows were even worse this time, stirred up by the magic energy flowing through our plane. Even I had difficulty seeing through the squirming mass. "Who?"

"Who else? The Immortal. And what's he doing here?" Dixon's trying hard to stay in control, but it's not working. He follows us into the living room, where I deposit Alex on the couch. He sinks into the cushions gratefully, taking deep breaths.

"He left. And Alex was there, so for now, he can stay."

"What? How could you let him leave? He—"

"I didn't 'let' him do anything. Where's Liza?"

My abrupt change of topic makes him pause, and her name sobers him. "I don't know. We were watching a movie, well, trying to, it was hard to pay attention to it since we were waiting for the laptop."

I wave my hand at him, urging him to hurry up.

"She said she was getting a drink, and she never came back. I searched the whole house. She isn't here."

"What about the—"

"Looked there too. Her phone's still here. She just vanished."

Anything could have gotten to her tonight. But how would it have gotten past the wards? "Shoes?"

"What?"

"Did she put on her shoes? If she did, then she left of her own free will. If not, then something took her."

"I didn't even think about shoes." Dixon races back into the kitchen, a step ahead of me. He groans, and my heart plummets. "They're gone."

"Okay. She could still be okay." Reassuring Dixon is hard. *Where in the world would she have gone? She's not stupid enough to leave the safety of the manor tonight.* Back in the living room I examine the laptop screen, scanning the information it's been compiling on magical activity. A lot of it is typical, harmless Halloween stuff. Seances. Curses. Practical jokes.

While I'm at it I start barking orders at Dixon. "You have her phone, so start calling her friends. Anywhere you can think of she might have gone. When you're done with the mundane stuff, start thinking of magical stuff. Find her, and I'll go and get her."

"What are you going to do?"

I punch in a few keys, isolating the category titled "Creature Sightings" and linking it to my phone. After a moment's hesitation, I highlight a few more and send them to Mason, a number I wish I didn't know by heart. He's probably already in the field, but this way he'll have the same information we do. "I'm going to go save lives."

I've already discarded the idea of tracking down the other worship-magic sites. Until I figure out how Hecate slaughtered a dozen sorority girls from beyond the grave, I don't dare interrupt any more rituals tonight. It takes a grueling ten minutes for me to be ready to leave the house again. First up, changing clothes. Not only do I not want to run around the country killing baddies dressed as Zena, it's also not practical for slaying monsters. Way too much exposed skin.

I keep the sword, just in case, and rearrange my silver knives. Then I visit Alex. "Hey. How are you feeling?"

"Better." He looks better. Exhausted, but better.

"Do you have any more potions on you?"

He startles at the word, as if surprised I know it. The air between us is heavy with the secrets we need to divulge, but we seem to have reached an unspoken agreement that now isn't the time. "You're going back out?" His eyes take in my new outfit: jeans, boots, long-sleeves, leather jacket thrown over my arm.

"I have work to do. Monsters to kill. Do you have anything that might help?" He doesn't flinch at my mention of monsters, confirming my suspicions.

"Not really. I was mostly thinking about keeping you safe, so everything I have is designed for humans. You can have these, though." He pulls out a couple vials of the same bright blue magic gatorade he gave me last week.

I stuff them in my pocket. "Thanks. I have to go, but I'll see you soon. I want you to stay here, where it's safe, and we can talk when I get back, okay?" Even with his secrets, Alex isn't a threat. The conversation we need to have can wait until there aren't lives on the line.

"What can I do while you're gone?"

I hesitate, wanting to make him feel useful and needing to get out of there. "Just, keep an eye on Dixon, okay? He's having a rough night." *We're all having a rough night.* I try to give him a reassuring smile, which I'm sure comes out wrong, then leave without saying anything else.

Dixon catches me at the door, but doesn't hold me up. "Be careful, okay? Check in every now and then."

"Will do." Then I'm gone, out of reach of the wards and into the Shadow Plane.

Some people raise creatures on Halloween. They don't mean to. Often they're a result of inexperience and magic gone wrong. A lot of shadows cross into the Mortal Plane on Halloween. Other creatures just get excited, drawn out by the energy and the extra people on the streets. I only have one way to differentiate between these normal occurrences and what may be Hecate: last time, she used hellhounds. It's a slim lead at best. All of these creatures will be looking for blood, but hellhounds will be looking for a massacre.

My first stop is the closest college campus on the list, Post University in Connecticut. Someone called the cops and reported a rabid dog chasing them to the bus stop. Might be a hellhound. Might just be a stray. There's no big event going on here tonight, but on Halloween, potential victims wander around in delicious clusters just waiting to be picked off.

The bus stop is busy when I arrive. Down the street, I can see the bus coming, and more than a dozen people are milling about the sidewalk. I scan the area, but nothing looks immediately wrong. At least, no one is screaming. The call was placed twenty minutes ago, which means the rabid dog could be halfway across town by now.

The bus pulls up, and people spill out as the doors open. I circle the crowd, looking for any sign of my target. Over the cacophony, I barely hear it. The lowest of growls, rumbling out of the bushes lining the sidewalk. My head snaps up, and I see what I've been missing: a smear of blood, hidden by the shadow of the stop's awning.

I draw my sword. "Everybody get back on the bus!" My yell does nothing but get their attention, but the gleaming sword in my hand convinces them to get far, far away. The crowd pushes away from me, fleeing into the street, as a dark blur hurdles over the bushes.

"Ventus!" The wind spell worked last time. The gust knocks the creature sideways, causing it to miss a step when it lands. As it stumbles I rush in, pressing my advantage and herding it away from the people now cramming themselves back onto the bus. The hellhound, as I can see now that it's in front of me, snarls and lunges at me, teeth snapping shut inches away from my wrist. My arms are already tired from squaring off against the Immortal, but I will new strength into them and meet the hellhound head-on.

The hellhound is fierce, but I haven't forgotten my fight with the last one. With the sword, I'm able to keep it at arm's length, and with my wind spell I keep it off-balance, unable to pick up speed. This fight is much shorter than my last, and minutes later I'm watching the hellhound's ash blow away in the breeze.

The bus is still there, but I ignore the faces pressed against the windows. Most of them will be telling this story for a long time, but I can't worry about the exposure right now. If the hellhound is here, that means the summoner is, too.

A prickling on the back of my neck pulls my attention away from the street and into the darkness. Outside of the streetlamps, I catch sight of my observer. Short stature, long billowing coat, face hidden in shadow: *the summoner.* Pulse racing, I head that direction, but the summoner vanishes before I can even get close.

No time to rest. I down one of Alex's magic gatorade vials and pick out my next target.

My next three potential hellhound sightings are a bust. I find a black bear, a coyote, and a barghest. The barghest is one of those creatures often drawn to the revelry of Halloween. The good news is, the large, spectral black dog is a stalker, taking only one or two victims a night. It was sighted in a small town in the hills of Kentucky. I spend longer than I want to tracking it down, but am able to kill it before it claims its victim.

I'm wiping the blood off of my knife when alarm bells start going off in my head again. "Aargh!"

Someone's worshiping Hecate. I feel a tug on my body again, telling me where to go, and for a moment I almost follow. Almost. This one is strong, even stronger than the sorority, and tempting. But I can't risk it. With a heavy heart, I choose to ignore the summons. With the choice the bells go silent. I wonder briefly about the Immortal. If I don't go, I'll never know whether he did or not.

I check my list, and head off to Mobile, Alabama. Nothing here is screaming "hellhound", but there's something weird going on in the bay.

A fight is already in motion when I arrive. With a start, I realize the person on the shore is a magi, throwing lightning bolts at something writhing in the waves. The water crackles as the lightning hits, and the creature roars in pain and anger. I race in to help, drawing a silver knife.

"Mason!" I call out, getting the magi's attention. The only light on the beach comes from the coals of a dying bonfire, but out here the moonlight is strong enough for me to make out his features. There's so much going on tonight I didn't expect to run into him, but no matter our personal history, the battle comes first. "Fire!"

Without waiting for his reply I race into the surf. I take half a second to gain control over myself, letting the water crashing into my legs center me and give me the focus I need. "Unda!" I cry, drawing on that water, pulling it away from the creature.

Mason appears at my side, intent on our quarry. His opportunity arises, and he pounces on it. "Ignis!" The exposed hide of the creature bursts into flame. I keep pulling the water, uncovering more of the massive beast, while Mason pours on the flame. Even from here, the strength of the heat has sweat rolling down my face.

Finally, the creature's screams die away, and after a moment Mason releases his fire. I release the ocean, letting it close back in and sweep away the body of the beast. Panting, we both trudge back to the shore, only fighting now against the pull of the waves.

"What was that?" I ask between gulps of air.

"No idea. Tentacles. Teeth. It got three drunk guys and a homeless man. Thanks. For the assist." Mason is a giant tool, but he knows his job and does it well.

"Any time."

"But it's not 'any time' though, is it?" Mason pauses for dramatic effect, while I wait for whatever biting comment is going to come next. "Dixon called. Said he couldn't get a hold of you."

"I was busy." His tone makes me bristle. Like I committed some grave sin. Part of me thinks he's right. I had a perfectly justifiable reason for not answering Dixon's call, but that doesn't make me feel less guilty about not being there when he needed me.

Mason knows what I'm thinking before I can articulate the thought. It's something he's always been good at, and one of the things I hate most about him. "The details don't matter. You're here now, and that's what counts. You can explain it to me later." And there it is. His uncanny ability to make me feel like a child.

"I'm marking this one as complete," I answer, pulling my phone out of my jacket pocket, thankfully still dry. "Which one do you want, so I can go somewhere else?"

His look says we're definitely talking about this later. He ignores my phone, though, and pulls out his own. "Um, I'll take the psycho in Indiana with the black altar in his backyard. You?"

"More creatures. Still looking for hellhounds."

"Hellhounds?"

I don't elaborate, just take a few steps back and cross into the Shadow Plane. I don't owe Mason an explanation, although he'll probably show up later demanding one. For now, there's a mauled corpse in Pennsylvania that needs my attention.

Pennsylvania isn't a hellhound. The night drags on, until finally the sun begins to crest the eastern sky. With its appearance, the laptop alerts stop. Just like that. The sun has that effect on wayward Halloween magic. I scan the rest of my list and decide none of it needs my attention at the moment. If there were any hellhounds still on it, they would have disappeared with the light anyway. Along with any chance of encountering the summoner again.

My feet are dragging when the manor comes into view. After a night like this one, I sorely need to decompress. But as the ranking member of the household now, I can't really dawdle on the way home anymore. I had to settle for emerging down the block and walking the half-mile back to the house. A shadow in the trees at the side of the house catches my attention. Not for any reason I can pinpoint, just a general feeling that something is there.

I stop and wait, staring into the shadows, willing whatever is there to appear already and get this over with. Glowing red eyes blink out at me. When it finally steps out I curse and go for my sword.

The hellhound is as tall as my hip, lean, almost skeletal. I wait, but it doesn't come any closer. It takes no defensive action, either. No growling, no hackles, not even a bared tooth. Still I wait, staring it down, as the minutes slowly pass and the sky grows lighter.

Then it does something impossible. It steps out into the emerging sunlight. Not only that, it whines at me, then lies down and rolls over, exposing its belly. My eyes flash to the razor-sharp claws dangling off its feet, but it only looks at me, imploring me as if it were just a regular dog. *Maybe my eyes are playing tricks on me. Maybe it really is just a dog.*

I inch closer, still brandishing my sword. The hellhound watches me, complete calm in its demon eyes. At two feet away I stop, sniffing the air. No trace of the burning smell I've come to associate with hellhounds, now that I know they're from the Ashen Plane. It definitely *looks* like a hellhound, though. The sun continues to rise, making the situation all the weirder.

An unlikely thought occurs to me, one I almost dismiss out of hand. It's too unlikely to even consider. And yet...

Under my breath, I utter a string of words every magi is taught, on the off chance they might need them someday. An acknowledgment and an oath. At the conclusion of my recitation, the hellhound leaps up and pounces on me, knocking me to the ground. Its muzzle descends, and its barbed tongue sends a scathing lick up my cheek.

My heart stops. I have a familiar.

FIFTEEN

"**D**ID SHE SAY ANYTHING?"

"No. I barely got her to the couch before she dropped."

Liza's face is serene in sleep, her breaths deep and even. Her hands are dirty, though, and her hair holds the stink of smoke. So does the duster coat she's currently wrapped up in, the one Heather got her for Christmas last year. It's so long it reaches her knees, and billows ominously when she doesn't have it buttoned. *Oh, no. Please, honey, no. Not you.* Something warm and scratchy rubs against the palm of my hand. I almost jerk it back, then remember who's nuzzling me. My new familiar, taking the form of a hellhound. My brain lacks the energy to process these new developments and is pretty much running on autopilot.

Dixon, to his credit, seems to be taking it in stride. He yawns widely, eyes puffy and bloodshot. We've had way too many all-nighters lately.

"Go to bed," I order him, bending over stiffly and gathering Liza into my arms. Whatever else she may be, she's still my sister, and I'll keep treating her that way until I have a very good reason not to. *The coat is circumstantial. It doesn't prove anything.*

"What about school?"

"We're not going." I don't mean to be terse, but it was a long, exhausting night. Dixon trails behind as I tromp up the stairs, arms trembling under Liza's weight. I deposit her into her own bed, tucking her onto one side so I can slide in beside her. I snuggle us both under the covers, holding her tightly, chin resting against her hair. One by one the rest of the household joins us. Pong curls up into a tight ball behind Liza's knees. Dixon comes in with a pillow and blanket and stretches out on the floor next to the bed. A dull thud tells me my hellhound has taken up residence by the doorway. *What am I going to do about this?* The thought barely forms before I pass out.

I don't sleep long. A few hours, best I can tell, but the nightmares won't let me sleep longer. I'm a little fuzzy on what time I actually made it home this morning. Carefully, I extricate myself from Liza's arms, who's turned in her sleep and is now latched on to me. Navigating Pong and Dixon without unsettling them is like an extreme sport, but I eventually gain the hallway unnoticed. The soft padding of paws tells me I'm not alone.

Eventually, I'll look at my familiar and not want to cringe, I'm sure of it. I study it now, looking up at me in the dim light of the hallway. Its red eyes are less glowing, more muted now. Like the banked coals of a campfire. Black fur covers its too-thin frame, long and shaggy. The part of my brain that sees a hellhound is telling me to kill it. And yet, a connection exists between us. I can feel it, deep in my bones, that it's a part of me now. I don't understand it, but there's no going back, even if I wanted to. I spoke the words. I bonded it to myself. We are one.

The living room is empty when I make it that far. Alex was passed out in the armchair when I came home this morning, and I decided to leave him that way. I find him at the kitchen table, a cup of coffee and an untouched muffin in front of him.

"Good morning," I say, alerting him to my presence.

"Good mor—" he starts, then scrambles to his feet. "What in the hell is that?"

"It isn't going to hurt you. Sit down." I get my own coffee as Alex lowers himself back into his chair. "No school for you, either?"

"Can you blame me?" He answers me calmly, but he keeps one eye trained on the hellhound. The beast pays him no mind and plops down onto the floor at my feet.

"No. You must have a lot of questions." Mug in hand, I join Alex at the table, sitting across from him instead of beside him. After last night, I don't know where we stand.

"Some, yeah. I don't even know where to start."

"I do."

"Shoot."

"You're a hedge witch."

"Yeah."

Silence reigns while we both sip at our coffee. Alex breaks it first. "I wanted to tell you. I did. I just, you know, didn't know how to bring it up."

"You knew I was a magi?" It didn't take me long to work it out, in the sporadic minutes I had between monsters. Why else would he have shown up with a bag of potions? And the more personal questions. How long has he known? Before he asked me out? Does his family know?

"Not at first. I've always been drawn to you; there was something different about you that I could never quite put my finger on. But I've known for a little while now."

"The lizard thing, right?"

"Yeah. I'd never seen that kind of magic in action before. I wasn't even quite sure that's what it was until I was thinking about it later. Hedge witches, we're not front-line practitioners. Most of what I know comes from old histories and family legends. I had to wait until I got home that night to even put a name to what I thought you were. It took me a while to process it all. That was a heck of a first date."

"It really was." I let a small smile grace my lips. Part of me wants to be angry that he kept something like this from me, but wasn't I doing the same thing? "Why did it take you so long to tell me?"

"At first, I figured you'd tell me when you were ready. Then I realized that was stupid. Knowledge like that has to be protected, and you had no reason to think I already knew. After that, it was a matter of finding the right time. You're a fighter. I saw that. I wanted to be able to help, to hold my own. To be worthy of you."

"*You* wanted to be worthy of *me?*" It's so completely absurd I burst out laughing.

"You're pretty intimidating. And not just because you know a hundred different ways to break every bone in my body."

I didn't even know how tense the kitchen had gotten until the mood lifted. I give Alex a wide smile, and he smiles back, and suddenly everything's okay between us again.

"So, what happened last night?"

I help myself to a muffin as I launch into an accounting of the monsters I took down last night. Alex is the perfect audience, cheering my successes and mourning the ones I was too late to save. When I get to my arrival home, my narrative flounders.

"The dog is a familiar? What's that?"

"How much do you know about magic?" I counter, trying to figure out where to begin.

"Very little. What we do hardly counts as magic. Hedge witches are benign, dealing in potions, with some dabbling in herbs and basic charms. My family comes from a very diluted bloodline, so we're not very strong. My parents are actually afraid of it; they don't practice at all. They let my grandfather teach me, but don't allow it to be discussed in the house."

"That blast last night was pretty strong."

"One of our few defensive potions. That's the biggest weapon I have."

"Effective though. So, familiars. Familiars are spirit creatures that have no form of their own, so they assume forms humans can recognize. They're drawn to strong magic, and occasionally present themselves to magi who show exceptional strength. They're connected to totality as a whole, rather than a single plane, and once bonded, can act as a conduit to make a magi even more powerful."

"Wow, that raises a whole bunch more questions. You're pretty strong, then?"

"No, I'm not. That's what's so confusing. I do okay, but my magic is nothing special. I have no idea why it came to me."

Both of us look at the hellhound, snoozing peacefully on the tile, just like a regular dog.

"So, what do you do now? Does it just follow you around, or…"

"That's a good question. I need to name it. Jeez, I don't even know if it's male or female. I need help. I need Heather." My voice fades, drifting off as I mention her name.

Alex, reading the change in my mood, comes around the table and takes my hand in his. "Where is Heather?"

"Gone."

"What do you mean?"

I sniffle, then swallow hard, pulling the emotions back in. Alex is very close, and I'm suddenly very aware of how long it's been since I brushed my teeth. Or washed…anything, really. "I'll tell you later. I'm disgusting, so I'm going to go upstairs and grab a quick shower."

"I'll come with you."

I give him a pointed look, and he chuckles. "Not what I meant. I just want to keep talking, and you look like maybe you shouldn't be alone right now."

He hits the nail on the head. I'm so tired of being alone. I let him follow me upstairs, the hellhound trailing us, and once I'm safely behind the shower curtain he takes up a position on the seat of the toilet. Now that he can't see me, it's easier to recount what happened to Andrew and Heather. And telling him feels so good. Just getting the words out, saying them to another person, is a release I didn't know I needed. He doesn't say anything when I finally run out of words, and I let my mind go blank, focusing on the sting of the hot water against the back of my neck.

I can't check out for long. It's kind of a curse. As the water begins to cool I let my eyes rove over my body. I didn't take any serious hits last night, so I didn't even consider first-aid before falling asleep. My hands now boast several scratches and broken nails, in addition to the new blisters from handling my sword. Bruises crisscross my legs, with a dark purple blotch blossoming right in the middle of my breastbone. A brief memory of being tackled by that barghest flashes in my mind, and my fingers find the puncture wounds its claws left in my right shoulder. From there, they move up to my face, where if memory serves I have a wicked cut across my left cheekbone, not to mention the bruising on my jaw from the Immortal. *How in the world did Alex sit there at the table with me and talk to me as if I wasn't the most disgusting person on the planet?*

Maybe it's a hedge witch thing. As a race, they tend to be more mellow and nonconfrontational, though the magi don't interact with them much. Their weaker magic doesn't have much to offer us, and we're a fairly exclusive group.

"You okay in there?"

"Just finishing up. Can you give me a minute?"

"Sure."

I wait until his footsteps leave the bathroom before reaching for my towel. I rub my hair vigorously with it, and wrap it around myself before stepping out onto the mat. It's a good thing, too, because even though he left the bathroom, Alex neglected to close the door behind him. His eyes widen as he sees me and realizes his mistake, and I choose to believe his surprise is genuine. He heads back toward the bathroom, but instead of closing the door, he steps back inside. A look of pain crosses his face as he sees my visible injuries, his eyes traveling up my body and locking with my own.

One hand cups my cheek, thumb hovering over the cut. I try to turn my head so he can't see it, but there's nowhere to hide all of my imperfections. He reads my mind, and turns my face back to his. "You're beautiful," he whispers, head lowering toward mine. Just before our lips meet he pauses, giving me the chance to refuse if I want to. I don't want to. I close the remaining distance, pressing my lips to his.

As far as kisses go, it's sweet and chaste. Not what I expected from our first kiss, but somehow better. And perfectly right, in this moment. Dropping his hand, Alex exits the bathroom, closing the door so I can change in privacy.

There's an intruder in the living room when we come back downstairs.

"Ahh, Ms. Young. There you are. Please, have a seat."

"You're the guest, Mr. Henderson. Shouldn't I be the one to offer you a seat?" My politeness is forced. This is the guy who dissed Dixon and argued with Andrew.

"Mr. Leavengood has already been most accommodating." Dixon reenters the room at that moment, bearing a steaming cup of coffee. For our guest, I presume. The liver spots on his hands shine brightly in the lamplight as he takes the cup and sips out of it delicately. Dixon makes a face at me over the old man's head that tells me he's as happy to have him here as I am.

I stay where I am, in the middle of the living room floor. Alex hovers behind me, not certain what to do in this situation. I can't help feeling bad for him. He's used to being the one in charge, but here he's completely out of his depth. "What can I do for you?"

"I'm here to assume charge of this house, of course."

I have to look at Dixon to make sure my jaw hasn't dropped to the floor like I think it has. "Maybe I do need to sit down."

Alex begins to follow me over to the couch, but is stopped by Mr. Henderson. "And who are you, young man?"

Alex changes course and stops in front of the recliner, extending his hand. "Alex Keller, sir."

"Do you live here, Mr. Keller?"

"No, sir, but—"

"Then you have no place in this conversation, and I think it best that you get home now."

That's it. "No. Alex, please stay, if you want to. You can wait up in my room until I'm done talking to Mr. Henderson. Mr. Henderson," I continue, drawing his attention, "I don't know you, or why you've chosen to come now after we've been alone for a week and a half, or what right you think you have to 'assume charge' of us at all, but you will not speak to a guest in my home like that and you won't order us about as if we were ignorant children."

A low growl fills the room as I finish, and for a moment I think it's coming from me. I certainly feel like growling. But no, it's coming from the doorway, where the hellhound has locked onto Mr. Henderson and looks none too happy.

"Oh my." I feel a tiny bit satisfied to see Mr. Henderson afraid, but only a tiny bit. After all, as a senior member of the council, he's still one of the good guys, no matter how rude and arrogant he is.

"Easy," I murmur, while at the same time examining my own emotions. As I let my anger at Mr. Henderson slip away, the growling ceases, and the hellhound pads sedately over to sit at my feet, allowing me to scratch it behind the ears. Alex retreats, choosing not to make a scene.

"I wasn't aware you had a familiar, Ms. Young." Mr. Henderson is looking at me with a new curiosity and, dare I say it, respect.

"It's new."

"I see. I'd like to talk with you more in depth about it later. I'm sure you have many questions."

I hate to admit it, but I do. *At his age, he's probably forgotten more about magic than I'll ever learn. I could learn a lot from him.* My inner voice is right. I should probably try to smooth things over and not let my pride get the better of me. "I'd like that."

"Good. Now, for the present. In the McGinnis's absence, I have accepted the role of moderator of the magi council. Many of us feel that the magi as a body would benefit from more structured leadership than it currently receives. To that end, it is my intention to mitigate the deficiency in your training and supervision. Until Andrew and Heather return, of course."

"Of course." What he means is, we need a babysitter.

"I'm sure you're still very tired, so tomorrow will be soon enough for you to walk me through everything that has been going on in your guardians' absence and get me up to speed. In the meantime, rest, and I will make myself at home."

Mr. Henderson settles into his chair, a clear dismissal. Catching Dixon's eye, I look pointedly at the door. "I think Mr. Henderson is going to be a problem," I mutter as we gain the privacy of the stairs.

"Yeah. You noticed all that about 'structured leadership' and 'mitigating deficiencies'?"

"Sure did. Andrew told me he wasn't happy about how the council is run. Seems he's taking advantage of their absence to institute some changes."

"Makes me wonder how hard he's actually looking for them." Dixon's comments cut right to the heart of the matter. Despite his words, Walter Henderson is looking out for his own interests. Not ours, and certainly not Heather and Andrew's.

Sixteen

"So, how many planes are there?" Alex asks the question as I land a side kick to the bag, grunting as my foot makes contact. I've been severely neglecting my training, eking out half a workout here and there but not actually training, and I'm going to need to be on my game to handle whatever Hecate throws at us next.

"Nobody knows for certain. There are a few we're sure about, like the Shadow Plane, and the Ashen Plane, but there are several in between that haven't been properly documented. The magi who have tried tend to not make it back."

"Ashen Plane?"

"The bottom of the pile, in simplest terms. Think darkness, fire, and ash. The evilest evil lurks there. There have been only a handful of reports in the last couple of centuries of anything from the Ashen Plane gaining the strength to make it all the way up to the Mortal Plane." I land another kick, Alex's eyes following my movements and not dwelling my skin-tight shorts and sports bra.

"But that's where the hellhounds come from?"

"Yes. They can't do it on their own, which is why they need the summoner. Someone on this side to leverage their own power to pull them through."

"Who's the summoner?"

"That's the question I've been trying to answer for the last few weeks. It was supposed to be a fairly simple case, but it keeps getting more and more complicated." I don't mention my new suspicions about Liza. I need to do more digging first. Alex's foot twitches as I kick again, and I can't help but giggle. "Come over here."

"Why?"

"I'm going to show you how to do it." His eyes light up as he smiles, and a wave of appreciation rushes through me. Appreciation that he's not so macho he can't take martial arts advice from a girl.

Alex is in amazing shape. As the star running back for an undefeated team, he kind of has to be. My nerves take over as he stands in front of me and I realize I have to put my hands on him. It was one thing when we were dancing last night, and both of us were completely in the moment. This is intentional.

"Nervous?" he asks when I hesitate.

"A bit. I've never taught anyone before."

"Is that the only reason?" Is it my imagination, or is his voice a tiny bit huskier than it was a moment ago?

"What about you?" I shoot back. "Aren't you nervous at all?"

"What do I have to be nervous about? I'm just standing here, waiting for you to decide to teach me something."

"Maybe because your girlfriend is standing in front of you half-naked?" It's the first time either of us has used the g-word, and I don't even know I'm going to say it until it leaves my mouth. But once it's out there, it's out there, and I hold his gaze, waiting to see how he's going to react to it.

"If I can resist you in a towel, I think I can resist you in sweaty gym clothes." The barb helps to break the tension and get me focused.

"All right hot-shot, let's see how limber you are." I snap into professional mode, running my hands from his shoulders to his hips and correcting his posture. "You want to keep your weight on this leg…"

An hour later we're both covered in a fine sheen of sweat, and I feel better than I have in a long while. Working out with a partner is always preferable to doing it solo, and teaching Alex was a bit of a workout for me, too.

Alex huffs in my ear as I help him unwrap his wrists from our bag work. "I thought I was already in shape. That was tough."

"You did a good job." My voice is a little breathless, and only partly from the physical exertion. Alex lost his shirt about half an hour ago, and being so close to him has turned my insides into jelly.

"You've been doing this how long?"

"The martial arts? Several years. I also box, wrestle, and train with sharp, pointy things."

"Like the sword."

"Like the sword."

"Why doesn't anyone know? You keep to yourself so much at school."

He's sweet. Naive, but sweet. "Drawing attention to myself is usually a bad idea. And my skills would raise questions.

Specifically, why do I do it? I don't compete. Why do I train so hard? What's the purpose? I already tell enough lies."

He nods, but I can see he doesn't fully understand. He doesn't really have to hide who he is.

"Shower?"

"Yes, shower."

The manor has a gym. Not a large one, and we rarely use it, but it does have one. It sits on the first floor, with the perfectly normal library in the mostly uninhabited end of the manor. As much as I trust Alex, there's no way I'm taking him down to the training room, where we keep all of our secrets. I'm a magi first.

Before leaving the gym, I scroll through the news alerts that popped up on my phone while we were training. I've been scanning them obsessively all morning, looking for signs of the Immortal. I remember every single ping I got last night on the worship magic. So far, there have been three murders that likely belong to him. Nothing new this time, though.

"It's not your fault."

"I know. If I'd been there, they'd still be dead. Hecate would have killed them for my interference. Doesn't make me feel less guilty about it." Somewhat more subdued, I lead Alex through the dusty halls and back toward the living room.

Mr. Henderson's voice floats down the hall as we come back to the lived-in part of the house. "My apologies, Mr. Sanders. The house has been in a bit of an upheaval since the departure of Mr. And Mrs. McGinnis. I would be delighted to meet with you to discuss Adrienne's progress. Yes, tomorrow at noon works for me. Thank you for your call."

He's hanging up as I storm into the kitchen. "What are you doing?"

"Handling things, Ms. Young, as is my job. It seems we need to have a discussion about your schoolwork, beginning with your failing grade in chemistry."

"Yeah, I've been just a little bit busy—"

"There is no excuse for you not completing your schoolwork. That is your prime directive."

"Actually, my—" I pause and glance over at Alex. He looks distinctly uncomfortable, and he shouldn't be listening to this conversation anyway. "You can use the shower in my room, if you want to. I'll be up in a few minutes." He recognizes the dismissal for what it is and doesn't argue.

"My prime directive," I continue once Alex is gone, "is to protect people. In case you haven't noticed, there's been a lot of activity on that front. Saving lives comes before homework."

"You're still a minor. Schoolwork comes first until you graduate."

"Fine. Take it up with Heather. Oh wait, you can't. She's *gone*."

With my parting shot I spin on my heel and march out of the kitchen, just in time to hear a strangled yell from upstairs. I race for the stairs, nearly colliding with Dixon as he stumbles into the hall on his way to my room. From the way he's wobbling he was sleeping soundly. Good.

A loud thump draws me through my door to find Alex on the floor, one arm twisted too high, Mason pinning him down with a knee in his back. Alex is struggling, uselessly, but he goes still when he hears my voice.

"What are you doing?" It's the same thing I said to Mr. Henderson, but it's my typical question when I find people doing things they shouldn't be in my house.

"Apprehending an intruder." Mason's voice tells me he knows exactly what he's doing. This isn't about Alex. It's about me, and our history, and how we grate against each other in every personal situation we're in together. Both of our blood runs hot, and we communicate best when we're pounding the stuffing out of each other.

I don't waste any more breath on words. In two bounds I'm across the room, right foot flying toward Mason's chin. He reacts just as I expected him to. Releasing Alex's arm, he catches my foot in midair and pushes, using my own momentum to send me spinning off into the corner of the room.

But my goal was accomplished. Alex scurries up and rounds to face Mason, fists up in the stance I just taught him half an hour ago. He must know he doesn't have a chance, but that doesn't keep him from standing his ground anyway. The thought makes me smile. I've been shunting Alex aside a lot the last couple of days, but maybe protecting him isn't the right move. I could use a partner.

Mason laughs at what he sees as Alex's pathetic attempt to defend himself, then throws his left fist out in a jab headed straight for Alex's nose. I'm too far away to stop it, but my magic's not. I thrust an arm in Mason's direction, muttering "Collido" as I do. Partner material or not, Alex isn't ready to take on Mason.

The spell shoves Mason to the side, slamming him into my bedroom wall. Dixon takes the opportunity to rush in and grab Alex's arm. His words are soft, but they make it to my ears. "Better to let them work this out." Alex resists a moment, shooting me a look. I nod and he backs away, retreating with Dixon to the open door. They don't leave, just stay out of range.

Mason recovers quickly. "Magic, Adrienne? Fine." He hits me with his own spell, knocking me back into the same corner he threw me into earlier. "What's your problem?" he demands, advancing on me.

I launch myself off the wall at him. "My problem is you showing up here unannounced, lying in wait in my bedroom, and attacking my boyfriend."

"Boyfriend?" he sputters. "Him?"

"Yeah. Him."

"Well at least you were actually here where you were supposed to be."

We tumble to the floor, limbs locked together. His mistake. Mason is stronger than me, but I'm wigglier. Grappling is the one area I've always beaten him. "You haven't been practicing," I pant, wrapping my knees around his waist and securing my elbow under his throat. I haven't been, either, but he doesn't need to know that. For now, I have the upper hand, and needling him is my prerogative.

Mason throws himself back, landing his considerable weight on top of me. Still, I hold on, tightening my hold on his throat. He'll give in eventually. He always does.

A moment later I'm proven right. Mason thumps a hand on the floor, yielding. I release him and he stands, then offers me a hand, which I ignore. "You still fight dirty."

"I fight to win." I chance a look at Alex, trying to gauge his response to what he's just witnessed. His face is serious, and I have no idea what he's thinking. I go to him, reaching out a hand, but he pulls back.

"What was that?"

"A long story. One I'm willing to tell you, but not right now. Mason and I have something to discuss, but-"

"Another conversation I don't need to hear?" His voice is brittle, a complete 180 shift from just a few minutes ago. It hurts, but I can't blame him. The last twenty-four hours have taken a tremendous toll on him.

"I'll explain later, I promise. Just, let me handle Mason first, okay. We have a...complicated history."

"Is there something I should be worried about?"

I shake my head vehemently, trying to convey how outrageous that idea is. "No. Definitely not. If you want to grab that shower, I'll make it up to you after?" I smile, trying to put some innuendo into my words.

Alex isn't having it. "I think it's about time I went home."

I don't try to stop him. My life is a lot to take in, and even though he knew I was a magi, there was no way for him to prepare for it. I totally understand the need to decompress.

"Your boyfriend's a bit skittish." Mason's voice grates on me, reminding me he's still in my bedroom.

"He has every right to be."

"Is he the reason you were MIA last night?"

"You're not a cop here, Mason, and this isn't an interrogation. It's none of your business."

"You missing from your post is 100% my business. Every single magi had a responsibility to be out there last night, dealing with the uncontrollable magic that Halloween spawns. Most of them can't do what you do. How many people died because you were too busy to do your duty?" He means the barb to sting. It does, but I don't let him see it. Showing weakness to Mason is never a good idea.

"I didn't answer my phone. Doesn't mean I wasn't on duty. I appreciate your help, I really do, but you're not my boss. You're not even my mentor anymore. So leave, now, before I have to make you."

"Not without an answer. And since you managed to lose Andrew, I'm the closest thing to a boss you have. Where were you? You say you were on duty, prove it. What were you fighting?"

I let my voice drop, so he has to listen hard to hear me. "If I thought you would believe me, I would tell you. I could use a fighter like you on my side. But that's the problem, isn't it? You're never on my side."

He's never going to be the one to leave first. I leave instead, walking out of the room without giving him the chance to answer. He doesn't follow, and I briefly wonder how long he's going to lurk in there. I'd like to go to bed at some point. My familiar is waiting for me in the hall, and it occurs to me that it didn't rush in and tear Mason's face off. Interesting.

Instead of going back downstairs, I pause outside of Liza's room. She's still asleep, and hasn't been able to tell us what happened last night. I crack open the door, just as I have about once an hour all day. The lump in her bed is breathing soundly, blankets moving up and down with her chest. The sunflowers that once covered the walls are drooping, evidence of Liza's neglect. The herbs in her window, though, are thriving. *The same herbs the sorority girls were growing. Coincidence?* A thump alerts me to Pong's presence as he drops down off the bed, and his body shows up blacker than the darkness as he heads for the door and freedom. My breath catches as he slides through the crack. Granted, I haven't been paying much attention to him lately, but he's definitely bigger. Like, mid-sized dog bigger.

Footsteps down the hall pull my attention away from the cat, and I take a moment to clear my mind, preparing to do battle with Mason yet again. But it isn't Mason who speaks.

"Ms. Young. Would you accompany me downstairs to the study? I think it's time we had our discussion."

I consider blowing Mr. Henderson off, but then reconsider. "Fine. I'll tell you everything I know. The rest of the council should know, anyway. There's something big coming." Mr. Henderson looks completely non-plussed by my pronouncement of doom. "But I want some information in return."

"About?"

"Liza."

Seventeen

"Liza was a very unusual case. We didn't find her until she was almost eleven, much older than children typically come into their power."

"I remember." The sun is long down, and my storytelling is over. Mr. Henderson listened attentively, nodding and taking notes as I described my interactions with the Immortal and my discovery of Hecate. Now it's his turn.

"What's also unusual is Liza's mother. As you know, in the case of the magi, magic is not an inherited trait. Best we can tell, it appears at random and cannot be predicted. But Liza's mother was an accomplished magi in her own right, so Liza being born with that same power was nearly unheard of. It has happened occasionally, of course, and those children always seem to be stronger in their magic than children born to normal parents."

"So, Liza's gifts are simply because her mother was a magi?" Mr. Henderson looks annoyed at the interruption, but I don't care. I need to understand.

"I wouldn't say so. The benefits are noticeable, yes, but not absurdly so. Liza is special."

"Why, then? Why is she so strong?"

"Because of her birth."

"But you said—"

"Perhaps if you stop interrupting me, you'll hear the entire story."

The rebuke rattles me, but I keep quiet. I know the facts about Liza's discovery, but I suspect the answers I want are in the details I wasn't privy to at the time.

"Now then. Not only was Liza born to a magi, she was also born under a convergence. Do you know what a convergence is?"

I'm allowed to talk now? "No."

"A convergence is an overlapping of celestial events. It can also apply to a mixture of celestial and ceremonial events, but those don't have quite the same kick as the purely celestial. For instance, Liza was born on the summer solstice under a partial solar eclipse. It boosted her power astronomically, and has spurred much interest in the council. She also began exhibiting powers at a very young age. Four years old, by her own account."

I can't help it; I have to interrupt again. "But if she was doing magic at four, how was her mother able to hide her from the council?"

"We'll never know exactly, but she likely used perception spells of her own devising. It was only when she was tragically killed in a car accident that we learned of Liza's existence. By then she was already strong, and a practiced magi in her own right. Her raw talent is off the charts, but she lacks the maturity and experience to channel it properly. That is why Heather kept her restricted, even though she has passed every exam set before her and exceeded the limits of every senior magi who has tested her."

"You knew her, didn't you? Liza's mother?"

"Briefly. Her strength was in perception, as is my own. I tutored her for some months when she was a student. But as these things go, we fell out of contact as she grew older. She pulled away from the council, and by the time Liza was born, had spoken to no one in years."

Mr. Henderson falls silent, and I ponder his words as I fight back a yawn. Despite my interest in the subject, my body is losing its fight against my exhaustion.

"Thank you, Mr. Henderson." His eyes widen slightly, apparently surprised at my politeness. "You've given me a lot to think about."

"Why this interest in Liza's past?"

I hesitate. I did promise to tell him everything I know, but I don't actually know anything here. I have suspicions and circumstantial evidence, but no proof. In my gut, I know that Liza is my summoner. The big question is, why? And does she even know she's doing it? What connection does Liza have to Hecate?

For Mr. Henderson, I opt for a partial truth. "I'm worried about her. She's been having nightmares. She told me she had them a lot when she was younger. I want to help her."

Mr. Henderson seems appropriately concerned, like a grandfather, but not unduly so. Good. I don't want Liza on the council's radar until I know exactly what is happening to her.

My room is empty when I get back upstairs, my bed soft and inviting. If Mason is still lurking in the manor, he's behaving himself and staying out of sight. Honestly, the house is so big, he could take up residence in one of the empty bedrooms and as long as he was careful about his trips to the kitchen, we'd never know he was there. The thought sends a quick shudder down my back.

A quick glance at my phone tells me Alex didn't call. I didn't expect him to, not after the way he left, but I still hoped he would. I'll give him the space he needs. I just hope he figures it out fast.

I didn't get my post-workout shower earlier, but I'm too tired to bother with it now. I do a quick wash of my face and brush my teeth, my green eyes staring back at me from behind a puffy raccoon mask, then crawl into bed, gym clothes and all.

The sun is up when Dixon shakes me awake. "Liza's up."

His words hit me like a cold shower. I scurry out of bed, tripping over my legs where they're tangled in the covers, and follow him into the hall. Liza's still in her room, sitting cross-legged on her bed, staring blankly into space.

"Hey, there." I flip on her desk lamp, sending a soft glow of light into the dark room.

She turns to me slowly, as if confused about where she is. When she finally registers me, a small smile crosses her face. "Hey, Adrienne. Good morning." Her eyes take in my gym clothes. "Is that what you're wearing to school?"

Dixon and I exchange a look, and without prompting he steps back and closes Liza's door. He approaches the bed first, sitting close enough to touch her lightly on the shoulder. "Do you know how long you've been asleep?"

She glances between the both of us, knowing something's up. "Too long, apparently. Did we miss school? What happened last night?"

My turn. "Liza, you've been sleeping for a day and a half. You went missing on Halloween. Do you remember?"

"What are you talking about? I was here with Dixon, watching that crappy movie. Then...then..." Tears spring up in her eyes as she struggles to recall what happened next. "Adrienne?"

"Oh, honey." I join her and Dixon on the bed, wrapping her in my arms as she begins to cry in earnest. It takes several minutes to soothe her, murmuring and smoothing her hair. When she quiets, Dixon tells her about her disappearance, being as gentle as possible.

"What happened to me? Where did I go?"

Why do I have to be the bearer of bad news? "We don't know. But we're going to find out."

"We are?" Dixon and I haven't talked about it yet. We haven't talked much since Halloween, period. I know I can count on his help, though. I give him a firm nod, and he nods back. "We are."

"Well, we can't put it off forever. You need to get dressed, Liza. It's time for you to meet Mr. Henderson."

Twenty minutes and a round of showers for each of us, and Dixon and I lead Liza into Heather's study. Mr. Henderson is exactly where I left him last night, making himself comfortable behind Heather's desk, her papers spread before him, stroking Cerise's head. The canary has her head twisted around, blinking up at him as he croons to her. "You're so pretty, Cerise. Pretty birdie. You were always pretty, but I like this yellow much better than the red. When you get strong again, you should keep the yellow."

"Mmhm." I clear my throat to get his attention.

"Ah yes, Ms. DuPage. I hoped you would be making an appearance this morning. Please, have a seat."

Liza sits tremulously on the overstuffed couch, Dixon and me flanking her. Mr. Henderson looks at us pointedly. "I'd like to speak with Ms. DuPage alone, please." Then when we don't move, "That wasn't a request."

A moment more, just to make a point, then we leave. "I don't trust him with her," Dixon whispers to me as we walk away from the closed study door.

"What do you think he's going to do, eat her? She's perfectly safe." Despite the quip, I don't blame him. I don't fully trust Mr. Henderson overall, but especially not with Liza. His presence here feels strange, and his motives are questionable. He's already owned up to taking advantage of Heather and Andrew's absence to make changes to the council. I don't know what his plans are for us, but he gives me the heebie-jeebies nevertheless.

I'm cracking eggs into a bowl five minutes later when I hear Liza scream, followed closely by a loud crash. I drop the egg I'm holding, shell and all, dimly registering the crack of it hitting the floor as I race out of the kitchen. Barging into the study, I find Liza curled up and shaking on the floor. Mr. Henderson is across the room, disentangling himself from the ruins of Cerise's perch. The drywall behind him is cracked. I ignore him, bending down to scoop Liza up.

"What happened?" I ask her gently, getting her settled back on the couch. She doesn't look hurt, but that doesn't mean she's okay. I round on Mr. Henderson, seething. "What did you do?"

"A spell," he answers, rubbing the back of his head. "Something went wrong." He takes a step in our direction.

I take a step to match him. "Details, or you're going back into that wall. I have no qualms about hitting an old man."

He stares at me, as if gaging my sincerity. Then he deflates. "It's a tricky perception spell. Liza doesn't remember what happened on Halloween, and I was trying to draw the memories out of her subconscious. It should have been painless."

"Should have been?"

"I hit a block in her mind. When I tried to breach it, she screamed as if in great agony. Then a wave of magic surged out of her, pure magic, without form or direction. It threw me like a rag doll." The admission is difficult for him, like he doesn't want to be perceived as weak.

Before I can answer, the glass shatters in the study's lone window and a black form comes soaring into the room. Pong lands gracefully on the thick carpet, panting like a dog. He must have raced from wherever he was off hunting to be at Liza's side. He struts over to the couch, settling himself on her lap, purring and glaring at us. The cat's comfort is exactly what she needs, and slowly her shakes fade away as she strokes his glossy fur.

I turn back to Mr. Henderson, reading the look in his eyes. "You're not going to try that spell again."

"I think you've forgotten who's in charge around here, young lady. I need to know what—"

"No. Liza's mind is officially off limits to you. There are other ways." I glare at Mr. Henderson, daring him to challenge me.

"Very well. I have a meeting to prepare for, anyway. If you'll excuse me."

Meeting? Oh, crap. Mr. Sanders. My neglect of my schoolwork is finally catching up with me. *It's not even worth trying anymore.*

Liza's eyes are open, watching the exchange. I wait until Mr. Henderson leaves before I let my guard down enough to talk to her. "Hey. Feeling better?"

She nods. "I agreed to the spell, Adrienne. It's okay with me if he tries again. This is important."

I'm shaking my head before she can finish. "You didn't hear the sound that came out of your mouth. I will kill him where he stands before I let him make you make that sound again."

She looks doubtful.

"I mean it. We can find out what happened without digging around in your mind. We just have to get creative. Now, let's go get you something to eat."

She allows me to help her up, dislodging an annoyed Pong. I wait until she's steady on her feet before I release her, carefully watching to make sure she's actually okay. I may have said the right things, but I'm having trouble making myself believe them. *How am I going to figure this out?*

Liza helps me finish making breakfast, a meal we all desperately need. The last several days have been spent scarfing in the kitchen whatever was available. It's been a while since the three of us sat down and had a real meal together. I go looking for Dixon while Liza sets the table. I wondered why he didn't respond to Liza's scream, but it makes sense when I find him in the training room. He's sitting cross-legged in the middle of the floor, eyes closed, mouth moving in obvious spell practice. A piece of paper is clutched in his hand, a picture from the look of it, but I can't see the faces between his fingers. I wait, but nothing noticeable happens. Which doesn't mean anything. A lot of perception spells don't have a visible effect.

"Dixon?"

"Hmm?"

"Breakfast."

"Up in a minute."

I wait a few moments longer, but he doesn't stir. Last I knew, he was still running algorithms on his computer. If he has a picture, he must be making progress. *Why didn't he tell me?* I eventually leave him, and he follows me upstairs soon after. Breakfast is a peaceful affair, the three of us eating in silent camaraderie.

Dixon's washing the last of the plates when my phone starts going crazy on the table. I jump for it, convinced it's Alex, then frown at the screen. "Monster alert?"

"I never shut down the laptop." Dixon runs out of the room, hands still dripping, and returns with the laptop. Sure enough, his Halloween program is still running, feeding me data on a potential monster in Miami.

Dixon starts pressing keys, but I stop him. "Leave it up. Without Andrew, this is the best way we have of finding out about attacks. I'll go get ready." My assignments always came from Andrew. I know a few of the spells he would use to track down monsters, but I'm not nearly as proficient as he was. *Is!* I still don't know they got their information for their own cases. That's level three stuff.

I may have neglected myself after Halloween, but I most certainly did not neglect my weapons. My silver knives await me in the training room, freshly sharpened and gleaming. The alert didn't tell me what I'm dealing with, but the options are limited in the daylight. The knives should be able to handle anything I'll come across.

Minutes later I'm in Miami, standing on a bustling street in the middle of downtown. People are running and screaming, and a news van has taken up residence in the mouth of an alley. Its breaking news story is what prompted the alert.

Taking a deep breath to calm my nerves and steel myself against the panic of everyone around me, I plunge into the crowd. The going is difficult, as I'm headed toward the commotion while everyone else is headed away, but in a minute I'm through, and my target appears directly in front of me.

Animal control officers have the creature surrounded, and it lets out a throaty snarl as one of them gets too close. Droplets of blood sprinkle the sidewalk where it got hold of someone. Rolling my eyes, I watch for a moment, then whisper a quick "somnus" under my breath. The sleeping spell doesn't work on monsters, but on a normal black bear it's more than effective. The bear stumbles, drops to its knees, then tumbles snout-first onto the concrete. *Dixon's program may need some tweaking.*

"The mighty warrior strikes again." His voice is completely out of character with my surroundings, and I spin around, searching for him. Strange how the Immortal doesn't stand out at all, here in the regular world.

"You just passing by, or were you looking for me?"

"I visited your home, but I only arrived to find you departing. I followed you here."

"To do what?"

"You fight well. I would enjoy watching you fight someone else for a change."

"Terrific. Would you like to accompany me home?"

"That would be acceptable."

"Great."

The Immortal follows me into the Shadow Plane, a place he is quite obviously comfortable. I don't take him directly home, though. There's a nagging problem I need to deal with first. The Immortal agrees to wait outside while I go into the school alone, and I feel reasonably sure he won't slaughter my classmates in broad daylight. At least, not without being provoked. A couple of signatures later and I'm back in time to meet Mr. Henderson as he comes out the front doors. He's carrying a large file folder, probably filled with all of my missed assignments.

"Ms. Young. I'm glad to see you here. I wish you had been on time for the meeting, but I think I have been able to convince your Mr. Sanders to allow you to stay in his class." His self-satisfied smirk makes me want to punch him in the face.

"I'm sorry to have wasted your time, but I won't be needing Mr. Sanders's class anymore."

"Chemistry is a graduation requirement, so yes, you will be finishing the course."

"No, I won't. I've just come from the guidance office. I'm dropping out."

EIGHTEEN

I DON'T KNOW WHAT looks more out of place: Mr. Henderson texting on his cell phone or the Immortal watching a football game on my couch. From the peek I got at Mr. Henderson's phone, he's messaging with Tamara, the magi who mocked me during the council meeting. When I told him about the Immortal and Hecate last night, he took in my account with studied indifference, promising to look into the matter. Now he's agreeing with Tamara that I don't have any hard evidence to support my claims.

The Immortal is waiting for me, I guess. Although he seems to be enjoying the game.

"Patriots fan?" I ask as he cheers their touchdown.

"Not so much. I favor the 49ers, but they are not playing today." His answer takes me by surprise. In my head, the Immortal is the mythical guy lurking in the shadows. I never thought about him having an actual life. *What does he do when he's not killing people or fighting magi?*

As if reading my thoughts, the Immortal grabs the remote and flips the TV off. Who knows, maybe he did read my thoughts. He's two thousand years old, give or take. Who knows what he can do.

He catches me staring and gives me a puzzled look. "You did not bring me here to watch football."

His observation pulls me out of my daydream. "You're right. I asked you here to tell me about Hecate."

He sighs. "That is a long story."

I plop myself down on the other end of the couch, grabbing a pillow and settling in. "I have time."

Before he can get started, footsteps pad across the room and my hellhound joins me on the couch, snuggling in against my side. The Immortal, to his credit, doesn't react. "I was not aware you had a familiar."

"It's new."

"What do you call her?"

"Her?" I sit forward eagerly. "How do you know it's female?"

"All hellhounds are female. They are in service to Hecate, and she does not suffer males of any kind in her service. As a virgin goddess, her acolytes, as well as her hounds, are unmated." He cocks his head at me, giving me that reading-my-thoughts vibe again. "You are uncomfortable with your familiar?"

I haven't told anyone about that. He hits the nail on the head, though. I'm bonded to her, and through that bond, I am at peace. But in my head, I know I don't deserve her. "I don't understand why she's here. Familiars come to magi who possess great strength."

"You feel you do not possess great strength?"

"Not in magic. I'm only a level two. I've tested for level three several times, but I just can't seem to get there."

"I do not understand these levels, but allow me to put your mind at ease. Familiars have allied themselves with magi for millennia, but it is not strength of magic that draws them. In ancient times, they were found alongside warriors, drawn to the strength of their character. You should name her. She deserves that from you."

I can't tell if he means that last line as a rebuke or not, but I decide not to question him about it. "So, Hecate."

"Hecate."

"Why don't we start from the beginning. How do you know her?"

"As I said, Hecate was a powerful sorceress. She envied the worship of the gods, and so she erected her own temple and created her own acolytes. By demonstrating her magic, she established herself as a goddess. Her magic gave her power over the people, and as long as they pleased her, she blessed them in mighty ways. But when they displeased her, she punished them severely.

"My sister was one of her favorites. Korinna loved Hecate, and devoted herself to the sorceress. Ever the dutiful brother, I kept a watch over my sister while she served in the temple, and so became enamored of Hecate myself. She was the most beautiful woman I had ever seen, and when she bestowed her favor on you, the rest of the world vanished into the background. She had other suitors, of course, but I surpassed them all. For Korinna and me, Hecate was all we needed in this life.

"But our bliss was not to last. The inevitable happened, and Korinna displeased Hecate. One of the suitors, tiring of Hecate's repeated refusals, came upon Korinna alone in the temple. He took his frustration out on my sister. I was not there. Hecate had told me of her desire for meat, and I was hunting for her table. When Hecate learned of the incident, she called Korinna before her, and assembled the rest of her acolytes to bear witness. She denounced Korinna for her impurity, for her wantonness, and for the grievous sin of stealing one of Hecate's own suitors. She killed her on the spot, beheading her on the steps of the altar.

"My eyes were opened that day. I did not act rashly, but plotted how I might kill Hecate. She was stronger than I, but I burned with the fires of vengeance, and was certain I would prevail.

"I did not prevail. Worse, when I tried, Hecate laughed at my attempt. As she held my life in her hands, my spirit as broken as my body, I begged for her to kill me. Instead, she did the cruelest thing she could think of. She cursed me with life. I have walked this earth for two and a half thousand years, broken, unaging, and alone."

The Immortal ends his tale abruptly, and I don't have the words to respond. We've gathered an audience. Dixon and Liza have joined us, drawn out of the depths of the house to listen to his story. Even Mr. Henderson is listening intently, his phone discarded on a side table.

"I'm confused." Dixon's the first to speak. "You said Hecate wouldn't allow males in her service. Yet you served her." Dixon has a good ear. Even I didn't catch that one, and I was listening hard.

"You misunderstand. I was not in service to Hecate. But I did pursue her. Many men, myself included, spent time in the temple, doting on her, hoping to win her favor. She allowed us to do so, enjoying the attention, but she did not welcome us into her counsels." He pauses, but no one else speaks. "Do you have other questions?"

"What was your name?" Liza this time. "Your sister was Korinna, but you didn't tell us yours."

"I have not used my given name in a very long time. I no longer remember it."

Liar. I lie quite often, so I can usually tell when other people are doing it. *Did anyone else notice? Why doesn't he want to tell us?*

I feel like it's my turn, but I'm not ready. It was a serious story, one that is still churning around in my head, and I need some time to digest it before I know where to go from here. One question I do have to voice, though: "Andrew and Heather. Now that we fight on the same side, will you return them to us?"

I see the answer in his eyes before he even opens his mouth. "It is not that simple. You and I have struck an alliance, yes, but we are still getting to know one another. The magi you request from me are strong, and hunted me down when no one in the last thousand years has been able to do so. I will not risk them turning on me upon their release, not when I am so close. Hecate's power is building, and will soon reach its zenith. I will not be detracted from my course."

"But if I could guarantee—"

"You cannot. It is not for you to make promises on another's behalf. Your magi are stalwart and morally pure. Duty would drive them to eliminate the threat I pose. No, it is too much to risk."

Silence falls over the living room. Though said respectfully, the Immortal's refusal to return Andrew and Heather has soured the relationship I'm attempting to build with him, and tension hangs heavily in the air. *Well, what now?*

Liza attempts to salvage the conversation. "Why do you like the 49ers?"

The question takes him off guard, but his voice is benign when he answers. "My home is in northern California." When no one else ventures to speak, the Immortal rises. "I feel there is much to think about. May I return at a later date to further discuss Hecate?"

My brain is still in a fog, and with my feelings hurt I don't trust myself to answer. Mr. Henderson does, though, speaking for the first time. I'm surprised he let me handle this, what with being bossy and full of himself. "Yes, Mr...Immortal. Can you return tomorrow morning?"

"I can."

"Very well. Thank you for your time." As he shows the Immortal out, Mr. Henderson's fingers flash over his keyboard, and my eyes narrow.

I told myself I would give Alex the time and the space he needs. I lied. Lying in the dark, I know it's not the Immortal's story keeping me awake. The clock reads almost midnight when I quietly slip out of the house.

Minutes later I'm standing outside Alex's window. His room is on the second floor, and unless I want to break in, the window is my best entry point. It's also a good time to practice my manipulation magic.

Liza likes to make plants grow, so when I practice with her, that's usually what we work on. I focus on the ground now, reciting the words just like I've memorized. It takes a moment, a really long moment, but then I feel it. A tiny vine, no bigger than my pinkie finger, pushes its way out of the dirt and begins creeping up the side of the house. I've seen Liza's plants shoot up, fully grown, in the span of seconds. Still, my little vine is making a valiant effort.

Ten minutes later, it's the best it's going to get. The vine is now as thick as my wrist and ends about a foot shy of Alex's window, but it's latched firmly to the house and should hold my weight. I begin climbing, hauling myself upward and wishing I had just launched myself at the window instead. When I reach the top I'm glad I didn't, because it's locked. That's one manipulation spell I can pull off every time. The latch clicks open, and I slip inside.

Alex is asleep, clearly not as troubled as I am. He's also shirtless, blankets thrown back so I can see his lean muscles in the moonlight. I slip off my jacket and shoes, careful not to startle him, and slowly crawl into bed beside him.

He stirs when I touch him, sliding my hand across his chest. I settle myself against his back, where I can speak into his ear without being too loud. The closeness reminds me of dancing with him on Halloween, and how well our bodies fit together. My face flushes as I breathe in the scent of his shampoo.

"Don't be afraid. It's just me."

"Adrienne?" He's coming awake fast, but thankfully he's not panicking. "What are you doing?"

"I had to see you. I want to apologize."

"This couldn't be done over the phone? Or during the day?" Irritation colors his voice. I get it. I'd be irritated if someone woke me up in the middle of the night, too.

"I couldn't sleep. I can't stop thinking about how things ended yesterday, and the longer we were apart, the more I was afraid you wouldn't come back." Dropping my guard is hard, but I try to let some vulnerability shine through. "Can I talk to you for a minute? Then if you still want me to go, I will."

He sighs heavily. "I don't want you to go, Adrienne."

That's the best opening I'm going to get. I start talking softly, the words rushing to get out of my mouth. "Alex, my job as a magi is to protect people. I don't know if I told you, but I'm a combat magi. That's why I train and fight the way I do. I kill monsters, and I hunt bad guys, and I save lives."

"This doesn't sound like an apology."

"I'm getting to it, I promise." I take a deep breath, ready to plunge into the deep soul stuff. "My first impulse is to protect you, to keep you out of harm's way. My second impulse is to protect our secrets. I know you understand that, but I haven't been doing a very good job of explaining it to you. I've been shunting you to the side, trusting that you'll be waiting there when I come back for you. That's not fair to you. Letting someone else in isn't easy for me. It's not supposed to be, because of the burden I carry. I still can't tell you everything, but I'm sorry for pushing you aside. You deserve better than that."

Alex shifts around in my arms until we're face-to-face. I can barely see his eyes, but I can feel them boring into mine. "I'm sorry, too. I understand the need for secrecy, I do. I keep secrets, too. I just want to be a part of this. I want to help you. You don't have to fight alone."

My heart flutters, and I open my mouth, but he keeps talking. "And I'll admit, I didn't like seeing you with Mason."

I knew it. "He's not a threat to you. He's not even a friend."

"Still. I don't even know why you two fought like that, but there was something very...intimate about it. Your bodies knew each other."

"I never thought about it like that. I was already pissed off at Mason, from something that happened before, and then when he attacked you...I just came unhinged. I wanted to pound his face in."

"He was waiting in your room."

"Because he knew I'd eventually be there. Mason's a jerk, and he wanted to take me off guard." My words aren't convincing enough. I can feel it in the way his muscles feel under my hand. He's still slightly tense, as if waiting for the other shoe to drop. "I told you Mason and I have a complicated history, and if you want to hear about it, I'll tell you. But I don't think now is the best time. Not when we're on the verge of making up."

"Is that what we're doing? Making up?"

"That's exactly what we're doing." I can barely see his face in the darkness, but we're so close it doesn't matter. I lean in, lightly pressing my lips to his. He doesn't respond, but he doesn't object, either. I kiss him again, parting his lips with my own. He lets out a groan, then suddenly he's kissing me back. His lips lock tightly onto mine, drawing my breath from me.

"For the record," he gasps, breaking our kiss to draw a breath, "you can't just kiss me whenever you want to avoid a discussion."

"Not avoiding. Just postponing." I chase his lips, scooting closer until our bodies are pressed tightly against each other. He lets me draw him back in, tongue sliding out to brush lightly against mine. He reaches out a hand, the first time tonight he's touched me, and lays it gently on the back of my neck. Gradually, our kisses deepen, hunger clutching at each of us. His skin is fire under my hands as they trace circles against his skin, holding him tightly against me.

Then the tenor of our little make-out session starts to subtly shift. Alex moves his lips down to my chin, kissing along my jaw until they land on the pulse throbbing erratically in my neck. My breaths come out in ragged gasps. His hand moves from my neck, sliding down my back, pausing at the base of my spine. I moan softly, urging him on. He responds with a groan, slipping his hand under the hem of my shirt and sliding it back up my spine in a torturous tease. I arch my back, thrusting myself into his chest, and his lips drop lower on my neck.

When his hand reaches the middle of my back he pauses. "You're not wearing a bra."

"It wasn't high on my priority list." I hook his leg with mine, bare skin rubbing against bare skin. *How did I not notice he wasn't wearing any pants?* I'd done little more than throw a jacket over my pajamas, and it's starting to hit me how little clothing is between us.

It's hitting Alex, too. He dips his head, resting his forehead against my shoulder. "I can't believe I'm about to say this, but...I think we need to stop."

I know he's right, but I desperately don't want him to be. I think about how easy it would be to convince him otherwise. *A kiss on the ear, run my fingers down his back, just like he did to me ...toy with the waistband of his boxers, that'll drive him wild...his hand is still in my shirt, it wouldn't take much prompting for him to pull it around to the front...*

"You're right." I force the words out before I do something I'll regret and destroy the fledgling relationship we're trying to repair.

Alex scoots away from me, flopping down heavily onto his pillow. "You can stay, if you want. I wouldn't mind waking up next to you."

"If I stay, neither one of us will be getting any sleep."

He groans at the implications, and I see a flurry of motion as he rubs his hands across his face. "I must be an idiot, kicking my girlfriend out of my bed. My incredibly hot, agitated girlfriend."

"Not an idiot. A gentleman." I give him a quick kiss on the cheek, then reluctantly untangle myself from his covers. Without another word, I slip out the window and back into the cold night air.

Nineteen

"Where is Hecate now?" This Immortal-as-a-regular-guy thing just keeps getting more bizarre. I slept late after my visit with Alex, and woke to find him scarfing pancakes at the kitchen table. Liza's the chef this morning, with no sign of the men of the house. Dixon is probably holed up in the training room, but I couldn't care less about where Mr. Henderson is or why he's skipping the meeting he specifically asked for.

The Immortal takes a moment to finish chewing his bite, then washes it down with a gulp of orange juice before he answers. "When I failed to kill Hecate, I retreated to my mother's kin. It was there I discovered the magi."

"Wait, you're not a magi?" *How did I miss this?*

"At that time, the magi were not what they are today. They were secluded, tribal, and secretive, even with one another. When I learned that I possessed magic, there was no one to teach me. Until Hecate, I did not know another magic user. But when I returned home, they found me. Word of my attempt on Hecate's life had spread, and the magi sought me out to find out what I knew. When I learned of their magic, I enlisted their help, believing that together, we would be strong enough to defeat her."

The table digs into my elbows as I lean forward, engrossed in the story. This is what I've been most wanting to learn: how to defeat Hecate. It doesn't even matter that he hasn't answered my question yet. He'll get around to it.

"My view of Hecate was small. I saw her as the murderer of my sister. But she was much greater than that. Hecate had grand aspirations. As her power grew, more cities fell under her influence. Admirers flocked to her, and all dissidents were swiftly removed. The steps of her temples were perpetually slick with the blood of those who lost her favor. In a matter of months, half of Greece lay under her dominion. Unhindered, it was the firm belief of the magi that she would not stop until the entire known world was under her control.

"My body was slow to heal, and even after, we spent months in preparation. It was our belief that we would have only one opportunity. That opportunity came during Thesmophoria, an annual festival in Athens celebrating fertility. Hecate was very busy during this festival, and would be distracted.

"Even taken by surprise, Hecate was too powerful for us to overcome. One by one, the magi fighting at my side were killed. When only four of us remained, our captain, Calix, made the decision to change our tactics. By joining our magic, we were able to work a mighty spell against Hecate. This spell broke her magic, splintering it into pieces and scattering those pieces far from her, leaving her unable to cast against us. However, her wards remained intact, so our casting was likewise futile. Even without her magic, Hecate was a formidable opponent, and slew two of my remaining companions in open combat.

"Only Calix and I remained. We knew, above all, that Hecate had to be removed from this world. We had agreed, if we could not kill her, then we would do the next best thing. Now, that time had come. It was my sacrifice to make, but Calix acted of his own accord. Seizing Hecate, he opened a rift and dragged her from this Mortal Plane."

"Dragged her to where?"

"The Ashen Plane."

Silence, deep and heavy, meets the Immortal's pronouncement.

Liza breaks it. "So, Hecate is weaker in the Ashen Plane?"

A look of relief comes into the Immortal's eyes. His story, no matter how necessary, was difficult for him to tell. It was the moment of his greatest triumph, and his greatest failing. Wounds like that don't ever heal. Talking about Hecate in the Ashen Plane, however, is more clinical. No personal involvement needed.

"Mortals cannot survive in the Ashen Plane. My friend and comrade, Calix, is dead. But Hecate has become more than mortal. For centuries, I believed she was gone forever. But slowly, her influence began to reveal itself. Through her curse, we are linked. I can feel her magic stirring within me. Her magic was broken, weak and scattered, but she has spent the last two thousand years collecting and rebuilding it. Any act committed in her name causes her power to grow. The untainted women who worship her. Those who grow the poisonous herbs she is so fond of. Sacrifices, claimed by her agents both human and beast. Now, it seems as if she is nearly ready to make her move."

"This spell that broke her. Can you teach it to me?"

"I cannot. It was of Calix's devising, and he did not share it with me."

I sit back in my chair, pondering. Hecate's in the Ashen Plane. I don't really know what I thought when the Immortal said she was banished, but this wasn't it. Something does click in my head, though. "Her wards, they were like yours? No matter what I cast against you, I can't touch you."

For the first time since we met, the Immortal looks ashamed. "My wards are a gift from Hecate. A part of her curse. I cannot remove them, no matter how I try." With this admission, the Immortal looks very...human. Not some otherworldly force out to thwart me at every turn.

The next moment, his vulnerability angers me. "You speak of the atrocity of Hecate's crimes, but your hands aren't clean, either."

"I have explained—"

"To stop their worship, yes. Cut off their link to Hecate. But why do you have to do it so brutally? Those children were...well, they were *children*. Little girls, and you slaughtered them like animals. Isn't there a better way?" I'm huffing by the time I end my rant, and the Immortal has the good grace to look ashamed.

"It is never my intention. When they are immersed in their worship, I feel Hecate's presence strongly, and I react blindly in my fury. The remorse I feel after is not enough to prevent me from doing it again, and again."

"I—" Whatever I'm about to say is interrupted by the storm of magi that come bursting into the kitchen. Some come through the door, some from the hall into the living room, and some from the second set of steps leading down into the basement. There are probably a dozen in all, with Mr. Henderson leading the charge.

Lips move, and spells go flying, and I dive out of the way. The Immortal can handle himself. Liza can't. She's already on her way to me, and I tackle her to the floor, dragging her with me to the far wall, where the door to the pantry is. I try to stuff her inside. "Stay here!"

"I can help!"

"No!"

The other end of the kitchen has erupted into chaos. The magi are trying to pin down the Immortal, but of course their spells aren't landing. He's backed into the corner, throwing his own spells, tossing magi out of his way but not hard enough to seriously hurt them. Opening his mouth, he lets out a roar like a caged animal.

An answering roar comes from the doorway, then my hellhound throws herself into the fray. Her body slams into a golden-haired magi, I think her name is Kendra, knocking her off balance and breaking her concentration. Their initial rush over, the magi have fallen back into battle positions spanning the width of the kitchen. Two lines, six staggered magi in each line.

I can't let them do this. I don't know what their master plan is, but it isn't going to end well for anyone involved. From the look on the Immortal's face, he's about done playing Mr. Nice

Guy. Following my familiar's lead, I join in, barreling into the magi closest to me. I can't hope to best their magic, but my combat skills are unmatched by any here.

By joining the fight, I succeed in dividing the magi's attention. Three of them turn to deal with me, and in less than a minute I'm pinned against the counter, steel bands securing my wrists to the soapstone. But they're all sporting minor injuries. The Immortal has won free of his corner and is fighting his way to the door. My captors' wards may defend them from my attacks, but I do excel with indirect spells. Centering my focus, I scream "Ventus!" and a tornado forms in the middle of the kitchen.

Even I'm surprised by the strength of the spell. It only rages for a couple of seconds, because one of my captors is able to fight their way to me and hit me in the head, breaking my focus, but it's enough. The Immortal vanishes through the kitchen door and out into the sunlight. The magi give chase, but it's no use. They won't catch him.

Moments later, Mr. Henderson storms back into the kitchen. The magi who pinned me, *Norman?*, releases the bands, dropping me to the floor. Mr. Henderson stops in front of me, yelling so hard spittle flies from his mouth.

"Attacking magi? What the hell were you thinking, Ms. Young?"

"Me? What were you thinking?"

"That man is a dangerous criminal!"

"'That man' is the same one you were having a civil conversation with yesterday. He is the only link we have to stopping Hecate, and you just tried to kill him!"

His expression softens slightly, adding in elements of pity and disgust. "Hecate doesn't exist. You have been taken in by a madman and a killer. I don't fault you for falling for his charisma, but I did hope you would exhibit better judgment. Your defense of him today is regrettable, but I will not allow you to be further swayed by his honeyed words."

"I haven't been swayed!"

His anger resurfaces at my objection. "What would you call it? He abducted Andrew and Heather, and murdered children, and you're eating pancakes with him!"

"I haven't forgotten!"

"Enough!" Liza stands in front of the open door to the pantry, completely forgotten by everyone, even me. Her one word is infused with so much power that the entire kitchen goes still. Or...

"Liza?"

"Yeah?"

"How did you do that?"

"I'm not sure..."

From their terrified faces, the members of the council aren't sure either. What they definitely are, though, is paralyzed. All of them that remain, that is, frozen in space, not even blinking.

"What do I do now?" The question comes from the girl, not the magi, the two sides of Liza once again at odds with each other. All that power, and not enough experience to handle it.

"You need to let them go."

"Okay." Liza closes her eyes and takes a deep breath, finding her focus. Her lips move as she figures out what she needs to say, then her eyes fly open again. The spell she utters is more of a song, the kind of rhyming song that children sing. When she finishes, the members of the council as one fall to the floor. They rise slowly, visibly shaken. They all know of Liza, of course, but they've never been on the receiving end of her power.

Even Mr. Henderson looks rattled. "Ms. Young, we shall discuss your insubordination later. You sided with our enemy over your own people, and that cannot go unpunished. For now," he shoots a sideways glance at Liza, who glares back at him, "clean up this mess. I have matters to attend to."

One by one the magi begin to vanish, but I'm not through talking yet. I snag the one who pinned me, tossing him back against the counter. "Hold on, Norman. I want a word."

"Norton."

"Whatever. What the hell was all this about? The council doesn't have a hit squad, and they certainly don't have the authority to bust in here and attack my guests."

The man before me is probably middle aged, a professional type that wouldn't merit a second glance on any city street. He held his own in the fight, but now that he's alone looks like he's about to pee his pants. "In the absence of the McGinnises, Walter has taken temporary command of the magi council. He believes your new friend to be a threat, and it would appear he was right." His last words come off as smug as any new disciple's.

"Doesn't matter what Mr. Henderson thinks. This isn't what the council does."

"It does now. Under Walter, the council is moving in a new direction. A more...dynamic direction. Magi need more than just advice. They need guidance. Supervision. Control."

I can't take it anymore. With the mess in my kitchen and the looming takeover of a vengeful goddess, I don't have the energy to deal with the hijacking of the council. Besides, when Heather gets home she'll put Walter right back in his place. Instead, I give Norton a shove toward the door. "Get out of my house. Don't ever come back."

Sagging, I collect Liza and give her a squeeze. "You okay?"

Her face appears drawn and haggard. "Yeah. I'm good."

Dixon chooses that moment to enter the kitchen. "Whoa. What did I miss?"

An hour later the kitchen is put back to rights, as much as it can be, anyway. Lots of stuff got broken in the ambush, including the kitchen table, which is now sitting out behind the house where no one will notice it until we can do something about it. Mr. Henderson vanished with the rest of the council, but I can't waste time dwelling on his ominous threats. I have work to do.

The corner where the Immortal was pinned is where he worked the bulk of his magic. It's been a while since I visited the girls' school with Andrew, and the spell we used there is a vague recollection buried under all the other information of the last couple of weeks. Liza helps me piece it back together, then she and Dixon leave me alone, giving me the quiet I need to work it.

Finding magic in the kitchen is easy. Finding the right magic, that's the trick. Once I successfully cast, the collective buzzing of magical signatures sounds like a swarm of bees frantically trying to escape from my head. I sift through them, one by one, hoping I'll know which one is the Immortal's when I find it. Some I discard immediately. With a pang, I remember the familiar comfort of Andrew and Heather's magic. Some of these magi are harboring such anger and pain that it can't help but show through, and I wonder what happened in their lives to make such an impression on their signatures. *No wonder they're so willing to fall in line behind Mr. Henderson. They're desperate for someone else to be in control for a while.*

Then I find it. Once I do, I wonder how it took me so long. The Immortal's magic is easily the strongest one in the kitchen, and the feelings it invokes in me are strange and foreign. When I hold tightly to it, I can feel the sun on my face and smell the salt of the ocean. I feel a deep yearning, and sorrow, and despair.

Focusing all of my energy on that magic, I cast the tracker spell Liza devised for me. It seemed an insignificant detail at the time, one I didn't mention to Mr. Henderson, and now I'm glad I didn't. If the council knew about it, they could find any magi, any time. Maybe that's too much power for them to have.

The spell is just as hard as I remember. As sweat breaks out on my forehead, a warm presence presses itself into my back. Risking my concentration, I open my eyes to see my hellhound curl herself around my body and lay her head on my knee. A disembodied feeling of calm courses through me, and my mind clears as if I didn't know I was sitting in a fog. I cast again, and immediately feel the spell take hold. "Wow," I whisper at the ease of the cast. "Where have you been all my life, girl."

There's nothing more I can do at the moment, not until the Immortal uses his magic. When he does, I'll find him. Hopefully before any members of the council.

My phone rings, distantly, from where I left it up in my room this morning. The only slightly cracked clock tells me it's just past noon, making me smile. *Alex.*

I don't rush, and the ringing cuts off before I make it. Picking the phone up to call him back, my eyes are drawn to the bouncing voicemail icon. It's been bouncing for three days. I don't have to listen to it to know what it says.

Three days ago I ignored a call from my mom. I can't really be blamed for that; I was kind of tied up doing Halloween things. Her voicemail will hold a little hesitation, a little concern. We've both been trying, but comfort and familiarity remain just out of reach. She'll ask how my training is going. She'll ask about school. She'll ask after Andrew and Heather, and Liza and Dixon. I don't feel like lying to her, so I've chosen silence instead.

My talk with Mr. Henderson about Liza definitely brought up some feelings I'm not ready to deal with. Liza's mom did everything she could to keep Liza safe, protected, and more importantly, with her. My own parents were all too relieved to hand me over when Heather and Andrew came knocking. I know, because I looked back at them when I was walking out to the car. It was the first time they'd smiled in weeks. I've tried telling myself it's different. Liza's mom was a magi. She knew what she was dealing with. Doesn't make it sting any less.

My phone rings again while I'm still staring at it, jolting me back to the present. *Alex.* "Hey, there."

"Adrienne? Is there maybe something you forgot to tell me?"

TWENTY

O *OPS.* M*Y* M*IND* R*ACES,* trying to figure out what he's talking about. It's been a crazy day.

My pause exasperates him. "School?"

"Oh! Not intentional, I swear. I was a bit preoccupied last night..." My face heats just thinking about last night. Part of me can't believe I was so bold, and the other part...well, the other part just wants to do it again.

Alex's tone remains serious, not taking the bait. "You really dropped out? What about your future? What about college?"

"What about Hecate?" I fire back. I'm not mad at him, not really. He's just concerned. But I really don't need him acting like a parent. "I can't do school right now, Alex. It's too much of a drain on my time and my focus. Once I deal with Hecate, and everything gets back to normal, I'll start thinking about the future again."

"Promise?"

"Promise."

Alex sighs. "I get it, Adrienne. I just...I just wish you didn't have to carry this burden alone. Isn't there a whole council of magi? Isn't there anyone who can help?"

"The council isn't what it used to be. They're under the thumb of Mr. Henderson now, and he's made it clear he doesn't believe me. And…and they tried to capture the Immortal." Briefly I describe the events of the morning, and how I intend to find him.

"Jeez." He pauses. "I worry about you. I don't want you fighting Hecate alone."

"I'm not alone. I have Liza and Dixon. And the Immortal, I think. The jury's still out there."

The ringing of the bell echoes over the line, indicating our time is up. "I gotta go."

"Okay. I'll talk to you later."

Girlfriendly duty done, I head off in search of Dixon. I find him down in the training room, once again chanting in the middle of the floor. He's holding a grainy black and white picture, like a still shot from a security camera. This time I interrupt, sitting down across from him and settling in for a potentially long chat. "You've been down here a lot lately."

"Yeah, well. It's important to me."

I sigh heavily, hands going up to support my suddenly very heavy head. "I know finding your parents is important to you, Dixon. Trust me, I understand the need to have that—"

"You don't understand." His voice is low and brittle, tinged with an emotion I've rarely seen in him. Anger. "You know who your parents are, Adrienne. You could call them up and talk to them right now. You could go through the Shadow Plane and see them in minutes. But you don't even care. They're right there, and you don't even…you have no idea what it's like to…"

Unable to find the right words, he shoves himself to his feet and paces in agitation.

"You're right. I don't know exactly how you're feeling. But I do know where my family is, Dixon. It's right here, and so is yours. You, me, Liza, we're all each other needs—"

"You don't need me." His words shock me into silence. "You see that look on your face? You haven't even noticed how you've shut us out. You have Alex now, and the Immortal, and me and Liza just don't measure up. We're not a team anymore."

My temper flares. "You're accusing me? You're the one who keeps disappearing on me. You missed the Immortal this morning, and the crazy attack from the council. You were missing yesterday when Mr. Henderson hurt Liza. Ever since Halloween, you've been more absent than you have present. There are bigger things going on right now than your identity crisis."

I regret the words as soon as I say them, but there's no calling them back. Dixon looks like I hit him. I reach for him, mouth opening in an apology, but he shrugs me off. "Don't touch me." He stalks away, but doesn't make it to the door. The artificial lights go dim as the room fills with shadows.

"Dixon!" I scream, watching him get pulled under, too far away for me to get to. The shadows come for me, too, swarming around me in an obsidian tornado.

Dixon's screaming, too, but not my name. He's screaming Liza's. I don't have the time to think about the implications, though. Of all the monsters I've hunted, shadows are my least favorite. Especially in the Shadow Plane. They're non-corporeal, so I can't just beat them down. I have to use magic.

"Quae! Quae!" The containment spell works on one shadow at a time, and it's too slow. I can't keep them off me. My wards are down, as they always are in the training room. It's supposed to be safe in here. I certainly don't feel safe now. The fear shadows spread is creeping over me, sending chills down my back and raising goosebumps on my skin. It's taking every ounce of willpower I have to stay on my feet, and keeping them at bay is preventing me from raising my wards to protect me from their influence. I need a bigger weapon.

Over the rushing of the shadows, a menacing snarl reaches my ears. A hole appears in the darkness surrounding me, the tiniest flash of light giving me a glimmer of hope. The shadows hiss in response. Another growl, and the snapping of teeth. This time a large hole opens, and the face of a hellhound pushes through. Fangs bared, tail whipping back and forth, she lunges for another shadow. Her jaws snap shut on empty air, but the shadow dissipates regardless.

Familiar magic. That's it! I don't need to understand how my familiar can kill a shadow to accept it. Not just contain or banish it, but kill it entirely. And if I can get to the weapons room, that power can be mine, too.

The next time she opens a hole, I'm ready. Diving through, I emerge on the other side of the shadow-wall, the light making my eyes tear up. I'm running as soon as I come out of my roll, hissing erupting behind me. The door to the training room is pitch-black, Dixon trapped somewhere inside. *I'm coming. Just hold on.* The weapons room is in the other direction, and I sprint for the door, legs protesting at the sudden exertion. As I run, I whisper the spells that will open the door, then crash through it without stopping. The door snaps back, hinges popping and wood crunching. One hand flies up to cover my eyes, the other hand already reaching for the sword.

The shadows are on me as soon as I stop, but I'm no longer afraid. The sword sings in my hand as I swing it, cutting through the oppressive weight in the training room as shadows are sundered. Frenzied, the shadows bear down on me, desperate to regain control. Only moments pass, but it feels much longer before the air around me is once again clear. No time to rest, though. Darkness still reigns at the other end of the room.

Attacking a wall of sheer blackness is intimidating, to say the least. The shadows surrounding Dixon are so dense I can't make out their individual shapes. I start at the edges, advancing carefully, aware that the slightest miscalculation could sever Dixon in half.

I don't get far before the shadows turn on me. They're stronger than the ones I've already killed, drunk on Dixon's fear, and they attack with abandon. Even with my sword and hellhound, the weight of them once again threatens to drag me under. They cluster around my face, blinding me. In a panic I drop my sword, clawing at my eyes, a high-pitched squeal escaping my lips. Defenseless, I sink to my knees, arms wrapping around my head in a last-ditch effort to hold them off.

"Aargh!" The wordless yell is less than human, and a weight crashes into my side. Light behind my lids has my eyes flying open to see Dixon standing his ground, arms up and fingers out in a defensive spell maneuver. Long scratches show on his cheeks where he was also clawing at his face, and his eyes are puffy and still holding tears. But he's on his feet, eyes steely with purpose and control. Bolstered, I scrabble around on the ground, fingers finally brushing the hilt of my sword. Between the three of us, with spell, sword, and teeth, the remaining shadows are defeated.

When they're gone I stand gasping for breath, but Dixon won't let me rest. "Liza." He grabs my hand and pulls, and together we race out of the training room and across the hall. Together we burst through the doors, ready for anything. Except, that is, to find Liza curled in an easy chair, book open in her lap and a bewildered expression on her face.

"Hey guys, what's up?"

"Are you okay?" Dixon rushes to check on her while I sweep the room. No sign of shadows.

"I'm fine. Why?"

"You explain. I'll do a sweep." I leave the two of them alone while I check the remaining rooms. Our pocket of the Shadow Plane isn't that big, with the training room and the library taking up the most space. But there are a couple of smaller spaces, like the weapons room, the changing rooms, and the artifacts room. The artifacts room is where we keep dangerous objects that we've confiscated and either don't know how or just plain can't destroy. The sweep only takes a few minutes, and Dixon's finishing up when I return to the library.

"You really didn't see anything?" *If the shadows got in, why were they only in the training room? How did they get in in the first place?* My mind zips back to the shadow that got in the house. That one also came through from the training room.

Then the less comfortable question: *Did Liza let the shadows in?*

"If I had seen shadows, do you think I'd still be sitting here?" Liza sounds offended that I asked.

"I'm just glad you're okay." I'm too distracted and confused to think of a less generic answer. "What are you doing down here, anyway?"

"Dixon brought me. After the Immortal's visit, I wanted to do some reading on Hecate."

"Find anything?"

"Not yet, but I haven't gotten very far. We don't have a lot on her."

"Okay. Well, let's all get back upstairs. I'll call Mr. Henderson and tell him about the incursion. I don't want either of you down here until he gives us the all-clear, got it?"

"Got it," they chorus, sounding none too happy. I'm not happy about it either, but it needs to be done. The rules that govern our pocket are beyond all three of us combined. If something's wrong, it needs to be handled by the council.

I usher Liza and Dixon ahead of me so I can watch their backs. As they leave the room, a dark smudge on the carpet catches my eye. My first thought is blood, though I don't remember either Dixon or me sporting any injuries. Shadows aren't a physical threat, and hurt the mind instead of the body. Still, I crouch down and probe the smudge with my finger. It comes up easily, and when I hold it up to the light I see that it's not blood. It's coarse, gray sand. The kind of sand you only find in the Shadow Plane. *How did this get in here? Someone had to track it in. And it's right by Liza's chair...*

"You coming?"

"Yeah." I wipe my hand off on my jeans, but it's not so easy to take my mind off of it.

On second thought...

It only takes me a moment to dart back and scoop up the book Liza was reading. A few more are littered on the carpet around her chair, and I take those too. Liza and Dixon have already crossed back over, and I'm able to smuggle the books upstairs without being noticed.

Mr. Henderson is waiting for me, saving me the trouble of calling. He speaks as though we weren't physically brawling just a few hours earlier. "Would you care to explain what's going on?"

I do, as succinctly as I can, successfully shoving down the impulse to knock him unconscious and tie him up where he can't cause any more damage. Throughout my narrative his eyes keep glancing nervously down at the sword I'm still holding at my side. I have the feeling I'll be keeping it close for the foreseeable future.

"And how did the shadows get in?"

"I don't know. I was hoping you could take a look at the defenses and find out if there's some sort of breach or—"

"Not necessary. The only way a shadow could get in would be if someone let it in."

"But that's—"

"The only way. Period."

"Would you take a look anyway?" It's difficult not to let my exasperation show. After his stunt this morning, all I want to do is chuck Mr. Henderson out the window, but I can't let that rule my decision here. Our safety from the monsters is paramount.

He rolls his eyes. "Fine. I'll have someone look into it." I turn to leave, but he catches my elbow. "There's still the matter of your actions this morning—"

"Later." I shrug him off and head for the stairs. He doesn't follow, and that makes me smile. *I think he's afraid of me.*

I find Liza in her room, lying on her bed in the dark. A moment of panic washes over me. *Maybe the shadows got to her after all.*

"You okay?"

"Just tired. Thinking about taking a nap."

"Still having nightmares?"

She doesn't answer, but the lights come on as she sits up. She stares at me until I meet her gaze, then drops her glamour. I gasp. I can't help it. Her face is gaunt, with sunken eyes and prominent cheekbones. Her thick black hair hangs limply down her back.

"Why didn't you tell me?"

"You have so much going on, much more important stuff."

"You're important." I sink onto the bed, pulling her against my side. My eyes roam around her room, which is slowly being bleached of the vibrant colors Liza usually surrounds herself with.

"Nothing helps, Adrienne. Not spells. Not tea. Not sleep aids. Nothing. What's wrong with me?" Now that she's being honest she can't hold back the hysteria in her voice. Searching for inspiration, my eyes fall on the herbs growing out of Liza's windowsill. The plants have taken over like a miniature jungle.

Hecate's plants? The Immortal said her acolytes grew poisonous herbs. With a whisper, I pluck a couple of leaves off each plant and draw them forward on a breeze. Liza is too upset to notice when I deftly snatch them out of the air and stuff them into my pocket.

"I have an idea, but you may not like it."

"Will it help?"

"I don't know. But it can't hurt."

"Tell me."

"A perception spell. For me. Something that will let me see your dreams tonight. If I know what you're dreaming about, maybe it will help us figure out how to stop it."

"Dixon doesn't know about the nightmares…"

"This wouldn't be Dixon's spell. It would be mine." The idea has been rolling around in my head, but I didn't think I'd be able to pull it off. Now, with my familiar's help, it finally seems possible."

It takes Liza a moment to answer. Finally, a soft, "okay". That's it.

"Okay. I'll come back at bedtime, and we'll see what we can do, all right?"

I'm at the door when another thought occurs to me. "Where's Pong?"

A puzzled expression crosses her face. "I haven't seen him today." She doesn't appear concerned, but I am. The last time she was in danger that cat broke a window, but he's absent today? Something isn't right. I don't say anything, but I can't shake the uneasy feeling creeping over me.

Twenty-One

NIGHTMARES. MOON. HELLHOUNDS. INSANITY. *Shit.* I don't say it. Not out loud. Saying it out loud will make it true, and I'm not ready for it to be true. Instead, I calmly put away the Hecate research and go in search of Liza. It's time.

It's hard to keep a straight face as I look at her, knowing what I know. At least, what I suspect. I still don't have any proof, not yet, but it would be too much of a coincidence otherwise. It's easier to keep my gaze averted as I circle the room, lighting cedar, rosemary, and sage. It may be a bit of an overkill on the herbs, but tonight I desperately need the help to focus. If Liza notices, she doesn't mention it.

I would never be able to pull off this spell without Enyo, and if I'm being honest with myself, I'm not so sure I can do it even with her help. Not now.

"What if I can't sleep?" Liza's voice is laced with apprehension.

"That's what the tea is for. Just close your eyes, okay? I'll be right here." There's nothing magical in her tea, just herbs to help her relax. I told her there was something stronger, though. If she believes it, it'll help. She's asleep in minutes, whether by tea or plain exhaustion, I don't know. As I listen for her breathing to even out, I silently prowl around her room. I only let myself feel guilty for a moment before brushing the unwanted emotion aside. *Invading Liza's privacy is a small price to pay for answers. Now, if I were a piece of condemning evidence, where would I hide?*

I only have a few minutes to search before I need to begin my incantation. The dresser drawers yield nothing obvious. Neither does the closet. I'm about to give up when I notice a small dish on the corner of her desk. *If I'm right, and she doesn't know she's doing it, then she would have no need to hide it, right?* Among a cluster of little collectibles is a dull-colored, sharply pointed rock. Finnigan's words come back to me. *A piece of the Ashen Plane...*

I don't touch it. But when I hover my hand over it, it emanates heat. *How did she even get it?*

My time's up. I can't just leave it there, though. Grabbing a sock from Liza's drawer, I scoop up the rock and stuff it into my pocket, then take my place in the chair by her bed. Her eyelids flicker, indicating her dreams have started. I need to get in there.

The spell is strangely worded, for me at least. I like my power words. The subtle magic in perception spells often slips my grasp. But I was determined not to bring Dixon into this, so this time the spell is all my own. Being left out again will hurt him, but I can't say anything until I know for sure. As I chant, the flowing words get tangled up in my mouth and I begin to doubt myself and my ability to help. Then Enyo comes. Leaping gracefully into my lap, the hellhound leans into me, and her touch stills my mind. I breathe deeply of the burning herbs, narrowing my focus, repeating the words, feeling them take effect.

It isn't like watching a movie. Liza's dream begins with ash. In the air, on the ground, swirling thick and gray like dirty snow. A woman is screaming, and a baby is crying. I can't see them; the ash is too thick, the darkness too dense. Despite this, or maybe because of it, their voices cut through me, threatening to rip the sounds of pain from my own throat.

Then the world explodes. Light and sound and cold and pain, all around, surrounding me, too loud and harsh for me to concentrate on any one of them. Once again, a woman is screaming. A child cries, no longer a baby. Slowly, the scene begins to take shape. Rain drums against asphalt, the steady sound of it drowned out by the scream of sirens. Broken glass and twisted metal litter the ground, unrecognizable if you don't already know what you're looking at. *Oh my. She's remembering the car accident that killed her mother.*

I want to shut my eyes tight as the paramedics haul a broken body out of the front seat, but I can't look away. These are Liza's eyes, and she can't look away. As she watches, a hiss of a voice begins to whisper in her ear. So light, I almost miss it. *Hello, child. I've found you.* Shivers race down my spine as the voice worms its way into my mind, and for a moment, I think she's talking to me. But no. That's ridiculous. Then the shivers I feel are Liza's. The dread, Liza's.

The accident melts away, like a gruesome Salvador Dali painting, replaced by an unyielding darkness. Liza's voice stammers out into the void. "Wh-what do you want?"

Are we still in a memory? Or is this new? I don't have time to ponder as the voice answers, stronger this time, but still hovering just out of reach.

Do not be frightened, child. Even through your mother's charms, you heard me calling. And you have answered. Come. I will show you everything you could ever be.

"N-no." Then running, through that blackness, pushing against the darkness like a tangible thing, clinging to arms and legs, straining to hold her back. Heat and fire, licking at her feet, the smell of brimstone filling her nostrils, a roar sounding out behind her, filled with anguish and fury.

Then she's burning, Liza's burning, the flames devouring her skin yet leaving her whole, and she's screaming, and I'm screaming, and—

What is this? The voice fills my mind, and I know it's no memory. *Who are you, child, to try and spy on me in this way?*

I try to flee, to break my connection to Liza, but I can't. Trapped within my own mind, I can feel her advancing, the owner of this voice, this voice that makes my whole body convulse, trying to vomit, trying to expel her like a toxin. The darkness before me bends and shifts, beginning to take form.

Yes, of course. I recognize your mind. You are the one who killed my hellhounds. I have been looking for you. Have you felt my touch? Have you enjoyed the visions I have sent to you? But I did not bring you here this time. You think yourself a warrior, child? Come to protect the innocent girl? You think you are a match for me? For me? Her last line is not whispered, but thundered, the outrage of a wronged goddess consuming my senses, pulling me apart, devouring the pieces. Not even with Enyo at my side can I withstand her.

Then another consciousness joins with us. Vast and alien, it surrounds my mind, shielding us from the might of the sorceress. I can hear her scream in frustration, the predator whose prey has been snatched from within its very jaws. Gasping, I come to, eyes flying open to find my face buried in Liza's bedroom carpet, my body thrown free of the chair. A warm pressure between my shoulder blades has me flipping around to find Pong's head pushing into my body, but it's not the Pong I remember. Gone is the tabby cat. Hovering over me stands an honest-to-goodness panther.

How did—

Before I have time to pee myself he abandons me for Liza, who's somehow still asleep, thrashing around in her covers as if she really were on fire. With a grace belying his size, he bounds onto the bed, stretching along her length and nuzzling his head under her chin. In a moment she goes still, chest rising and falling in gentle breaths, and I can picture what's going on inside her head. Pong, mightier than Hecate, rescuing his magi and giving her mind rest. The same thing he did for me.

How did he do it for me? We're not bonded. How did he get inside my head? I decide it doesn't matter. I don't know what would have happened if Hecate had had her way with me. If I dwell on it too long I'll probably turn into a drooling mess on the floor.

Hecate. I finally allow myself to form her name. She's definitely the voice tormenting Liza. *How did she get her claws into her?* I think back through the memories I witnessed, trying to form a timeline, but they're all tangled up together in my head. It's going to take some thought to figure it all out. Until then...

My bed is warm and inviting when I make it back to my room. It felt like only minutes passed in Liza's nightmares, but my clock reads well past midnight. I missed a call from Alex. I've barely talked to him in the last couple of days, and I'd love nothing more than to curl up and fall asleep with his voice in my ear. I resist, though. No need to make a habit of waking him up.

I have a missed call from Mason, too. Weird. I don't think he's ever called me on the phone, not once. On the rare occasion he wants to speak to me he just shows up at the manor. I don't call him back, either. That would imply wanting to talk to him.

Morning comes before I'm ready. Not ready to wake up, and definitely not ready to talk to Liza.

"Pong's back." She's awake when I come in, stroking the panther between his eyes.

"Yeah, he showed up last night." I pause, then continue when she doesn't mention the obvious. "He's quite a bit bigger than the last time I saw him."

She rolls her eyes at me, which I decide to take as a sign that she slept well for the rest of the night. "Obviously. That's why he wasn't around yesterday. He had to find a new body."

"Liza," I begin, then stop and move to sit next to her on the bed.

She senses my hesitation. "It's the spell, isn't it? It didn't work."

"No, it worked. Perfectly, actually." I can't stop myself from studying her eyes, looking for some sign that she's not Liza. "How much do you remember?"

"Nothing. I told you, I don't remember my nightmares. That's what makes it so hard." She's studying me back, suddenly afraid I'm going to give her bad news. She's not wrong.

Like ripping off a band-aid, right? "Hecate's causing your nightmares."

She just stares at me, like she's waiting for the punchline to a bad joke. "What?"

I say it again, slowly and carefully telling her about what I saw. What I heard. About the voice.

"No. That can't be right. No. You made a mistake. Something went wrong, or, or the spell. That's it. Your spell went wrong. Maybe—"

She knows I'm not wrong. I let her talk, though, working through it. When she finally quiets, I know we've come to the hard part. "I need to ask you some questions."

"I don't know—"

"I know. But I need to ask anyway. Okay?"

She nods, looking much younger than she actually is. Sometimes I treat her that way, too, which doesn't help, but in times like this, she just looks so tiny and vulnerable.

"When did you go to the Ashen Plane?"

"What? Never. Are you crazy?"

"That's the only part I can't make sense of, Liza. This is the way I see it: You were born under a powerful convergence. Hecate felt it, and came looking for you. You told me you had nightmares when you were really little, right? That's when she found you. Your mom cast spells to hide you, not from the magi, but from Hecate. When she died—"

"Please stop." Silent tears roll down Liza's cheeks. We don't talk about her mom's death. Ever.

"When she died, her spells failed, and Hecate could find you again. I don't know what she wants with you, but it's nothing good. She's already made you..." I trail off. I can't say it. *How can I tell her that so many deaths are her fault?* Liza is my summoner. Maybe if I'd known what to look for, I would have seen it sooner. She was MIA the night I killed the hellhound. When I thought back on it, I realized she wasn't around the three full moons prior, either. She'd vanished, and we hadn't noticed, because stopping the carnage was more important. Liza slipped through the cracks.

I backtrack, going back to what I really need to know. "But one thing doesn't fit. That memory where you spoke with Hecate? She said she called you. Something broke through your mom's magic, and you went to her."

"No."

"You went to the Ashen Plane, Liza."

"No."

"You brought something back with you. A piece of a rock, something so inconsequential you probably didn't even notice you did it. Hecate's making you use that rock to summon hellhounds—"

"No!" For the first time since he showed up on our doorstep, Pong growls at me. Not a sweet kitty growl, either. A try-it-again-and-I'm-going-to-eat-you growl.

"Have it your way, but you know I'm right, even if you don't want to admit it, and we're going to have to talk about it sooner or later." I leave Liza's room in a huff, blowing past Dixon in the hallway. I mumble a good morning but don't even stop.

"What's going on?" he asks as I walk away. I don't answer, and I hear him talking to Liza as he moves into her room.

I lied to Liza. I know what Hecate wants with her. She's the most powerful magi alive. Young, nubile, and virgin, just like Hecate likes them. Hecate wants to use her to cross back into this plane. How, I don't know, but I think I'm finally getting a handle on the big picture.

Twenty-two

"You guys need to get back to school." I feel like a broken record. "Monday is the perfect day for a fresh start."

"You really expect me to go to school like this?" 'Like this' meaning possessed, or whatever. We're still not sure exactly what Liza is. At least she's talking about it now, which is a major improvement from a week ago. With the new and improved Pong guarding her dreams, Hecate hasn't made any more appearances.

"Come on, Adrienne. We've probably missed more days than we've attended this semester. They probably wouldn't let us come back, anyway." Dixon's interjection is at least rational, while Liza's is completely emotional.

"You can't just not go to school."

"You're not." Liza's barb stings, and it's a struggle to not take it personally. She's been lashing out at everyone, and who can blame her? Learning Hecate is in your head isn't an easy thing to deal with.

"Mr. Henderson, in his infinite bag of negotiation tricks, has persuaded the principal to let the absences slide as long as you guys can get caught up on your work."

"So, what, you guys are friends now?"

I sigh, digging the palms of my hands into my eyes until little spots appear. "Definitely not. His day of reckoning will come. But he comes in handy sometimes." 'Sometimes' being the operative word. Officially, Mr. Henderson is still living at the manor and acting as our legal guardian. Unofficially, none of us has seen him since the day he attacked the Immortal in the kitchen. Council members drop in to check on us and pass along messages, but the man himself is keeping his distance. Most often we see Tamara, who makes all of us uneasy. She doesn't say much, but looks at Liza as if she knows something.

"And we're just supposed to do what he says? You haven't even told him about me, have you?"

"You know I haven't, Liza, now stop biting my head off. You're going back to school, end of discussion." The snap in my voice makes me cringe, and Liza stomps out of the kitchen without another word.

Dixon appears at my side as she leaves, hovering at the edge of my peripheral vision.

"You want a piece of me, too? Let me have it. Tell me how badly I'm screwing everything up."

"The only thing you screwed up was not telling me right away. You can't expect her to be calm about all this, and you can't expect her to go to school like her world isn't ending."

"Her world isn't ending. Hecate is after her, yes, but she's not going to get her. I'm not going to let her. She's not even giving her nightmares anymore. She can't get past Pong." Pong, in all his massiveness, has spent every night since his return at Liza's side, wrapping her mind up so tight Hecate can't get through. I don't know how it works, and I don't need to. For now, she's safe, and that's all that matters.

My own sanity may not be so certain. Hecate knows me now, and since she can't get Liza, she's coming after me. My dreams for the past week have been plagued with monsters and all the people I was too late to save. Horror-movie stuff, dredged up out of my own memories. Worse, she's sending me nightmares of the future, too. At least, the future as she envisions it. A future where all nations bow in fear before her, where eternal darkness crowds out the sun, and where the streets run red with the blood of any who dare oppose her.

"She's twelve, Adrienne. She can't see all that. She's just scared."

"I know that. That's why getting back to a normal routine is a good idea. Get her out of this house, occupy her mind with normal, twelve-year-old-girl things instead of bogging her down in anxiety and despair. I'll handle Hecate, but there needs to be something for her to come back to once Hecate is gone."

Dixon nods. We haven't fixed whatever's broken between us, but at least he's on my side in this. "Okay then. We'll go tomorrow." He's almost out of the kitchen when he adds, "You know tomorrow's a full moon, right?"

"I know." He doesn't ask me what my plan is, which I'm grateful for. He wouldn't like it. Liza's definitely not going to like it.

At my elbow, my phone buzzes, preventing me from shoving a large forkful of scrambled eggs into my mouth.

"Alex?"

"Hey there. I—"

The rest of his words get drowned out by a sudden ringing in my ears. It's so sudden it makes my head spin, and I thump it down on the table, wrapping my arms around it. *This is so weird. It feels just like Halloween...*

"Adrienne? Talk to me, are you okay?" Alex's voice breaks through and gives me something to focus on.

"I'm here, but I gotta go. I just got a bead on the Immortal. I'll call you later, okay?"

"Want some backup?"

"Thanks, but I'll be all right. He won't hurt me."

"Okay. Be safe."

My relationship with Alex has come a long way. I'm still doing my best to keep him out of the craziness that is my job, and my life, most days, but as long as I'm honest with him about it then we're okay. He's at the manor every evening after practice, enduring a whole second workout with me. He's an eager student, and teaching him comes easily to me. It's a nice hour when I can let go of the cacophony in my head and just focus on the feel of my body. Without Andrew, my workouts have been sporadic and disorganized. Stepping into the teacher role has refocused my energy and given me some clarity.

The ringing stops as soon as I pay attention to what it's trying to tell me. How the Immortal has gone a whole week without using any magic at all is beyond me, but now that he finally has,

I know exactly where to find him. *Pacific Shores? When he said northern California, he wasn't kidding.*

It doesn't take me long to get ready, and I feel a little naked without being armed to the hilt, but considering how our last conversation ended, showing up looking like I'm ready for a fight doesn't seem like the best idea. The knives I do take are well hidden, and Enyo's a weapon in herself.

I'm mobbed by shadows as soon as I cross into the Shadow Plane. They can't hurt me with my wards up, but they can cluster around me and clog my vision, which they do in earnest. Surprisingly, Enyo passes unscathed. They fall behind as I walk, though, which I'm only grateful for for a minute. Once I'm clear, the sight behind me becomes all too disturbing. More shadows than I've ever seen in one place are congregated in a single spot: the manor. Chills run down my spine, and it's almost enough to make me lose control of my wards. *They're here for Liza.* I know it as certainly as I know my own name.

Much as I want to, I don't have time to dwell on the shadows or their purpose here. I have to get to California, before the Immortal moves on me.

The emptiness of the Shadow Plane will never cease to unsettle me. The dimness, the lack of light, the utter silence and stillness. The complete absence of life. If I didn't need to travel quickly I would probably never come here at all.

The Immortal's house is not what I would have imagined, if I had spent any time imagining his house. Sleek and modern, it sits high up on a rocky cliff overlooking the coast. Walls of windows and a dual-layer wraparound deck give it a oneness with the open sea air surrounding it.

The Immortal is waiting for me. "It took you long enough to find me."

"It took you long enough to use your magic."

"Ahh, so that is how you did it." In workout shorts and a tank top, with a tall glass of iced tea in his hand, he's definitely not expecting trouble. "Are you alone?"

I spread my arms out to the sides. "If I weren't, I think you'd know it. You just want to know if I'd lie to you."

"That is true." With his beverage hand he gestures out at the hellhound on my heels. "You have claimed her, then? She stands proudly, as one bearing a name."

"Enyo." For a moment his face darkens, and I fear I've made a tasteless mistake. "I've been doing a lot of reading on Greek mythology lately. Did you know her?"

"As the others, Enyo was only ever a myth. A minor war goddess, though she did have her devotees. The wind can get chilly out here. Come inside." He disappears through a sliding glass door that's barely visible behind him without waiting for me to follow.

The inside of his house is just as surprising as the outside. Once again, the money can be seen in the solid wood furniture and the gleaming stainless steel. *I guess he's had plenty of time to make some long-term investments.* The entire first floor is open concept, with the living room, kitchen, and dining area all blending into each other. Hardwood floors trace dizzying geometric designs, accented by strategically placed plush rugs. The Immortal catches me staring, and I can't swear that my mouth isn't hanging open just a little.

"You have good taste."

"For a murderer?"

"Right to it, then." I take a seat on one of the barstools by the counter as the Immortal refills his glass. "I didn't have anything to do with that attack."

"I know."

"But?"

"Your council was not wrong. I have killed. I have committed atrocities. I deserve to be tried for my crimes."

"You don't sound apologetic."

"I am not. I regret none of the things that I have done. But you have requested my help, and I will admit that I may be in need of your aid as well, as you have already observed. Can you reconcile yourself to working with a murderer?"

His question takes me off guard, and in my hesitation he asks me another.

"What of the sins I have committed against you? The people of yours I have taken? You tried to kill me for them once. I have already refused to return them to you. Am I to believe you have moved past this?"

"Is this why you haven't contacted me?" I fire back, my temper flaring. "You think I'm going to turn on you? And instead of asking me about it, you hole up here in your fancy beach house and twiddle your thumbs? The full moon is tomorrow night, and Hecate is wreaking havoc, and you're just sitting here drinking iced tea?"

The Immortal's eyes flare at Hecate's name, but he doesn't rise to the bait. "I am aware of the moon, but Hecate will not rise tomorrow night. A simple full moon is not strong enough to pull her into this plane. I would have your answer now."

He actually expects me to answer? I assumed his questions were rhetorical. Taking slow, even breaths, I work to calm my temper and reply evenly. "I can't deny your crimes, but I can't fight Hecate without you, and for now that's all that matters. Whatever you did with Andrew and Heather, I believe they are safe, and I assume you wouldn't give them back to me even if I were to ask a hundred times."

"You are correct. Once my business is done, they will be returned to you, unharmed."

"I know that. Now, can we move on? Because Hecate is inside Liza's head, and—"

The Immortal's head whips around, pinning me to my stool with the strength of his gaze. "She has chosen a vessel?"

"I don't know what that means." *Liar.* "But she's been giving her nightmares and tormenting her, and Liza's been...doing things."

"Explain."

I do, telling him about Liza's missing time, her unexplained absences, the shadows in the training room. He listens intently as I recount Liza's nightmare, and it occurs to me that I didn't ask her permission to tell him. The stuff about her history is pretty personal, but any little tidbit could be helpful, so I don't hold back.

"The child is strong?"

"The strongest."

"Then it is as I feared. Hecate is attempting to bring the child under her control in order to gain access to her body. She already exercises a good deal of influence over the child's mind."

"Her body? What does she need her body for?"

The Immortal looks at me like I've just asked the stupidest possible question, and for a moment I actually think I did. *What did I miss?*

"Hecate does not have corporeal form. The human body cannot exist in the Ashen Plane. For Hecate to rise, she must take possession of a vessel."

Liza. "But that's not right. Liza went to the Ashen Plane, and she obviously came back with her body. I saw it myself."

"You saw a vision in a dream, a dream that Hecate created. You cannot prove it was true."

I don't argue the point. I know what I saw, and it wasn't some fabricated vision. It was a memory, a real memory. Instead, I focus on the important part. "She's going to come back for Liza, isn't she?" I already know she is, but I need to hear him confirm it.

Finally, some measure of emotion shows on the Immortal's face. The barest trace of sadness, but it's there. "Yes. Her expulsion from the child's mind will not keep her away for long. She will renew her attack, more strongly and more fiercely than before."

"How do I keep that from happening?"

The look the Immortal gives me sends me back to the first time we met. Sizing me up, determining my worth. "Our next step is clear. Sever the link between the child and the sorceress. It will not stop her from rising, but it may perhaps delay her long enough."

"Sever the link…" His meaning hits me like a wrecking ball to the chest. No wonder he was looking at me like that. "No. Absolutely not. We are not killing Liza. There has to be another way." Panic threatens to overwhelm me, and I fight to keep it at bay. *If he decides Liza needs to die, I won't be able to stop him.*

"Our time is drawing short, and we cannot afford to pursue flights of fancy. The regathering of Hecate's power has been slow, but has increased exponentially in recent months. I did not know why, but now, knowing that her vessel has been assisting her, I understand."

"Liza has not been—"

"Willingly or unwillingly, it makes no difference. She has played her part, and I fear Hecate now stands poised to enact her plan. Yet, she still requires a major source of power to rip through all of totality and regain this plane. A simple full moon is not enough, but a larger celestial event—"

"The comet." A memory flashes into my mind, of Liza and her partner, what was her name? Laughing in the kitchen, working on a project, she told us all about it at dinner, *how could I have forgotten?* Sandiphan's comet. It only crosses our solar system once a millennia. I do the math on my fingers, picturing the display in the hallway at school, the one counting down the days until the comet. How many times did I walk past that display this semester and not realize its significance?

"December twenty-first." The date comes out on a gasp. "The comet is due on the same day as the winter solstice."

TWENTY-THREE

THE KITCHEN IS SUSPICIOUSLY vacant when I return from California. Not that I expected Liza and Dixon to just be sitting around waiting for me, but that doesn't stop the disappointment I feel in having to track them down. I find them together, practicing spells in the training room. At least, Dixon is practicing. I haven't seen Liza cast since we discovered Hecate in her head. I think she's too afraid.

"Hey, guys."

"Hey." My entrance is met with monotone voices and less than joyful expressions.

"Don't you want to know what happened?"

"He didn't kill you, so it must not have been too bad." Dixon keeps his eyes trained on the target against the far wall. He's not aiming for it, rather using it as a focal point to keep his mind from wandering. Liza avoids my eyes and stays silent.

Exasperated, I stalk over to stand in front of Dixon and block his view of the target. "Is it too much to ask for a little of your attention? This is important."

"Fine." His eyes meet mine, but the indifference in them is plain. "What did he say?"

I could smack him. "What is it now, Dixon? Let's have it all out, right now, so we can finally move past whatever this is. Liza's life is at stake, so it's time to stop acting like a sulky child."

Liza squeaks at my words, and her face goes ashen.

Dixon rises to his feet, his face struggling to stay neutral and not betray how hurt he's feeling. "You used to tell us things. Share your plans with us. Ask for our help. Remember when Heather assigned you this case? We had a meeting and everything. We were supposed to be a team, all three of us, but you keep shutting us out."

"We've already been over this—"

"Actually, we haven't. You got mad at me, and then we were attacked by shadows. Nothing's changed. You stopped telling us stuff. You didn't tell us you invited the Immortal *to our house*, or that you were planning on teaming up with him. And you didn't tell me about Liza's nightmares, or your suspicions that she was the summoner, or that freaking Hecate was *living in her head*!"

I can't help it. My temper flares in response to his own, and I reply in kind. "I am doing my best to be the leader in this house, until Andrew and Heather come home. Neither of you are trained in the field, so yeah, when I find other warriors that can actually help me fight, I'm going to do everything I can to convince them to. You're not some innocent victim, Dixon, being so distracted with finding your parents that you keep missing all the big events. You keep disappearing, and you're never around when I need you, and you're so wrapped up in your own little world that you're ignoring the bigger picture.

Which is Liza, by the way, and the sorceress who is trying to body-snatch her."

I realize my mistake the instant the words fly out of my mouth, but it's too late to take them back. Dixon looks like I punched him in the gut. Liza's actually looking at me now, working the words over in her mind, understanding crashing down on her face. "Liza, I'm so sorry, I didn't mean it to come out like that."

Leaving Dixon, I cross the room to kneel down in front of her, letting the anger fade out of my voice. "I'm not going to let that happen, okay? That's what the Immortal and I were discussing." I put my hands on her shaking shoulders, but she shrugs me off and bolts.

"You see? Look what you did to her. You just can't stop messing things up, can you?" Dixon stalks from the room with that parting shot, and I let him go. He'll keep. Liza won't.

Liza's in her room when I finally find her again, hugging her pillow with her back to the door. "You crossed by yourself, didn't you?"

"It's not like it's hard. Those rules are just stupid, anyway." Hearing that snarky tone come out of her sweet mouth makes my heart hurt.

"I really am sorry, Liza."

"Save it. Just tell me what's going on."

She can't be angry with me forever, right? I relate my conversation with the Immortal to her, not omitting any details. She has a right to know.

"When?"

"We believe it will be during the comet."

She's already nodding. "That makes sense. It's at the same time as the winter solstice. The power that she'll have..."

"You knew that? Why didn't you say anything?"

"I didn't know it was important. You didn't tell me to look for a celestial event."

Silence falls between us, and her words dig at the wounds Dixon left. "Is he right, Liza? Have I been shutting you guys out?"

She doesn't answer right away, and I'm pretty sure that's my answer. Then, "Not so much me. I'm patient zero, so you don't have much of a choice. But Dixon? Yeah, I guess. All he has is his brain, but he can't use it if you don't tell him what you need. He's feeling pretty useless and unwanted."

Ouch. "Is that why he spends so much time on his parents? Because he thinks I don't want him around?"

"How would you react, if it were you?" Her question hits me hard. *She sounds so...adult. When did she get so perceptive? But then she's had to grow up fast...*

Liza isn't done raking me over the coals, though. "Imagine you're Dixon. You spend your entire life feeling discarded and unwanted, and then you discover you're special. Someone gives you a home, and a family, and tells you they love you. But then they find someone more powerful than you, and suddenly you're on the sidelines again, and those feelings of being unwanted start coming back. How would that feel, Adrienne? Can you blame him?"

"I'm not discounting his feelings, Liza, but what's going on right now is so much bigger than Dixon's feelings. He needs to see that."

"Would you be able to?"

I sigh. "When did you get so smart?"

"Just one of my many gifts." For a moment the old Liza peeps through, smiling and carefree, but the glimpse is gone before it can fully manifest. Instead, that haunted look comes over her face, the one I've seen too much of in the past week. "So, what's the plan for tomorrow?"

"In a nutshell: keep you inside. It probably won't be that easy, though. We're stealing Hecate's vessel right out from under her nose, and she isn't going to take that lying down." Tomorrow night, Hecate is going to have the power to work her influence in the world, and deep in my gut, I know she's going to come for Liza. I don't know what it's going to look like, but something is going to happen.

I could use some time to myself. Enyo follows me as I wander through the manor, leaving the lived-in homey parts for the abandoned halls and rooms that haven't been used regularly for decades. It's a gorgeous house; there's just too much space for the few people currently living here. It used to be used more regularly as a kind of magi headquarters, before we spread out and integrated into society. Andrew used to come here. There's a sun-filled parlor where he'd sit after a particularly difficult mission. The couches are comfy, the stained glass is mesmerizing, and the windows give a perfect view of the forest stretching behind the house. It's very secluded and peaceful. Drawn there now, I run my hands along the edge of an end table and sneeze at the dust that billows up. One corner of the room is free of dust, though. Andrew's favorite chair, surrounded by all the things that help him relax: Western novels, record player, spicy candles. Just seeing them there, waiting for him to return for them, makes my eyes tear up.

Where are you, Andrew? I need you here. There's so much going on, and I don't know if I can handle it all...

Sitting in his chair feels like an imposition, so I perch on the cushioned window seat instead. And from that vantage point, I see something I've never noticed before: a seam running along the underside of the chair. It takes me several minutes to find the latch, but when I do, something falls out into my hand.

Andrew's journal. His professional journal is in his study, detailing his work as a magi, but this one is different. Personal. I've only caught him writing in it a handful of times, and he's certainly never let me read it. The cover is embossed leather, faded and cracked with age. I only hesitate a moment before opening it. *We never learned how they found the Immortal. Maybe something in here can help.*

Most of the pages I skim, truly not wanting to invade Andrew's privacy. The dates go back about ten years, and I have to flip forward to find anything recent. He writes a lot about his emotions in dealing with the girls' school murders; he was having trouble sleeping. Nothing about the Immortal, though. *He must not have had time. They found him, and just went. He would have written about it when they got back.* Except they never came back.

Before putting the journal away, an idea comes to me, and I flip backward three years. I have to search a bit to find what I'm looking for, but I finally do, a few weeks after Heather and Andrew brought Dixon home.

Dixon finally appears to be settling in, though his attitude is still withdrawn and it is difficult to engage him in conversation. Our visits over the past year while working out the legal issues surrounding his guardianship have helped him to control his magic, but he is still not certain that he can trust us on a personal level. He has been deeply wounded. I do not envy the day when Heather and I will have to tell him the truth about his birth. For now, we have done our best to bury the information deeply enough that the casual investigator will not be able to find it. The persons involved have been encouraged to remember certain details differently, and the documents have been altered so as not to give anything away. When he is ready, we will tell him that his parents are wanted fugitives. For now, his psyche is too damaged to handle such news.

The entry is followed by several newspaper clippings. One of them has mug shot photos: a woman who shares Dixon's close-cropped curls, his light brown skin, and his slight stature, and a large, hulking man with an evil look in his eye. I skim the articles, but the extensive list of their crimes doesn't matter. For a few moments I just sit there, allowing my heart to ache over everything Dixon has been through. The circumstances of our lives aren't that different, but the details do matter. Dixon was right about one thing: I don't feel the same sense of loss and abandonment that he does. And not just because I know about my past. My future may be a mystery, but the present is crystal clear. I know my place in this world. He's still struggling to find his.

There's no question about showing him the journal entry. He deserves to know, and the sooner the better. Not to mention, keeping it a secret will only further damage our already strained relationship. Maybe he'll finally be able to let the past rest.

Dixon's no longer in the training room, and his door is shut when I go back upstairs. He doesn't answer when I knock. "Dixon? Can I come in?" Nothing. "Dixon?"

Still nothing. "We need to talk. I'm ready to listen, Dixon, to whatever you have to say. And I have something to show you. Please?" I give it another minute, then open the door anyway. It's past time for us to get this sorted out.

The door opens to a dark room. *Weird*. Not completely dark, though. The glow of a computer screen beckons me to the desk, where Dixon's laptop is sitting open. A program is running in the background, the same one I've glimpsed before but didn't understand. A dozen tabs are open, most showing files and various scanned copies of paperwork. The foremost tab is a map with a blinking marker over Hong Kong.

A sticky note is stuck to the right of the trackpad, the few scribbled lines barely visible in the glow. *Adrienne-I know you'll be the one to find this. If I'd told you, you would have tried to stop me. I can't make you understand how important this is to me, but they're my parents. I have to go. I have to know. I'll be back before the full moon, but you said it yourself. I'm not a fighter. I won't be any help to you anyway. You have this under control.*

I have to read the note four times before it finally sinks in. *Dixon's gone.* I stare at the computer screen, my eyes riveted by the blinking map marker. "He found them." The room doesn't answer.

Twenty-four

"WHERE'S DIXON?" LIZA CAN read my face almost as well as Dixon can, so I don't even bother trying to hide it.

"Gone."

"What? Where? Why?"

I want to tell her everything. Unburden myself of the weight of this secret I'm now carrying. But I can't. Dixon has to be the first to know, and it'll have to be his decision who to share the information with. I can tell her where he went, though. "Hong Kong."

"Why would he go to...He found them, didn't he?" She gets it. She always did. The drive Dixon felt to know and to understand. To her, it's perfectly logical that he would go.

"He left a note." I let her read it. There's nothing personal there.

"See, he'll be back. He isn't going to miss the full moon." And with that her mind is settled. He said he'll be back in time, so of course he'll be back in time. No doubt. My mind is less settled. Dixon's parents are dangerous, and magic takes full control and intention to wield. His control is getting better, but this meeting is going to wreak havoc on his mental state. A growing sense of foreboding makes me shudder.

Liza goes to bed early, snuggled deep into Pong's belly fur, his legs wrapped tightly around her. I text Mason, asking him to come tomorrow, then ignore him when he tries to call and talk about it. I call Alex instead, knowing that it's time. If I expect him to fight at Mason's side tomorrow night, I need to clear the air between all of us.

"I'm ready to tell you about Mason." I start talking as soon as he answers, knowing if I let him draw me into small talk that I'll never get back around to it.

A deep breath on the other end of the line. Then, "You slept with him, didn't you?"

It's that obvious? I hesitate a second, wanting to hold onto our relationship just the way it is for this last, brief moment. "Yes, I did."

I pause to let him respond, but he doesn't say anything, so I press on. "When I first came to the manor, Mason was already here. I had just learned I was a magi, and I was terrified. He's two years older than me, and he seemed to have this whole magic thing under control. He's combat, just like me, and I was in awe of him. He knew how to do everything that I wanted to learn, and he did it well.

"At first, he was my sparring partner. When I got older, he was my hunting partner. Or more like, I was his apprentice. He did the job I do now, keeping people safe from the monsters. Andrew was our teacher, but I hunted at Mason's side. He was much like he is now, strong and decisive, acting without hesitation. Watching him was intoxicating. It didn't matter that he was also condescending, or that every compliment he paid me came with a backhanded twist. I was socially isolated, completely entrenched in my training, and spent nearly every waking non-school hour with him. I idolized him."

The admission is difficult. I've never told anyone what I'm telling Alex now. Dixon and Liza are both new to the Mason-and-me story, and missed those early years. There were older teens at the manor back then, but we were never close. For a long time, it was just the two of us. How much Andrew and Heather knew, or suspected, I have no idea.

"When did you…"

"Almost two years ago. I was sixteen, and we had just gotten back from taking down a particularly difficult werewolf. Adrenaline was high, we had moved in perfect sync with each other, and the manor was empty when we got back. I kissed him on impulse. Our bodies reacted accordingly."

It's almost as if I can see the warring emotions on Alex's face. He wants to ask about what happened next, while at the same time wanting to run far away and never finish this conversation. It's an easy decision to spare him the intimate details he doesn't really want to know anyway. "Things weren't the same between us afterward. Not that they were good to begin with, but our encounter brought all the things I'd been ignoring about Mason crashing down around me. Opening myself up to him like that, he seemed to see it as further evidence of my weakness. A few months later he graduated, moved out, and I took up his mantle."

This time I pause intentionally, letting Alex digest my words and making sure he's really listening to what I say next. "I don't have romantic feelings for Mason. I never really did. You're the only guy I want. And if we ever decide that we're ready, I know it'll be different with you."

We don't spend much longer on the phone. After such a heavy conversation, we both need time to decompress and absorb everything that was said. Even after we hang up, I lie in the dark for a while wondering if I made the right call. We're all going to need to be at the top of our game tomorrow. I'll just have to hope this new information isn't too much of a distraction.

Mr. Henderson arrives at the manor bright and early the next morning. In a last-ditch effort I messaged him last night, acknowledging that more people on my side would be a good thing, regardless of who they are. Unfortunately, he's not alone. Tamara lurks behind him, her eyes haughty and smug. Just seeing her puts me in a grumpy mood.

"I didn't realize you'd be bringing company."

"Tamara is my right hand. She accompanies me on all official business. This is official business, is it not? You said you wish to request the aid of the council in overcoming your Hecate fantasy?"

Tamara, is it? Not Ms-whatever-her-last-name-is. They must be getting pretty familiar. "Official business, yes. Fantasy, no. Look, I know we don't see eye-to-eye here, but I'm reaching out anyway. Liza's life is in jeopardy, and I need all the help I can muster to keep her safe."

There it is. Bluntly, my cards laid out on the table.

Mr. Henderson considers a moment. "Where is Ms. DuPage now?"

"Upstairs, sleeping."

It's the wrong thing to say. Tamara's chin goes up even higher when Mr. Henderson responds with condescension. "If she is in such danger, how is it that she is even now safely tucked away in her bed? You have indeed sunk deeply into your delusions if you expect me to believe such an outlandish claim."

Something inside me breaks a little. Despite everything, I guess I was still holding out a little bit of hope that he would believe me. That a real adult would swoop in and save us, and I wouldn't have to do it all alone anymore. The voice that comes out of my mouth next is defeated in a way I've never heard before. "What happened, Mr. Henderson? When you first came here, you seemed like you actually cared. When I told you about Hecate, you seemed at least open to the idea, even though I didn't even know who she was yet. For better or worse, you're the head of the council. There are children pleading with you to help them. How can you just brush us aside?"

Mr. Henderson blinks, and a strange light moves through his eyes. His expression softens, confusion flickering across his face. That's when I see Tamara's lips move. Her voice is too low for me to hear, but I can almost feel her words worming their way into Mr. Henderson's ear. His face clears, hardening once again into the heartless mask I now know he's wearing.

"Ms. Young. I have had more than enough of this. I had hoped that you would eventually come to your senses, but it is painfully obvious that you will not. So no, Ms. Young, the council will not aid you. In fact, it is high time you were held accountable for your actions in assisting the criminal known as 'The Immortal', as well as your negligence in the disappearance of Andrew and Heather McGinnis. Do not leave the premises. I will return for you forthwith."

There's nothing to say. I watch Mr. Henderson and Tamara leave, eyes trained on the back of that woman's head. Questions swirl inside my own. Who is she really? How is she mind-controlling Mr. Henderson? And for how long? And most importantly, what's her interest in keeping him from helping us?

No time for dwelling. Not that I have the head space, anyway. If we all survive the night, I'll put more effort into untangling Mr. Henderson from Tamara's influence.

Alex makes it to the manor as evening falls. The purr of his finely-tuned motor sends me running down the stairs to meet him nervously at the door. If he's nervous, too, he doesn't show it, catching me up in a deep, lingering kiss. "Hey."

"Mmm," I answer, pouting when he breaks the kiss off before I'm ready. "We should keep doing more of that."

"We kind of skipped over this part, so you'll get no objection from me. I don't think now's the right time, though."

"Now is the perfect time. It's not like we're going to have any later."

"You make a good point." Alex leans in for another kiss as Mason enters the kitchen.

"Can't you two get a room?" Shirtless and sweating, Mason makes a beeline for the cold water bottles in the fridge. He showed up at noon, and has been training since he got here. Tai chi, kickboxing, even a little yoga, making me look bad for not training today.

Alex stiffens in my arms. "Why's Mason here?" While his attitude toward me hasn't changed, his attitude toward Mason definitely has. Before there was suspicion and confusion; now there's a coldness I've never heard in his voice before.

"For the same reason you are. It's all hands on deck tonight, and I need fighters." My voice drops without my permission. "If something happens to me, he's the only one who can protect her."

"Nothing is going to happen to her." Empty words, but I appreciate the attempt.

"Not if I can help it."

Ten minutes later our team of four is holding a strategy meeting in the living room.

"Training room? We're stronger there, and it's a defensible position." Mason's question indicates he's letting me run the show. Or at least pretending to.

"No good. Even with the wards, it's still a part of the Shadow Plane, and will be more easily breached by Hecate's magics. And Liza's already proved it's vulnerable by letting in shadows."

"Seriously?"

"Seriously. If there's going to be a fight, I want it done on this plane. The wards on the manor are sound, so no beasties are getting in. Or human acolytes, thanks to our vandal."

"So, as long as we stay inside, we won't be attacked?" Alex's question is way too light-hearted for the situation. "Sounds too easy."

"That's because it is."

"Liza's right. The real threat isn't outside. It's in here with us."

At their looks of confusion, Liza jumps in again. "It's me. If Hecate is able to break through Pong's shielding, then she'll be able to take my mind over completely. I could kill you all."

Her announcement is met by silence. I can't help looking at Alex. As a hedge witch, his life has just a touch of magic in it. Nowhere near as much as mine does, and certainly not as much danger as mine does. We both know he's in over his head, but he's not the kind of guy to sit back and not try to help. No way he wasn't going to be with me in this fight. I'm glad he's here, but at the same time, I really want to send him home. Even now I'm still not sure he fully understands what he's getting into.

"Where's Dixon?" Alex's question is an innocent one, but it still makes the lump of concrete in my gut lurch.

Liza saves me from answering. "He isn't here." The lack of emotion in her voice kills any follow-up questions.

Before the silence gets too heavy I redirect everyone back to the task at hand. "Okay then. Let's do another round, make sure the house is locked up tight. I want to—"

"Um, Adrienne?"

"Yeah, Liza?"

"Shoes?"

My own stocking feet wiggle up at me from the carpet. *Come on, Adrienne. Get your head in the game.* "Right. Shoes. I guess I'll start in the kitchen. Let's go."

My boots live on a mat in the kitchen, right next to Dixon's. Of course his boots are still here. He wore his sneakers yesterday.

I'm still staring at the boots when Mason finds me. "We've got this under control, Adrienne."

"I should have gone after him." I hadn't wanted to tell Mason about Dixon. Or about Andrew and Heather. Or about the Immortal. Didn't want to admit my own failings to him. But he needed to know the stakes tonight.

"Sounds like he didn't give you much of a choice."

"I still should have tried. Stupid. Why does he have to be such a stupid kid? There's still time. If I left now, maybe I could—"

"No, Adrienne. There's not time. Dixon is fine. You know that. Your priority tonight is Liza."

From anyone else, I may have accepted the rebuke, but not from him. Not when I know he's right and my nerves are so frazzled I'm about to snap in two. "So, this is your play? Telling me what to do? Bossing me around, just like old times? You've just been waiting for this all to fall apart on me, haven't you, so you can swoop in, pick up the pieces, and make me feel like shit. Just like old times, all right."

"That's not what this is about, and if you were thinking clearly—"

"Get your hand off me." I snarl the words at Mason as he attempts to touch my shoulder.

"Hey, easy." Alex slides between us, like we're beta fish who won't attack if we can't see each other. He places his hand over mine, stilling it as it frantically yanks on my laces. "Mason's right, Adrienne. Look, it's already dark outside. I hate to say it, but Dixon is going to have to wait. Tonight's about Liza. We'll make do without him."

"Where is Liza?" None of us noticed that she didn't follow us into the kitchen. I mentally kick myself for flying off the handle at Mason. He didn't even deserve it. This time.

"I'll find her." Trusting I'm in my right mind, Alex stands back up and leaves me with Mason, who's busy looking out the window.

"Adrienne?"

"Yeah?"

A long, lingering howl from outside interrupts us. Then a hundred more voices join it in chorus, howls and yips echoing from all directions.

"Finish getting those boots on."

Twenty-Five

"They're just dogs, right?"

Alex's naivete makes me grimace. "On their own, yeah. See that one? That's Mrs. Wallace's shih tzu, Fluffykins. He's just a dog. A really sweet one, actually. But tonight? Tonight they're an army."

We wait for the wards to stop them, even though we know they won't. They're just dogs. The manor isn't warded against regular animals.

"How is she doing this?"

They all look at me. "The literature says Hecate's associated with dogs, but she's always pictured with hellhounds, not regular dogs."

Mason's look says I dropped the ball on this one. He's given me that look a lot today. For once, I don't think he's wrong. "Remember, these are people's pets. Nonlethal force if you can, but don't take any stupid risks. Kill them if you have to." A collective shudder passes over the room, the thought of butchering all of our neighbors' pets not sitting well with anyone.

That's all the time we have to think it over. Glass shatters, and the house fills with the barks and growls of our attackers. We closed all the first-floor doors we could to hamper their progress, but nothing could be done about the large picture windows in the living room. Through them leap a pair of rottweilers and a great dane, followed by a rainbow of labradors. Their front line.

Mason is the quickest with a spell, stopping the dane in his tracks. "Ventus!" My gust of wind, bolstered by Enyo, knocks the rottweilers into the labradors and sends two of them flying back out into the yard. Liza is working on the window, vines bursting up through the carpet and stretching toward the ceiling. For a split second, I think we have a chance.

Then a crash comes from down the hall as one of the doors gives way. At the same time, Liza lets out an ear-splitting scream and collapses to the floor, her vines withering and dying without her to sustain them. Still conscious, she claws at her head, screaming incoherently.

"They're a distraction!" I call to the guys, rushing to Liza's side. Pong is already there, snuggling into her neck, snarling softly as he battles Hecate for control of her mind. Because that's exactly what this attack is about. The dogs are to keep us busy while Hecate takes back what is hers.

"A little help here!" I've hesitated long enough. Alex is besieged in the doorway, fending off canines with a baseball bat. Mason is covering the window, but they're coming in too quickly for him to handle them all. As I watch, a yorkie slips past and latches on to his ankle. Any other time, the dance he does trying to shake it off would have given me many amusing memories.

"Alex! Get down!" He drops to the floor, and I send a gust of wind roaring down the hallway. It gives him the breathing room he needs, but only for a second. I change tactics. "Quae! Quae! Quae!" One by one, dogs drop as the containment spell takes hold. They tangle in the feet of the dogs behind them, slowing them down, but not enough.

I'm so focused on the hall I've forgotten about the window. I pay for it with a set of fangs in my calf, tearing straight through the leg of my jeans. I spin, which is probably the worst thing to do, because it rips my leg out of the labrador's mouth, tearing muscle along with it. The dog doesn't miss a beat, lunging for my throat instead. *Why don't I have anything in my hands?* It's an oversight I need to immediately rectify. I let the dog hit me, falling backward into a roll and using its momentum to pitch it over my head. I hear it hit the far wall, but can't spare the time to look for it.

Another crash, this time from the direction of the kitchen. "They're through the back door!" And suddenly we have three fronts instead of two. Mason appears at my side, breathing heavily and bleeding from several long scratches. "We can't keep knocking them back. They just get up and come back again."

"I know. We need a change of venue."

"Upstairs?"

"Upstairs."

Easier said than done. The press of canines in the living room makes navigating the space nearly impossible. When I have a breath, I hit the little ones with a containment spell and kick them over against the wall. The big ones, though, can't be deterred. Fangs bared, they go for the throat at their first opportunity. With reluctance, I draw my silver knife, the familiar weight of it for the first time not the least bit comforting.

I spare a glance at Alex. He's holding his own, though he's bleeding freely from bites and scratches on all of his exposed skin. As I watch, his foot snaps out in a kick I taught him, giving me a quick flash of pride. The saint bernard before him takes it on the chin, reeling backward and shaking his head. Liza has managed to rise onto her knees, swaying back and forth, mouth moving silently in whatever spells she's using against Hecate. The dogs are leaving her alone. Of course they are.

A sudden whimper snaps my attention back to the dog fight, and Enyo gets barreled over as the pair of rottweilers return, slamming into my chest. My knife hand comes up of its own accord, the wet squelch of impact making my stomach lurch. I toss the body into its companion, freeing my legs and allowing me to roll back to my feet. I'm facing off against the second rottweiler when he appears in the doorway of the living room, coming through the rarely-used front door. The Immortal, looking imposing and avenging and righteous all at the same time. He wades into the fray, seemingly unconcerned about the slavering dogs rushing to meet him. *Duh. They can't touch him.* He shoves them out of his way as he moves, as he might an errant chair. He doesn't stop to engage.

He isn't here to help. "Liza! Run!"

I spin in time to see her hear my warning, her eyes snapping open to locate the new threat. Her lips don't stop moving, though. She can't stop, can't let her focus waver, can't give an inch, or Hecate wins. Her gaze stops on the Immortal. He's halfway across the room, unhurried, hampered by the press of the dogs but still moving determinedly forward. Pong at her heels, Liza runs, slipping and staggering, trying to flee despite the onslaught against her mind.

"Mason!" He can't help me. He's even farther away from her than I am, taking the high ground on the back of the couch. Alex has disappeared, but I can still hear the sounds of conflict from down the hall. Neither of them could get to her in time.

I run. It's hard, slogging through the sheer mass of bodies stuffed into the living room. My motion attracts the attention of every dog in the room. True dogs at heart, they can't resist the sight of fleeing prey. The Immortal disappears into the kitchen, where the coast is clear and he can gain ground. I'm only a few seconds behind him, but in that time he's already out the back door. My sword is waiting for me on the back of my chair, forgotten in the rush to get my boots on and get back to a more defensible position. I snatch it up and bolt outside.

The dogs follow, picking up speed on the open ground. I can hear the pounding paws behind me, then the Immortal flicks his hand and the pounding turns to yelps of pain. A quick glance back shows me the mob of dogs leaping and snapping at some kind of invisible wall. *He couldn't have done that inside?* Trapped with them is Enyo, lagging behind to guard my exit.

"Immortal!" He slows, turning to face me, expression cold and harsh. He may not be in a hurry, but I am, sprinting until I can swing in front of him, ignoring the shooting pain through my torn leg muscle. "I won't let you do this."

"You cannot stop me, little mage. You know this."

"Like hell I can't."

He sighs, and that stony visage cracks, just a little. "Do not fight me on this. You know it must be done."

"No, I don't, and it doesn't! She's just a girl!"

"She is the vessel of Hecate, and I cannot allow her to live."

"So be it." I brandish the sword, and he sighs at me again, more in exasperation than anything else. Hoping against hope, I glance wildly around for Liza, praying I don't see her. She didn't make it far. In the moonlight I can make out her huddled form crouched on the grass, once again holding her head and rocking violently.

"She will lose this fight." He advances again, daring me to swing first.

I do. The sword slices through empty air as he evades the attack, but he doesn't counter. "Fight me," I growl at him.

"No."

"Fight me!" I swing again, driving forward, aiming for where I think he'll end up after he dodges.

We're both surprised when the sword finds its mark. The blade cuts deep, thudding into the bone of his shoulder. He roars in pain, lashing out with raw magic that sends me flying. The sword is wrenched from my grip and I land hard.

I don't even have time to recover. The Immortal is there, yanking me up, blood pouring down his arm. "Why are you making me do this?" he roars into my face. It's the first time I've seen him lose control, truly lose it, and it's terrifying. In the next breath, he slams me back down into the ground, hard enough to make the frosted earth give way beneath me. "Stay down."

I couldn't get up if I wanted to. It's taking everything I have just to draw breath through the crushing pain in my ribs. The

Immortal leaves me behind, staying on target. "No," I try to rasp, but only a cough comes out.

Across the yard, a ring of fire springs up, encircling the Immortal and Liza. Through the flames I see the glint of silver, and I know the Immortal has drawn his blade. "No," I hiss, stronger this time, forcing the air out, forcing my limbs to move. A low growl rumbles over the property, fierce and menacing. Pong. Liza's last line of defense.

The Immortal's words float back to me as I stagger to my feet. "I have no quarrel with you, beast. But I will kill you if I must." Pong's answering growl says yes, he must.

The Immortal's attention diverted, I'm able to make my way toward the ring of fire. I can't stand fully upright, and I can only take half breaths, but I can't let her down. I have to attack, now, while he's distracted.

I'm not the only one who has that thought. With a barbaric yell, Alex hurdles the flames and rockets toward the Immortal. He catches him around the waist in a full tackle and takes him down. Pong leaps onto the two of them as they go down, and they become a thrashing mass of limbs and fur and grunts. I make my way to Liza, dropping to the ground beside her and wrapping an arm around her shoulder.

"Come on, we have to go." My voice comes out as barely a whisper, but I know she hears it.

"Adrienne!" The voice screams my name, and the shock of hearing it makes my head snap up. "Adrienne!"

The young woman holding the gun is only one of half a dozen present, sporting burns on her arms and singed hair where she came through the fire. She takes in the current events with an air of detachment, then fixates on me again. "You."

My mind takes only a fraction of a second to register the long, silky gown the young woman is wearing, embroidered with the symbol of a torch on her left shoulder. "You serve Hecate." Only my mouth moves, but she seems to understand.

"We serve the Infernal Goddess, yes. We are here to see that her desires tonight are met and usher her into this world with all the glory due her name." The young woman continues, spouting out Hecate's virtues, but I tune her out. The flames all around us flicker in the lenses of her glasses, but it's like she doesn't even see the chaos. I see it. The fire still rages, lighting up the backyard like the noonday sun. Pong lies motionless in the grass. Alex is down, too, still conscious but clutching his stomach. The Immortal is still, staring in confusion at the woman with the gun, waiting for the scenario to play itself out.

"You're not listening!" Her nearly hysterical screech brings my attention snapping back. "The Infernal Goddess told me you were not worthy, and now I understand. Count yourself blessed to meet your end in such a quick fashion." The young woman raises the gun, pointing it deadlocked at my forehead. "Goodbye, Adrienne Young. May Hecate have mercy on your soul."

I try to draw on my magic, but between the eye I'm keeping on the Immortal and my own inability to draw breath, I can't achieve the focus I need. I try to think a wind spell in her direction, but all that happens is a breeze that swirls the leaves around by her feet.

She clicks the safety off. I'm still staring at her, straight into her eyes, so I know the exact moment hers go dead. She stays upright a moment, blood pouring from her eyes and nose, before her legs crumble and she crashes to the ground. Beside me, Liza's hand drops, and it's then I realize her chanting has gone silent.

"No!" This time the whisper comes through, and I grab her with both hands, shaking her. "Liza!"

A manic giggle bursts from her lips, and her eyes snap open, boring into mine. Instead of Liza's chocolatey brown eyes, I'm staring into orbs darker than the abyss, with flecks of red glowing like charcoal.

"Hecate."

Twenty-six

I CAN'T MOVE. MY brain registers that I'm holding Hecate, but my eyes still see Liza. I just crouch there, staring down at her, willing it not to be true.

Then suddenly it's no longer my decision. A hand on my shoulder shoves me roughly backward, and metal sings as the Immortal swings his blade. My heart stops, and I lurch forward, reaching uselessly for his arm, trying to call it back somehow.

An oof, and a thud, and a giggle. The voice that speaks is the most beautiful sound I've ever heard, and it chills me to my core. "The girl's magic is...strange. Benign. Like it doesn't want to hurt you."

The Immortal answers from the ground. "Maybe the child is stronger than you thought." Hearing him come to Liza's defense after he just tried to kill her is too much. Strength floods my limbs as my adrenaline surges, and I rise to my feet, hobbling back to where Liza now stands over the Immortal, the cruel smile foreign and disturbing on her lips.

"How does it feel to know you have lost, Deacon? That you have wasted your immortality in your foolish pursuit to prevent this very thing from happening?"

"You have not yet triumphed, you putrid daughter of a toad. You wear the child's body, but the magic you wield is hers, not your own. There is still time."

A thoughtful expression comes over her face. "Perhaps there would have been. Perhaps you and the mage would have been able to stop me. Too bad you will not get that chance."

Before I can do anything, before it even occurs to me to do anything, Hecate raises her hands and shouts something unintelligible at the sky. The words are sharp and brutal, and the Immortal flinches away from them as if just the sound of them causes him pain. *Why is he still down? Get up!* As she finishes speaking, a mighty crack sounds through the night, and the earth opens beneath the Immortal. It just splits right open into a gaping chasm and the Immortal falls. I stumble toward it, mouth agape, but it snaps shut before I can reach it. I whirl on Hecate, who is watching me carefully but making no move to attack.

I force the words out past my screaming ribs. "What did you do to him?" It takes everything I have to keep my voice from shaking. I will not show weakness in front of her.

"He is alive. My curse holds, and the child cannot kill him."

"Why? Why are you doing this? Why do you need her?" I can feel my control slipping through my fingers, my last words coming out more of a plea than a demand.

There is no emotion in her response. "I am only reclaiming what was stolen from me. The child is a tool, nothing more."

"Then take me instead. Please, let her go."

This time a sneer crosses her lips. "I would never occupy a tainted vessel, child. I can smell your impurity from here."

She turns in a slow circle, surveying the scene around her, seemingly satisfied. Then in the firelight, which is beginning to dim without the Immortal to sustain it, her eyes flicker. For the barest moment, those chocolatey pupils emerge, wide and terrified.

"Liza!"

In a flash they're gone, and Hecate's anger blazes out into the night. With a flourish, she waves her hands again, and once more the earth shakes. At her feet, skeletal arms burst forth from the ground, wrapping themselves around her legs. As one, they wrench her down, pulling her with a single fluid motion into the earth.

"No!" My hands collide with the solid dirt only an inch behind her hair, little bones snapping in my fingers at the force of the impact. "No!" Despite the pain I scrabble at the dirt, clawing it, raking it back, frantically trying to reach her. I shove back the little voice that says it's pointless, that she's gone, that I failed her. Sobbing and screaming and digging, I go and I go and I go until I have nothing left to give, until my nails are broken and bloody, until I can no longer see past the gunk in my eyes, until I collapse shuddering and wheezing into the hole.

The next time I see the sky, the sun is coming up. It isn't visible yet; just a pink streak announcing that morning is on its way. It isn't fair. The sun shouldn't rise on a world without Liza in it.

There's a blanket draped over my shoulders, and the ground is cold beneath my body. Enyo is snuggled against my side, sharing what heat her lithe form has to spare. Someone is sitting next to me, close enough to be available but not too close to crowd me. Alex.

"Hey," he says softly when he notices my open eyes.

I squeeze them shut again, not willing to accept a position in this world anymore.

"I know you don't want to hear this, but you should probably go inside. I didn't know how badly you were hurt, and I didn't want to move you until you could tell me." Then, softer, "We're going to get her back, Adrienne."

How does he know? That's right. He was here. He saved her from the Immortal.

I still don't answer, but something in my face must make him think it's okay to approach me. "I'm going to pick you up, all right? You need to get off the ground. Just tell me if it hurts too much."

Of course it hurts too much. But that's not what he means, so I keep my mouth shut. Even when he jostles my ribs and knocks all the air out of my lungs, I keep my mouth shut. There's nothing to say.

Ever so gently, Alex carries me inside and deposits me on the couch. The living room looks...normal. No sign of the chaos that reigned in here last night or the destruction we wreaked. Alex notices me noticing. "Mason's been busy. He was trapped inside, with that wall thing, but when...and then, the dogs, they just left, like nothing ever..."

He trails off and sits down beside me, wrapping an arm around my shoulders, the same way I used to snuggle Liza when she needed me. The thought brings fresh tears, and I allow him to draw my head down onto his shoulder.

The sound of footsteps gets my attention. Mason's are heavy and decisive, but the others are light and plodding, almost hesitant. "Here she is." Mason's voice is quiet and tender, almost reverent. When I see his companion I understand why.

"Willow." It's the first word I've spoken, and my voice is husky and cracked. I've always liked Willow. She rarely leaves the reservation, but on the occasions I've met her, she's been kind to me.

"You poor thing. Here, let me have a look at you." Her brown hands are warm and soft on my face, yet firm and supportive on my back as she navigates me into lying down. "You should have called me earlier," she scolds Mason.

"I'm sorry, grandmother. I judged her injuries non-life threatening, and did not wish to wake you." She isn't his grandmother. Most of the magi call her that.

"It is not her injuries that concern me. It is her heart." With no more ado, she lays her hands on me again, one on my forehead and one on my chest, and begins to intone in a steady rhythm, like the beating of a drum. Almost immediately something shifts inside me, and I'm able to draw a full, deep breath. She keeps chanting, and warm tingles spread all over my body. They're relaxing, like a massage, and I feel myself fading out again. Before I fall all the way under, I hear her orders to Mason: "Let her rest. As long as she needs. Only she can heal what is truly broken inside."

The next time I wake up, I'm in my own bed. The sun is bright through my window, and something warm is pressed against my back. I reach for Enyo, to stroke her head, and hit Alex instead. He wakes in an instant.

"Adrienne?" His voice is panicked, like he caught me trying to sneak away.

"Mmff."

A moment later he's hovering over me, concern clouding his sleepy eyes. "How are you feeling?"

"Like I got trampled by a herd of horses and then a goddess stole my sister." There's no humor in my flat response, but he seems happy just to hear my voice.

"I'm glad you got some sleep. Can I get you anything? Some food? Water? I can run you a bath."

What I want is for him to stop worrying over me like a mother hen to her chicks, but I can't tell him that. He cares, and it's sweet. It's just suffocating. "A bath would be nice."

He grins like that's the best thing I could have said, and bounds out of bed. A minute later the bedroom starts to fill with steam, the scent of lavender reaching my nose from my stash of bubbles. Now that I'm thinking about it, and about the sweat and dirt and blood that's probably covering my entire body, a bath actually does sound kind of nice. I drag myself out of bed and into the bathroom as Alex turns the faucet off. Ignoring his presence completely, I start peeling off my grimy clothes and tossing them into a heap in the corner.

"Oh, um, I'll just, yeah, I'll be outside..." Alex stammers his way out of the bathroom as I step into the scalding water. I sink down into it, letting the heat seep into my body, chasing away the memory of lying on the cold ground. But then the reason

I was lying on the cold ground pushes its way to the forefront, and I have to choke back a sob. *She's really gone.*

"Adrienne? Are you okay?" He heard me. I don't answer, hoping he'll take the hint and go away.

He doesn't. A soft knock on the bathroom door, and then, "Can I come in?"

"Why not."

"Do you want to pull the curtain closed, or..."

"I have bubbles."

"Okay, then." Alex's face appears, peeking down at me in the tub, that same concern in his eyes. He takes a seat on the toilet and stares down at his hands. "Last night..."

I stiffen, and he flinches, like he doesn't want to hurt me but has to do it anyway.

"Last night, some crazy shit went down, and I'm not sure I understand it. I know you probably don't want to talk about it right now, but when you do, I have some questions."

"Hecate took over Liza's mind. Then she took her body away. The end."

"That's not...I know that's not all there is to it. I'm sorry. This is a bad time, and I'm being a jerk. I'll ask Mason about it later."

Now I feel like the jerk. Not only that, I feel weak. Here I am, drowning in the bath and being depressed, when I should be taking action. Making a plan. Getting her back. That's what a real leader would be doing.

"I'm sorry." My words come out barely louder than a whisper, but he hears them. I slosh around, sitting up a bit more so I can see his face. "I haven't even asked how you're doing."

"I'm fine, Adrienne. I really am. Only minor injuries, and Mason was able to fix me up last night. He-he didn't feel comfortable handling yours."

A pause stretches between us. I get his need to talk about it. If I'm being objective, I probably need to talk about it, too. It's hard to make the words come, though. "You were there. You saw it. You saw all of it."

"Yeah. I saw it. Whatever it was. And...and that girl..."

That girl. "Liza saved my life. That girl was going to kill me, and she...she shouldn't have. She stopped fighting to save me. It was only a second, but it was enough to let Hecate in."

Now we're looking at each other, really looking at each other. My voice drops, intimacy and gratitude bleeding through. "You saved her."

"I tried." He opens his mouth to say something else, but closes it abruptly, his gaze dropping. "You, um, you're losing your bubbles."

So I am. Not only that, my water is now a disgusting shade of grayish brown, and I haven't even gotten my hair wet.

"I should go." Alex leaves abruptly, without even giving me the chance to respond. I almost smile. Almost, but not quite. My heart still hurts too much to commit to a smile. Holding my breath, I dunk myself all the way under and begin to scrub.

Alex is sitting on my bed when I finally emerge, pruny and clean but no less sad.

"Hey, I'm sorry about all that." I let him draw me into a hug, actually raising my arms and hugging him tightly back. The physical touch is nice, and I burrow my head into his neck, just feeling him breathe.

A knock at the door interrupts our hug. "Adrienne? You awake?"

"Come in."

Mason pops his head in, making a face at the sight of me snuggling Alex in only a towel. "You need to come downstairs."

Alex interjects. "She's supposed to be resting. Anything you have can wait."

Mason ignores him, looking me straight in the eye. "Dixon's home."

Dixon's waiting anxiously on the couch, where I assume Mason threatened him into staying. He jumps up when I come into the living room. "Adrienne! What happened? Where's Liza? What's—"

"Shut up." He falls silent at the vehemence in my voice. I advance on him, hands trembling. "You left us."

"I—"

"You left us. You left her. Hecate took her, and you weren't even here!" I can hear the edge of hysteria in my voice, but I don't even try to reign it in. I don't want to.

His face drains of color, brown skin taking on a grayish hue. "What did you say?"

I stop in front of him, emphasizing our height difference as I stare down into his face. I want him to feel small. My voice goes deathly calm. "Liza is gone. Hecate broke her, and then she took her, and you weren't here to protect her. I'll never forgive you for that." I stalk away, leaving Dixon gaping behind me. Somewhere deep down, very deep, I know my words are unfair. Dixon couldn't have saved her. But I don't care. I want him to feel every bit as bad as I feel, every bit of grief and guilt and mind-numbing pain. I don't look back as I leave the living room, avoiding the stairs and heading down the hallway that hardly anyone ever uses, searching for some hidden, forgotten room where I can sink into myself in peace.

Twenty-seven

T HE LIBRARY IN OUR pocket plane is creepy. It smells musty and makes old house settling noises that sound like footsteps sneaking down the hall. One of these noises stirs me from a nap, but it's gone before I can pinpoint it. I needed to wake up anyway. I've lost track of the time I've spent hidden away down here, but it's longer than I should have. They've come looking for me a few times. At least, they've made a show of it. Walking around, calling my name, not actually expecting me to answer. Just checking to see if I'm ready yet.

I wasn't ready. But I am now. With each passing hour the gloom that settled over me with Liza's abduction has slowly melted away, revealing the slow-burning fire I'm going to need to get her back. I *am* going to get her back. I'll need help, though.

It takes a lot of bending and stretching to be able to stand upright once I manage to get myself uncurled. The rocking chair looked comfy when I flopped down into it, but in time it turned against me. At my feet, Enyo stretches herself awake, too. She's been my constant companion, not even leaving to eat or drink. By the emptiness in my own stomach, I know she's got to be hurting, too. Friends first, though. Then food.

Morning or night, I have no idea. Alex finds me before I take more than a couple of steps, and he smiles to see me upright. He's carrying a plate with a sandwich and some carrot sticks, and a bottle of the magic blue gatorade. "Hey, you. Mason let me in."

"Hey, yourself. I was just coming to find you. I want to talk to everybody, I—"

"Food first," he interrupts. I open my mouth to protest, but he won't let me get a word in. "It's been more than a day, Adrienne. Food first."

"Fine." I snatch the plate from him and settle onto an ottoman, far away from the tortuous rocking chair. I take a big bite to show him I'm behaving, then start talking around the mouthful of food. "I'm going after Liza, but there's something else I need to do first."

Alex starts. "Liza's gone. You know that. Right now—"

"Gone, yes. Dead, no. Hecate still needs her. I heard it from her own lips. Liza's lips. Whatever. She was using Liza's magic, not her own, because she was only controlling Liza's body. She hasn't taken full possession of her yet. She still needs the comet to be able to rise. That means Liza's still alive."

"Slow down, Adrienne. I want to talk about this with you, but you need to take care of yourself first. Starting with swallowing that bite. Then maybe a shower. Some sleep in your own bed. Then tomorrow, when you're rested, we can decide on a plan."

Alex's logic makes sense in my head, but my body rejects being rational. After so many hours of inaction, my body is humming to get moving. To pummel something. To make progress.

"Come on." I can barely focus on eating. My body needs something else, and it's not going to let me rest without it. Physical activity has always been my outlet. It's how I find clarity, dissolving the world into simple things like sweat and breath.

"What do you—Adrienne? Where are you going?" I'm out the library door before Alex catches up, still stuffing sandwich in my mouth because I know he won't be happy until it's gone. My stomach rumbles, pleased with the offering but a little uneasy at the sudden movement. I ignore it. This is what I want. It's what I need.

Alex pipes up again when I lead him into the training room. "Are you sure now is the best time to—"

"Yes, I am." When he enters, I knock his feet out from under him with a sweep kick. He recovers before he hits the floor, landing in a roll and popping back up to face me. "Very good. You're improving."

"You're supposed to be eating."

"All done. See?" I wiggle my empty fingers at him to prove it. "Now hit me."

"I still don't think—"

"Hit me." I swing at him, slowly, giving him the opportunity to block, which he does. Then he retaliates with something I didn't teach him. "You've been training with Mason, haven't you?" *He got over his animosity quickly.*

"Once, yeah. I wanted to be ready for, you know, whatever comes next. He's not nearly as fun a teacher as you are though."

"Of course not. He probably enjoyed the opportunity to beat on you, too." That's all the time I allow for banter. The restless energy building in my body has reached the breaking point. We spar for the next hour, and I'll admit I whail on Alex a little harder than I probably should. He takes it in stride, defending himself the best he can, and even gets in a couple good hits of his own.

With a tackle, I take him down to the mat. I haven't taught him grappling yet, but he still does a decent job holding his own. It's only a few minutes later that we're lying next to each other, panting and still.

"Tell me what's been going on up there." I haven't wanted to think about it. About what could have changed the night of the full moon. What havoc Hecate could be wreaking while I've been catatonic.

It takes Alex a moment to catch his breath before he can answer. "It's been tense. Mason did a patrol last night, and he saw hellhounds."

That gets my attention. "But—"

"I know. Hecate's strength has grown now that she has Liza. She's strong enough to send the hellhounds without a human summoner or the added boost of the full moon."

"How do you know about—"

"Mason and Dixon do a lot of talking. I do a lot of listening. Other things are weird in town, too. Half the school didn't show up yesterday. Teachers, too. The ones who did looked like they'd been up for days. The timing can't be a coincidence."

"No, it can't. One of Hecate's weapons in this plane is nightmares. They can be pretty intense. Trust me, I've had my fair share of them. If she's affecting people en masse, things could get bad pretty fast. Especially now that she's not limited to the full moon." A world where Hecate can exert her influence without restraint isn't a world I want to see. There's a lot of damage she can do in the three weeks until the comet.

"So, do you think you're ready to head back upstairs?"

"I think I've been putting it off long enough." Once we exit the training room, though, I veer back to the library instead. Enyo didn't follow us to the training room, preferring to stay behind and devour the plate of food Alex brought for her. I hadn't even noticed the second plate. Now, sated, she's waiting patiently for me to return for her.

"Hey, girl. I didn't forget about you. We have a big job ahead of us. Are you ready?"

Her thumping tail would be answer enough, but the bond between us also thrums with both eagerness and contentment. Eagerness to get back to work, and contentment to follow my lead, wherever I might take her. Before we can leave, though, Alex notices the books. They're across the room, but there's no missing the haphazard way they're piled around the tables, four of them currently propped open.

"Hecate?"

"Mostly. A few on non-combat spells, upping my defensive capabilities. This one here," the book I heft up is four inches thick and bound in some kind of animal skin, "is a journal from a sixteenth century magi named Matilda Cowle. It's the oldest one we have, and the sheer amount of forgotten magic in it is astonishing. Dixon went through it a few months ago and he..." My voice trails off as the happy memory punches me in the gut. I made a lot of progress today, but the thought of Dixon still sends me spinning through a whirlpool of emotions that I'd rather not examine too closely.

Alex notices my distress. "He hasn't said anything. About you, or about the other night. He does a lot of reading though."

That's Dixon. Doing a lot of reading. "We should get upstairs."

Dixon's disembodied voice interrupts our return to the manor. "Mr. Henderson is here."

I'm unprepared to hear his voice, but those words trump the tension it brings. "Come again?"

"He brought friends."

"Shit."

Alex's eyes are full of concern when they meet mine. "This isn't going to be good, is it?"

"No. I have the feeling it's going to be very, very bad." I rub my face, digging my palms into my eyes until I see spots. It doesn't help.

"What do you want to do?" The question brings a smile to my lips. Instantly on my side. To hell with the rest of the world.

My training kicks in and my mind instantly clears, shoving my turbulent emotions to the side in favor of decisive action. "I have to go in there. They're here for me. You don't need to be a part of this, though. In fact, I'd rather you weren't. The less the council knows of your involvement with magi, the better."

"I can't just leave you to—"

"Yes, you can. Mason and Dixon are still here. I won't be alone. Hide out in the dark end of the manor. Hopefully, I'll be coming to get you. If not, sneak out when you can and go home. There's something I need you to do, and it's big."

"Anything."

"Eventually, we're going to have to wrench control of Liza's mind away from Hecate. I don't know if we can do it with brute strength, and we already know she's smarter than me. Is there some kind of potion that can help with that?"

He chuckles, a rough, desperate sound. "Here I thought you were going to ask for something hard."

"I told you it was big."

"I didn't say I couldn't do it. At least I'll have plenty of time to figure it out."

"Thank you. I have to go in there now, but I'll call you when I can."

"If you're sure..."

"I'm sure."

Leaving Alex isn't hard. It's my nature to protect him, and allowing him to follow me into the living room would be the exact opposite of that. Mason's in the living room, talking to Mr. Henderson. They both go quiet when I walk in, flanked by the pair of magi I picked up in the hall. Another pair are trying to be unobtrusive in the far corner. Tamara stands behind Mr. Henderson and slightly to the side.

I address Mason. "You let him in?"

"I didn't know I wasn't supposed to."

"Mr. Chandler did the right thing, Ms. Young. You were warned that this was coming. I am here to take you into custody. I would appreciate it if you accompany us of your own free will."

Yup. It's bad, all right. "What law have I broken?"

"Aiding and abetting a known murderer. Conspiracy with said murderer. And you have played some role in the disappearance of Ms. DuPage, the details of which I'm unclear on but will soon get to the bottom of."

He stops talking, seemingly pleased with himself, but nothing happens. None of the bodyguards step forward to take me. *Are they afraid of me? Or do they just not see me as a threat?* "You're on the wrong side, Mr. Henderson. Arresting me is very big mistake."

"Wait a minute," Mason interjects. "You can't just take her away. There are protocols. There are—"

"Shut up, boy. This doesn't concern you." As mind-boggling as it is to hear Mason coming to my defense, I have to agree with Mr. Henderson. He's only going to get himself into trouble.

"It most certainly does concern me. It concerns every single magi that hasn't agreed to give the council any more power than it already has. You can't just declare yourself the ruler of all of us and cart Adrienne away. If you have a grievance against her, you have to convene the entire council, not just your favorite members, and allow a mediation to take place. There has to be notice given, and affidavits filed, and—"

"Enough! Hold your tongue, boy, or you'll find yourself charged as her accomplice. Do you have any idea what she's done?"

"Tried to save the world?" Time to bring this back to me.

"Save the…? I warned you about getting tangled up with that criminal, but no, you wouldn't just let us do our jobs. How could you be so stupid as to actually believe that nonsense he was spouting about some resurrected goddess? All to cover up his own madness and justify his own crimes! And now look what your delusion has cost you. He's taken Ms. DuPage, and he's probably killed her by now, all because you—"

"Don't you dare!" I was doing fine, honestly I was, until he decided to blame me for Liza. Now the bodyguards step forward. Shaking with barely controlled rage, I take a step toward Mr. Henderson. "Don't you dare lay this one on me. I told you about Hecate. I shared information with you even when it became clear you had made up your mind not to believe me. If you were in your own mind, you would see that what I am saying is the truth. You're being controlled by Tamara, and I don't know why she wants you to believe that Hecate—"

"Hecate isn't real!" He roars the words at me, losing what little control he still had over his temper. "She's just a figment of a madman's imagination to justify the slaughter of children. Children, Ms. Young!"

"Not real? Not real? I've spoken with Hecate. I've battled her for control of Liza's mind. And I watched as she overpowered that little girl and dragged her into the earth, so don't you dare tell me she isn't real!"

Strangely, my words have a calming effect on Mr. Henderson. The mottled purple in his face fades away, and his next words come out evenly. "Thank you, Ms. Young, for making this easier. My comrades were reluctant to come here with me tonight. They were having difficulty believing you to be a threat." Then to the guards, "Take her."

The room explodes into motion. The two guards standing behind me grab for me while the other two send spells flying my way. I duck as Mason charges, taking out my guards with a tackle. Dixon appears out of nowhere, grabbing for my hand to pull me to safety. Life-or-death situations have a tendency to put personal quarrels on hold. Enyo goes for the head honcho himself. Snarling, she launches herself as Mr. Henderson's face.

"I need to get outside," I huff to Dixon as we run for the kitchen.

"Get her!" Mr. Henderson screeches as he wrestles Enyo off and is able to draw a breath. She doesn't attack again, though. She did what she needed to do, and races to catch up with me.

"I've got this," Dixon tells me as he pulls away, shoving me out the kitchen door while beginning to chant, working a perception spell to keep them from seeing me as I make my getaway. I don't argue. There will be plenty of time to repair my relationship with Dixon, I just have to remain free long enough to do it. I run with everything I've got, which is a lot. In no time I'm past the wards and slipping into the Shadow Plane.

One thing Mr. Henderson has succeeded at is turning me into a criminal. I managed to grab my shoes on my way out the kitchen door, but have nothing else on me except the clothes I've been sleeping and now sweating in for way too long. With a little perception magic I manage to shoplift some protein bars and a burner phone. Alex picks up on the first ring.

"Bad?"

"Very bad."

"What happens now?"

"I can't avoid the council for long. I've had Mr. Henderson on the back burner, thinking the issue could wait, but it all came to a head sooner than I expected. I need you to tell Mason that Tamara holds some kind of control over Mr. Henderson's mind. Maybe he can do something about it before things get any worse. As it is, I won't find any help from the council."

"So…"

"So I'm going after someone who's on my side. I already had to, anyway. He's the only one who can help me get Liza back."

"The Immortal."

"Yeah."

Alex hesitates, then asks the question anyway. "Didn't he try to kill Liza?"

I have to force those images back down where they belong. "Yes."

"Didn't he get sucked into the earth?"

"Yes."

Hesitation again. "Then what makes you think he's even alive? And if he is, how do you expect to find him?"

"He's alive. Definitively. He can't die. As for where he is…that one's tougher. But I have a few ideas." I let my voice go soft. "I'm going to be okay. You know that, right?"

"I want to believe that, Adrienne. I believe in you, I do. But there's major stuff going down, and it's a whole lot bigger than you are. I'm afraid for you."

"I'm afraid too. But I'm coming back. I promise. And I'm bringing everyone home with me."

Twenty-eight

I ASKED LIZA ONCE about the magic tracking spell she created. It's an incredible piece of magic, and after experiencing it firsthand on Halloween, I wanted to know more about the methodology behind it. She gave me a long and complicated answer, rooted in magi history and magic theory that I didn't fully understand, but the crux of it is this: our magic is connected to us on a personal, fundamental level. Andrew and Heather knew this, too, being able to separate and identify magical signatures in their investigative work, but Liza took it a step further. Following that trail of magic back to its source was unprecedented, and as far as I know, I'm the only one to attempt it successfully. Liza's spell made me a pioneer. Now, I need to go even further.

Wherever the Immortal is, he isn't using his magic. I still have his tracker active, and it's been silent. I'm hoping that through that link I'll be able to locate him anyway. His magic is as much a part of him as mine is of me, and it's still there, whether he's using it or not. In theory, I should be able to find it.

There's a place in Greenland, a glacial cave discovered by a magi named Einar Matsen in the sixteenth century. The remains of his journal are currently buried in the pile I was just showing Alex earlier. Something about this cave makes it impervious to magical detection. He theorized it was due to the unique geological makeup of the floor of the cavern, but died before he could determine anything conclusively. If anywhere in totality is safe from the eyes of the council, this cave is it.

The Shadow Plane gets me close, but the subfreezing temperatures make the half-mile I have left to hike deadly for anyone without access to fire magic. In addition to being invisible, the cavern is a magical marvel. It's lit by a dull yellow glow without an obvious source. The internal temperature is nearly tropical, and giant ferns are not only sprouting from the bare rock, but thriving. The air hums with the sound of buzzing insects and birdsong, but none are visible. I arrange my pilfered and shoplifted herbs within reach, part of me wishing this was a social trip and I could just explore the cave instead. "Ignis," I whisper, setting bundles of herbs alight. The smoke flares up, pungent and sweet, filling my nostrils. Enyo settles herself against me, ready to lend a hand if I need it. "Here we go, sweet girl."

There's not a spell I can whisper to show me what I'm looking for. Soul searching is an obscure branch of magic, much like worship magic, fallen out of style and only remembered in texts and journals. Fortunately, I read every single one of our journals looking for the Immortal, and some other miscellaneous information stuck around in my head, too.

Like soul searching. Andrew and Heather never even mentioned it. Centuries ago, the magi believed that one could know everything there was to know about oneself by examining all their inward parts. Their body, their mind, their magic, all of it was accessible through rigorous discipline and absolute control. Those that practiced it spent a lifetime perfecting their control before attempting it. Some who weren't ready got lost inside their own minds and never found their way back out. Soul searching is dangerous and not to be undertaken lightly, especially by a novice. A novice like me.

Pushing those thoughts aside, I settle into position and rest my hands gently on my knees. There's no room for fear here. Nor doubt, nor indecision, nor guilt, nor any of the negative emotions I've allowed to take root in my mind. I spend the next hour clearing those out, one by one, identifying them and cleansing them from my mind.

Finally, I feel ready to begin. I breathe deeply of the cedar and sandalwood, close my eyes, and wait, not quite sure exactly what I'm supposed to do now. I sit like this for a while, until a dim light appears behind my right eyelid. A shadow walks in front of it, low to the ground, gangly and lean. Enyo.

The hellhound keeps walking until her full form is in view, as if she were standing in candle glow in the middle of a darkened stadium. "Hey girl," I say to her softly, out loud as well as in my head. "Are you here to help?" *Dummy. Why else would she be here?*

I walk toward Enyo, and without a sound she turns and walks back the way she came. As we walk, the darkness begins to lighten, until I'm able to detect movement around me. I stiffen, and the vision of Enyo begins to fade as my control wavers. *Easy, Adrienne. You're inside your own mind. Nothing is going to attack you in here.*

Enyo flickers back into view as I recenter my focus. Keeping her in my peripheral vision, I look at the scenes playing out around me. My own memories, crackling like a movie reel, all jumbled and mingling together. There I am playing in a sandbox, no more than six years old. A younger boy plays with me. He has my dark hair and my green eyes. Then a werewolf tears across the scene, with fourteen-year-old me in pursuit. There's a boy in this memory, too. Brown-haired and hazel-eyed, Mason is sporting the first dusting of stubble on his chin and screaming at me as our quarry gets away. I'm too slow, but Mason catches it, blood spraying all over the sandbox. Six-year-old me doesn't notice, just keeps shoveling sand into a hot pink bucket. I look away. This isn't what I came here for.

With that thought, the motion around me ceases, as if I were in control of it. *Well, this is your mind. Who else would be in control of it?* Still, I don't really know how I did it, so I keep following Enyo and thinking about what I'm looking for: the Immortal's magic. The moment I think of the Immortal, his face pops into my mind, and memories begin to flow around me again. My first sight of him, standing over Heather's body, our fight forever seared into my brain. I remember every detail: the way he moved, the way his voice sounded, the rage and frustration I felt when I couldn't hurt him. The knowledge that in my anger and my desperation, I would get myself killed if it meant killing him.

A moment later I look for Enyo, ready to resume our journey, but she isn't there. There's nothing except my memories of the Immortal. No, wait. There she is...wrong again. It's just a memory of her, sleeping stretched out on my bedroom floor.

I know she's a powerful being with a brand of magic all her own, but it's hard to remember that when she's whimpering and twitching her feet like she's chasing a dream-rabbit. More memories tumble in: Enyo devouring a mouse she found in the pantry, Enyo launching herself at Mr. Henderson's face, Enyo bumping her head against my chest while I sit on the floor and cry.

A snarl sounds in my ear, then I feel myself being hauled roughly backward. The visions in front of me splinter, then shatter like glass, and I'm left blinking into the sudden blackness. Then my head slams down onto the rock of the cavern floor and I'm breathing cedar and sandalwood again. A hunger pang tears through my stomach as if I haven't eaten in days. *How long was I in there? It only felt like a moment...*

Enyo is still sleeping beside me, giving no evidence that she just ventured into my mind. Or that she pulled me back out again. Now I understand why soul searching is so dangerous. One stray thought and I was swamped in my own memories without ever realizing I was trapped in them. If Enyo hadn't found me...

I give an involuntary shudder. Still, I have to go back in. I didn't find what I was looking for, and I have no way to mark the passage of time while I'm inside. Already I'm sure more time has passed than I can afford to lose. "You coming with me again, girl?" I give Enyo's head a scratch, and she grunts and shuffles herself around. "All right then. No time like the present."

I close my eyes again, and this time Enyo is waiting for me. "I won't wander off again," I promise. "Lead on."

This time I ignore the flow of memories. As much as I'd like to examine some more closely, I can't take that chance again. The tighter I hold my focus, the less movement I see. I'm unprepared for the emotions, though. Rage, elation, shame, lust, they all come rushing in, taunting me, begging me to spend just a little while with them. They're surface emotions, though. My magic is at the core of my being. It makes sense the remnants of my spell would be there, too. I need to go deeper.

Still Enyo leads on. It feels like forever, and who knows, it might be. The few minutes I spent in my head last time turned out to be hours, maybe days, of real time. Finally, my foot touches down, and the rumble of a gong thrums through my entire body. We're here. My...center, for lack of a better word. My core. Who I am.

I don't look at anything. Don't let myself wonder what might be contained down here. That's information I don't need or want to have. No one should know exactly who they are, one hundred percent. Instead, I keep my intent focused on my goal. Enyo waits patiently by my side, her task complete. A shimmer appears in the darkness, growing brighter the more I concentrate on it. I step forward, entranced, straining to see it clearly. I hear my own words, reciting the spell that linked the Immortal's magic to mine. With the reflection, a tether appears in my hand, glowing silver-white. It stretches infinitely forward, fading into obscurity in the distance. "This is it," I whisper to myself in my excitement.

I try to move, to follow the tether, but my feet are stuck fast. I try pulling the tether forward, hand over hand. It doesn't budge.

I pull harder. Still nothing. I strain against the invisible force keeping me immobile. Nope.

"Enyo. Come on. I need some help." The hellhound just stares at me, sadness in her eyes. She's not strong enough, either. Frustration knifes through me. "No!" I scream into the darkness, my voice echoing around me. My control slips, and the darkness spins, trying to draw me in.

Sinking to my knees, I let a few tears fall. The emotions come tiptoeing back, and this time I reach out and touch one. Despair. How appropriate. It snuggles into the forefront of my mind, gluing my eyes to the tether. I came all this way. I found it, I'm here. I'm just not strong enough.

A growl rumbles though the blackness, and for a moment I assume it's Enyo, coming to wrench me out of the pit again. But it's not. She's here with me, head hanging low, sharing my despair with me. Besides, the growl is too deep, too primal, too angry to have come from her. Then I sense a presence intruding into my mind, something big and powerful, shaking my foundations as it approaches.

Alarm bells go off, warning me to protect myself, telling me I'm vulnerable here. I leap to my feet, a spell flying to my lips, but I'm too late. Another mind overlaps mine, sweeping me up in its vastness and...familiarity?

"Pong?"

The panther growls in acknowledgment, and the tether still clenched in my hand burns red-hot. The next instant I'm flying along it, shooting off into the darkness so fast my figurative stomach rolls.

I come to a sudden stop, head snapping forward hard enough to smack my teeth together. It's no longer dark. Instead, the air glows orange and shimmers as if baking under the hottest sun. The landscape stretches endlessly in all directions, unbroken by the slightest rise. The ground beneath my feet is parched and brittle, deep cracks waiting to snag my shoes if I try walking carelessly.

The Immortal lies at my feet, for all appearances dead. His body makes no movement; even his chest doesn't rise and fall with breath. His eyes are open, dry and shriveled like his lips. Insect-like creatures swarm over his body, the same lifeless brown color as the ground, giving it a ripple effect. Their shells clack together as they bump into each other, endlessly moving but never going anywhere.

"Found you," I whisper, half-expecting him to answer. He isn't dead. But then I'm not really here. That realization snaps me back into my own mind, and the light fades as the darkness crowds back in. Enyo is waiting for me, mouth clamped down on the tether. "Not going to lose me again, huh? You want to get out of here?"

I come to myself more slowly this time, Enyo carefully leading me back through the intricacies of my mind. It's a struggle to even open my eyes. My herbs are long burned out, piles of ash that aren't even smoking. The hunger has vanished from my stomach, replaced by a dull, empty ache. I try to push up with my arms, but they're too weak to lift my body, and just the effort sends my head spinning fast enough to make me retch. Only a thin stream of bile comes out. A dark shadow has me lifting my eyes, straining to see the form hovering over mine.

Pong's head lowers and bumps against my shoulder, somehow comforting and unnerving at the same time. He isn't my familiar, yet he's been in my head twice now, saving me and helping me. When he vanished from the backyard after Liza was taken, I assumed he had followed her. So, how did he end up in this cavern with me? My voice comes out as a raspy whisper, barely audible. "Pong, buddy, you're a conundrum. Did you want me to find the Immortal? Is that why you're here?"

Enyo whimpers beside me, claws scrabbling weakly as she also fails to rise. "My poor girl. I'm so sorry I did this to you." The effort to speak is too much, and my mind drifts, neither awake nor asleep. Dimly, the thought manifests: *I'm dying. And Enyo's dying with me.*

Then with a suddenness that has me retching again, I'm hauled into the air and dragged forward, head-first back out into the biting cold. The shift is too much for my body to bear, and I lose consciousness.

TWENTY-NINE

"**S**HE DOESN'T LOOK GOOD."

"Where's she been? It's been weeks, and not a peep from her. And now this?"

"Why are you here, anyway? There's nothing you can do for her that we can't. She needs to be with family right now."

"I don't even know where 'here' is. One minute I'm asleep, the next this massive cat is yanking me out of bed and dragging me into the Shadow Plane. He must have thought I needed to be here." A pause, then, "I obviously didn't get here on my own. Even you know that."

The bickering drags me out of a hazy sleep, and I open my eyes to see the owners of the voices flickering in and out of the edge of my vision. I must moan or something, because they cut off abruptly and hurry over to my side.

"Adrienne? Are you okay? Can you talk?" The worry in Alex's eyes is strangely comforting.

Mason's bedside manner could use some work. "Drink this." The cup he presses to my lips is brimming with cool water, and I manage to choke some down before my stomach lurches and spews it back out again. Mason's look of disgust is only tinged with concern when he goes for a towel.

"Here. Try this instead." Alex's strong arms lift me into a sitting position, propped against a giant mound of pillows, and he holds a spoon to my lips. It smells rich and salty, and the warmth feels good in my dried-out mouth. I swallow a couple of spoonfuls before he takes it away again.

"What are you doing? I told you you're not giving her any of that crap." Mason's scolding precedes his return, his look warning Alex not to test him.

"It's not a potion, just some bone broth. Not everything is about magic."

It may be just food, but the broth certainly feels like magic as warmth once again floods my limbs. My head stops spinning, and I'm able to focus on more than the two faces staring down at mine. Namely, the solid wood beams overhead and the wall of windows directly in front of me, looking out over crashing ocean waves. *The Immortal's house? Why would Pong bring me here?*

An important question, but not the most pressing issue at the moment. My first attempt at speaking fails, but the next time the word comes out. "Dixon."

The boys stop snapping at each other and focus their attention back on me. "What did you say?"

I swallow dryly, and Alex hurriedly feeds me a few more spoonfuls of broth. *No magic, my ass.* "Where's Dixon?"

"He's outside, checking the wards, but he'll be back in soon. Why do you want him? What do you need?" Straight to business.

"I just...do." Even with Alex's broth, my newfound strength is fading rapidly. He's still at my side, kneeling down beside my couch. I flop my arm at him, and he gets the hint, wrapping his fingers around mine. "Don't leave me." His mouth opens in reply, but I'm gone before I can hear it.

Alex is still holding my hand the next time I wake up, and this time there's no disorientation. "Hey."

"Hey." His smile scares me. It's too relieved, too genuine. It makes me think I almost died.

"Dixon?"

"Right here." The casual greeting belies the tension that thrums underneath.

I may be weak, but my head is clear, and my voice is strong as I address him. "Dixon. I'm so sorry. What I said to you...it wasn't fair. I was angry, and hurting, and I lashed out. Even if you'd been home, there's nothing you could have done. There was nothing any of us could have done."

"Adrienne, you don't need to do this now. Just rest, and when you're stronger—"

"No," I cut Alex off. "Now."

Dixon waits for us to finish before he answers. "I know that. I need you to know, though, I'm not sorry I left."

The admission leaves me speechless. I just assumed he was wallowing in regret and guilt. It never occurred to me he wasn't.

He reads the expression on my face perfectly, and his own tightens. "I found my parents, Adrienne. It wasn't what...they're not...but I got some answers about my past. I refuse to feel guilty about that. I am sorry about everything that happened, but if I had to do it again, I would still go."

An uncomfortable silence falls between us. *This isn't right. We've always gotten along. We're a team.* None of that matters, though. I can't forgive him for abandoning us, and he won't admit he was wrong to do it. We're at an impasse.

"I need your help." Personal issues aside, there's still work to be done.

"Anything." His voice isn't the eager young Dixon I used to know. It's suddenly older, calmer, confident. Like he grew up overnight.

"I found the Immortal. He's in the Barren Plane."

"Shit."

I do a double take. That's my line. "When did you start cursing?"

"The coming end of the world seemed like an appropriate time to pick up a few vices."

"Fair enough."

"No magic. No oxygen. If you go there, you'll be trapped, and dead within minutes. I know you think we need him, but going after him is suicide. You have to see that."

"I have an idea. I just need you to tell me it's possible."

Dixon sighs. "Probably, somehow. But if I think it's too risky, I'm not helping you do it. Liza comes first, and you can't go after her if you're dead."

"Duly noted. So, the Barren Plane is two levels deeper than the Shadow Plane. In a normal scenario, I would cross over plane by plane until I got there, then cross back, one by one." We both know this, but I feel it's important to begin with context.

"Getting to the Barren Plane isn't the problem. It's getting back out."

I ignore his observation. "The Immortal told me when they banished Hecate, his partner, Calix, opened a rift straight into the Ashen Plane."

A familiar light sparks in Dixon's eyes. "If a rift can be opened into the Ashen Plane, there's no reason we can't open one to the Barren Plane."

"The magic would be performed here, in this plane. If we could somehow keep that rift open, I could walk through it, like a door, find the Immortal, and walk back out." For a moment, it feels like old times. Then a cloud descends over my thoughts, reminding me those old times are gone. My relationship with Dixon will never be the same.

"It could work. In theory." He stresses that last part. "It would take a whole lot of power. I need to do some research. There are books here I've never even heard of. And we'd have to find someone strong enough to work the spell."

"I've got the strength covered. Just do what you need to."

Alex watches our exchange in silence, but when Dixon walks away he scoops me up in his arms as if I were as light as a feather. Who knows, maybe at the moment I am. I'll never admit it to him, but my talk with Dixon took more out of me than I expected. I let my head slump against his shoulder as he bears me away, up the stairs and into a spartanly decorated bedroom.

"This must be a spare. The master bedroom is a lot more comfy." Alex supplies the context as he tucks me into the covers, then climbs onto the bed beside me, careful not to jostle me too much.

"I've never thought about the Immortal's bedroom. I'm surprised he doesn't sleep upside down from the rafters like a bat."

"This is the Immortal's house?"

"Yeah."

"Huh." Once again the broth appears at my lips, and he lets me have more this time, until my stomach starts to actually feel a little full.

"You lied to Mason."

"It was a well-intentioned one. He doesn't have a high opinion of hedge-witches. Or of me, personally."

I let a smile cross my face as my eyes drift closed. Not sleeping. Just resting. "Remember what happened the last time we were in bed together?"

"I don't think you're capable of compromising my honor at the moment." An easy silence falls, and I'm considering going back to sleep when he speaks again. "If you're not up to it now, I understand, but I'd like to know what happened."

The words are said so casually I almost miss it, but I see it when I crack my eyes back open. The look on his face that says I really did almost die. The hell I put him through by disappearing, then turning up weeks later barely alive. He deserves an explanation. I do my best, giving him the most succinct explanation of soul searching that I can in my current condition. What I can't do is stop the pain that reflects back at me when I describe the risks of the task I undertook.

"Was that your plan when you left?" His words are clipped. Terse.

"Yes. I wanted to do it at the manor, but Mr. Henderson..." I trail off as that look crosses his face again. The one that says I betrayed him. Again. I left him out of the loop and did something dangerous, and it cuts him deep. The realization pains me for a moment, but the pain abruptly fades away as my temper begins to rise. "You don't have the right to be angry with me."

"I don't? What you did was stupid, Adrienne, and—"

"And it had to be done. We've already had this conversation, Alex. Being a magi comes first. That means finding Liza, finding the Immortal, comes first. I'm sorry I had to put myself in danger to do it, but I would do it again in a heartbeat if I thought it was necessary." I let my tone soften, trying to convey the deep feelings I have inside. "I want you in my life, Alex. But there are times I'm going to have to make my decisions alone, and if that's not something you can handle..."

The question hangs there, floating in the air. Whatever potion he's been feeding me is really doing the job. I feel energized. Strong. Strong enough to have this discussion, at least.

Finally, Alex heaves a sigh. "I want you in my life, too. That's why this bothers me so much. I don't want to lose you."

"Trust me, I'm doing everything I can to not get lost." I crawl forward on the bed and press a light kiss to his lips. A look of alarm flies into his eyes when he sees me move, and his arms come up, ready to catch me if I should fall. I can't help it. I giggle. "Don't have any faith in your own potion?"

"Just being careful," he murmurs, kissing me again. "Nothing's going to happen to you if I can help it."

"Good." I allow him to lay me back against the pillows again, pulling him down to snuggle with me. "Now it's your turn."

"For what?"

"Apparently I've been gone a long time. I assume you guys would have told me if I'd missed the comet. How much time do we have left? What's been going on?"

He hesitates, making me suspicious. "Four days."

Four days! "What happened after I left? With Mr. Henderson?"

"Mason said he was royally pissed off. Wanted to haul both of them in for questioning and containment, but one of the other magi stepped in. Mr. Henderson moved back into the manor, along with what Mason says is half the council, to keep it under surveillance. Your disappearing act really threw them for a loop."

"You guys seem...chummy."

"We've been spending a lot of time together, but trust me, neither of us is happy about it. They couldn't keep staying at the manor with the council goons, but Mason didn't want to leave town until you got back. He drops in, interrogates me on if I've heard from you, sometimes lets me train with him."

We lost the manor? Tears threaten, but I manage to hold them back. It's a trivial thing, in the grand scheme. And when Hecate is dead and my family is put back together, we *will* get our home back. "And they can't find us here? Are the Immortal's wards blocking us? Is that why you guys came here?"

Alex gives me a puzzled look. "We thought you chose this place. Pong-that is his name, right?-snatched us from our beds and drug us here, where we found you sprawled on the floor."

"I was barely conscious when Pong pulled me out of the cave. He chose this place for us, but why? And when did Pong become our de facto leader?" I ask the question in jest, but there's a serious observation behind it. Pong's been moving a lot of pieces lately.

"Because we all know you're the leader. No matter how much Mason hates it."

I allow the change in subject, and the lightening of the conversation. "Mason's a follower. He just won't admit it."

"Why?" Alex asks.

"Because he's too proud. He has a very high opinion of himself, and he is quite skilled, I'll give him that, he just doesn't—"

"No, not Mason. You. Why are you the leader? Why is all of this," he whips his hand around in a circle, indicating all the craziness that's going on right now, "your job? Not just right now, but the whole thing?"

"The whole thing? Not asking for much, huh?"

"You know what I mean. All of this started with you hunting a werewolf, right? Why were *you* hunting the werewolf? Why wasn't somebody else?"

I've asked myself the same question over the years. It's a simple answer as far as protocol, but not a simple thing to come to terms with. "I've told you about the three major branches of magic."

"Yeah."

"Manipulation is by far the most common, and the easiest to integrate into a normal, mundane life. Combat, not so much. And we're rarer. I'm one of the few people in the world qualified to kill monsters. But there are also traditions. I'm essentially Andrew's apprentice, making me the official first responder when the monsters show up. It's for the experience. I already told you Mason did it before me. Once I graduate, assuming I ever do, the three of us will split the responsibility until a new combat magi comes along who needs training."

"It seems like a lot of responsibility for just one person."

"It is."

We fall into silence again, and this time we let it last. We're both tired. Alex's skin is warm against mine, and he smells like pine needles. The peace I find in his embrace doesn't last long, though. Without the distraction of talking to him, my mind is pulled back to Hecate. And the Immortal. And the impossible task facing us.

The Barren Plane is a magic dead zone, setting it apart from all the other planes that make up totality. The ones we know about, at least. Dixon is working on a way to get me there, but I still have to figure out how to handle the complete lack of oxygen. The air is one hundred percent not breathable. No wonder the Immortal looks like a desiccated corpse.

He's still alive. I repeat the words to myself, willing them to remain true. They have to be true. I don't know how, but his curse is keeping him alive in there. I know it.

Hecate sure knew what she was doing. And I don't.

Thirty

"Your boyfriend's an idiot."

"Mason," I warn, snagging the plate of eggs out from under his fingers. He doesn't object, just fills another.

"Fine. Naive, then."

"I'll take it." I dig into the eggs, surprised at how light and fluffy they are. He mixed in ham and cheese and spinach, and they may be the best eggs I've ever had.

"Stop making that face."

"What face?"

"The one that's surprised at how good of a cook I am."

"I'm always surprised to learn there are positive aspects to your personality." Our teasing this morning is lighthearted with only kernels of truth, evidence of my still-delicate condition. Mason's being careful, which is yet another positive aspect of his personality. One I'm not mentioning, though, else he'll shove it back down and go back to being a jerk. "What is Alex being naive about?"

He takes a long swig of his coffee, making me wait for my answer. "Things are changing. It's subtle, but there if you're looking for it. Which I am, and he's not. It hasn't even occurred to him to look."

"You were eavesdropping last night."

"Of course I was. You didn't think it odd that I didn't haul you back down here for a debriefing? I tuned out the personal stuff, don't worry."

Sure he did. "So you know what happened in the cave."

"Yes."

"And you're not angry?"

"You did what I would have done. Of course, I never would have allowed myself to be put in that position in the first place, but the soul searching was the right call. I'll have to do some reading up on it, see if it's something worth knowing."

And there's the jerk. "You were talking about changes?"

He doesn't mention the segue. "I read your notes. About Hecate. And now that her power has grown, her influence is starting to show itself. She's preparing the world for her resurrection. At least, this part of it."

"That's weird, right?" I interrupt him as the thought occurs to me. "You would think she would be aiming for Greece, her old stomping grounds. What does she care about the U.S.?"

Mason gives me a puzzled look for a moment while he thinks it over. "I don't know. Maybe because there's a greater concentration of magic here for this age. Maybe it's because Liza lives here. She found Liza, and formed her plan around her?"

"Maybe." Hecate's motivations don't matter as much as her intentions, but I still wish I understood them better.

"Her signs are everywhere, now that I know what I'm looking for. In the future, you need to do a better job of properly educating the members of your team. With you missing, I was left in the dark and had to ransack your room for the information I needed."

"Noted." I let the first hint of annoyance slip into my tone, hoping he'll feel guilty about picking on me in my weakened state. If he notices he doesn't show it.

"The first sign is dogs. They're everywhere. Humane societies are suddenly full to capacity and turning people away."

"What are the dogs doing?"

"Nothing, really. Roving around, howling, just doing dog things. They're an annoyance more than anything else. I don't think Hecate's controlling them, they're just linked to her somehow. They can feel her."

"Weird." I shiver as a cold chill runs down my back. "What else?"

"Reports of lunacy are up. More people are going crazy than ever before. And there have been altars. Not many, but even a few is enough to draw attention. They're popping up at three-way crossroads."

Three-way crossroads? Yep, that's definitely a Hecate thing. Even the students in Vermont and the sorority girls in California had that part down. I didn't know what I was looking at at the time, but the random places they chose in the sidewalks wasn't random at all. They were both three-way crossroads, albeit makeshift ones.

"Torches are showing up posted on the doorways of her followers, like they're announcing their allegiance or something. And people are growing these." Mason pulls a clump of leaves from his pocket, ripped and crumpled, but still familiar. I never got around to identifying them.

"What are they?"

Mason points to each as he names them. "Aconite. Belladonna. Dittany. Poisons that Hecate favors."

A shudder runs through me. *These were in my house.* "People are just growing these?"

"Yeah. In little herb gardens on their porches. Only single women, though. Married people and families just get driven insane." The look on my face makes him pull back on the morbid humor. "What is it?"

"Liza was growing these."

Before he can respond we're joined by Dixon, who looks like he hasn't slept and based on the wild look in his eyes is running on pure caffeine. "I've got it."

"Got what?"

"Your door."

My heart jumps. Mason and I speak at the same time, "Already?" and "What door?"

"What, you weren't listening to that part?"

Dixon talks over us, his words tumbling over themselves in his fevered state. "It isn't going to be easy, but I can open the rift. I won't be able to keep it open more than a few seconds, but I will be able open a second one after a short period of time. I think that'll work better anyway, because you'll need time to find the Immortal once you get there and get him back to the door." He ends in a gasp, doubled over and heaving.

Mason catches him as he starts to teeter and steers him into a chair. Then he spears me with a look. "You neglected to tell me something."

"Not neglected. I just haven't gotten around to it yet. I'm going into the Barren Plane to fetch the Immortal."

By the time night falls, we're ready. The delay has me chafing, but Dixon can't be rushed. He needs to be comfortable in the ritual, and it's an incredibly difficult spell to work in the best of circumstances. We definitely don't have the best of circumstances. Mason took advantage of the time to liberate oxygen masks and tanks from a nearby hospital. He didn't give me the details, and I didn't ask. He put me under orders to rest and recover today, which I ignored the moment he left. When he comes to find me, I'm still in the Immortal's weapons room, gaping at the walls in awe.

"I've only dreamed of weapons like this." I assume the person intruding into my solitude is Alex, and Mason's voice has my defenses going up on instinct.

"I don't think you should go."

"That sucks."

"Let me rephrase. You're not going. You're still weak, and I'm not letting you take that chance." He crosses his arms and stares me down, maintaining the high ground on the stairs.

"It isn't your decision to make. This is my mission."

"Not when you're compromised, it isn't. It's my job as your second to relieve you of command when you're no longer fit for duty."

"I'm sorry, when did I name you my second? For that matter, when did you ask to join my team?"

Mason seethes. I watch, waiting for my answer, curious what he'll come up with. With our history, I don't need him to ask, and he would never do it anyway. It's just understood.

"We're partners. Always have been, always will be. The other miscellaneous people in your life won't change that."

A not-so-subtle dig at Alex? I raise my chin. "I don't need you to tell me what to do anymore, Mason."

"You're not going."

Stalking forward, I snatch the sword I was eying off the wall, then turn back to face Mason. "If you think you can stop me, prove it. First blood gets to go."

He can't resist a challenge. Neither of us can. He takes a moment to choose his own weapon, then meets me in the middle of the floor. "First blood. I'll try to take it easy on you."

No, he won't. Which is why I attack first. Despite my bravado, my strength isn't one hundred percent back, and I don't know that I can defend against him. He parries my blow, and I release the hilt of the sword, letting it fly from my grip. The change in momentum unsettles him, and I drive my other fist into the bridge of his nose. Blood spurts onto his shirt.

"I win." Without looking back at him I collect my sword, returning it to its place on the wall. I'm actually glad this happened. Now I know the blade isn't balanced properly for my hand, and I can choose a weapon better suited to me.

"You cheated."

"You bled. That was the extent of the rules." I turn my attention to the Immortal's collection of daggers instead. The only sword I want to wield is my own, which Mason cleaned and stored in the training room beneath the manor after our last battle, making it currently unreachable. I select four daggers, stowing them on my body, then after a moment of indecision tie a silver-bladed machete onto my belt.

"Like that won't draw attention."

"It has a longer reach without being unwieldy." He doesn't answer, but I see him snatch up its mate as I leave the room. Alex and Dixon are waiting for us upstairs.

"What took you so long?" Mason appears behind me, and Dixon answers his own question. "Never mind. Let's get going."

"Hey, Dixon?" I let the others move ahead as I pull Dixon back.

"What?" A worried look shadows his determined eyes. Distracting him right before he needs to cast a really big spell probably isn't the best idea, but just in case I don't make it back...

"At home, on your desk, I left—"

"Andrew's journal, yeah. I saw it."

"Oh." *Is that all he has to say about it?* "Did you read it?"

"I read it. Now isn't the time, Adrienne. We can talk about it later." Putting on speed, he catches up to Mason at the door while Alex drops back.

"Are you all right?" Alex whispers into my ear, sliding an arm protectively across my shoulders and casting Mason and Dixon a sidelong glance.

"Everything's fine. Let's get to it." Dixon and I haven't talked about what happened when he left. He said he found his parents, but didn't offer up any details. Knowing who they are, I'm burning to know how that confrontation went down.

We can't cast the spell from here. At least, not without a better understanding of the Immortal's wards. Dixon did his best, but the spell work is more complex than any he's ever seen. We're not even sure how we managed to get past, unless Pong did something to bring us through. Instead, we're heading to a remote location where we can work without being seen.

That plan lasts as far as the yard. The moment we step onto the ground and outside the wards, hellhounds begin appearing all around us. Their ghastly howls fill the night, striking fear into each of our hearts.

"Back inside!" Mason's cry makes Alex and Dixon stop in their tracks, backpedaling toward safer ground.

I charge ahead.

"Adrienne!"

"I need my sword!" No time for more explanation than that. Mason curses as I sprint out of reach, but stays behind to protect the others. I put on speed, managing to stay ahead of the pack as it converges on me. Enyo appears at my side from wherever she'd been hunting, snapping and snarling. Machete in hand, I slash at the hounds closest to me as I slip into the Shadow Plane.

The Shadow Plane turns out to be a bad idea. The hellhounds are faster here, teeth grazing my ankles before Enyo can shoulder them out of the way. The blood trickling into my shoes makes me wince, more from memory than from pain. It took more strength than Heather could muster to save me from hellhound injuries last time. Here's hoping the Immortal knows the spells needed to cure me this time.

Home is every bit as cold as winter in New England can be, and as we burst from the Shadow Plane a weight lands square in my back, knocking me face first into the snow. Teeth close on my throat, and I feel them hit their mark just as Enyo tackles their owner, freeing me. I've lost my momentum, though, as the rest of the hounds are on me before I can regain my feet.

Snow is water, right? "Unda!" It's the same command I used to help Mason with his ocean monster. Now, instead of pulling the water, I push it, forcing the snow away from me in all directions. The ground lurches from the force of the spell, snow flying into the air and taking the hellhounds with it. They don't go far, but it's enough. My head light from the sudden exertion on top of my run, I stumble forward in the direction of the manor. Enyo takes the lead when I hesitate, guiding me with sure steps. The pack recovers quickly and gives chase, but not fast enough. The first three hellhounds that try to follow us through the wards disintegrate instantaneously. The rest take up residence outside, prowling around the perimeter, ready to tear us to pieces the moment we step back out.

"First things first, girl," I say to Enyo as she snarls at the pack. She doesn't follow me into the house, but rather stays planted at the back door, facing down the hellhounds outside. If the council is still residing here, there's no sign of them when I enter. I sneak as quickly and silently as I can, through the kitchen, down the stairs, into our pocket training room. I'm only here for the sword, and I snatch it up without even breaking stride. Anything else we might need I'm sure I can find somewhere in the depths of the Immortal's house.

On my way back out I hear the soft murmur of voices coming from the library. Unable to help myself, I cast my bending-light spell and peek through the door. Mr. Henderson sits stiffly in an overstuffed chair, eyes glazed and unfocused. Tamara leans over him, holding something shiny and crooning softly into his ear. I shudder, forcing down the rush of pity I suddenly feel for the old man and turning away. I have more important things to do tonight.

Keeping the machete in my non-dominant hand, I march back through the kitchen. "Ready?" I ask Enyo. She meets my eyes and lifts the corner of her lip in a savage doggie smile. Together, we charge into the pack of hellhounds amassed on the other side.

THIRTY-ONE

EVERY LIGHT IS BLAZING in the house on the cliff. Mason stands watch on the deck, weapons drawn, daring the creeping things of the night to come for him. Too bad the only thing charging out of the darkness is me.

"Adrienne!" His shout brings the others running, just in time to catch me as my legs give out on the steps. "Holy shit. Get her inside."

"Enyo."

"I've got her." My poor hellhound is scrawny enough even Dixon can lift her. Mason scoops me up in his arms, shouldering Alex out of the way and relegating him to holding the door. I don't object. The amount of blood leaking out of my body is a time-sensitive issue.

"What happened?" Alex is by my side the moment Mason deposits me on the couch, hands clamping down on the largest of the gashes.

"Hellhounds. What else?" Mason's tone is brusque as he examines my injuries. "Not that one. This one. It's smaller, but deeper." He barks the order, rearranging Alex's hands to keep me from bleeding out.

It only takes a minute for Mason to make his assessment. "You ready?"

My teeth are clamped tightly, to keep myself from crying out, but Dixon answers for me. "You can't heal them. Not completely. They're infected."

"Infected with what?"

"Ash," I gasp out, unable to hold back any longer. "Just do as much as you can. Get me upright, and the Immortal will do the rest."

Mason doesn't argue. He's saving it for when I'm not actively dying in front of him. Again. Silently, he closes his eyes and begins to chant, reciting the more complicated first-aid spells I never got around to mastering. His hands rove over my body, and I scream as my muscles attempt to knit themselves back together. Alex curses beside me. My eyes are drawn to his lips, moving as he chants something, too. Not a spell. The lyrics to the song we danced to on Halloween. A second later his voice reaches my ear, singing just loud enough for me to hear him. The song cuts through the pain, but isn't enough to completely distract me.

Suddenly the pain intensifies, fire racing across my skin. Mason abruptly stops chanting and begins cursing instead.

"What is it?"

"It's not working. The magic's too strong. I can't break it."

"Neither could Heather," I grind out, bracing myself against another wave of nausea-inducing pain. "She needed Cerise's help."

"Then why am I even bothering?" Mason spits out the rhetorical question and vanishes. He reappears a few minutes later, bearing alcohol and a needle. "Guess we're doing this the old-fashioned way."

The old-fashioned way takes much, much longer, but eventually the bleeding is stopped and all of my wounds are sewn tightly shut. I can feel the infection resisting being bound, but Mason's work is true and the stitches hold.

"Take it easy," Mason cautions as I rise to my feet. My legs are wobbly, but they hold my weight, and that's good enough.

"Good as new." The joke falls flat on even my ears.

"Not even close. The wounds are closed, but not well. You lost a lot of blood. And the infection is minor right now, but it'll spread quickly."

"Then we need to move quickly, too. We need to get the Immortal out before the infection spreads. Dixon, are you ready?"

"I'm ready, but we can't go back out there. The hellhounds—"

"Are gone. For now. Hecate may have others, but I think if she did, she would have sent them, too. We have a window, and we need to make use of it. We'll do it here, on the cliffs, where we can retreat back to the house in a hurry if we need to."

Dixon's already in motion, grabbing his things. Alex and Mason don't move.

Mason goes first. "The situation has changed, Adrienne. You're not up to this mission. Hecate already had a target on your back, and now she knows where you are. If you go out there again, she'll make another play. You may not be so lucky next time."

"Lucky? You think this is luck? Do you know how many hellhounds there were? Twenty-two. Twenty-two! You don't best twenty-two hellhounds with luck."

"You're good, I know, but that doesn't change the fact that Hecate is gunning for you. When you ran, every single one of them followed you. She doesn't care about us. You're the threat, and she'll stop at nothing to take you out."

I drop my voice, low and menacing. "Are you really trying to talk me out of battle? You want me to stay here, where it's safe, like a coward?" That does it. I see the defeat in Mason's eyes before he knows it.

"Dixon. Let's go."

"Adrienne, no."

"Not now, Alex." The look in his eyes is almost my undoing, but I harden my heart against his raw display of emotion. "This is who I am."

Dixon steps to my side. "We're only missing—"

"He'll be here."

"Then let's do it." Dixon lets me lead the way, keeping close on my heels in case we're attacked again. Enyo wags her tail but doesn't rise to follow. While Mason was busy saving my life, Dixon was busy saving hers. Her wounds are closed, but she lost a lot of blood, too. She'll be weak for a while until she recovers. I was right about the window. If Hecate has another round, it's taking her time to put it in motion.

A minute later we're standing on the cliffs, facing out over the waves with the house at our backs. The steady churn of the water is soothing, and I take just a moment to breathe it in, calming my nerves, easing my anxieties. Dixon does the same beside me. Of all of us, he's the one who needs to remain in control the most. Despite his recent control issues, I have no doubts about his abilities tonight. The young man standing next to me is calm, focused, and determined.

We wait while Dixon gets settled on the cold, damp ground. Alex looks around nervously, while Mason fidgets at the lack of activity. I get it. We're sitting ducks, standing out here in the open and waiting to be attacked.

"Okay," Dixon murmurs, his voice low and even. "Where's—"

A low rumble cuts him off. Pong melts out of the darkness, striding into our group like he's king of the jungle and we're merely scavengers he has allowed to continue existing. On silent feet, he takes up residence behind Dixon and lays his massive head on the boy's bony shoulder. Dixon takes a sharp intake of breath, and I know their minds have joined. As one who's joined minds with Pong in the past, I don't envy him.

The minutes tick by. Above us, the moon climbs higher, the lack of light pollution making every body in the night sky shine forth ten times brighter. Dixon's lips move, the words of his spell drowned out by the crash of the waves below us. Sweat stands out starkly on his brow, and his breathing becomes labored with the force of his concentration.

Finally, it happens. The air in the middle of our circle shimmers, then explodes in a shower of orange light. When my eyes adjust, a pulsing orange mist is hovering in midair, filling our little circle. Through it, I can make out only Mason's outline on the other side.

"I can't hold it long," Dixon grits out. "Remember, three hours, and you have to be there."

Without hesitation I slide my oxygen mask down to cover my mouth and step into the mist. Just as my foot touches down, a cold hand slips into mine. Alex, sporting his own mask, steps through the door with me into the Barren Plane. Through the mist, a primal shriek reaches my ears, and before I can think it through I turn to go back. I don't make it. The mist vanishes as Dixon releases the door, sealing us in.

A single click starts the button on my stopwatch. Three hours exactly. Any more and we'll miss Dixon, and risk becoming stranded in here forever. A deep breath, and I pull my mask away to talk to Alex. "I should have known."

"You insisted on coming. How else was I supposed to keep you safe?"

"Just stay close, okay? Neither of us knows what to expect."

Alex casts a glance at where the door used to be. "What do you think that scream was?"

I take a long breath before answering. "I don't know. And it's pointless to speculate about it. Let's find the Immortal."

"Why is the sun up here?"

"There is no sun. It's always this light here. Harsh, blinding, unyielding light. Now hush."

Finding the Immortal's magic is easy this time. When I came back from inside myself, I kept hold of the tether. Figuratively speaking, I tied it to a post in my brain where I could easily access it again. Now it's just a matter of stepping inside my head, grabbing the tether, and following where it leads. With a nod in the right direction, I show Alex where we're headed.

We begin walking, leaving a small blue flag planted in the ground behind us. The utter lack of ambient noise is unsettling. Even our footsteps are silent; no crunch of loose gravel, no scuff of our soles against the rock. With the masks, I can't even hear Alex breathe. The very air is thick and oppressive, blazing hot with not a drop of humidity. We soldier on, staying within arm's reach of each other as we go.

The Immortal isn't far. The deeper one travels into totality, the smaller the planes become. I see him long before we reach him. The mound of beetle-like creatures is the only thing protruding from the otherwise unbroken landscape.

Alex points at the beetles, then holds his hands up in a questioning gesture. I assume he wants to know if they're dangerous.

I shrug back at him. *How should I know?*

The beetles don't seem to notice our approach. Or, maybe they really are harmless. I nudge the mound with my boot. The beetles part at the contact, then resume their coverage when I draw my foot away.

Only one way to find out. Squatting down, I reach my hand into the seething mass. Once again the beetles part, allowing me to reach through and grasp what I believe to be the Immortal's leg. It feels dead. Sunken, shriveled flesh clings to the protruding bones. When my arm doesn't pull back, a group of daring beetles climb up onto it, spiny legs clutching at my skin.

Alex starts forward, but I hold up my other hand to keep him back. The beetles aren't attacking. They're just exploring. As I watch, the lead beetle nuzzles my arm, then probes my skin until a thin wafer of white skin breaks loose. It tickles. The beetle eats the dead skin, emitting a buzz-like hum, and suddenly the rest of the beetles covering the Immortal surge toward me.

I back up in a hurry, hands coming up to direct my spell. Once the beetles are clear of the Immortal, I release the fire, waiting for the bugs to be incinerated in a fiery blaze. Nothing happens.

What? I know this spell backwards and forwards. Why is it flaking on me now? I keep backing up, leading the beetles away as my mind races for the answer. It takes longer than I'll ever admit for it to click. *Duh. No magic here.*

I keep backing up, and the beetles follow, deserting the picked-over body of the Immortal. They're not even frightening. They're not being aggressive, just excited about finally getting a meal. All of them are humming now, scurrying toward me as fast as their tiny legs will allow.

Once the beetles are clear, Alex squats down next to the Immortal. I circle, trying to keep as close to them as I can while still staying out of reach of the beetles. "How is he?"

"He looks dead."

He really does. Eyes open and unblinking, his face twisted in pain, he looks like the mummy I saw once in a museum. "Do you think you can carry him?" I have to raise my voice as the distance between us grows. I would offer to help, but the words would be wasted. No way he'd let me, not when I'm barely being held together as it is.

In response, Alex hoists the Immortal, dragging his stiff body across his own shoulders. He lets out a grunt, but doesn't look like he's straining too much. "Let's just get out of here. This place gives me the creeps."

It takes longer to walk back to our rendezvous than it did to get here, due both to our fatigue and the Immortal's weight on Alex. He isn't an easy burden to bear, but Alex doesn't complain. Our entourage does nothing to improve our spirits. They scurry slightly faster than I walk, so I can't let my pace waver. Some abandon me for Alex, swarming onto his shoes before he can shake them off. When at last I see the blue flag ahead of us, my heart jumps in my chest.

Ten yards out, the silence is shattered by the sudden beeping of my watch. *We're late!* Alex and I both pick up the pace, him shuffling just a little bit faster, me breaking into a slow jog. I train my eyes on the air in front of us, not daring to miss our door. It doesn't come. We reach the flag as the watch stops beeping, signaling the end of the minute. Still no door.

I trade nervous glances with Alex. *It doesn't mean anything. He's just a little late, that's all.* No matter how many times I say it, though, I can't convince my heart not to pound. Alex lets the Immortal slide to the ground, sighing audibly at the release. The beetles catch us, but there's nothing we can do about them now. Neither of us says anything. We just keep watching, waiting, praying for our door to appear.

An hour later, my oxygen tank beeps. Alex's has been beeping for ten minutes. He went through his air faster than I did, carrying the Immortal. The ground is hard under my feet, where I squat, tensed and ready to spring the second the door opens. Some of my stitches have popped, the dripping blood being sucked down into the scorched earth. Beetles crawl over my body, devouring any piece of dead skin they can find. *Where are you, Dixon? What's going on up there?* No reply comes from the still, dead air.

THIRTY-TWO

W HEN THE DOOR FINALLY comes, it doesn't explode into being like the first time. It flickers, barely visible, winking out twice before finally holding steady. As one the beetles hiss and scurry in all directions, fleeing the sudden surge of oxygen-rich air. Alex is sleepy, lying across my lap. It takes some hard shaking to wake him, but he finally notices the door and crawls toward it. Scooting out from under him, I seize the Immortal under the arms and begin to drag him toward the orange mist. The door wavers, making my breath catch and spurring me to move faster. The Immortal is not a small man.

Alex reaches the door before I do, but I'm right on his heels as we fall through to the other side. The sudden darkness of the Mortal Plane has me stumbling blindly, tripping over Alex as he lies gasping on the rock, swallowing as much air as he can.

"Adrienne! We have to get inside, now!" Mason's arms wrap around me, but I push him off.

"Take the Immortal." Relinquishing his weight to Mason, I haul Alex up instead. His strength is coming back quickly with the influx of oxygen, and our eyes are adjusting fast. What I see drives me forward, triggered by Mason's urging to get back inside the wards.

Bodies are strewn about the cliffs, clad in the same torch-bearing robes as the woman who almost shot me. *Acolytes.* They don't matter. The one who matters is two feet to my left, lying face-down on the rock and not moving. "Dixon!" Beside him lies Pong, but the big cat is beyond my help. Blood from multiple blade wounds coats the ground around him, still steaming in the chill night air. Wrenching my gaze away, I scoop Dixon's feather-light frame into my arms and stumble after Alex and Mason, each struggling to get themselves to safety.

"What happened?" I demand of Mason as we lay Dixon out on the floor. He isn't breathing. I start CPR as Mason murmurs spells over him, spells to restart his heart and fill his lungs with air. They'll only work if we got to him in time.

Ten minutes later, we begin to accept we didn't get to him in time. Magic is a powerful tool, but it can't bring back the dead. Not in any way that matters, at least.

Deep cold spreads over my entire body. It starts in my hands, still poised on Dixon's chest, willing it to move. The cold moves up my arms, through my chest, and in less than a minute has encased me in ice. Alex draws my hands away, wrapping them in his own and pulling me back against his chest. Even his body heat can't penetrate the cold.

Mason thumps heavily against the floor. When he speaks, the words come out in a monotone. "They were on us as soon as you left. I held them off, got us back to the house. We had three hours; surely we'd figure out something. They just kept coming.

"I did as much as I could. I kept them off him as he tried to open the door. But they weren't after me. Or him. They were after Pong."

"Because he's strong enough to go after Liza." My whisper trembles in the thick, heavy air.

"Dixon couldn't open the door without him. We fought, all of us. Finally, they were all down, but Pong...he held on, as long as he could. They got the door open, but then his body gave out, and Dixon had to keep it open all by himself. He wouldn't...he wouldn't..."

Mason breaks, dissolving into sobs. I know what he was going to say, though. Dixon wouldn't leave us there. He gave himself to save our lives. To save Liza. My tears join Mason's, less vigorous but no less raw.

Alex is the first to move, sometime later, when my joints are stiff and sore, and losing the support of his body makes them scream in protest. He returns a minute later with a glass bottle half-full of dark brown liquid and three crystal glasses. He pours us each a liberal portion and raises his in the air. "Dixon."

"Dixon," Mason and I echo, downing the liquor in a single gulp. It burns sharply in my throat, the first thing to penetrate the cold.

Alex doesn't return to his previous seat. "Now isn't the time to mourn," he says softly, making my eyes snap to his.

"How dare you. Dixon is dead, and—"

"Yes, Dixon is dead. He deserves to be mourned. And he will be. But now isn't the right time, and you know that. Adrienne," he calls softly, taking my chin in his hand, "don't let his sacrifice be for nothing. The job isn't done. You still have to save Liza."

Liza. The one word that has any hope of shaking me out of the stupor Dixon's loss is threatening to drag me down into. Alex wields the word like a weapon, driving it into my heart and my mind and making me hate him for daring to use it in front of me. The feeling passes quickly, though, as logic and reason take his side. With an effort, I swallow my tears, pulling my shirt up to scrub at my face. Alex is giving me a gentle smile when I emerge, and he holds out his hand. I take it, allowing him to pull me to my feet.

I don't look at Dixon's body, still lying sprawled on the floor as if he were sleeping. I can't. Instead I focus on the other corpse in the room.

"What do we do now?" Alex's question is like a jump-start, sending my mind whirling as it tries to come up with an answer.

"I have no idea." The first thing, I guess, is to examine the body. Find out exactly what we're dealing with. Hands trembling, I place a finger under the Immortal's chin, searching for a pulse.

The instant I touch him, the Immortal convulses, lurching into the air. His skeletal fingers close around my wrist in an unbreakable grip. His mouth opens as he screams something at me, but only rasps and puffs of dust come out of his lips. Alex and Mason both jump on him, pinning him to the floor, taking my arm with him. As they hold him thrashing, I begin to notice the subtle changes that have taken place. His skin has darkened by several shades, and his chest is moving in irregular, shallow breaths. Though still gaunt, his limbs are beginning to thicken as his muscle mass rebuilds itself.

"Shh, shh, we're not going to hurt you. It's Adrienne, remember? The little mage? We're trying to help you, Deacon, and—"

Wild eyes snapping open, the Immortal throws off Mason and Alex and lunges at me. As his hands close around my throat, his voice breaks through, barely audible. "How do you know that name? Only She uses that name!"

He's getting stronger by the second. Alex and Mason manage to pry him off me again, but they can't hold him down any longer. "Hold on," I say, scrambling backward until I'm out of reach and jumping to my feet. A quick run to the weapons room and I'm back with something I'd seen and glossed over earlier: a long, heavy chain ending in a pair of manacles.

"Get him over here." The boys wrestle the Immortal, now trying to escape with all his might, into the center of the room, where I've attached the chain to one of the massive pillars supporting the second story of the house. It takes all three of us to get him into the manacles, and even then he chases us to the end of the chain, throwing himself backward as it snaps taut.

"What now?" Mason's question is lacking even an ounce of enthusiasm or genuine interest. I get it. I'd much rather go curl up under a blanket and forget the rest of the world exists, too.

"We wait."

"For?"

"For him to regain his sanity. His body is healing. His mind will get there eventually, too." The Immortal snarls at me, apparently done talking for the time being. I take a moment to eye the manacles, until I'm mostly certain they're going to hold.

I don't know how long I stand there, staring at the Immortal chained to a post like a dog, but when Alex takes my hand Mason is gone. Dixon is gone, too, covered by a dark green blanket. "Come on. We have some time. Let's get cleaned up."

I let him lead me upstairs, where my brain re-engages again. The guest room we slept in earlier has its own bathroom, and Alex gets the shower going while I pry off my bloody and less than pleasant smelling boots. My stitches are still leaking. "You go first. I'd like some time to myself."

Alex doesn't fight me on the issue, but I can see he wants to. "Fine, but I'm leaving you plenty of hot water."

The moment he closes the door, though, the silence of the room presses in on me and I realize that being alone is the absolute last thing I want. I don't even think about what I do next.

Despite Alex's promise of hot water, the bathroom is full of steam when I step inside. The damp feels good on my dry, chapped skin.

"What—"

"Shh." I cut off Alex's protest with a kiss, not even flinching as the scalding water rains down on my body. Pressing into him, I pin him against the shower wall and deepen my kiss, sliding my tongue across his top lip.

He responds, drawing me in closer, hands wrapping around my waist and making me shiver under his touch. Every inch of my skin is buzzing, acutely aware of our naked bodies pressing into each other.

Alex is aware of it, too, but his head is in a much better place than mine. He lets out a low groan, then pulls his head away from mine. "Adrienne, what are you doing?"

"Do I really need to spell it out for you?"

"Not like this. It shouldn't be like this."

"Like what? Don't you want me?" I can hear that girl in my voice, that girl who whines and needles and manipulates to get her way, and I hate it, but I keep doing it anyway. "Don't you care about me?"

He lets out a heavy sigh. "You know I do, to both questions, but you're not yourself right now. Can't you see that?"

"I want this."

"You think you do, but trust me, you'll regret it later."

"Trust you? What do you know about it? You're still a virgin."

The barb hits home. Hands on my hips, Alex forces me back a step. "I think I'm clean enough. Shower's all yours."

I don't try to stop him as he grabs a towel and disappears back into the bedroom. I'm not stupid. I know he's right. That doesn't stop me from seething at him, and his refusal to give me the distraction I was looking for. I stand there under the blazing hot water, head hanging down, feeling the water scald the back of my neck and run through my hair before finally landing in the tub. I stand there until the water runs cold, but I still don't get out. I don't want to be part of the world outside of this shower. Instead, I sit down on the floor of the tub, wrap my arms around my legs, and bury my face in my knees. It doesn't take more prompting than that for the tears to start flowing again. This time I cry more like Mason, hacking sobs and gasping breaths, drool and snot mingling with the water rushing down the drain. I sob until my throat hurts and I can't see out of my puffy eyes, and then I sob some more.

I don't hear Alex come back into the bathroom. He shuts off the water, wraps me in a bathrobe, towels off my hair, and lifts me out of the tub like a child. Wordlessly, he bears me back into the bedroom and snuggles me into bed, just like he did last time. Neither of us sleeps. We just lie there in the dark, listening to each other breathe and waiting for the sun to come up.

Thirty-three

T HE MORNING SUN BRINGS fresh perspective for everybody. Mason is acting like a hothead. Alex is acting like I wasn't a raging bitch, and I'm acting like I'm in complete control of the situation. Most importantly, the Immortal is acting like himself.

"How long?" is his first question to me when I appear in the kitchen. His manacles lay in pieces across the floor, and he smells like baby powder and lemongrass.

"Tomorrow is the equinox. The comet will begin its passage in the late afternoon. We expect Hecate to rise with the night." It's just an estimate, but one I feel confident in.

He nods deeply. "It is her way."

He turns back to the counter, where an impressive array of blades are shining with a fresh coat of oil. I hesitate, then venture forth anyway. "How are...um...do you want to talk about it?"

The Immortal doesn't look at me, but I can see the corner of his eye go dark and hard. "Would you wish to talk about it, if it were you?"

His question gives me pause. *Would I?* My immediate response is to say yes, of course, but is that really how I would feel?

The Immortal takes my silence as my answer. "I pray you never know the agony, to be in all respects dead, yet unable to die. It is yet another sin that Hecate will pay for." And with that, the subject is closed. In my head, it sounds like a cell door slamming shut. I'll never ask again.

We're joined the next moment by Alex and Mason, the latter of whom pulls a blade the moment he struts into the room. Shouldering past me, he whips it up against the Immortal's Adam's apple. "Where is he?"

"Mason!"

The Immortal doesn't flinch. "The body of a magi is a precious thing. I attended him with honor, and he now awaits his final resting downstairs in my weapons room."

"You had no right to touch him!"

"As he was resting in my house, I had every right." I hadn't even noticed Dixon was gone. I couldn't bring myself to look into the living room.

Mason's hand trembles, but he lowers the silver machete and offers it handle-first to the Immortal.

"Keep it. You fought for your comrade's life with it, and paid for it in his blood." Mason trades a glance with me, but I don't know what the Immortal means either. Is he blaming Mason for Dixon's death? Or just saying that Mason earned the blade? Honestly, it could go either way, but neither of us is willing to press him on it.

The Immortal turns his attention to me again, this time meeting my eyes. "What is your plan?"

My plan? Right. This is my show. "We go with the comet. The scant lore we have says Hecate is weaker in the daylight, so she'll wait until darkness to rise. The comet will give us the juice we need to get there, and she'll be pinned waiting for darkness to fall. The Ashen Plane is the center of totality, and as such isn't large. We fight through Hecate's minions, find Liza, and get out. I kill Hecate."

I expected resistance, but the Immortal doesn't argue that last point. "You believe yourself capable, when so many others have failed?"

"I am a servant of good, and I fight for a righteous cause. My belief in that is strong enough to kill her."

He nods, apparently satisfied. "And surviving the Ashen Plane? It cannot be done by a mortal."

"Hecate has been doing it for thousands of years. Whatever she would have the world believe, she is still a mortal and can be killed as one. And she needs Liza's body. Liza is alive, and has survived the Ashen Plane before on at least one occasion."

"And you know how they accomplish this?"

It came to me in the night. It's not like I was sleeping, anyway. "Ash. They're infected, the same way I am."

Alex jumps in. "Your injuries. I thought you were going to ask the Immortal to heal them?"

"You are injured?"

"She is, badly. She—"

"I'll be okay. But the infection that will kill me here is the same one that will keep me alive there." I can see them about to cut me off again, so I hurry on. "Liza has a scar on her shoulder. She told me it was a dog bite, from when she was small. We already know that Hecate has been influencing her for her entire life. What if that bite is from a hellhound?"

"But her mother was a magi. She would have healed any bites Liza received, magical or not. There wouldn't be any scar."

The only way to answer Mason convincingly is through show-and-tell. Before any of the guys can protest, I undo my shredded jeans and slide them down to my knees. There, on my thigh, my own hellhound scar gleams faintly against my skin. "Heather did mine, and she's the best. If mine scarred, why not Liza's?"

Silence. I can see the wheels turning on their faces as I pull my pants back up. The Immortal, the only one of us able to view this situation with anything resembling objectivity, breaks the silence first. "Your reasoning is sound. How many fighters accompany us?"

I wish I had a better answer to give. "It's just us." Then somewhat defeatedly, "The magi have turned against me."

Unexpectedly, the Immortal grins. "A few loyal comrades are stronger than a host of the double-minded." He sobers. "I am honored to fight alongside you, little mage. Tonight we bury your friend. Tomorrow, we kill Hecate."

Alex draws me aside as the Immortal departs, pulling me back upstairs. "I need to talk to you."

Back in the bedroom, he closes the door tightly and pulls a vial out of his pocket. "The time hasn't been right to show you this, since I assume you haven't mentioned it to the others yet."

"Is that—"

"It's the best I can do. There isn't a potion that can free the mind. I reached out to every obscure relative my parents forbade me to talk to, and they all agree. We might be able to do it indirectly, but if it doesn't work—"

"No." I know where he's going with this. The only thing that surprises me is that he's the first one to bring it up.

"Adrienne, we have to accept the possibility that we aren't going to make it in time. I'm really hoping Liza's okay, somehow, but we're going in blind. Hecate could have already taken full possession of her. If she has, and the potion doesn't work..."

He can't bring himself to say it. I can, because it's never going to happen. "Nobody is killing Liza."

"But if it's the only way—"

"It won't be." My voice drops, taking on a pleading tone that I can't hide. "It can't be."

He doesn't press the issue, which I'm grateful for. I'm not stupid. I can't deny that no matter what I do, Liza might not make it out of this alive. But the second I admit that, killing her will become a primary objective, and I'm going to fight like hell to save her. In the end, the world is what matters. If Hecate rises, she'll bring death and destruction with her. She has to be stopped. No matter the cost.

I take comfort in Alex's brief, chaste kiss, but when I open my eyes again my attention is drawn to a folded piece of paper laying on the nightstand. "Alex?"

"Hmm?

"Do you know what this is?" My fingers tremble as I lift the paper, as if somehow knowing that whatever is inside is going to punch me in the gut.

"No. I didn't even notice it there."

Heart pounding, I unfold the paper. Dixon's handwriting jumps out at me, and my eyes fill with tears. My shaky legs no longer want to hold me, so I sink onto the bed. Oblivious, Alex disappears into the bathroom to brush his teeth.

Adrienne: There isn't much time. The house is surrounded, and I don't see how we're going to be able to open the door in time. I promise I'm going to do everything I can to get you out, and if you get the chance to read this, then I'll have done my job right. I hate how awkward things have gotten between us, and if we all survive this I'm going to make sure we fix it. I understand now what you were trying to tell me about my parents. I thought you didn't care, but that wasn't it. We just saw things differently. It took a while, but gradually the truth began to sink in. It doesn't matter whose blood I share. My family is, and has always been, at the manor. Heather and Andrew stepped in to be the parents I never had, the only parents I ever needed. They made me who I am. For the first time, I know exactly who I am, Adrienne.

The letter crumples in my hand as my chest constricts and my lungs gasp for air. For a few moments I just sit there, allowing the hurt to come rushing in, all the pain and guilt and sorrow I feel over Dixon's loss utterly consuming me. *If only I'd been paying more attention. If only we'd found Andrew's journal sooner. If only they'd told him all of this long ago. If only...*

A sharp shake of my head interrupts the string of 'if only's. Sitting here dying won't change the past. It won't bring Dixon back, and it certainly won't make killing Hecate any easier. Fleeing before Alex can find me in such a wretched state, I return downstairs, where I'm assaulted by Mason, who seems to have been lying in wait for me.

"You're going to get yourself killed."

The jibe is just the kickstart my emotions need. "Nice to see you, too."

"I'm not kidding, Adrienne. The only reason I agreed not to call Willow is because you assured me the Immortal could handle your healing. Now you're not even going to let him try, and your injuries are too high risk to let them fester for two days."

"If you're going to berate me, at least do it while we walk. And I feel fine."

Mason falls into step with me as I turn toward the stairs leading down to the weapons room. "Really? Do you always feel fine when your eyes are too bright and you have a sheen of sweat on your temples?"

"You're looking awfully closely at my temples."

"I take it your boyfriend didn't even notice?"

"He's preoccupied. And he's not used to examining me for signs of my imminent death."

Mason makes a disapproving noise in the back of his throat but thankfully doesn't pursue that line of discussion. I kind of like Alex's naivete and predilection for optimism.

The Immortal heard our bickering on the stairs and is waiting for us in the weapons room. I start talking immediately, before Mason can hijack my conversation. "There's something we need to talk about, but it's a little awkward, and I'm not sure how to bring it up."

"I believe you just did."

Parking myself on the end of one of the long benches, I meet the Immortal's gaze. I don't look at the other end of the bench at all. Dixon lies there, his body wrapped tightly in strips of linen, like a mummy. "Yeah, I guess so. When we discussed the infection upstairs, you seemed satisfied, but you didn't ask me the obvious question."

"Obvious, yes. I did not see the need to ask. I will require infection as well, and so I assume I need to be attacked by a hellhound." He says it so casually, like being attacked by a hellhound is no big deal.

"You do. Enyo will do it, assuming you can keep yourself from killing her out of reflex. My bigger concern is when. I've seen you heal from a stab wound within minutes of the injury. How quickly will your curse heal you from this infection?"

"I will not hurt your familiar, little mage. Rest easy. As for the infection, I cannot say. If it leaves a scar past the point of magic, then it is possible my curse will not be able to best it. But it is better not to take that chance. I believe it best to leave it until the last possible moment."

"Okay then."

"Where is Enyo?" Mason was so quiet I'd almost forgotten he was there. He's been interrupting less often lately, which is an interesting change in our dynamic.

"She's resting. She almost died, remember? If it weren't for Dixon—" Just saying his name makes my throat close up. I swallow past it, then continue in a small voice. "She's coming with me to the Ashen Plane. She needs her strength."

As if summoned by the mention of her name, Enyo appears in the doorway. She's moving slowly, but looks recovered from her injuries. "Hey there, pretty girl. We were just talking about you. Are you feeling better?"

She gives me a lingering look, then looks pointedly at my weeping stitches and lets out a low whine. I feel Mason open his mouth, but give him a "shh" before he can speak. In a silent and watchful room, Enyo begins to lick my wounds, her tongue pulling at the stitches with a gentle pressure that seems to pull my infection out with it. A quick glance at Mason's and the Immortal's faces tells me I'm not imagining it. Somehow, with the foreign magic of her race, Enyo is drawing the ash infection out of my body.

"Make sure she doesn't—"

"She won't, Mason. She knows what's at stake." A moment later, Enyo ceases her licking and curls into a tight ball at my feet. I feel...rejuvenated. The infection is still there, but the strength of it has been muted. My fever is down, and my body feels strong. The silence lingers for several minutes, while Enyo, oblivious to our wonder, begins to softly snore.

Thirty-four

W E BURY DIXON AT sunset. I don't cry. I can't. I spent a good portion of the day summoning the steely resolve I'm going to need to see this mission through to the end. If I let it crack now...

Mason cries. It's weird. Seeing him show any genuine emotion is weird. For the past couple of years he's been this caustic presence in my life, someone to be avoided and thwarted and defeated whenever possible. How did he become my right hand?

Alex doesn't cry. Neither does the Immortal. They knew Dixon, sure, and his death is a tragedy anyone can acknowledge, but they don't feel it like we do. I lost a brother. Mason lost a comrade-in-arms, a comrade he couldn't save. We'll both mourn him far longer than this simple service under a flaming red sky.

When the time comes, I step forward and lay my rose on top of the freshly turned earth. "I'm sorry," I whisper into the ground, too low for anyone else to hear. "I'm sorry for shutting you out. I'm sorry for breaking us apart. And I'm sorry for leading you into a fight you couldn't win. You put a high price on my life, Dixon, and I'm going to try to live worthy of that."

The words are almost my undoing. Hardening my heart, I reign back the tears and simply lay my hand on the ground. "I love you, Dixon." At my side, Enyo gives a whimper and nuzzles my hand. I let her snuggle in, then use her body as leverage to haul myself off the ground. Mason takes my place as I move away, and I tune him out until I'm far enough away to not hear his words.

The bodies of Hecate's acolytes are gone. I'd forgotten all about them. After Dixon, well, they just didn't matter. I'm guessing the Immortal took care of them, seeing they were scattered around his front yard. Someone who matters would eventually notice.

"Are you okay?" Alex takes my hand and gives it a squeeze.

"Fine." His look says he doesn't believe me. "Okay, I'm not fine, but I don't want to talk about how not fine I am, okay? For now, I have to be fine."

The buzzing in his pocket cuts off whatever he's about to say next. It catches me off guard, and I stare at him for just a moment, trying to place the sound. My phone is too easy to track, even without magic. I haven't seen it since Liza was taken, and the burner I picked up got left behind when Pong dragged me out of that cave. There's no one to call me, anyway. Everyone is already here.

"You're not going to answer it?"

"Not at a funeral, no. It's just my mom, anyway. She's been trying to get a hold of me all day."

That one simple sentence brings reality slamming back down. "Shit. Your mom. You haven't been home in days. She must be worried sick. And school. And football. And—"

"Hey. Hey." He grabs my hands as I start to flail them about, freaking out over the life I've ripped him away from. "It's all okay."

"No, it's not. You have to go to school. You have to graduate. You have to not vanish from your room in the middle of the night without a trace. She probably called the police. What have I done?"

"Adrienne." His stern tone brings my eyes to his. "She hasn't called the police. I just talked to her yesterday. And school is out for Christmas break. You were gone for three weeks, remember? I still went to school, I still played football, and I still had dinner with my family."

"But Pong—"

"Yes, Pong did drag me out of the house without warning, but I've been sleeping with my phone in my hand for the past three weeks, waiting for you to call. I knew this comet was coming, Adrienne. We made preparations. My parents think I'm spending break with your family, camping in the mountains where cell service is spotty and I'm often unreachable. When we found you here, I sent her a text that said we decided to get an early start and I didn't want to wake them before I left."

"You did all that for me?"

"No. I did it because Hecate is more important than any part of my life, and I'm going to do everything I can to help defeat her, which I know isn't much, but I'm here anyway. You being here too is just a bonus."

Talk about cracking my steely resolve. I throw my arms around his neck, and his tighten around my waist in response. "You can't say things like that. You're going to make me break."

"I'm not trying to make things harder for you. Although, I guess I should wait to ask you to go to the Valentine's Dance with me."

"What? A dance?"

Alex chuckles. "You're all set to march off and fight a goddess to save the world, but a school dance makes you nervous?"

His laugh is just what I need to lighten the mood and ease the tension I've been holding in. "Well, yeah. Dances are scary."

Somehow we've become the last people still in the clearing where we buried Dixon. Hand-in-hand, we make our way back through the pine until the Immortal's house is once again in view. It's risky, spending this much time in the open, outside of the Immortal's wards as the darkness closes in, but having the Immortal around makes me feel safer. More in control. He's watching from the balcony, waiting to see that we made it back okay. When he sees us, he gives me a nod and goes back inside.

"Let's not go back in just yet."

"Don't you need to talk to everyone? Rally the troops?"

"It can wait." Forever, preferably. Right now, I just want to hang on to this moment. This moment where no one is trying to kill me, and Alex's hand is warm and strong in mine, and the cold air smells like salt and clean earth, and the sun is sinking like a ball of fire into the ocean.

Alex doesn't object, just pulls me in closer, wrapping his arms around me to keep us both warm as the temperature continues to drop. It isn't until the light is completely gone and darkness stretches across the sky that we finally meander back up to the house.

The morning of the equinox dawns cold and white. The cliffs outside are dusted with a thin layer of snow, and isolated flakes continue to drift by on the light breeze.

"It's almost Christmas," I observe to the person moving up behind me to peer out the window.

"A few more days," Mason agrees. "You missed your birthday."

"I hadn't noticed." I really hadn't. My eighteenth birthday came and went, one of the lost days I spent lying in a cave wandering around my own head. "I don't feel like celebrating, anyway."

"It's all strange, isn't it?" Mason answers. "I don't think I've ever had less holiday spirit."

"*You* have holiday spirit?" The joke is light, but it doesn't land.

Mason responds with sincerity. "You know, there was a time you didn't hate me."

"I don't hate you."

"You know what I mean."

"Yeah, I do." There isn't time to explore this conversation further. The comet is still several hours away, but we want to be in place in plenty of time to be ready.

"You're absolutely sure about this?" Alex asks one more time as we get ready to leave.

"I'm not absolutely sure about any of this, other than the fact that we have to do it. But when Hecate took Liza, she ripped a hole through totality. The Ashen Plane is accessible from the manor, and it's the best place to pick up Liza's trail once we cross over."

"And if the council is there?"

"Then we deal with it. Once the comet comes, they won't be able to stop us." The Immortal is opening our door, using Dixon's notes. It's going to be even harder than the one to the Barren Plane, since the Ashen Plane is so much deeper. None of us, not even the Immortal himself, knows the limits of his strength, but he is certain he won't be able to accomplish it without the comet's help. That presents one final problem, one that will only matter if we manage to win the day: comets are so rare, it's impossible to predict how long its influence will last. If we are in the Ashen Plane past the comet's influence, we may not have the magical juice to get back home.

Past the Immortal's wards, we cross into the Shadow Plane and feel it immediately. Something is off. "We haven't been attacked yet, so it can't be too bad, right?" My question to Mason is more a reassurance to myself, but he answers anyway.

"Not necessarily."

"Great." Still, it doesn't feel like there's a threat coming. More like a tension in the air, like when someone in the house has been having an argument. Just being in the same space as them feels wrong. Today, the Shadow Plane feels wrong. "Think it's the comet?"

"Or Hecate's movement. Did you notice the shadows?"

No, I didn't notice the shadows, because there aren't any shadows to notice. "Maybe they're just somewhere else?"

"Somewhere other than surrounding the delicious magi who just worked some pretty heavy magic casting wards? I don't think so."

"You think they fled?"

"Fled. Hiding. Whatever it is that shadows do when bigger, badder predators are on the prowl."

"Let's not stay any longer than we have to."

"Way ahead of you." Mason is already moving forward, staying a few steps ahead just in case. He leads the way on silent feet, looking back over his shoulder every few steps to make sure we're still behind him. Enyo guards our rear. Together, we form a silent procession through the gloomy emptiness.

We exit the Shadow Plane down the street from the manor to assess the situation from a distance. "The town is quiet," the Immortal observes, "but Hecate has been making her presence known. I can feel her influence in the air."

I'm beyond questioning the Immortal's connection to Hecate. If he says he can feel her, I believe it. "House looks quiet, too."

"Sure does."

The driveway hasn't been plowed. There are no tire marks or footprints to be seen. "Do you think the council would abandon the manor if they thought you weren't coming back?" Alex's question only reveals his ignorance of the ways of the magi.

"Even if they thought that, the manor holds too many secrets. Someone's inside. They have to be. It's best to steer clear.

We're going to swing wide to avoid the manor's wards and any detection spells the council may have put in place. Keep close to Mason; we may cross back over abruptly." It takes a level of skill to navigate the Shadow Plane in relation to the Mortal Plane, and know where you'll end up when you cross over. I'm competent, but Mason is more finely tuned than I am. The commands come easily to my lips. It wasn't so long ago I struggled to take charge of this investigation, allowing my self-doubt to keep my confidence in myself side-lined. Today, I have no doubts. Liza's abduction and Dixon's death have galvanized me into the leader I should have been three months ago.

Once more, we slip into the Shadow Plane, and once more, there are no shadows to be found.

"Maybe they're not here because nobody is afraid."

"Hecate gives nightmares. Of course they're afraid."

"The shadows must be afraid too, then, to not take advantage." It's a chilling thought. Shadows aren't the scariest monsters on the block, but when something makes the monsters wary, you know it's bad.

Mason ignores Alex's and my conversation, but not out of arrogance this time. His eyes are shut tight, hands up, and he's muttering under his breath. He's keeping one eye on the Mortal Plane, so to speak, to make sure we bypass all the wards.

I sneak a glance back at the Immortal, bringing up our rear. He's been uncharacteristically silent all day. Not that he's ever chatty, but this is different. The normal stoicism on his face has been replaced by a look of such intense concentration and seriousness that I almost hesitate to break it.

"How are you doing?"

"I am not one of your friends."

Ouch.

"Apologies. I only meant that I do not wish to engage in some kind of heart-to-heart on the cusp of battle. I will perform my duties to the best of my ability, as I expect you all will also. You need not worry about my emotional welfare."

His little speech has the opposite effect. We're standing on the brink of everything he's ever worked for, the culmination of the last couple thousand years of his life. That has to be messing with his head.

"We haven't talked about—"

"I have not forgotten, little mage. Your guardians remain safe, and my word stands."

"Here." Mason vanishes, preventing me from contemplating the Immortal further. As one, we follow his lead and emerge in the woods at the backside of the manor. No sooner do my boots sink ankle-deep in the snow than alarms start going off.

Thirty-Five

"Mason!"

"It's not us. It can't be."

"Do you have another explanation?"

"Wait," Alex interjects, stepping between us. "Wards don't go off like car alarms. And that sounds familiar."

We all listen. The alarm blares for another minute, then falls silent. Pushing through the ten feet or so to the edge of the tree line, I peer out at the manor. Nothing's moving, although it does sound like someone is yelling.

"What do you wish to do?" The Immortal appears beside me, somehow silent in the deep snow.

"I don't know yet. Give me a minute." No sooner do the words leave my mouth than the alarm blares again. "Shit."

"Hold on a second. Hold, hold…" Mason trails off as he rips his glove off and starts digging around in his coat pocket. He comes up holding his phone, which he looks at for a moment, than waggles at me. "Dixon."

"That's it! I knew I'd heard it before. Halloween."

It clicks. "The monster alert? But there's no way we'd hear the laptop all the way out here."

A smile crosses Mason's face. "You would if Dixon connected it to a mundane burglar alarm."

I burst out laughing. I can't help it. Melding magic with technology is a very Dixon-like thing to do. "He did that?"

"He was working on it. Thought it would drive the council members insane. I didn't know he pulled it off. Something about the wards interfering with the sensors or something or other, it was all very technical."

"Yeah. That sounds like him." For a brief moment, we all enjoy the levity, the pleasant feeling that comes with fond memories. Then we have to sober. "So, if the alarm's going off…"

"That means monsters." Alex finishes the thought for me. "Lots of monsters," he adds as the alarm sounds again.

"It is Hecate."

I forgot the Immortal was there again. We make a good team, he and I, but he doesn't quite fit with a group full of teenagers. I have a feeling, when this is all over, he's going to disappear without a trace, and I'll never see him again. I shake off the thought, and instead say, "It would be a big coincidence otherwise."

"She knows we are coming. She seeks to distract us, divide our forces, keep our attention on this plane."

"She won't succeed." My heart skips at the thought of how many people are going to die today while we're busy ignoring the incursion. *Hecate's the bigger threat, and she'll rack up a much bigger body count than they will.*

"It seems the coast is clear, then."

"Alex is right. Let's get into position."

We cloak ourselves again, but the tracks we leave behind betray our presence to anyone paying close enough attention. We enter the true backyard of the manor just as someone comes outside, staring right at us. *Tamara.*

I pause in my step, allowing the Immortal to draw alongside me. "Do you think we have time to deal with her before the comet hits?" It's like the mention of her trips some kind of alert. Her eyes narrow, and I feel my perception spell fading away until her eyes are boring into mine.

"What just happened?"

"How did she do that?"

"Doesn't matter," I snap at the boys. "Weapons at the ready. Defense first, questions later."

The Immortal is still invisible. His strength must outmatch whatever she cast at us. I can't see him either, but I feel his absence as he leaves my side and begins to circle.

"Walter!" Tamara calls, her eyes never leaving mine. "I have something you need to see."

Maybe we should have moved, tried to hide or something, but the three of us are still standing frozen in the backyard when Mr. Henderson joins Tamara on the back steps. "What is it now, Tamara? In case you haven't noticed, I'm a little busy—"

"Look."

It takes Mr. Henderson a moment to adjust to the brightness of the sunlight glinting off the snow, but when he does, he doesn't smile like a cartoon villain like I expect him to. I honestly don't know how he's going to react, so I speak first.

"Mr. Henderson. I know this is unexpected, but we mean you no harm. Keep your distance, and we'll do what we came here to do and stay out of your hair."

He laughs. He actually laughs. "What exactly do you think is going to happen, Ms. Young? I'm just going to let you traipse around the manor after you attacked me and spent nearly a month in hiding? I don't think so. Do you have any idea how many magi are currently in this house? It will be best for you, all of you, if you come inside calmly and allow me to convene the council. Leave your weapons outside."

He steps aside, as if he actually expects me to obey. "No. I'm sorry, Mr. Henderson, but nothing has changed. It will, though, if you leave us to our business." I take a deep breath, pausing just a second before saying what I don't want him to know, but what he also needs to hear. "I'm going after Liza. Right now. I may not come back, so this is your last chance to do the right thing and come with me. Afterwards, I promise I will do whatever I can to release you from Tamara's influence."

"Are you crazy?" Alex hisses in my ear.

"Crazy to bring more players to the team? No."

Mr. Henderson grows visibly agitated. "Did your time away do nothing for your senses? Or did you spend it converting the weak-minded to your cause? Mr. Chandler, I was lenient with you for the part you played in Ms. Young's escape because I believed you to be merely defending your friend, which is an admirable quality. When you and Mr. Leavengood began to have extended absences from the manor, I suspected you may know more than you were telling. But now you stand firmly on her side. This is disappointing indeed."

"I stand on the side of good and right, just as I have always done. Your refusal to see the truth in this makes you unfit to lead the council, and your cowardice makes you unfit to be a magi."

While Mason antagonizes Mr. Henderson, Alex whispers in my ear again. "Why is he still talking?"

"Because he likes the sound of his own voice?"

"Not what I meant. He's trying to convince you to surrender, but last time he brought a small army to take you out. If that house is really full of magi, why hasn't he summoned them yet? Or, why haven't any of them peaked out the window to see who he's talking to?"

Hmm. I start walking forward, Alex and Mason on my heels, not sure what I'm up to but trusting my judgment.

"Stop right there young lady!"

"I think not. All this time, I was afraid. I was afraid the council would come after me, and I didn't want to have hurt them for the simple sin of being wrong. Magi are not my enemy, but you made me their enemy, and sicked them after me because you were too weak to do it yourself. But it turns out I was wrong, too. I don't know what happened between you and your disciples, but I do know they're not here to back you up. Nobody was ever coming after me, because you were the only one looking. There are no other magi in the house. Even Tamara here, after whispering lies into your ear, is distancing herself from you."

"Not quite." In one fluid motion, Tamara reaches up from her position behind Mr. Henderson and snaps his neck.

It all happens so fast, I don't say anything. None of us say anything. We just stare.

"He was an irritating, tiresome little man, wasn't he?"

"Tamara?"

"I didn't want it to go down this way. You think I enjoy killing magi and exposing myself like this? I don't. Walter was supposed to be the bad guy. But he lost. He couldn't stop you, so now that task falls to me."

"You didn't have to kill him!"

"Yes, I did. Don't look so surprised. Did you think the Infernal Goddess would not have her devotees among the magi?" Tamara tsks, shaking her head. "It wasn't difficult to convince the old man that you were a liar. Yes, I whispered in his ears, but he already yearned to believe my truths over yours. His own aspirations and greedy desire for power made him easy to manipulate. His following, though, proved more difficult. The magi turned to him quickly enough, but they're not stupid. As Hecate has made her presence known, they realized their error and abandoned him. They may have failed, but I will not. There is no disappointing my goddess." Raising her voice, Tamara calls out, "I know you're out there somewhere, Deacon. You were a worthy adversary. Hecate wants you to know that."

The use of his real name is too much for the Immortal. In a flash he reappears directly behind Tamara and swipes at her with a blade. She dodges, faster than her age implies she should, and the Immortal catches only air.

His movement stirs the rest of us. "Take her out!" I give the order as I scramble to the side, trying to find a defensible position instead of being mired down in the snow. Alex follows. Mason goes the other way, splitting our front. Adding to the confusion, the monster alarm begins blaring again, and it's much louder up close.

"What do you have?" I shout to Alex, struggling to be heard over the alarm.

"Let me see." Slinging his backpack around, he begins digging through the collection of potions inside.

"You know what, never mind. Stay back here, out of striking distance. Stick to potions you can throw. Hit her whenever you see an opening, and for goodness' sake don't hit any of us."

I leave while Alex is still nodding and rummaging through the backpack. The fight hasn't progressed much, but it has moved over to the driveway where the footing is slightly more stable. Tamara is keeping the Immortal at a distance and not letting him land any blows. Her specialty is manipulation magic, and that's a battle she's fighting on two fronts. Pulling moisture from the air, she's shooting tiny blocks of ice at the Immortal while keeping Mason and Enyo busy fighting a feral snowman. It takes only a moment to make my decision.

"Unda!" Snow is impossible to run in, but it's only water, after all. My spell sends snow flying in all directions as the path between me and Tamara becomes clear. As I race forward I launch a wind spell at her, trying to knock her off balance. Her wards deflect it, but it does draw her focus. Out of the corner of my eye I see the snowman falter, giving Mason the opening he needs to lop off its head. Even decapitated, the pieces still roll toward him, fueled by Tamara's magic instead of any life of their own.

Tamara smiles and raises her sword, more a prop than anything else. Something to have in her hand in case her magic fails. The look in her eyes dares me to strike her, confident that her wards will protect her. The funny thing about wards, though, is you have to be specific when you cast them. I doubt it occurred to Tamara to ward herself against fumes.

The tiny glass vial, launched by Alex, bounces off Tamara's wards and smashes at her feet. Black smoke billows up, and I have to backpedal to avoid getting caught in it. Behind the smoke, Tamara lets out a bloodcurdling screech. As the air clears, I see her huddled on the ground, folding in on herself. Her skin is melting in big fat drops off her bones and sizzling down into the snow. Her screaming lasts only a moment longer before her throat dissolves and she crumples forward, gasping and shuddering. I'm the closest. One swing, and her suffering is ended.

"What was that?" I ask as Alex appears at my side.

"No idea. I took three different ones and mixed them together, then threw it before it could blow up in my hand."

"Don't do it again." We all look at him. "No one deserves to die like that."

A pall descends on the backyard. The monster alarm goes off again, shrieking into the stillness. *That's going to royally piss off the neighbors.* "Will someone please shut that thing up?"

"On it." Alex runs from the backyard as if anxious to escape the scene.

Mason sidles up to me. "Has Alex ever killed anyone before?"

"No."

"Damn. Tough break. We'll have to keep an eye on him."

The alarm goes silent, and Alex emerges from the house. "Shut down the program on Dixon's laptop. It shouldn't go off anymore."

In the next moment, we're no longer alone in the driveway. Half a dozen elderly magi appear from the Shadow Plane, led by Willow. The only one not confused by their presence, Mason meets them. "You got my message."

"Walter Henderson lost our loyalty long ago. The younger generations fear him, but some of us still remember a time when his influence was not so powerful."

Stepping to Mason's side, I take over the conversation, asserting my command. "Walter Henderson is dead. Killed by Tamara, one of our own, and a devotee to Hecate." None of the assembled magi react to the name of Hecate, though Willow's expression grows somber.

"I have heard the claims of Walter Henderson, but my own eyes reveal the truth to me. We have come to lend our assistance, such as it is. But I fear we are no longer young enough or strong enough to enter into a fight of this magnitude."

The brief hope that flared in my chest flickers out. Of course they're not up to the task. Taking them to the Ashen Plane would be akin to murder. However... "If you wish to help, there are other actions to be taken. Monsters are roaming freely today, and I can't be in two places at once. There's a laptop in the manor with all of the details. Spread the message that Mr. Henderson is dead. Rally what troops you can, and get out there and save people."

My order is met with much nodding. I'll admit, I never paid much attention to the elders among us. Their knowledge is extensive, but oftentimes the strength of their magic has faded with age. They're nice enough, but never seemed particularly relevant to me.

Willow answers for the group. "We will do our duty, Adrienne. You go and do yours."

Before I can respond, a tingle washes over my entire body. Looking around, I know I'm not the only one. The Immortal is the first to put it into words. "The comet has entered Earth's atmosphere. It is time."

THIRTY-SIX

As the Immortal begins his preparation, I draw Alex up close to the house. "Talk to me."

"About what?"

"About what? Seriously? You just killed a woman, Alex. Talk to me about that."

"There's nothing to talk about."

I give him a look.

He gives me one back. "I'm taking a page out of your book, Adrienne. I'm fine, because I have to be. I did what I had to do, to help you, to help everyone. Tamara needed to die. Am I happy that I dealt the killing blow? No. But I'll deal with it later. When I can afford to."

I can't argue with that. Just one more thing to deal with when this is all over. *When this is all over...* That's been my mantra for so long now. Strange to think it could actually be tomorrow. *We're all going to need some serious therapy.*

The Immortal is sitting in the snow. Eyes closed, lips moving in a silent chant, the same pose I've seen hundreds of times from Liza and Dixon but never from him. He's never needed to reach so hard for concentration. The magic comes so easily to him, a true second nature. Maybe a first nature. Seeing him like this is...disconcerting.

It takes a long time. An incredibly long, heart-wrenching time. *We're so close. Come on, come on, come on!*

The Immortal gives a shudder, like the last oomph before a feat of great strength, and the smell of ash fills the air. In the next instant, the ground in front of him falls away, revealing a gaping, bottomless black hole.

Mason whistles softly. The Immortal pants and leans his hands on his knees, catching his breath.

"This is it," I whisper, just loud enough for everyone to hear. "If anyone wants to turn back, now's the time. Nobody will think any less of you." Silence.

I catch the Immortal's eye. "Are you ready?" He nods and pulls his shirt up over his head. "Enyo?"

It isn't a pretty sight. Enyo launches herself at the Immortal, burying her fangs in his shoulder. He winces, but doesn't cry out. Blood runs freely down his arm, fouling the snow. Alex and Mason both look away. They received their bites this morning, on the leg where the injury would cause less trouble. The Immortal's needs to be nearer his heart, to make sure the infection spreads as fast as possible before his body can heal him from it.

It's over quickly. The wound begins closing before the Immortal even stands up. "I can feel it," he says to my look of concern. "The injury is inconsequential. The ash remains."

"Good enough. Let's go." Without ceremony, I leap into the hole.

Enyo lands beside me, my stalwart familiar and most loyal companion. The Immortal is next. Through the dim light, his eyes are shining with a ferocity I haven't seen in them before. He's finally here. The apex of his vengeance. A shudder runs through me, making me glad we're fighting on the same side. Mason and Alex are half a second behind, and we're silent as we examine our new surroundings.

The air is toxic. That's my first observation. It prickles against my skin and stings in my throat, and it's so clogged with ash I have to fight against gagging. The stench of sulfur burns in my nostrils. Ash covers the ground and hangs in the air, reminiscent of blizzard conditions. There's light, but not much; more like the glow from a flickering campfire. The ground isn't level, either. Black, ragged crags tower overhead, further blocking the light and our line of sight.

"How are we going to find anyone in this?" Mason asks me.

"I have a feeling they're going to find us."

"Hecate is this way." The Immortal takes the lead, stalking off in a seemingly random direction. Shrugging my shoulders, I fall in behind him. He felt her presence up in the Mortal Plane. For all I know he has some preternatural sense telling him where Hecate is. My visibility is only about three feet, so I have to stay right up behind him or risk losing him in the obscurity. I can still feel the comet, vibrating through my body, telling me I'm capable of anything. Urging me to do something big and crazy. Like kill a goddess? The only problem with that is she'll be jonesing on the comet, too.

Our procession is silent as we make our way through the ash. For my part, I can't help but gawk at the spectacle around me.

At one point, our path leads us along the edge of a chasm. For a moment there's a break in the ash, and the air is clear enough to see out into the dark emptiness awaiting the slightest misstep.

However quiet we've tried to be, our presence doesn't go unnoticed. No sooner do we cross the chasm than threatening growls rumble at us from out of the darkness.

"Hellhounds." My warning is unnecessary. The beasts are already leaping at us, going straight for the killing blow. Enyo intercepts my first before I really register the attack. With a snarl, she takes the monster to the ground and slashes into it, leaving it thrashing and whimpering behind her as she marks another target.

I'm ready for the next one, cleaving it in two in midair. My mind flashes back to my very first hellhound, scrambling around an alley in the shadow of a stadium, thinking I could kill it with a silver knife and a little bit of magic. Now, I'm a hellhound-killing pro, thanks to my copious amount of experience and my trusty familiar-magic imbued sword.

Mason and Alex aren't faring so well. Despite a few weeks of basic sword training with Mason, Alex is no fighter. And while Mason has the skill, he doesn't have the fancy familiar magic I do, so every opponent is a serious struggle. The Immortal is...well, the Immortal. He tears through the hounds like a beast himself, ignoring their fangs and simply ripping them in half. Unlike in the Mortal Plane, though, these hounds don't just dissolve into ash, only to be reborn later. Killing them here means killing them for good.

Alex takes a hit to the knee before I can back him up and goes down. Three hounds pile on. One of those hounds is Enyo, wrestling the other two off of him. They hit the ground in a squirming pile, snarling and snapping at each other. By this time I've made it to Alex's side, and we face off the remaining hounds together.

Before I know it, it's over. We're bruised and bleeding, but all still standing and accounted for.

"Not to push our luck," Mason heaves, doubled over, "but that didn't seem so bad. Is that all Hecate's got?"

"Idiot!" I scold him as the ground begins to tremble. "Why did you have to go and say something stupid like that?"

"This is somehow my fault?"

"Silence!" The Immortal orders, eyes fixed on the ground. The ash is shaking, too, quivering as the ground beneath it shifts and moves. Then I see what the Immortal is staring at. Horrified, I kneel down for a better look. I have to be sure.

"Run!" I scream, as a thin line of ash sinks out of view.

They obey without question. Above us, a chunk of black rock breaks off and comes crashing down, missing Mason by inches. The cracks in the ground open wider, swallowing ash and racing our feet as we flee to safer ground. Heat wafts up around us, and tiny flames leap up to lick our shoes. We try to stay together, but the Ashen Plane has a different plan. The crevices force us farther and farther apart, until we have to split to navigate the jutting crags. I crash into one in the darkness, and it leaves a six-inch slice down my arm at the contact.

The Immortal and Enyo are with me. Mason and Alex are lost, but we can't turn back to find them. We enter a broad, flat expanse of emptiness, and suddenly the ground stops shaking.

Light flares in front of us, and we stagger back, unaccustomed to the brightness.

"Apologies. The change can be...abrupt. Take your time to adjust. I'll wait."

Liza. Her voice is ingrained in my head. While I squint at her, Enyo doesn't hesitate. With a snarl that would turn any mortal's legs to jelly, Enyo leaps. Her snarl morphs into a whimper as Liza raises an arm, sending my familiar crashing back to the ground and trapping her there. Enyo thrashes and growls, but can't rise.

"Hecate." The name comes out with a snarl of my own.

"Foolish dog. Don't you know that hellhounds are *my* domain? You may be your own creature, but I command the body you wear. Now, be a good dog. Stay."

The Immortal has also recovered, and stands stiffly beside me, so tense he might shatter into a thousand pieces. Ignoring me, Hecate advances on him. As she gets closer I can once again see her eyes, black and red, alien in such an innocent, delicate face.

"Deacon. It is good to see you again. Did you enjoy your vacation in the Barren Plane? I'll admit, I did not expect you to return so soon. I underestimated the girl."

At that she casts a sideways glance at me, catching me in the act of trying to sneak into her blind spot. "Rest assured, it will not happen again."

If a surprise attack won't work, perhaps a direct one will. "Quae!" I leap as I scream, crashing into Liza and taking us both down to the ground. We land in the ash and I bounce back to my feet, hoping to see Liza lying immoveable on the ground.

She rises, dusting off her clothes, the same clothes she was wearing when Hecate sucked her down into the earth. "Did you honestly expect that to work?"

"It was worth a shot," I answer, ducking as the Immortal's blade sings. It stops short of her throat while his other huge, corded arm wraps itself around her chest.

"Show yourself," he hisses in her ear. "Let us dispense with games and be done with this."

Hecate laughs. "You will not harm the vessel. The only game that remains is to decide how each of you die. If we're being honest, I'm leaning toward abandoning you here and simply letting the beasts have you."

"Your hellhounds?" I scoff, filling my voice with as much bravado as I can. "They didn't do much damage last time."

"They weren't supposed to," she spits, for a second dropping the cordial facade. "If they happened to kill you, fine, but their purpose was just to spur you on. Surely you thought it strange you encountered nothing upon your entrance here? That you were able to pass unmolested? I had a vested interest in facilitating this little meeting, and it is only due to my protection you made it this far at all."

"Your protection? From what? From the ash? The darkness? The crags? There's nothing here."

This time her laugh is sinister, a low chuckle that makes my skin crawl. "Is that what you think, you ignorant fool? I have been here for thousands of years, but the Ashen Plane has existed since the world began. What do you think populated it before me? Oh, there are beasts here, girl, beasts who will rip the flesh from your bones and devour you whole before you even have the chance to scream. This plane may be my prison, but it is their home."

As if on cue, the darkness around us shifts, and heavy footfalls thud dully in the carpet of ash. Hecate notices my hackles rising. "Yes, they're out there. All around us. It is only by my mercy they hold themselves at bay."

"Enough," the Immortal growls, giving Liza a shake, but my mind is no longer here. It's trying to drag me back, into thinking about Mason and Alex, out there all alone, fighting demons they don't know about and aren't prepared to face, and if they're not dead yet they soon will be, and it'll be all my fault, just like Dixon was my fault, and—

"Adrienne!" The Immortal's voice cuts through my spiral and brings me back to the present. I see the emotions in his eyes and I know what he's thinking. If he kills Liza now, Hecate can't rise. Her plan will be stopped, and we can hunt her down at our leisure.

"Yes, enough," I repeat, allowing a deadly calm to settle into my voice. I can't help Mason and Alex. But I can still accomplish this mission. *Enyo? She has your body, but your mind is still with me. It's time. Find Liza.* The thread connecting me to Enyo is thrumming with tension, my familiar's rage and frustration pouring out in all directions. My request gives her focus, and unleashing her on my enemies gives me a thrill.

"Enough of this back-and-forth. You know why we're here. If you're going to kill us, get on with it, but it's time for you to stop hiding behind a little girl. Show yourself, Hecate, and let's put an end to it."

Liza's body stills, unnaturally so. She looks right at me, and Hecate's ember eyes burn with a hatred that can't be disguised. "If you so wish," she whispers, and Liza faints in the Immortal's arms. In the same instant the light vanishes, replaced by a darkness so thick I can feel it on my skin.

I move. I don't know where, but no way I'm going to be standing in the last place Hecate saw me. I slide silently through the ash, confident the Immortal is doing the same thing, preparing myself to meet whatever happens next with the strongest magic I can muster. In a tiny corner of my mind I can feel Enyo, searching for a hole where she can slip through Hecate's defenses. It's our job to keep the sorceress too busy to notice the intrusion.

Despite all our planning, all the research, all the power at my disposal today, I'm still not ready when Hecate makes her entrance. Seconds after the darkness falls, light begins to filter back in. It's not the same glaring, orange light from before. Rather, it's a brilliant, pure white light that stands in stark contrast to the nature and landscape of this plane. Out of the gloom overhead a full moon appears, shining down benignly yet giving me a chill. Nothing good ever happens under a full moon.

Then I'm hit by some invisible force, catching me in the chest and launching me back into the base of one of the cliffs ringing our little stage. Thousands of tiny cuts open as I connect and drop to the ground. Ringing laughter sounds, clean and beautiful, like the tinkling of a bell. "Are you cowed so easily? Is this not what you wanted?"

I regain my feet, noting the Immortal doing the same not too far from me. "Where is she?" I holler at him, no longer concerned about giving away my position.

"Everywhere," he grunts out, popping his right shoulder back into place. "She is not corporeal."

THIRTY-SEVEN

*N*OT CORPOREAL? MY IMMEDIATE reaction is shock. *The Immortal tried to warn me, but I wouldn't listen. It never occurred to me that her spirit could endure while her body withered.* She hits me again, rushing in like a gale-force wind and flinging me up into the open air. Air is something I know, though, and my magic responds before I realize I've made the decision to. "Ventus!" Fueled by the comet, my wind spell forms a whirling tornado around me, bearing me safely back to the ground and standing sentinel against Hecate's attacks. The next time she comes the tornado falters, but holds.

She's still playing with us.

The Immortal is fighting back, throwing up spells to turn her back each time she comes for him. He's holding his own, if not gaining ground. *How can we kill her if she doesn't have a body to kill?*

The Immortal lets out a scream of pain, telling me I've been idle too long. *Think think think think. This isn't what I do!* My only experience with non-corporeal entities is fighting shadows, but my go-to containment spell already failed. My strength lies in hand-to-hand, so what do I do if I can't fight? I lash out in my frustration, letting magic flow from me without direction or control. The ground buckles beneath me, a chunk of black rock comes crashing down into the middle of our arena, and lightning flashes out from all ten of my fingers.

The smell of ozone rises above the stench of sulfur for just a moment, and the air around me stills. *Where'd she go?*

Taking advantage of the breather, I rush to the Immortal, who has regained his feet and is flexing the fingers of his left hand. "The lightning," he greets me, knowing we have precious little time. "Do it again."

"Lightning. Got it."

I glance around for some indication that Hecate has recovered, but the Immortal grabs my arm and pulls my attention back. "We cannot hold her forever."

He doesn't have to articulate the warning. Liza's body lies helpless in the ash, abandoned while Hecate toys with us. Vulnerable. If Enyo doesn't find Liza's consciousness soon...

I don't have time to finish the thought. Hecate returns with a vengeance, her magic pushing me to the ground and sucking the air from my lungs. Panicked, I try to gasp, but get only a mouthful of ash instead. As it forces itself into my throat, gagging me, I hear the Immortal bellowing commands. The pressure on my back loosens as Hecate divides her attention, and my mind begins to clear. I still can't breathe, but that's only temporary.

I usually use my hands to direct lightning, but this time it needs to be erratic. Pushing all of my comet-boosted power into one coherent desire, I let the lightning fly, thinking *fulgur!* with all my might. It's like a million gunshots going off at once. Several explosions sound as random bolts connect with flammable minerals in the surrounding rock. The charged air zings across my skin as I scramble up, hacking and coughing, instantly freed from Hecate's attack.

The sorceress may be gone for now, but that doesn't mean there's no threat. Under the light of the moon, a shadow emerges from the gloom and dives straight for me. It's fast, too fast for me to see more than glinting talons and scaly, rubbery wings. Opening its beak, it shrieks in delight, so close something pops in my ear and warm blood spills out.

"Down!" The shout comes half a second before the whistling blade, and the creature is cleaved in two by a blood-soaked silver machete. The droplets that spray across my cheek sizzle like acid. "Are you all right?"

"How did you find us?"

"You're my partner. I'll always find you."

"Alex?"

"Alive. Hecate?"

"A bitch." Pulling Mason along with me, I search for the Immortal, but can't find him. I can hear sounds of battle from somewhere in the darkness, outside of the moonlight, but the sounds echo and I can't tell which direction they're coming from. For the moment, the Immortal is lost to us, occupied with keeping the inhabitants of this plane at bay. We do find Alex, though, propped where Mason dumped him, presumably so he could rush in and save my life. He's bleeding. A lot.

"Hey." His voice is weak and scratchy, and the hand he tries to wave at me doesn't raise more than a few inches.

"Hey, yourself." Dropping to my knees beside him, I give him a once-over before returning my eyes to his. "How are you?"

"Holding on." The words come out on a cough, blood flying out between his lips. I cringe, but don't let it show.

"You're going to be okay. We're getting out of here soon, all right? You'll be good as new once we get topside again."

He nods, not believing me. I'm not sure I believe me either. We all agreed, though. No healing, except for immediate life-threatening stuff. Healing takes time and energy we're going to need elsewhere. Alex needs to hold on, just a little longer. He does have an amber potion on him, though. The same one he used on Halloween to fix my jaw and get me on my feet. It only takes a second to pour some between his lips.

I'm straining to hear the Immortal again when I feel it. A shift in my mind, barely there, like an extra-long blink. A tiny voice asks, *Enyo?*, as the familiar forges a connection with her mind.

My heart races. *Liza?*

Adrienne?

Liza!

"Find her!" I bark to Mason, rushing off back into the arena. Of course he doesn't know what I'm talking about, but it doesn't matter. Liza is right where we left her, the Immortal dropping her body when Hecate cut the lights. She's lying cradled in a pile of ash, smack dab in the middle of the arena, surrounded by debris that looks like it should have hit her but was deflected at the last moment. I never thought I'd be thankful to Hecate for anything, but the wards she placed on Liza's body make me come close.

She's stirring by the time we reach her, returning to herself as Enyo leads her through whatever hole she found in Hecate's defenses, just as she once led me out of my own mind. Pushing herself up on trembling arms, Liza stares in horror at the scene around her. Dropping to my knees, I wrap my arms around her and pull her tightly against my chest, squeezing way too hard.

She struggles against me, writhing until I finally release her, ducking to look into her eyes. Familiar chocolate orbs look back at me, filled with fear and anger and relief.

"Are you—" I try to ask, but she cuts me off.

"I don't have long. Hecate will realize she's lost control, and I won't be able to keep her out. What's your plan?" Her words are careful and controlled, the swirl of emotions in her eyes the only indication that she's freaked out of her mind.

"How much do you know?"

"Everything."

"Good." I fish a vial out of my pocket, holding it up so Liza can see it in the moonlight. We're all carrying one. The familiar blue color makes my mind flash to Alex, and the amount of hope contained in this little vial. *Here's hoping he came through.* "Drink this. Right now."

Liza doesn't hesitate, snatching the vial and downing the contents before asking, "What will it do?"

"It's going to help you win. You're strong, nearly as strong as Hecate, but not quite. Alex used the same revival potion he uses for energy and mingled it with the Immortal's essence. Don't ask. The point is, the two of you are now connected. You can—" I don't get to finish my instructions. Mason disappears from my side, skeletal hands sucking him down into the ash in a scene so terrible and familiar my mind refuses to believe it just happened again. More hands latch onto my knees and ankles, dragging me down and away from Liza.

She screams my name, the sound dying on her lips as her eyes blaze crimson. "A valiant effort, child, but futile. I wasn't going to make you watch your friends die, but now I think you shall. This knowledge will pain them in their final breaths."

The hands hold me immobile while Hecate, back in control of Liza's body, steps slowly toward me. Cast as I might, I can't break free. In desperation I draw my silver dagger, plunging it into one of the hands, but it doesn't let go. The dead don't feel pain. It's close quarters for a sword, but I scrabble for it anyway as Hecate draws closer...

"No!" Mid-stride, Hecate stops, one hand going to her own open mouth. Then her mocking tone comes back as a cruel little smile plays on her lips. "Child? Are you feeling brave once more?"

Liza doesn't answer, but she's obviously discovered what Alex's potion can do. Her connection with the Immortal allows her to draw on his immense strength and combine it with her own. The skeletal hands still hold me, but I no longer struggle as I watch Liza's battle unfold.

I can't see it, but the expressions that play across Liza's face tell me what's going on. Hecate is silent, focusing on regaining control. At first the sorceress is confident, using minimal effort to quash Liza's uprising. Then there's shock as she realizes the depth of Liza's opposition. Determination, fury, and finally, panic.

Hecate doesn't give up yet, though. She may be losing the battle for Liza's mind, but that's not the only front from which she can attack. In an impressive display of strength, Hecate deals a major blow to Liza, metaphorically knocking her down. Before Liza can retaliate, Hecate presses her advantage, but not against her. Against us.

The ground begins to tremble. That split second was long enough for Hecate to set a spell into motion. With a resounding crack and a belch of smoke, the ground breaks open, splitting the arena neatly in two. Shapes pour forth, climbing out of the bowels of the earth and stalking forward, red eyes gleaming in the light of the moon.

In my peripheral vision Enyo leaps to her feet, her body released as the hellhounds are given free reign. There are too many to count. The hands holding me down tighten their grip, preparing to serve me up to the beasts, but I have no intention of going quietly. I draw my sword as I begin to cast.

When the hands first took me, my focus was on breaking free, but no matter what I tried, I couldn't break their grip. Now, it's time to try something else.

"Ignis!" Like I did with the lightning, I fuel the power of the comet into the spell, and balls of flame erupt around me as the skeletal hands ignite. At the same time, I cry out in pain as the fire sears my own skin. The stench of roasting meat fills my nostrils as the fire gets hotter, blue light shining through. But the pressure lessens.

The moment my legs are free I end the spell, but I still can't move. Charred scraps are all that remain of Hecate's minions, but my emancipation comes at a high price. Pain clouds my mind, and I instinctively draw inward where I can cower in peace. Instead of peace, though, I find a sharp growl and new pain lances through my hand. The bite is piercing and startling enough that my eyes fly open to find Enyo standing between me and the advancing hellhounds. The weight of her mind on mine is a small comfort, but comfort nonetheless. If we're checking out, at least we're doing it together. Gritting my teeth, I brandish my sword and wait for the beasts to come.

Fighting with a sword while sitting on your knees is difficult, but doable. Fending off attacks from multiple directions is difficult, but doable. Blocking out incapacitating pain is difficult, but doable. Doing all three at once is nearly impossible.

It would be completely impossible without Enyo at my side. Linked as we are, she dances between my blows, evading my blade while beating back hounds. She doesn't kill any, though. Neither do I. Trapped as I am, all we can do is keep them at bay and pray our luck holds.

Movement out of the corner of my eye catches my attention. The Immortal, bloody and staggering, reappears in the moonlight and lurches my way. His weapons are gone, and he's hunched over and panting, but he still comes on. A few of the hounds take notice of him, but the majority stay right where they are, choosing the weakest, most vulnerable prey. Lightning flies from the Immortal's fingers, single bolts that lack the sizzle and pizzazz I've seen from him before. The bolts hit their targets, knocking them aside but not doing the damage they need to. *Liza's draining him.*

"Yes!" Liza's voice rings out triumphant, tearing my gaze away from the weakened Immortal. An unearthly glow emanates out from her body, too bright to look at, and all movement around me ceases. The glow pulses out, washing over all of us, mortals and hellhounds alike. The glow gives me a feeling of hope, while the hounds around me crumble into ash.

Liza fades, her skin resuming its normal cocoa complexion, and her eyes seek out mine. "I've got her."

THIRTY-EIGHT

I HAVE TO MOVE. I have to get to her. My legs still don't work, so I sheathe my sword and pull with my arms, plowing my way through the deep ash. Liza meets me, tears shining in her eyes.

An ear-splitting shriek echoes through the plane, and Hecate rushes back in a mighty wind. Needles of rock burst forth from the ground as ash rains down from above. "I thought you said you had her?" I ask as she throws her arms around me, for once being the one supporting me.

"I have her mind. She still has everything else."

The Immortal roars, an inhuman sound, and in her fury Hecate turns her ire on him, pounding him with magical blows. He goes down, trying to hold her off, but he barely managed it when he was at full strength.

"Well, expel her already, so we can kill her."

"How are we going to kill her, Adrienne? Her body died a long time ago. If I expel her, we'll be right back where we started." There's no more fear in Liza's eyes. There's calm, and resignation.

"No."

"I have a body, Adrienne-"

"No!"

"It's the only way."

"No, it's not."

"Then tell me another one."

There isn't one. We both know it. Liza releases me, and helps prop me back up into a sitting position. Reaching up with one soot-covered hand, I pull her forward and press a kiss to her forehead. "I love you, sister."

"I love you, too."

In the next breath Liza begins to chant, her voice deep and guttural. Hecate pauses in her assault, the words of her own possession spell weighing down the very air. I can only imagine how confused she must be. How wary. In the reprieve, the Immortal struggles to his feet and stumbles toward us, dropping to his knees a few feet away. He doesn't ask. He already knows.

Liza chants on, eyes vacant and fixed on a point in the distance. Her voice rises, gaining volume with the power behind her words. Hecate begins to laugh as her plan unfolds, glorying in her victory.

Then Liza pauses. Her eyes focus, swiveling before coming to rest on the Immortal's face. He meets them with sobriety and peace. "Finish it."

The chant bursts forth once more, rising to a crescendo, and the Immortal's eyes go blank. He teeters, then topples face-first into the ash.

Immediately, Liza's chanting stops. Hecate's laugh stops. Everything stops. Even the ash seems to hang motionless in the air. I keep my eyes trained on her face, searching for some indication that my girl is still in there.

A minute passes, then Liza's eyes snap open, beautiful and brown. I let out the breath I was holding, but don't allow myself to feel relief. It's good that the spell was successful. But now it means...

"Now, Adrienne." Clipped and terse, Liza's voice tells me just how hard Hecate is fighting for control of her new prison.

I draw my sword, but it suddenly feels too heavy for my hand. I stare at the blade, familiar sigils shining through the gore and the ash, then swing my eyes up to Liza's. She reads the expression there with a knowing look. I can't do it.

Her brown hand covers my own. "It's okay, Adrienne." Then the sword is gone, reappearing in Liza's hands. It's almost as big as she is, a picture too tragic to ever be funny.

The scrape of boot against rock draws both of our attention to the crevasse still bisecting the arena. A moment later, Mason appears, crawling up from beneath the earth. He doesn't approach, though, just stares at the two of us, sitting in the ash, the Immortal lying lifeless beside us.

"It's a good note to end on."

"I'm not ready," I whisper, my control cracking and my emotions leaking through.

"Neither am I. But that doesn't matter, does it?"

"No, it doesn't." Without another word, and without hesitation, she drives the blade into her chest.

My heart breaks. Literally. I can feel it bursting into a million pieces, each one clawing its way out between my ribs. Sight, sound, smell, they all vanish. The only thing in my world is the line of blood pouring from Liza's open mouth, the weight of her body in my arms, arms I don't remember lifting to catch her. Then there are arms around me too, strong, masculine arms, clutching me to a blood-soaked shirt as wordless sobs wrench themselves out of my throat.

Alex strokes my hair, the healing potion having worked its wonders on his injuries, shushing me and whispering nonsense words into my ear until I calm down enough to hear him. "Listen to me, Adrienne. I can fix this, but we need to act fast. Can you help me?"

I understand the words, but their meaning eludes me. I just rock and stare, stare down at the little girl I moved heaven and earth to save and still ended up losing.

"We need to get out of here." Mason's voice cuts through, ringing with authority.

"Wait."

"We don't have time—"

"Just wait. I can fix this, but I need some help."

"What are you talking about?" Mason's tone turns harsh. He's hurting.

In response, Alex pulls my arms away from Liza, tugging her out of my grip and laying her flat on the ground. I scrabble for her, trying to get her back, but Alex easily knocks my hands away. "Get the sword."

I don't know whether he's talking to me or Mason, but Mason's the one who responds. The sword slides free of Liza's body with a squelch, making my gorge rise. Then Alex leans over her, fingers under her chin.

"What are you doing?"

"Making sure she's really dead."

"Are you a moron? Of course she's dead. And we will be too if we don't get out of here."

Ignoring Mason, Alex pulls the split edges of Liza's shirt aside and pours something dark blue into the wound. Immediately it froths and bubbles, but Alex watches it intently. "Come on, come on."

Mason gasps when he notices it. It takes me longer, because I can't tear my eyes away from her face, but finally I look down and see it. The wound is closing, slowly but surely, as Liza's body regenerates the destroyed tissue.

Finally, the last blue bubbles pop, and Liza's skin is once again intact. Alex springs into motion, blowing into her mouth and pumping her chest. My mind scrambles to find the right word. *CPR.*

On impulse, I begin to chant, the same life-saving spells Mason and I worked over Dixon. We were too late to save him. Is it too late to save her?

Mason joins me, placing his hands on Liza as Alex continues chest compressions. The seconds tick by, each one lasting an eternity. Enyo squeezes in between me and Mason, laying her head in my lap and letting comforting warmth flow from her mind into mine. Something moves around us in the darkness, emboldened by the absence of the moon, but none of us pay it any mind.

Liza coughs. Sputters. Gasps. Then suddenly she's breathing again, hacking and twitching and squirming and *living*. Alex sits back with a sigh of relief, but I claw at her, pulling her toward me and hauling her head into my lap, ousting Enyo.

"Ignis." The whispered spell brings a spark to my fingertips. I'm not good with subtle spells, but I've never had such laser focus as I do at this moment. The light is tiny, but it burns just hot enough for me to see down into Liza's face. Into her eyes. Her wide, confused, beautiful brown eyes.

"Adrienne?"

"Family reunion later. Escape now." Mason's back to taking charge again, but I don't care. One of us has to be in charge, and I'm certainly in no shape to do it. "Get the Immortal. Liza, can you open a door?"

"I-I—"

"He's breathing!" Alex's cry is like the breaking of some invisible dam. Shrieks and screeches sound all around us as the inhabitants of the Ashen Plane descend.

"Liza?"

"I can do it." Gone is her confusion. The Liza that rises on shaky legs stands poised with confidence and control. She takes one long breath, then throws her arms open wide and screams a spell out into the darkness. The ground before us churns and cracks, then falls away. Daylight rises up from the abyss, and a draft brushes against my cheek.

"Let's go!" Mason's command comes as he scoops me up into his arms. With no ceremony, he chucks me into the hole, then turns back for the next person. I land in a pile of snow, much deeper than the snow at the manor when we left. Liza lands beside me, but her legs buckle and she goes sprawling. Enyo leaps gracefully through, then Mason and Alex, supporting the Immortal between them. The moment their legs touch snow the door vanishes, sealing the Ashen Plane behind us.

For a moment, none of us move. Then I feel it bubbling up inside. I can't contain the laugh that comes out, and soon we're all laughing hysterically, the sound bouncing around the wide-open field we've landed in in the middle of nowhere.

"We actually did it." My words sober all of us, and the laughter dies out.

"Hey, you guys okay?" The voice doesn't belong to any of us, and comes accompanied by a low growl. Three heads shoot into the sky as Mason, Alex, and I sit up. Ten yards away from us stands a hulking man covered in several layers of something furry, carrying some kind of fishing gear and restraining a hound.

"Where are we?" I call out in answer.

The man obviously thinks something strange is going on here, but he answers anyway. "St. John's." At my look of confusion, he clarifies, "Labrador."

The names still aren't ringing any bells, but they connect for Alex. "We're in Canada?"

Mason, as always, cuts right to the heart of the matter. "Can we borrow your cell phone?"

Three hours later I'm on my feet again, wrapped in a blanket and standing in the driveway of the manor, watching the comet blaze a fiery trail across the night sky.

"We did it," I say again as someone comes up behind me.

"You did it," the Immortal answers, his voice weak and wavering. He hasn't recovered from the toll Alex's potion took on his body. His skin hangs limp and sagging on a frame hunched over and stiff. He looks...old.

"Not by myself. I may have gotten us there, but I never could have—" I trail off, not needing to articulate the rest. The Immortal knows. He always knows. Instead I turn to look at him. "You're not healing."

"No, I am not." He sighs, but a contented sigh. "Hecate is dead. I believe my curse died with her. Your healers are skilled, but I am not their usual patient. I am...something else."

Something else indeed. I don't interrupt, though. The Immortal's tone has turned reflective and pondering. It's not something to be intruded upon.

He continues. "I owe you many thanks, little mage. You rid the world of a great evil, but I am only human, and my greatest appreciation is for the boon you have given me. You gave me my vengeance. You gave my sister justice. And you have given me the most precious gift of all. You have given me death."

"Wait a minute—"

"No, little mage. I am done waiting. My death draws near, and I am anxious for the rest. Before I depart, however, there is something I still owe you."

Stepping back, the Immortal crosses his arms over his chest and begins to chant. A shimmer appears in the air, then two still forms descend out of the darkness and land gently on the snow. Andrew and Heather, hands crossed over their chests and faces serene. They could be simply sleeping. A single tear falls from my eye. After all we've been through, the journey I took to get them back...I can't put those emotions into words.

After a moment I notice they're not alone. A dozen other figures have descended, pulled from wherever the Immortal kept them, landing in a circle around me. Even now they're stirring, eyes fluttering open and fingers twitching. A sound of shattering glass comes from the house, and a fluffy yellow bullet pelts straight at me. It stops short, though, and is gentle as it alights softly on Heather's hand. Heather's lips twitch, then pull back in a tiny smile. "Cerise."

More tears flow from my eyes. "Thank you," I whisper, turning back to the Immortal. He isn't there.

EPILOGUE

LIZA

A WEEK AGO, I died. Adrienne says I'll eventually come to terms with everything that happened to me, but I don't see how. Even my body refuses to heal. Willow is the best healer the magi have had for decades, and even she can't explain why my skin still feels raw and why the air burns in my throat.

Alex was the easiest. He was already well on his way, jacked up on his own potions. And that stuff he used to close my stab wound and bring me back to life? He's not giving up that secret.

Adrienne was the hardest, and she'll have scars on her legs for the rest of her life. Even manipulation magic has its limits. But they've recovered, infection and all. So why not me?

A fuzzy head pushes itself under my hand, noticing I'm awake. Pong returned the day after we got back, as big as ever, a fact Heather and Andrew have yet to come to terms with. I'm not the same girl they knew. I don't really know who I am, either. And the one person who could definitely help me figure it out is gone forever. *Dixon.* I didn't even get to say goodbye.

As I swing my legs out of bed, a glint of sunlight on the far wall catches my eye. I couldn't leave it behind, but Adrienne can't even look at the sword anymore. It holds a macabre fascination for me. Some day she may want it back, though, so I'm saving it for her.

My face looks the same in the bathroom mirror. It shouldn't. There should be some sign, I think. Something to mark the changes. I shouldn't look exactly the same as I did three months ago.

Flush toilet, brush teeth, wash face. The monotony of my morning routine carries me forward. Just keep doing the same things, over and over, and eventually it will all feel normal again, right?

The towel is soft, and I bury my face in it, breathing in the sweet scent of laundry detergent. It's a normal, comforting smell. Then I see my face in the mirror. I'm almost smiling, but that's not what caught my attention. For just a moment, my eyes glowed red like a burning ember. A blink later, it's gone. And in the deep recesses of my head, a bell tinkles.

Acknowledgments

I'd like to take a moment to thank all the people who helped me get this far. My husband, who first gave me the courage to try writing a book. Our boys, who are too young to remember but always inspire me to chase my dreams. My mom, my biggest fan. My beta readers, Jake, Katy, and Chloe, for showing me problems in the story I didn't know existed. My editors, Karli and Kelley, and my cover designer, Eugene, for helping to make this book everything it could be.

ABOUT THE AUTHOR

Jessica Goeken is a graduate of Indiana State University. She loves reading, hiking, and having adventures. She is married to an Army helicopter pilot, and they have 2 sons and a chocolate lab. They are currently living in North Carolina.